Henry James Coleridge

Passiontide

continuation of the public life of Our Lord, Volume 3

Henry James Coleridge

Passiontide
continuation of the public life of Our Lord, Volume 3

ISBN/EAN: 9783741194832

Manufactured in Europe, USA, Canada, Australia, Japa

Cover: Foto ©Andreas Hilbeck / pixelio.de

Manufactured and distributed by brebook publishing software
(www.brebook.com)

Henry James Coleridge

Passiontide

THE LIFE OF OUR LIFE

PART THE FIFTH

PASSIONTIDE

PART THIRD

QUARTERLY SERIES. SEVENTY-SIXTH VOLUME

ROEHAMPTON
PRINTED BY JAMES STANLEY

PASSIONTIDE

CONTINUATION OF THE PUBLIC LIFE OF OUR LORD

BY

HENRY JAMES COLERIDGE

OF THE SOCIETY OF JESUS

PART THE THIRD

LONDON

BURNS AND OATES

LIMITED

GRANVILLE MANSIONS, W

1891

✠

SICUT TU ME MISISTI IN MUNDUM

ITA ET EGO EOS MISI IN MUNDUM

ET PRO EIS EGO SANCTIFICO MEIPSUM

UT SINT ET IPSI SANCTIFICATI IN VERITATE

NON PRO EIS AUTEM ROGO TANTUM

SED ET PRO EIS

QUI CREDITURI SUNT PER VERBUM EORUM IN ME

UT OMNES UNUM SINT

SICUT TU PATER IN ME ET EGO IN TE

UT ET IPSI IN NOBIS UNUM SINT

ET CREDAT MUNDUS QUIA TU ME MISISTI

UT EGO CLARITATEM QUAM DEDISTI MIHI

DEDI EIS .

UT SINT UNUM SICUT ET NOS UNUM SUMUS

✠

PREFACE.

THE present portion of the series of volumes on the
Life of our Blessed Lord on which I am engaged,
embraces the second part of the important chapters
on the sayings and doings of the last evening
spent by our Lord in the Cenacle, before He went
forth thence to begin His Passion in the Garden of
Gethsemani. As the reader knows, St. John gives
as many as five chapters to the narrative of the
sayings and doings of this Thursday evening, and
his narrative is all the more invaluable to us, from
the fact that without it we should be left unprovided
with any record of the great mysteries which he
relates. This, moreover, is a portion of the Gospels
in which the characteristic method of the fourth
Evangelist is more than ever conspicuous. For it
is common with St. John, beyond the other sacred
writers, to devote himself specially to the sayings
rather than to the actions of his beloved Master. But
this exclusive attention to the relating of our Lord's
words is so predominant a feature in these chapters

that it may be said, of the last three of them, to which the following pages are devoted, that they hardly leave room for anything but what our Lord said. We have, therefore, in the contents of the present volume, very little matter of great importance besides the actual words that He uttered on this occasion—certainly second to none, if we except the Passion itself, of all that the Sacred History has had to relate to us.

The particular portion of the words of our Lord which comes before the reader of the three chapters of St. John's Gospel, which I have had to try to explain in the following sheets—chapters xv., xvi., and xvii.—naturally seem to call for great study and care in the endeavour to trace the meaning of our Lord most faithfully. The first of these chapters begins the second division of the great discourse to the Apostles, which follows on the short break in that discourse made by the words, ' Arise, let us go hence,' at the end of the fourteenth chapter. This division seems to have been occasioned by the arrival of the time at which it was our Lord's intention to celebrate for the first time the Adorable Sacrifice of the Altar, and to impart to the holy company assembled in the Cenacle the most precious Communion of His Sacred Body and Blood. The words with which the resumed discourse begins afresh, speak of Him as the True Vine, and the great doctrine of Unity is immediately set forth under a parable of the Vine and its branches. This need only be mentioned here for the sake of showing the importance of the chapters of which we are speaking. But the great subject which is raised by our Lord in immediate connection with the image of the Vine and its branches, is not by any means the only topic of high importance of which it has been necessary to speak in the chapters of this volume. The vital doctrine of Unity, of which our Lord there lays the foundation, has been developed from His teaching in the Epistles to the Corinthians, Romans, and Ephesians in so beautiful a manner by St. Paul, whose language and imagery show that the teaching of this evening in the Cenacle took a deep hold on the minds and memories of the Apostolic Body who listened to it. For St. Paul could hardly have spoken of the doctrine as he has if it had not been familiar and welcome to those for whom he writes. His words on Unity are immediately followed by his great passage about charity.

After this they are instructed with regard to what must certainly have fallen upon them very much to their surprise, namely, the savage and continual persecution to which the Church, and themselves as its leaders and founders, were to be exposed immediately after the departure of our Lord Himself. This must have been an unexpected feature in the conditions under which they were to be called to labour for our Lord—not that He had not been Himself treated in the same way by the world, not that He had not often led them to look forward to the enmity of the world, and especially of the Jewish people, who they were even to see the murderers and executioners of His Sacred Person,—but that so little had as yet happened to prepare them for the entire rupture between the Jewish people and rulers, whom our Lord had even lately taught His disciples to obey, and the followers of the New Kingdom of the Catholic Church were to be gathered by them. There can be little doubt that the storm of persecution with which the Church was received almost from her first entrance into the world, might have been much less violent, if the Jewish rulers had been willing to follow the tolerant advice given them by Gamaliel and his party.[1] And although the heathen world could not long have permitted the teaching of the Church to continue without an attempt to drown the new religion in the blood of its professors, it is reasonable to think that the attempt was hastened, and the violence enhanced, by the fact of the furious hatred of the

[1] **Acts v.**

Jews, who seemed to be handed over to a spirit of malignant perversity after their dreadful cry in answer to Pilate's remonstrance at the time of the Passion. Our Lord's warning to His friends, therefore, in regard of what was at hand for them from their own nation, which He there speaks of under the general name of the world, must have struck them deeply, and have afterwards seemed to them a very important confirmation of His Divine foresight.

Time and space would fail me if I were to mention in the most cursory manner the great subjects which are set before us in these wonderful chapters of St. John. I need only add the prediction and prophetical description of the coming Paraclete, which will be found in the sixteenth chapter. This was the great immediate and overwhelmingly important Gift which was to be the fruit of the Sacrifice of the Cross, and which was to fill the whole world after our Lord had left it. It is clear that He did not think it well to say very much in detail about it on this occasion, yet it cannot be said that the great though few words in which He spoke, leave any doubt on the devout mind as to its full greatness and magnificence. His way of speaking of it may be compared to His manner of mentioning His own great personal gift of love, the Blessed Sacrament, concerning which He spoke so little, and that chiefly in a controversial discourse on one occasion—as far as we know—in the synagogue of Capharnaum. The words of our Lord about the Holy Ghost are enough to show the Divine Person of the Paraclete, and the whole theology of the Church concerning Him is built upon them.

Another very remarkable feature in this chapter is the manner in which our Lord has sketched in a very few words the office of the Holy Ghost in what He calls the conviction or reproval of the world by the Paraclete, which He sums up in three distinct sentences, the full meaning of which it requires a very long commentary to unfold. And yet this ' conviction of the world ' of which our Lord speaks so briefly has gone on from the Day of Pentecost until our own times, and will last in ever fresh vigour and power until the end of the world. No prophecy has ever been delivered so perpetual in its fulfilment, age after age, as this.

Of the chief remaining topics which strike us in these three chapters of St. John, it is hardly necessary to speak of more than two. The first is the tender and considerate love with which our Blessed Lord breaks the tidings of His own approaching departure to the Apostles, and in which He contrives, if we may use the word of Him, that the moment of His actual leavetaking should find them in a state of joy and peace, occasioned by His having told them just before the full truth about Himself, His Divine Person, and His Mission from the Father. The faith on which that outburst of joy was founded was to outlast the storms of many a trial and many a sorrow. But the most important of all the disclosures of the Sacred Heart made on this evening, may well be deemed the long and Divine prayer which our Blessed Lord poured out to the Eternal Father in the presence of the Apostolic band before leaving the Cenacle.

It has been necessary to comment at some length on this wonderful revelation of our Lord's interior thoughts and affections, which it is to be feared does not live so continually in the memories of Christians as it might have been intended to live. If it is lawful to speak of the times in which we live, there surely never has been a generation or a period in the history of His religion in which the constant meditation of the disclosures here made could have been more necessary or more salutary. Our Lord has willed that these words of His, of which the faithful of the very earliest age had no Gospel record—for the Beloved Disciple wrote the last of all the Evangelists, and not far from the end of the first century —should have been preserved for the faithful of the ages after the first. It seems as if it had been His will that the last thing put on record by St. John, or one of the last things, should be this Divine prayer for Unity—not as something which would add a bloom of perfection to the Church, which she might possibly exist without—a counsel, as we have seen it said, which it might be well indeed if possible to keep to, like the observance of poverty or of celibacy, without which Heaven might still be reached—but not only as the dearest boon from the Father's love, to be begged for by our Lord on His way to death, but as a condition absolutely essential to the work for which He came into the world, a condition the ascertained failure of which might involve the proof that His work also had failed. I will venture to ask the readers of this volume to pray continually and earnestly, that our Lord's desire here expressed may have more weight on the hearts of so many who strive to love Him, and that the thoughts of many, who are content to remain estranged from Unity, may be turned powerfully to the accomplishment in themselves of this His great desire, 'That they may be made perfect in one, that the world may know that Thou hast sent Me.'

H. J. C.

Manresa House, Roehampton, S.W.
Feast of St. Ethelbert, 1891.

CONTENTS.

CHAPTER III.

The Hatred of the World.

St. John xv. 11—27: *Story of the Gospels,* § 156.

CHAPTER I.

The Doctrine of Unity.

St. John xv. 4—8; *Story of the Gospels*, § 156.

WE have considered in our last volume the few words with which our Lord began His discourse to His Apostles, which He delivered after bestowing upon them the ineffable gift of the Blessed Sacrament and the Priesthood. We considered how those words of His which St. Luke has recorded about the fruit of the Vine, led Him by an easy connection of thought to the declaration that He was Himself the true Vine. The similitude contained in itself the further truth that those who were so closely one with Him were to be as the branches, through which it is that the Vine bears its fruit, and from this we have seen how He went on to describe the difference which there may be between one branch and another in point of fruitfulness. This again led Him to speak of the different manner in which the Almighty Dresser of the Vine had to deal with these different branches, removing those which are unfruitful, and pruning, by the wholesome discipline of afflictions of various kinds, those which were fruitful indeed, but not so fruitful as He desired, for His own glory and for the good of souls. He may, as we have seen, have had in His mind the unfruitfulness of the poor traitor Judas, whom it had been necessary in the providence

B 14

of the Father for Him to take away, as also whatever there was of imperfection about His other Apostles, to whose care He was to entrust the great work of the foundation, after Him, of the Kingdom of Heaven. He now approaches, as we have said, a new subject, most closely connected with this of fruitfulness for the Kingdom of Heaven, and we may judge of its importance in the affections of the Sacred Heart of our Lord from the fact that He makes this the subject of His first direct injunction to them, immediately after having given them Himself in the Adorable Sacrament. He is very anxious they should pray much, ask much of the Father, bring forth much fruit, and procure great glory to God. But His first word is not for prayer, not for fruitfulness, not even for the glorification of the Father—His first word is, ' Abide in Me, and I in you.'

' Abide in Me and I in you. As the branch cannot bear fruit of itself, unless it abide in the vine, so neither can you, unless you abide in Me. I am the Vine, you the branches. He that abideth in Me and I in him, the same beareth much fruit, for without Me you can do nothing. If any one abide not in Me, he shall be cast forth as a branch, and shall wither, and they shall gather him up, and cast him into the fire, and he burneth. If you abide in Me and My words abide in you, you shall ask what you will and it shall be done unto you. In this is My Father glorified, that you bring forth very much fruit and become My disciples.' In the natural vine there is no possibility of any action on the part of the branches, by which they can be separated from the parent stem. But our Lord tells us, by the mere fact that He makes the abiding in Him the subject of a most earnest exhortation, that in the mystical Vine it will turn out to be but too possible for the branches to separate themselves. He speaks as if this was the danger that He foresaw, and against which He was most anxious to warn and arm His Apostles. As St. John says of Him, when He would not commit Himself to many who would fain have joined themselves to Him at the outset of His Ministry, ' He knew what was in man.' This prevision of our Lord in more respects than one comes strongly before us in this last discourse. It must have occurred to the mind of the Apostle who gives us the report of what He then said, how truly both the promises that were then made to the Church had been fulfilled, so early in her history as the date at which he penned his Gospel, and also how many things which had been the subject of warnings and cautions, which were, in fact, prophecies of what no one could have expected, had also been verified in his own experience.

Alas, the prophecy which the words before us implicitly convey, was but too truly fulfilled in the experience of St. John. It might have been thought that the danger which is here foreshadowed was one from which the faithful might feel secure. Could there be any possibility of the branch separating itself from the parent stem ? it must be torn off by violence, and against the law of its being—could any one expect that a branch could become fruitful in a state of separation ? The life of the branch entirely depends on the sap which must flow into it from the stem, however far be the distance which it has to travel. Was it not to be so in the mystical Vine of which our Lord was speaking ? Were the branches of that Vine to be able to live when torn off ? Alas, the branches were to depart of their own accord, only too frequently and too fatally, from their connection with the stem. They were to imagine that they could live by themselves and bear fruit by themselves, and so incur by their own will the curse of sterility. When the blessed Apostle who reports this discourse to us came to commit it to writing, he must have felt that this warning of our Lord had been proved, by the history of the first age, to have proceeded from that perfect intelligence of what human nature was capable of, which He had shown before. For the continuance of that life and fruitfulness which they were to receive from our Lord as the parent Vine, it was necessary not only that they should receive them as the branches receive the sap from the stem, but that they should continue always unsevered from Him, by the abiding of which He speaks, and this abiding union with Him it was to be possible for them to forfeit by their own wilfulness and folly. St. John could see also, when he came to write this, many years after the Church had entered on her pilgrimage of conflict and tempest through the world, that our Lord's words here, like so many other of His sayings on this great evening, implied and conveyed a prophecy which it must have been most painful to His Sacred Heart to make. St. John, as we shall see, speaks in his First Epistle of the many who had separated themselves from the communion of the Church, that is, had torn themselves off like branches from our Lord. He had seen those who had once been fruitful branches going forth to prove the dreadful truth of this implied prophecy, separating themselves, and reaping the fruit of their separation, in incapacity for any good that might rejoice the heart of the great Vine-dresser, and then in the further sad fate which our Lord sketches so particularly and carefully in the paragraph which follows upon this.

We have supposed that our Lord, in His former words about the Apostles being clean or purified, as He had said to them, that is, in the sense in which He had spoken of purification at the time of the Lavanda, had perhaps in His mind the case of that one among their number who had left the Cenacle unclean and gone forth to throw himself into the deepest ruin. So we may think that the same contrast was still in His mind when He added these words about the necessity of abiding in Him, almost as if to say that for fruitfulness it is not enough to be free from stain, they will also have need of the continual influx of grace from Him, which is so beautifully figured in the sap which runs through the whole body of the tree, according to the image which our Lord uses. For He seems to keep the instance of Judas in mind in the description which He presently gives of the case of those who separate themselves from Unity. 'Abide in Me, and I in you. As the branch cannot bear fruit of itself, unless it abide in the vine, so neither can you unless you abide in Me. I am the Vine, you the branches. He that abideth in Me and I in him, the same beareth much fruit, for without Me you can do nothing.' Our Lord uses a very intelligible similitude. Those who do not abide in Him are as incapable of profitable work for God, as the branch, which is separated from the vine, is incapable of bearing fruit. The organization, so to speak, of the branch is the same as that of the tree, but the tree can live of itself and bear fruit of itself, even if it be maimed by the separation of the branch from it. The stem can even put forth fresh branches, which will supply the place of those which it has lost. Their loss does not affect its power of fructification. It does not depend on them for what makes it live and be fruitful. But the branch is at once useless from the moment of separation.

Our Lord does not explain the image further, because the truth which He wishes to insist upon is not so much the fruitfulness of the branches that retain their union with the vine, as the decay and destruction of the branches which lose that union. He might have described, in beautiful language, the various measures of glorious fruitfulness which He foresaw as gladdening His Heart, in the future labours and merits of those who were to abide in Him and He in them. He simply adds of such that 'he that abideth in Me and I in him, the same beareth much fruit, for without Me you can do nothing'—which last words may be an explanation of the double necessity of which He had just spoken, that He must abide in them as well as they remain united to and connected with Him, that He must in truth live and work in them who are to be His fruitful branches, as St. Paul takes such pains to declare in more places than one. 'There are diversities f operations,' he says, 'but the same God Who worketh all in all.'[1] He says in another Epistle that He 'Who wrought in Peter to the Apostleship of the Circumcision, wrought in me also among the Gentiles.'[2] He brings this truth constantly forward, when he is urging the image of the Body of Christ and its various members, an image in which we see a still further development of this parable of our Lord's of the Vine and the Branches, and in which the mutual relation and inter-dependence of the members of the Church is still more

[1] 1 Cor. xii. 5.   [2] Galat. ii. 8.

forcibly set forth, than in that before us. We shall have to speak of this presently.

In the passage now before us it is clear that the object which our Lord has in view is to follow up the instruction which He has just given, about the pruning and purifying process to which the Apostles were to be subjected in the Providence of God, by the further instruction which is contained in the words which we are now considering, on the subject of union with Himself. They are all, He has said, branches of Him as the Vine, but when He speaks of them as such He implies that they all together make up the Vine, or, as St. Paul would put it after Him, they are all members of His One Body. But first He speaks of the union between each branch and the parent stem, that is essential to the spiritual life, from which follows the union between each branch and all the rest, of which we shall have presently to say more. The result of the first union we have already mentioned—'the same beareth much fruit.'

The phrase used by our Blessed Lord, to 'abide in Him,' is one which seems to be used in more than one precise signification in different passages of the New Testament, at least, it seems to cover, in different passages where it is found, various stages or degrees of the same loyal and faithful adherence, either expressly or virtually. In itself it signifies the union of the heart with Him in its completest stage, in which that union involves faith, love, obedience, devotion, and whatever external profession and adhesion to Him in the Church, His Body, that He requires, or enjoins, or counsels, or takes pleasure in. The expression itself is one of those which the blessed Evangelist who lay in His bosom caught from Him,

and has made familiar to himself, beyond the other
writers of the New Testament, as expressing an order
of affection in which he took especial delight. The
Epistles of St. John, especially the first, which, as
has been said, seems almost as a kind of preface to
his Gospel, are full of this strain, and seem to
breathe the atmosphere of the Cenacle during these
last moments of our Lord's conversation with His
disciples. The manner in which these expressions
are used by the Apostle may serve somewhat as a
clue to their meaning in the mouth of our Lord.

Thus St. John uses the sacramental word communion,[3] which is rendered in our English version
by the word 'fellowship,' in a sense which seems to
be nearly identical with the 'abiding,' of which our
Lord here makes mention, and which includes the
union among themselves of those who are united
with God. Thus he says 'that which we have
heard and seen we declare unto you, that you
also may have fellowship with us, and our fellowship may be with the Father, and with His Son,
Jesus Christ.'[4] And again, 'If we say that we have
fellowship with Him, and walk in darkness, we lie
and do not the truth, but if we walk in the light, as
He also is in the light, we have fellowship one with
another, and the blood of Jesus Christ His Son clean-
seth us from all sin.'[5] The expression 'walking in
darkness' may fairly be taken to signify a life in sin,
and especially a life in which brotherly charity is
not practised. 'He that saith he is in the light,
and hateth his brother, is in darkness even until
now. He that hateth his brother is in darkness,
and walketh in darkness, and knoweth not whither

---

[3] κοινωνία.

[4] 1 St. John i. 3.   [5] 1 St. John i. 6, 7.

he goeth, because the darkness hath blinded his eyes.' Again, 'We have seen and do testify that the Father hath sent His Son to be the Saviour of the world. Whosoever shall confess that Jesus is the Son of God, God abideth in him and he in God.'

Again, St. John is speaking of the false doctrines concerning our Lord's Person which were even then rife, which were manifested in the denial of the truths of faith, and he says, 'As for you, let that which you have heard from the beginning abide in you. If that abide in you which you have heard from the beginning, you also shall abide in the Son and in the Father.'[6]

Again, the keeping of the Commandments is the evidence of abiding in Him. 'He that keepeth His Commandments abideth in Him and He in him, and by this we know that He abideth in us by the Spirit which He hath given us.'[7] Again, it is the confession of the true faith that is this abiding or fellowship. 'Whosoever shall confess that Jesus is the Son of God, God abideth in him and he in God. And we have known and have believed the charity which God hath to us, God is charity, and he that abideth in charity abideth in God and God in him. In this is the charity of God perfected with us, that we may have confidence in the Day of Judgment, because as He is, we also are in this world.'[8] It may also be said that the separation from the unity of the Church, in which schism consists, is a breaking off of that abiding in our Lord of which there is here question. The Apostle, speaking of those whom he calls Antichrists, who were doubtless schismatics as well as heretics, says in this same

[6] 1 St. John ii. 24.
[7] 1 St. John iii. 24. [8] 1 St. John iv. 15—17.

context, 'As you have heard that Antichrist cometh, even now there are become many Antichrists, whereby we know it is the last hour. They went out from us, but they were not of us. For if they had been of us, they would no doubt have remained with us, but that they may be manifest, that they are not all of us.'[9] For schism, being an offence against Unity, is an offence which cannot be concealed or mistaken, whereas heresy and other sins may often lie hid and undetected. The Unity of the Church is visible to all the world, like an established kingdom under a legitimate sovereign. To use our Lord's image, the branch that is torn off is seen to be torn off, and to use St. Paul's image, which is derived from our Lord's, the limb that is cut off from a living body is known to be cut off by every one who sees the body. The schismatics of whom St. John speaks were manifested, no one could doubt that they were schismatics, for their separation from the Unity of the Church could not fail to strike the eye.

We thus see that there may be various manners of this abiding in our Lord of which He speaks in the passage before us, increasing in intensity and in the perfection of the union that is maintained with Him, whether by faith, or by the state of grace, or by that of love, and conformity to His example and the keeping His Commandments or counsels, or by devotional and ascetic practices, or by ways of thought like His, which become habitual and, as it were, instinctive in those who serve Him with great closeness and fervour, or again by the participation of the privileges and rights of those who are members of His external Body in the

[9] 1 St. John ii. 18, 19.

Catholic Church. Conscious and wilful departure from Him in these ways cannot be without grievous sin, extinguishing at once the life of grace in the soul and all that abiding in Him of which He here speaks, indeed the whole spiritual existence, although the habits of faith and of the moral virtues may survive the separation from Him. We may now examine what He here says as to the two contrasted states spoken of, the state of those who do not abide in Him, and the state of those who abide in Him and His words abide in them. With regard to the first, the history of the man who departs from Him is described in several consecutive sentences, each of which has its own particular meaning. First, such a man shall be cast out as a branch, secondly, he shall wither, thirdly, he shall be gathered up, fourthly, he shall be cast into the fire, and lastly, he burneth. There the holy sentence of our Lord leaves him, as if the words 'he burneth' were to be understood of a state which lasts after all the other stages are finished.

The words 'he is cast forth, shall be cast forth as a branch,' seem to remind us that it is not enough to be a branch of the Vine, a member of the Body of Christ, for there may be branches that are separated from the stem of the Vine and so can have no sap. The soul whose lot our Lord is describing seems to be a branch and is so, but the state of separation is enough to put him at once in the way of all the disastrous processes which are to follow. He has no chance of the remedial care of the husband-man of which our Lord in the foregoing sentence has so spoken as pruning, for it is of no use to prune a branch of a vine which has already lost all power of bearing fruit by its separation from the stem. The soul may continue, to outward appearance, in the participation of the means of grace, but the state of sin makes them inoperative, and the community of Christians separated from Unity may seem like a flourishing tree in the eye of the world, and may even retain its hierarchy and its sacraments and the preaching of the Word of God, but the state of schism is enough to render all incapable of true spiritual fruitfulness, except in the case of those who in the eye of God have really no part in the sin of separation, and who only continue in it till they become aware of its character.

The next feature in the state of such souls or communities is that they wither. The loss of what answers to the sap in the Vine naturally leads to the incapacity to produce the life which the sap alone can supply, and the consequence is that in the eyes of God, and of man also, such souls 'wither.' They may lie under this ban of sterility without more as the dead branch of a tree may lie long on the ground before it is removed. But in truth it is dead. In the history of the decay of souls which our Lord is here sketching there is always room to be allowed for the action of His ineffable mercy in particular cases, for we know that though the dead branch cannot be restored to life save by a miracle, souls are never dead beyond hope as long as their time of probation lasts. Perhaps the leisurely manner in which our Lord speaks of these sad stages, one by one, may be set down among other things to His unwearied and inexhaustible compassion, and the tenderness of the Sacred Heart, which lingers over the downward process of the declension of the sinner as if each step in that process was an individual pang felt by Him most keenly. In the resources of His love for souls, there is that which would answer to the restoration of the branch to the stem from which it has been cut, and to the revival of life by the fresh infusion of sap, and the flourishing again of that which seemed to be the withered branch. But it is worse to be withered than to be torn off and cast out, and so the process is described in detail, and our Lord is speaking in parable of that which may ordinarily and legitimately take place, without reckoning on the extraordinary richness of mercy which may sometimes be vouchsafed. But withering unto death is the natural consequence of the separation of the soul from Him from Whom all grace flows.

The next step in the decay of these souls is that they are gathered up. 'They shall·gather him up,' He says, meaning apparently the Angels, as the executioners of the justice of God, as they are represented in the Parable of the Cockle among the Wheat. This perhaps is the ordinary way with our Lord in speaking of such execution of justice, not attributing it directly to God Himself, as if He was loath to act so against His creatures. It is so in the account of the Rich Fool in the parable where God says to him, 'Thou fool, this night do they require thy soul of thee,'[10] and of the Rich Glutton that 'he was buried in Hell.' The word, which is translated in our version, 'gather him up,' has in the original the sense which is conveyed by the Latin *colligent*— that is, the sense of gathering up with others, and thus we have three ideas expressed as to this part of the punishment. The first is simply the taking up, the second the gathering with others, and the third the kind of binding up and the restraint of

10 .St. Luke xii. 20.

liberty which befals those who are thus punished, one element of whose misery is their inability to free themselves by the exercise of any will of their own. For free will to choose between good and evil is lost in the fixity of the heart towards evil. Another element is the enforced society of wicked souls like themselves. The third is, that the destination of the whole to eternal torments is already fixed. These miseries may be in some measure anticipated in the case of hardened sinners even here, for the habit of evil becomes a tyranny—their life has almost perforce to be led with associates of their own sort, and the atmosphere which they breathe serves to confirm them in its own bonds. They strengthen one another by the maxims and rules and ways of thought and judgment which there prevail all around them. But the fulness of the evil state which our Lord describes is to be found in those who are already separated from Him beyond hope of deliverance.

Last among these steps of perdition come two more. The soul is 'put into the fire, and he burneth,' or rather, as our Lord puts it, 'they cast him into the fire and he burneth.' The dry branch blazes up in a moment, but it is not in this case to be consumed, it continues for ever burning. This is the end of one who was once a branch in the living vine, drawing from the stem the sap of life, and teeming with pleasant foliage and fruit which delighted the eye of the great husbandman. As we have supposed more than once that our Lord in this part of His discourse may have had in His mind the case of the one poor Apostle whom He had lost, and whom we shall find Him mentioning with sorrow, even in His great prayer to the Father with which the sayings and doings in the Cenacle were to conclude, it seems not unnatural that He may have had Judas in His mind in the words before us also. For the description which He here gives, in so much detail, of the soul which does not abide in Him, is general indeed in its language, but it seems to read as an account given by our Lord of the process through which the apostate Apostle had passed. Judas had begun by being unfruitful, to how great a degree it is difficult to imagine, when we remember that a year before the Passion our Lord had spoken of him as a devil. There had, then, been a long time during which this branch of the heavenly vine had borne no fruit, while the patience of the great Husbandman had waited, time after time, to give him every opportunity of recovering himself. Then the moment had come for the final breaking off, which had been his own act, the yielding deliberately to an evil passion which involved him in the foulest treachery against his loving Lord, His betrayal by a kiss, the bringing about His death, the renunciation of all his own privileges and hopes, his separation from the community which was in truth the body of Christ, and his abandonment of all hope of pardon, which was a denial of our Lord's love and mercifulness, and a deeper wound to His Sacred Heart than the betrayal and the murder itself.

The first judicial step taken by God, in punishment, as the Husbandman of the Vine, was, in our Lord's words, to take away Judas. Then came the casting him forth, by which we may suppose to be meant his separation from the body of the Vine, and consequently from all the supplies of grace which had besieged his soul in vain up to the last. It has been said that the Angels are the ministers of these judicial punishments of God, but we may add that there are some cases in which they seem to be carried out by evil angels rather than by good angels. Judas had been cast forth as a branch, and had become the prey and the companion of devils, the atmosphere in which his lot was now cast was that which they breathed, his thoughts and ideas and judgments and wishes, his attitude towards God and towards good and evil, his prospects and anticipations, as well as his present state and condition, were all those with which they were familiar. He was gathered together with them, made their associate and companion perforce, their slave, too, and their sport, he had been cast into the fire, and he was to burn with them for ever, the condition and state in which he now found himself was to know no change or relenting throughout eternity. Each particular detail, in the words before us, on which our Lord seems to linger purposely, was a special cause of grief and sorrowful compassion to the Sacred Heart of his Master, Who would so willingly have saved him at every stage of the ruin, until that at which it became irreparable.

The contrast to this picture is contained in the words of our Lord next following, ' If you abide in Me and My words abide in you, you shall ask whatever you will and it shall be done unto you. In this is My Father glorified that you bring forth ·very much fruit, and become My disciples.' The first thing to be noted here is that a clause is added which has no counterpart in the other picture. For our Lord, in speaking of the disciple who did not abide in Him, had not added, ' and My words do not abide in him.' For to abide in our Lord is not the same as for His words to abide in us. We may abide in Him in ways which fall short of His words abiding in us, as, for instance, if we keep the faith rightly and yet do not obey the commandments, and if we become negligent in any works of zeal or of charity. There is also a considerable difference in the other part of the contrast, between the disciple that does not abide in our Lord and the disciple who does so abide, and it is well to notice exactly how our Lord draws it out. What we might have expected on the side of the faithful would have been something which relates to fruitfulness, and the like, in contrast to the withering of the branch which was cast out. What our Lord says is not that if they abide in Him and His words in them, they shall not wither, but flourish with fruit, but that they shall ask whatever they will and it shall be done unto them. This, then, is the boon which He promises here, a general gift, placing at their disposal all the riches of God, according to the prayers they shall make to Him. It is not exactly fruitfulness, or success, or protection, or power, as of miracles, and the like, but that their prayers shall always be heard, whatever they ask.

We cannot doubt that our Lord's Sacred Heart was full of desire for the great fruitfulness of the Apostolic work, which indeed was to be the cause or instrument by which that was to be produced which He spoke of once as the fire He had come to cast upon the earth, and ' What will I but that it be kindled ? ' and, as has been said, some mention of the effects of their work for Him would seem to have been the natural antithesis to the picture which He had just drawn of the unfruitful branch of the vine. But fruitfulness in labours for God is the result of great prayer to God, and it is meant to be derived from prayer, and not to put it aside. We are reminded here of the saying of the holy Apostles themselves, when they announced to the faithful that they could not any longer undertake to discharge by themselves the charitable work of seeing to the distribution of the daily alms collected for the necessities of the community at Jerusalem, but were about to delegate it to the seven deacons. ' We will give ourselves continually to prayer and to the ministry of the Word.' [11]   We are thus taught by implication that the key which secures fruitfulness, or those other things just mentioned, is prayer, and that there is nothing which their prayers shall not obtain if they abide in our Lord, and if their obedience and faithfulness to Him is persevering.

Prayer must then be to apostolical men the one great means of keeping up their communion with Him, the exercise in which all their aims and designs of good are to be embodied and laid before Him. They are to have what they ask for, not simply what they think of or desire, but whatever they put before Him in prayer, rightly formed and perfect in all its conditions. A project or plan or design may occur to them, but it must be moulded and shaped by prayer. Of course it must be understood that the prayers to which this great promise is made are prayers according to the will of God and the rules of His Kingdom, and for things which He sees it good to grant. Otherwise the prayer is best heard by Him in granting something else, which He sees to be more advantageous for the good of their souls than the thing actually asked for. Thus when St. Paul asked to be delivered from that which he describes as the ' sting of his flesh,' [12] it seems to have surprised him, as something

<hr>

[11] Acts vi. 4.   [12] a Cor. viii. 7.

unusual, that the petition was not granted immediately. But he was informed that it was better for him that it should be left for him to battle with, for the grace of God was sufficient for him. The limitations which are to be assigned in such cases to general promises of this kind have been spoken of elsewhere, but it is a matter for great thankfulness that the promise is given, and blessed indeed are they who accustom themselves to live upon it. The promise here is not like that made to faith, 'as a grain of mustard-seed,' about the power of 'moving mountains.' It does not speak of graces which amount to miracles, or to the obtaining of favours to others, who may frequently be themselves obstacles to the impetration of what is asked for them. Our Lord seems to speak directly of personal graces asked by Christians for themselves, when they are abiding in our Lord in the state of grace, and when there is no serious fault in them to hinder their power in prayer. But there is no reason why it should not extend even to greater boons. When our Lord says, 'It shall be done unto you,' He seems to mean that He will do it, though the original word signifies only, 'It shall come about to you.'

He adds, 'In this is My Father glorified, that you bring forth very much fruit, and become My disciples,' and the order in which the words are placed by Him seems to have some reason, as we should rather have expected it to be inverted—that you become My disciples and bring forth very much fruit. It may be that the formation of the character of our Lord in those who belong to Him, and especially in those who have in any sense the Apostolic commission and the work of the Ministry, is the chief and most important fruit of the prayers and labours of such men, and that this is a process which is ever in progress, ever beginning again and again until it is finally consummated, not by the attainment of absolute perfection in the imitation of our Lord, but by the accomplishment of the measure which God desires to see in each individual soul. So that we are to be always ' becoming ' the disciples of our Lord, however great may be the fruit which we bear, and this fruit consists, as has been said, more in the exercises of the virtues, and the interior acts of the affections which are manifested in that exercise, than in great outward works and prolonged services and sufferings, which may meet the eyes of men. God may have been more glorified by the inner life of St. Francis Xavier than even by his external labours, and by the short life of St. Aloysius than by long years of some indefatigable missionary. The measures of Heaven are not those of earth, and the real history of the saints is that of their becoming more and more the disciples of their Master.

Very near to the thought of the abiding in Him, which our Lord desired to see in His disciples, lay in the Sacred Heart the thought of their love for and union with one another. Indeed, the two thoughts may be said to be in truth the same. The words on which we have been lately commenting are precious to us as being those in which He has laid the foundation, as we may say, of the doctrine of the unity of His Body, the Church, which we shall find to have been particularly prominent in His mind at this time. He had just, as we suppose, instituted the great sacramental feast of the New Law, one most conspicuous object of which was to bind them together in one as He and the Father are One.[13] He says this in His final prayer, the burthen

----

[13] St. John xvii. 22.

of which is an urgent petition and demand for the grace of unity among them. We shall see that when He says, ‘The glory which Thou hast given Me I have given to them, that they may be one as We are One,’ there is good reason for thinking that He meant to speak of the Blessed Sacrament. This will have to be explained later on. But it seems well here to point out how the passage before us seems to show that He desired His disciples not only to preserve with the greatest care and faithfulness their union with Him, their abiding in Him in the truest and fullest sense, but also to be most closely united one to another in the body of the Catholic Church, their close union with Himself producing, and as it were fructifying in their union one with another. This desire of our Lord is continually making itself manifest in the discourse of which these words are a part, and it seems evident also that He means the great boon of the Blessed Sacrament, which He had just bestowed upon them, to be the source and principle of their union one with another.

This great doctrine of unity was afterwards unfolded most fully by St. Paul, who is that one among the New Testament writers who had the office of drawing out the relations of Christians one to another as members of the Body of Christ. It is easy to see how the image which our Lord here uses, of the vine and the branches, is, if we may say so, the foundation of the other which is used by St. Paul, and how it also seems to require it as its completion and fulfilment. It was the object of St. Paul to bring out more fully the relations of the members of the Body one to another, and for this purpose the image of the vine was less apt, for it left untold the mutual subordination and duties of the members, their need of one another, and their sympathetic sharing in the welfare or the calamities one of another. On the other hand, there is no one member of the human body on which all the other members depend so entirely as the branches of the vine depend on the stem. Thus the image used by our Lord was the one more fit for the purpose of insisting on that dependence. We can imagine other reasons why our Lord left the image of His own Body to be drawn out by the Apostle, under the guidance of the Holy Ghost, at a later date in the history of the infant Church. And it may be said with truth that these two images, which may be called parables, are sufficient, when duly combined by Christian contemplation, to set forth the whole doctrine which must have been so very dear to the Sacred Heart, and which perhaps for that very reason among others the powers of Hell have most persistently and virulently assailed, and, as it is sad to add, with, in some sense, the greatest success.

Heresy and schism are the two sins which came into the world in consequence of the gifts of infallible truth and perfect and visible unity which were to be bestowed upon the Church, and on which our Lord's Heart was now dwelling with infinite joy and complacency. If God had not confided to the Church the infallible teaching of the truths of faith, there would be no heresies to rebel against that teaching. If the Church were not by Divine institution, as St. Paul tells us, one Body, there would be no schisms rending that Divine Unity. Thus these two sins may be considered as peculiarly antichristian in character, and the language of the New Testament treats them as such, as sins against the Person and Body of Christ. The sin of the rebel angels is a sin which man cannot parallel in its malice, not that man cannot rebel against his Creator, but that he cannot rebel in the light and privileges of Heaven. In the same way, heresy and schism rise above other sins which the children of the Church can commit. It is because they are by Baptism children of the Catholic Church that they are capable of committing them. Each of them is an appeal to some of the strongest, though perhaps not the grossest, instincts of degenerate nature—to the pride of intellect, or to the love of independence of authority. These two evil principles are always wrestling against the yoke of law, which is administered in the name of God by a succession of human instruments in the ever-living and always present Church. The world is always ready to aid human nature in its revolt.

The Church in every age, and her children who have caught her spirit, turn with a kind of nausea and loathing from both these sins, more especially that one of them which it is less possible to attribute to ignorance or mistake. Schism reminds us more of the treachery and disloyalty of Judas than of the malignity of Caiphas. The language of the Apostles concerning these sins is such as to surprise some readers, who have perhaps never understood their full character. St. Paul speaks as if one of the greatest of possible dangers had been introduced into the Church of Corinth by the divisions against which he writes, and the words of St. John about schismatics sound to us even more severe. Our Lord's own words do not imply any other truth— there can be no more dreadful lot for a Christian than to be cut off from the true Vine. We can only remember that in His merciful distribution of the recompence for good or for evil in the next world, the children are not punished, except temporarily, for the sins of the fathers, and that, especially in times like those in which we live, it is quite possible to have been born and educated in schismatical and heretical communities, without the act of personal disloyalty to our Lord, which consists in a deliberate adoption of the disobedience in which the schism or the heresy had its origin. There are therefore multitudes of such souls, we may believe, in communities separated from the Church, who will not have to bear the guilt of the authors of the schism or heresy which was accomplished centuries ago, and in such there are many who may be so faithful to our Lord as to be true consolations to His Sacred Heart, which is infinitely pained and grieved by the existence of such evils. But the case of the great mass of such Christians must be considered as most anxious and dangerous, for they have to bear, besides the possibility of a share in the guilt itself, the numberless disadvantages and spiritual losses of the condition which the guilt has entailed upon them— the imperfect teaching of the Catholic Creed, the certain, and in other cases the probable, absence of a true hierarchy and priesthood, mutilated or fictitious sacraments, and a perpetual alienation from the body of the living Church, together with the absence of the inestimable privileges which belong to the condition of her children. We cannot be surprised at the stern way in which the Saints speak of such a condition, or at the language of our Lord about Unity, which implies that He foresaw that the greatest triumphs of the kingdom of Satan against the Church would be won by means of the defection of Christians from their obligations in this respect, as to which He speaks as if the great work of the conversion of the world depended upon them in a singular manner.

St. Augustine[14] has a well known passage concerning the verses on which we have lately been commenting, in which he most naturally, and as a matter of course, puts his finger upon the true bearing of the whole context. 'This place of the Gospels,' he tells us, 'in which our Lord calls Himself the Vine and His disciples the branches, is spoken in the sense that He is the Head of the Church, the Man Jesus Christ, the Mediator between God and man, and in which we are the members of His Body.' He says that the union between our Lord and us could not have been without the Incarnation, for God and man are not of the same nature. Thus we are capable of being branches of Him, by His taking our nature. When our Lord spoke the words of this passage, there was only one part of the great truth of His Body as yet drawn out before the minds of the Apostles, that is, the doctrine of the union with and dependence on Him as the stem of the Vine, separation from Whom was death to the branch.

There was the further part of the same doctrine, which it was to be the office of the Holy Ghost to unfold, that is, the mutual relations and most intimate connection between one branch and another, and all the branches or limbs in the one body, and for this the image of the Body made up of many members, was the most appropriate, and we know how much use St. Paul has made of it in various places in the Epistles. We shall have little more

14 Tract. 60, in Joannem.

to do than to remind ourselves of the language of the Apostle in the great passages which have become classical in reference to the subject.

The illustration of the doctrine by the figure of the body, which has many members, first meets us in the First Epistle of St. Paul to the Corinthians. After dealing with a number of most important questions of various kinds, the last of which, before the passage of which we are to speak, relates to the abuse which had crept in among the converts at Corinth, with regard to the celebration of the *agapæ*, which followed after the great Eucharistic feast, in the place where they were accustomed to meet, St. Paul passes to the rivalries and ambitions as to the possession of the spiritual gifts of various grades, which were then common in the Churches, and apparently nowhere more common than in the favoured community to which the Apostle was writing. The point to be cleared up did not, as far as we know, touch directly any point of order or discipline, and in consequence the doctrine laid down by St. Paul was rather thrown in, if we may say so, for its own sake, than on account of the necessities of the case. We may suppose that it must often have occurred to the Apostle to introduce an important subject like this, as it seemed, by the way, for he must often have felt the usefulness of giving instructions of this kind, which he might not have other opportunities of mentioning. At the same time, it is natural that, on occasions of this kind, he might not treat a subject so leisurely as when he had other reasons for introducing it. St. Paul begins on the present occasion by a rapid enumeration of the various and manifold operations of the Holy Ghost, of which he has to speak. At the same time he is most careful to insist on the unity of the source from which they all proceed, 'and the manifestation of the Spirit is given to every man unto profit, to one indeed by the Spirit is given the word of wisdom, and to another the word of knowledge according to the same Spirit,'[15] and so the Apostle goes on enumerating the different gifts, but he says, 'all these things one and the self-same Spirit worketh, dividing to every man according as He will.' Then immediately, and without any preface, as if it were a contemplation familiar at once to himself and to those to whom he writes: 'For as the body is one and hath many members, and all the members of the body, whereas they are many, yet are one body, so also is Christ'[16]—where the name of our Lord is put for the body called after Him, 'For in one Spirit were we all baptized into one Body, whether Jews or Gentiles, whether bond or free, and in one Spirit we have all been made to drink.'

St. Paul goes on, as we all remember, to argue the point of the unity of the body and of the interdependence of the various members one upon another, as if this were the matter which he had before all others in his mind at the time. 'For the body also is not one member, but many, and if the foot should say, because I am not the hand, I am not of the body, is it therefore not of the body?' And he goes on at some length, as if it were a matter of great importance. We need not quote the whole passage, which will probably be sufficiently present to the mind of our readers. He argues from the need which the members of the body have one of another, from the care taken of those that are the

[15] 1 Cor. xii. 4, seq.   [16] 1 Cor. xii. 12, seq.

least independent, and from the mutual assistance
which all render one to another. A moment's
reflection will show us that there is less in the image
of the vine which could have served parabolically in
this way, and on the other hand, there is one thing
which the image of the vine brings out more forcibly
than this other of the body, namely, the absolute
dependence of the branches on the one parent stem.
The Apostle proceeds, that all this is arranged ' that
there might be no schism in the body, but that the
members might be mutually careful one for another,
and if one member suffer anything, all the members
suffer with it, or if one member glory, all the members rejoice with it.'

St. Paul then applies his argument, ' Now you
are the Body of Christ, and members of member,'
words which seem to mean that the Christian idea
is, that all form the one Body of Christ, and that
each individual belongs to it, as one of its members,
and each to all the rest. Then he enumerates the
various orders in the Church from the Apostles
downwards, though not precisely in the hierarchial
arrangement. He ends by the question, ' Are all
Apostles? are all Prophets?' and the rest, and
passes at once into the showing them a more
excellent way, which is no other than his wonderful
description of charity. It is not necessary to repeat
this chapter here, for it is one of the passages of
St. Paul that few readers of the New Testament are
likely to forget. But it is worthy of remark, that in
adding this wonderful passage about charity to his
statement on Unity the Apostle, we can hardly say
of set purpose, exactly follows the lead of his Master.
For in the chapter of St. John, on which we are now
occupied, the verses in which our Lord lays down so

strongly the doctrine of the Unity of the Church under the image of the vine and the branches, and with the repeated injunction to ' abide in Him,' He proceeds, as will be seen presently, to pour forth, one after another, sentences which either are expressions of His own love for the disciples, or exhortation to them to ' love one another.' There is a sort of instinctive recurrence on the part both of our Lord and of His Apostle to the topic of charity, after they have spoken of the obligation of Unity, which can hardly fail to strike thoughtful minds. We may say something more on this subject before we part from it altogether.

The great Epistle to the Romans was written in the same period of St. Paul's preaching as that which we have been lately quoting, and we may well confirm what has been said by the words of the Apostle in it on the subject of charity and unity. It does not appear that the Romans were at all torn by intestine divisions like the Corinthians, and the passage which we shall quote on this subject does not seem to have been called forth by any particular circumstances in the Church to which the Apostle was addressing himself. But as soon as he has finished his long and difficult argument on the rejection of the Jews and the admission of the Gentiles in their place, he turns to practical exhortations, and for the last five[17] chapters of the Epistle he speaks in the same affectionate strain. Almost at once he comes to the point of unity and charity. ' I say by the grace that is given me, to all that are among you, not to be more wise than it behoveth to be wise, but to be wise unto sobriety, and according as God has divided to every one the measure of

[17] Chaps. ix.—xiii.

faith. For as in one body we have many members, but all members have not the same office, so we, being many, are one body in Christ, and every one members one of another. And having different gifts according to the grace given us, either prophecy, to be used according to the rule of faith, or of ministry in ministering, or he that teacheth in doctrine, he that exhorteth in exhorting, he that giveth with simplicity, he that ruleth with careful-ness, he that showeth mercy with cheerfulness. Let love be without dissimulation.'[18] Here again we see how useful is the image of the Body for the doctrine of Unity.

There is another famous passage of St. Paul which must be added here, without which we should not have given the full witness of the great Apostle. The Epistle to the Ephesians is of a considerably later period in the career of St. Paul than those which we have already quoted, but this passage again can hardly have been suggested by any necessity peculiar to those for whom it is written. We shall find hints that the subject has somewhat developed in the mind of the writer, as is often the case when we find St. Paul taking up again a familiar thought. The Epistle is one of those written while St. Paul was a prisoner at Rome. ' I, therefore, a prisoner in the Lord, beseech you that you walk worthy of the vocation in which you are called, with all humility and mildness, with patience, supporting one another in charity, careful to keep the unity of the Spirit, in the bond of peace; one Body and one Spirit, as you are called in one hope of your calling, one Lord, one faith, one baptism, one God and Father of all, Who is above all, and through

18 Romans xii. 3, seq.

all, and in us all. But to every one of us is given grace according to the measure of the giving of Christ. Wherefore He saith, Ascending on high, He led captivity captive, He gave gifts to men . . . and He gave some Apostles, and some Prophets, and other some Evangelists, and other some pastors and doctors, for the perfecting of the saints, for the work of the ministry, for the edifying of the Body of Christ, until we all meet into the unity of faith and of the knowledge of the Son of God, unto a perfect man, unto the measure of the age of the fulness of Christ, that henceforth we be no more children tossed to and fro, and carried about with every wind of doctrine by the wickedness of men, by cunning craftiness by which they lie in wait to deceive, but doing the truth in charity, we may in all things grow up in Him Who is the head, even Christ, from Whom the whole body being compacted and fitly joined together, by what every joint supplieth, according to the operation in the measure of every part, maketh increase of the body unto the edifying itself in charity.'[19]

It is remarkable, how in this and other passages of the New Testament, coming from the pens of Apostles and their companions, the idea of the one Church rises above that of the particular communities which were, naturally enough, the points of immediate interest to the Christians of whom they were composed. The Churches of Corinth, or of Ephesus, or of Thessalonica, had each their own praises, or boasts, or their remarkable men, but the object of the Apostles seems to have been to teach the members of each particular city to forget their own domestic glories in their loyalty to the one

[19] Ephes. iv.

Church to which they all belonged. Another thing
that must strike the reader of a passage such as that
before us, is that St. Paul furnishes here what he
had not drawn out so fully in the earlier Epistles,
namely, the great object and purpose which it here
assigned for the unity on which so much stress is
laid. That object is drawn out in the last sentence
of the passage. That object is partly security in
doctrine, that 'henceforth we be no more children
tossed to and fro by every wind of doctrine,' in
which words the Apostle seems to point to some
danger to which the Christians to whom he writes
had been exposed, and which would be obviated by
the unity which he is speaking of, but chiefly perhaps
by the fact that the growth and progress of the
whole body in spiritual perfection was in great measure dependent on this unity and charity of which
he speaks. This is a point which it might require
much explanation to draw out in full. It is quite
certain, however, that the words of St. Paul set
before us a picture of the growth of the whole body
in spiritual stature, depending not only on the
advance of each member in the knowledge of our
Lord, but aided and made more perfect by the
simultaneous growth of the other members, each
contributing what belongs to him to supply, being
'compacted and fitly joined together by what every
joint supplieth, according to the operation in the
measure of every part.' The whole result is that
each one profits by the simultaneous increase of the
others, and that the body increases in perfection,
and especially in charity, at the same time that each
individual member becomes more perfect, and con-
tributes to the growth of the rest and of the whole.
The idea that they have a great deal of advance

still to make, indeed an almost unlimited capacity of growth and increase in knowledge, meets us over and over again in this wonderful Epistle, as the careful reader will be aware. Here we need say no more than that if it be indeed true that the advance of the Christian community, whether the whole Catholic Church or any smaller body a part of her in any particular city, is indefinitely furthered or partially stunted, by the peaceful atmosphere and invigorating glow of unity in the one case, or the chill of division in the other case, we learn to understand more completely why our Lord and His Apostles seem to speak with an almost passionate intensity of unity, as the condition of all true spiritual life, and why there is nothing which they seem so unable to tolerate as separation from unity. It cannot be a mere sentiment of what is beautiful or becoming, or in keeping with the atmosphere of peace and charity, which prevails in the Kingdom of God, that makes the saints, as it seems, so fierce, with regard to the very shadow of division and heresy. They see, as our Lord Himself and His Apostles saw, that schism is a sin by which the true temper of the soul is tested, whether it has what St. Paul calls the mind of Christ, or not; it is the sprouting of an evil root, which poisons the very life of the Spirit, and when it is once fixed in the soul, all hope is gone of life or progress.

It is in the same Epistle to the Ephesians that we find, for the first time in the New Testament, the use of the image of the union between a man and his wife as applied to our Lord and the Church. It occurs in that part of the Epistle in which the Apostle turns to the exhortation of the Christians for whom he is writing as to the right discharge of their duties one to another, a topic as we know which frequently finds its place in the writings of the Apostles, even when they have begun to write on account of some special and occasional necessity. St. Paul in the place of which we speak begins by general instructions, and then comes to the particular duties of married persons to one another, children to parents and parents to children, servants and masters, and so forth. He seems to go out of his way, so to speak, to bring in the application with which we are concerned. ' Let women be subject to their husbands in the Lord, because the husband is the head of the wife, as Christ is the head of the Church. He is the Saviour of the body. Therefore as the Church is subject to Christ, so let the wives be to their husbands in all things. Husbands love your wives, as Christ also loved the Church, and delivered Himself up for it, that He might sanctify it, cleansing it by the laver of water in the word of life, that He might present it to Himself a glorious Church, not having spot or wrinkle, or any such thing, but that it should be holy and without blemish. For this ought men also to love their wives as their own bodies. He that loveth his wife loveth himself. For no man ever hated his own flesh, but nourisheth it and cherisheth it, as also Christ doth the Church, because we are members of His body, of His flesh, and of His bones. For this cause shall a man leave his father and mother, and shall cleave unto his wife, and they shall be two in one flesh. This is a great sacrament, but I speak in Christ and in the Church.'[20]

We need not stop to draw out the full doctrine contained in these verses. It is enough for us here to note how readily the relation between Christ and

[20] Ephes. v. 22– 2.

the Church rises to the mind of St. Paul on this occasion, and how the use he makes of it, enlarging as he does upon it, seems to confirm our idea of the importance which he attached to it, especially as showing the tender care and jealous watchfulness which he devotes to it, and his care to draw out the significance in all its bearings. St. Paul seems here to lead the way for scores of other writers, Saints and Fathers of the Catholic Church, in the use of this image, which we know to be taken from Holy Scripture, and which occurs again in the closing book of the Holy Volume. The image of the bride is here brought into the illustration of this doctrine, and we must not forget that we owe this image, like the other beautiful figure of the Lamb of God, to the Blessed Precursor of our Lord, St. John Baptist himself, who was the first to speak of Him under the name of the Lamb, and also under that of the Bridegroom: ' He that hath the Bride is the Bridegroom, but the friend of the Bridegroom, who standeth and heareth Him, rejoiceth with joy because of the Bridegroom's voice,' and the Apostle must have had some particular reason for the language here used, beyond that of enhancing the dignity and sanctity of the marriage tie. Having spoken so strongly just before in the passage we have already quoted, it would seem as if he returned to the subject of the dignity of the body and its great nearness to the Sacred Heart of our Lord, no doubt taking occasion, as was often his habit, to enhance the impression of the truth he had before insisted on by adding something which he had then passed over about the very intimate relations between our Lord and His Spouse. The special truth which is set forth in these last words concerning the Church

seems to be the singleness and indissolubility of the
union.   The words remind us of those in the
Canticles, *Dilectus meus mihi et ego illi*, and others
like them.   We may imagine what St. Paul would
have said to a theory of more than one Church—as
far from his thoughts as that of a divided or defec-
tible Church.   The passages which have been quoted
might be supplemented by those in the Apocalypse
of St. John to which we have already referred.

There are, of course, other passages which might
be quoted from the New Testament writings which
would illustrate the passage before us, in which our
Lord seems to have laid the foundation in words of
His own of the great doctrine of Unity, which we
shall find coming once more to His lips at the close of
this evening, in the last words He uttered before He
went forth to His Agony in the Garden of Gethsemani—words addressed indeed to His Eternal
Father, but of even more significance to us than
others, because He must have uttered them as He
did, and have ordained that they should be recorded
as they have been, by His Beloved Disciple, in order
that they may fall on our ears with more than usual
weight and solemnity.   The few words about the
vine and its branches are plainly our Lord's con-
tribution, if we may use the term, towards the
formation in the treasures of the Church of this
doctrine of Unity, and we may well think that no
essential part of that doctrine has been omitted by
Him in them, especially when they are taken, as
we shall see, in connection with the immediate context and sequel.   After the Ascension and the Day
of Pentecost, the Church grew up under the guidance
of the Holy Ghost, and its principle of life was that
Unity which had been foreshadowed by our Lord in

His words about the vine. In process of time we find the other image of the Body of Christ used by St. Paul in the various places which have been quoted. It is like what was done by our Lord when He changed one parabolic image for another in order to bring out in one the truth which was more adapted to it than another. Thus the truth which is set forth in the Parable of the Cockle sown in the Wheatfield could not have been conveyed so well by some earlier members of the same series. It is plain that our Lord has taken into His own mouth the all important truth of the absolute necessity of union with Him, on which He has so much insisted in the verses before us, while He has left to the Apostles under the direction of the Paraclete the other part of the same doctrine which is virtually contained in the same image, the multiplicity of the functions of the members of His Body and their beautiful harmony among themselves. This was a part of the truth which required the organization which the Church had hardly received in its fulness before the Day of Pentecost, and perhaps for some time after that day.

It was not our Lord's manner to lay down, with His own lips, the rules which were afterwards to be in force in the Church for the preservation of unity. He showed plainly enough the immense importance it had in the system which He came to found, and He established Himself, in words never to be forgotten by the Apostles who heard them, the central throne which He was to leave behind Him, by which unity was to be preserved without any chance of mistake in the simplest way which all the world could always recognize. He provided, moreover, that that throne should never fail or err, and that thus the children of the Church should never be at a loss for their guidance as to this point, so urgently recommended to them by Himself as the darling desire of His Heart. But He left the disciplinary regulations which were to be called for from time to time, to those who were to come after Him in the Church in this and in other matters not less important, just as He left her to choose who was to take the seat among the Twelve which had been forfeited by Judas.

No one who has studied the New Testament will be surprised at the reticence which is observed by its writers as to matters relating to the constitution of the Church, the methods of dealing with rebellious members, and the like, though this silence is not universal. These were matters dealt with by the ordinary authorities as occasion arose, and were taken for granted without being made matters for special mention in the Epistles, unless there was some particular reason for it. Incidentally, we find some strong expressions against the persons who cause divisions, which show that they were, in the minds of the Apostles, the greatest of all sources of mischief in the early Church. ' Little children,' says the Beloved Disciple, whose words we need not scruple to repeat again and again, ' it is the last hour, and as you have heard that Antichrist cometh, even now there are become many antichrists, whereby we know that it is the last hour. They went out from us, but they were not of us, for if they had been of us, they would no doubt have remained with us, but that they may be manifest that they are not all of us.' Their true character is shown by their separation from the one Body of Christ.

CHAPTER II.

Love of the Brotherhood.

St. John xv. 9—17; *Story of the Gospels*, § 156.

THE next words of our Lord seem to follow very naturally on those of which we have been lately speaking, but they enter on what is in some sort a new topic. 'As the Father hath loved Me, I also have loved you. Abide in My love. If you keep My commandments, you shall abide in My love, as I also have kept My Father's commandments, and do abide in His love.' He does not say that our love for Him is to be equal to that love between His Father and Himself to which He refers, but that our love for Him is to be shown in the same way in which He showed His love for the Father, by keeping His commandments. It seems likely that we are to understand Him as speaking of His Sacred Humanity, of His love to us therein, and of the love of His Father to that Sacred Humanity, from which flows His own love to us and to the Church. The Eternal Father loved the Sacred Humanity of our Lord, in the first place, with a love that was perfectly gratuitous, for the gift bestowed upon it was a gift given out of pure love, and could not have been won or merited by anything in that Sacred Humanity, because it was the gift of the Personal Union with the Son of God. In giving that ineffable and gratuitous gift,

God gave all that He had to give, the whole substance of the Godhead, once and for ever, and all the
gifts and graces that could be conferred on that
Human Nature which was personally united to the
Divine Son. Our Lord's love for us has the same
characteristics of gratuitousness and immensity. For
His love for us could not have been merited by any
pure creature, and also He has given Himself to us
without reserve, all that He has to give, as far as we
are capable of receiving it. These words before us,
as we must not forget, were spoken by Him immediately after He had given Himself to the Apostles in
the Blessed Sacrament, in which gift all the wonders
that He has wrought for us are summed up, and
which would not be to us the gift of excessive love
that It is, if It were not what the Church calls It in
the words of the Psalmist, the 'memorial of His
marvellous works.' He gives Himself to us whole
and entire in the Blessed Sacrament, and with the
communication of the graces He has received in His
Sacred Humanity, the application of all the merits
of His Life, and Passion, and Death, the whole
fruits of His humiliation in the Incarnation. There
is, therefore, much similarity between the gift He
received from His Father's love, and the gift which
He has Himself given to us.

When our Lord bids the Apostles 'abide in My
love,' He means, as it appears, to tell them to be
careful above all things to keep themselves such as
those must be on whom His love rests continually.
He represents His love, with all the benefits it
conveys to them, as a home in which they are to live
and dwell, as the ocean encompasses the creatures
that live therein, or the air which is the element in
which the birds move and live. It is to be all

around them, and shelter them, and foster them, penetrate their whole being and surround their whole life. How this is to be, He tells them at once. 'If you keep My commandments, you shall abide in My love, as I also have kept My Father's commandments, and do abide in His love.' For, from the very beginning of the existence of that Sacred Humanity of which we are speaking, He was conscious of the end for which He existed, and He accepted the precept of the Father for the salvation of the world, and every single act which it involved. The whole subsequent history of the Incarnate Son was a perpetual act of obedience to the Father in every detail, as He said of Himself, 'I do always the things which please Him.' This is the model which He here sets before us, as the secure condition on which we may always abide in His love, the perpetual keeping of the commandments which He gives us, which He presently seems to reduce to one single commandment, which can be no other than the precept of brotherly love.

But it may also be remembered that while the tender love of the Father encompassed our Blessed Lord at every moment of the Life of the Sacred Humanity, so that in that sense it was true that He always abode in the love of the Father, that life itself was nothing but a continual and most energetic exercise of acts of love to the Father, a ceaseless, uprising stream of most sweet incense from the Sacred Heart, so that in that sense also He abode in the Father's love, actively, as well as passively. And this too is the life of the servants of God even on earth, the lovers of our Blessed Lord. He sheds down on them unintermittingly His showers of love, while they in their turn are always making their hearts altars from which a perpetual cloud of incense rises up to Him in return, consisting of their acts of love and obedience, which have a heavenly beauty and fragrance of their own. So that their life consists in the perpetual reception of the fruits of His most wonderful love, and in the continual giving back to Him of love for love, in the exercise of the virtues. This is indeed an abiding in His love.

He adds now, ' These things I have spoken to you, that My joy may be in you; and that your joy may be filled.' This saying of our Lord, that He has spoken to them certain things for this or that purpose, occurs several times in the course of this discourse, and is not always to be restricted in its meaning, as if it referred to the words immediately preceding. Our Lord sometimes refers to actions as well as to words, especially when the words have been explanations of actions, or connected with them as a part of the same whole, as had been the case with the Blessed Sacrament. The greatest joy of the Sacred Heart was in the thought of the Father, His whole Life as an offering of the intensest love to Him, in obeying His precepts, as He said, ' I do always the things that please Him.' After His joy in doing every moment of His Life what was the Father's will that He should do, then and there, the great joy of His Heart was the sight of those whom the Father had given to Him, and who by His teaching and prompting were like Him, always engaged in doing what the Father willed. For the Sacred Heart could rejoice in nothing more than in seeing His Apostles such as the grace of God had now made them, and the object He had in view in His teaching, as He now says, was that that joy of His might abide in consequence of their perseverance in charity. We find this affection of our Blessed Lord echoed in the language of the Apostles themselves, St. Paul speaking of His disciples as his crown, and joy, and rejoicing, and boasting, and entreating them to make his joy in them fuller and fuller. It cannot be doubted that it forms a great part of the joys of Heaven, that the saints are able to see the fruit of their labours in the souls of others, as it is of that of the Holy Angels to see the graces and glories of the souls over whom they have watched. It is not often that we are told by the Evangelists that our Lord expressed in words the joy which He felt in His Heart. But both St. Matthew and St. Luke tell us of the occasion on which He did this, ' At that hour He rejoiced in the Holy Ghost and said, I give thanks to Thee, O Father, Lord of Heaven and earth, that Thou hast hid these things from the wise and prudent, and hast revealed them to little ones.'[1]

' And,' He adds, ' that your joy may be filled.' This abiding in Him by means of obedience to His commandments, He knew well to be the real fulfil-ment of their joy, although they might have been inclined to place it in something else short of this, as in the enjoyment of the delights of His company, His bodily presence, or other things of the same kind. For the true joy of the soul is in abiding union with God, in which all graces are included. It is that which secures peace of conscience, which puts us in possession of perfect confidence towards God, and enables us to feed our souls without fear on the blessings which we have in the Church, and the hopes to which we look forward hereafter.

' This is My commandment, that you love one another as I have loved you. Greater love than this

---

[1] St. Matt. xi. 25 ; St. Luke x. 21.

no man hath, that a man lay down his life for his
friends.'   He had already spoken of the keeping of
His commandments as the same thing as the abiding
in His love, and now He tells them what these commandments require.   Instead of saying, 'These are
My commandments,' He uses the singular number,
and adding the Greek definite article, 'This is *the*
commandment, that which is Mine,' as if He meant
to say, 'This is the one which sums them all up in
itself, that you love one another as I have loved
you.'   And the words which follow leave no doubt
what is the measure of His love, which He wishes
to be the measure of our love also.   'Greater love
than this no man hath, that a man lay down his
life for his friends.'   And St. John, in the Epistle to
which we have referred, shows us how he and the
other Apostles understood the words.   'In this we
have known the charity of God, because He hath
laid down His life for us, and we ought to lay down
our lives for the brethren.'[2]   It sometimes seem to
us strange that our Lord should have so often insisted on the commandment of brotherly love, and
that His Apostles, especially St. John, should have
dwelt so much upon it and in words so strong.   He
seems almost to speak as if it were the greatest
danger which could beset the first Christians and
those who were to come after them in the Church,
that they would be so much tempted to fail in this
respect of brotherly charity.   St. John, for instance,
says in the same passage: 'This is the declaration
which you have heard from the beginning, that you
should love one another.   Not as Cain, who was of
the wicked one, and killed his brother, and wherefore did he kill him ?   Because his own works were

<hr>

[2] 1 St. John iii. 16.

wicked, and his brother's just. Wonder not, my brethren, if the world hate you. We know that we have passed from death to life, because we love the brethren. He that loveth not abideth in death. Whosoever hateth his brother is a murderer. And you know that no murderer hath eternal life abiding in himself.[3] . . . He that hath the substance of this world, and shall see his brother in need, and shall shut up his bowels from him, how doth the charity of God abide in him?'[4]

It seems clear that the precept of loving the brethren, loving one another, both in our Lord's mouth, and in that of His Apostle, means the love that is manifested, or rather that consists in works, as the Apostle goes on, 'My little children! let us not love in word nor in tongue, but in deed and in truth.' It is a love that is inconsistent with the neglect of any power that we possess of helping our brethren when they are in need. And St. John gives another test of this true love in another place which we have already quoted, in the same Epistle. As He calls those who do not relieve their brethren when in need, murderers, so He calls those who break the bond of Catholic Unity, antichrists. 'Little children, it is the last hour, and you have heard that Antichrist cometh. Even now there are become many antichrists, whereby we know that it is the last hour. They went out from us, but they were not of us, for if they had been of us, they would no doubt have remained with us; but that they may be manifest, that they are not all of us.'[5] It is plain enough to all that call themselves Christians, that the neglect of the succouring the poor in their necessity is an infallible mark of the

---

[3] 1 St. John iii. 11—15.　　[4] 1 St. John iii. 17.　　[5] 1 St. John ii. 19.

absence of charity. But how many are there, even
among those whose hearts and purses and services
are ever open to the cry of the poor, who do not
reflect that their love of the brethren, if it is not
to be in word and in tongue only, and not also in
deed and in truth, must be shown by their observance of the law of Catholic Unity, and that as
St. Augustine says, ' How can he have the charity
of God, who does not love the Unity of the
Church ? ' There have been many martyrs who
have laid down their lives for this Unity. Our Lord
foresaw the great dangers that would arise from two
most hateful of sins among Christians, the hard
worldliness which would freeze up Christian charity,
and the spirit of independence of authority which
would give birth to so many schisms, and thereby
place the greatest of all obstacles in the way of the
conversion of the world, besides ruining thousands
of baptized souls. He thought no repetition super-
fluous of a commandment regarding the essential
conditions of that union with Him, and abiding
in Him, to secure which He had just given to the
Church and to the world the inestimable gift of the
Blessed Sacrament.

Our Lord seems never weary in telling the
Apostles of the proofs of the love which He bears
them, and as He has in the last sentence called them
by implication His Friends, He now seizes the
opportunity of explaining why He has used that
loving epithet, which implies, in those of whom it
is used, some kind of equality with the person who
speaks, ' You are My Friends, if you do things
which I command you. I will not now call you
servants, for the servant knoweth not what his lord
doth. But I have called you friends, because all

things whatsoever I have heard of My Father I have made known to you.' It seems that these words are intended to add a fresh argument for the mutual love which our Lord has been enjoining. It is that this mutual love is a condition or qualification for the great privileges which belong to the Gospel covenant, wherein men are raised to a state which entitles them to be called the friends of God. The abiding in Him and in His love cannot be without a great illumination of the mind, a great extension of knowledge of God's will and mysteries, and this is the characteristic grace of the Gospel dispensation, which makes us children of God instead of servants. For it is the characteristic of the friend that he knows what his friend's plans and wishes and intentions and designs are, whereas a servant may have the execution of certain particular things entrusted to him, but he does not know why his master orders or desires this or that, even if it be committed to him in part to carry it out. We have said that it is certain that many things, the knowledge of which is now the common property even of Christian children, were not known commonly to the faithful of the Old Covenant, such as the doctrines of the Trinity in Unity, the Incarnation, the Redemption by means of the Sacrifice of the Cross, and the like. They were known to the Prophets, perhaps, and the saints who were, like Abraham, specially friends of God, and indeed that reason is given when Abraham is allowed to know of the imminent destruction of the Cities of the Plain, that he was so great a saint and had received the promise that the future Redeemer should come of him.[6]

St. Peter, in his Epistle, speaks as if the Prophets

[6] Genesis xviii. 17.

themselves were fain to inquire and seek out certain details and features in the future scheme of salvation which it was committed to them to foretell, 'to whom it was revealed that not to themselves but to you they ministered those things which are now declared to you by them that have preached the Gospel to you, the Holy Ghost being sent down from Heaven on whom the angels desired to look.'[7] St. Peter here speaks of the new Revelation, which was imparted to those to whom the Gospel was preached, and it cannot be doubted, as has been said, that even ordinary and not specially instructed Christians had then, as they have now, a clear and full knowledge of many Divine truths, which under the Old Law were only imparted to the special friends and favourites of God.

Our Lord Himself began the revelation, as it is said of Him by St. John at the opening of his Gospel, 'the only-begotten Son Who is in the bosom of the Father, He hath declared Him.' The Apostles received much of this new revelation from our Lord Himself, in the course of the years during which He was their daily companion, though it may have been frequently in germ, and what He calls 'proverbs' or parables only, as they were able to bear the truths which He had to declare. Then the Holy Ghost, as St. Peter says, was sent down from Heaven to complete and expand, as we see in the whole teaching and in the Epistles of the Apostles, the explanation of the Great Counsel, of which our Lord is called by Isaias the 'Angel.' In the present passage it appears that our Lord speaks of the truths thus imparted by Himself to the Apostles as the message which He had heard and received from the Father to deliver to

<hr>

7 1 St. Peter i. 12.

the Church, and as ·sufficiently explaining the whole
counsel of God for the salvation and perfection of
men, so as to constitute those to whom they had
been imparted as the instructors of the world, truly
the ' friends of God,' in the sense in which that name
was bestowed upon Abraham. As has been said
before, a revelation of the manifold wisdom of God
is continually made through the Church, not only
to mankind, but to the Angels themselves, whom
St. Peter describes as eagerly gazing down on the
great work of the Holy Ghost, from which they
learn continually fresh marvels of the Divine wisdom
and magnificence, giving them ever new and new
occasions for glorifying God in His dealings with
His creatures, which are to them fresh manifestations
of the Divine attributes and ways. We have gathered
from our Lord's words, in which He says that He
has made known to the Apostles already all that He
has heard from the Father, that He may have spoken
to them that evening of many things relating to the
application of the fruits of the sacrifice He was to
make on the Cross, by the sacraments and the
adorable Sacrifice of the Altar, of which no mention
is made in the accounts of the Evangelists. For the
manifestation of doctrine concerning the sacraments
and the like seems here to be included in the general
revelation of which our Lord is speaking, though it
belonged to that class of truths concerning which it
has more than once been said, it does not appear
that the Church was at first commissioned to put it
into writing.

Our Lord seems to pass naturally to the mission
of the Apostles as the preachers and ministers of the
New Testament which is the issue of their having
received the revelation of the ' whole counsel of God,'

E 14

as St. Paul speaks. He tells them that the high vocation which they have received in this respect was a gift as gratuitous as the love which He had showered upon them. 'You have not chosen Me, but I have chosen you, and appointed you, that you should go and bear fruit and that your fruit should remain, that whatsoever you shall ask of the Father in My Name, He may give it you.' Having received from Him the communication of the saving truths on which the new Kingdom was to be founded, it followed naturally that they should be sent forth to deliver them to the world. Yet it is implied that the mere reception of the Gospel message was not of itself enough to enable them to deliver that message fruitfully and with the blessing of permanence on their labours. The words in which this is implied are those in which He speaks of having chosen them of His own free will, when, as St. Luke tells us, the Twelve were first called. On the call of our Lord must follow the particular mission and institution of those so called, their consecration, as it were, to the special office and special work, as is always the way with Divine appointments, the gift of specific graces for the accomplishment of the work rightly, and also a special blessing on its discharge, extending itself to the protection and the guidance which might be necessary or convenient, and to the preparation of the graces which those who were the subjects of their ministrations required.

Our Lord had already told them, speaking of His love for them, that He had loved them as the Father had loved Him, and this is explained, among other ways, by the fact that the Sacred Humanity had been created by God and united to the Divine

Person of the Son without any merit on its own part which there could not be in such a case. In the same way we are saved by our Lord the Incarnate Son, without any merits of our own to purchase that incomparable boon. There is, as our Lord now says, the same character of gratuitousness and absence of preceding merit about the choice which our Lord had made of the Apostles for the high calling which they had received in the execution of the Divine counsel, for carrying on the economy of the Kingdom founded on the Incarnation. This seems here to be insisted on as another title for our Lord's claim of that obedience to His Commandment which is the chief topic in this part of the discourse, and especially to obedience in respect of the precept of charity. For the fact of their having been chosen instead of themselves having made the choice, is a reason for unity among them, as St. Paul uses it, when he reminds his disciples that they have been called in one hope of their calling.

The calling is not human but Divine, not the result of individual predilections, happening to fall on the same object in many different persons. 'You have not chosen Me, but I have chosen you,' and more than that, 'I have appointed you,' that is, 'I have made this your work, preparing you for it and it for you, and arranging in My providence all the aids and helps and opportunities and occasions fitted for its great success, that you should go and bring forth fruit, and your fruit should remain.' These words imply and promise the continuance of the Apostolic power in the Church as the great means provided by our Lord for the permanence of the work till the end of time. And then again we have the words, which imply that the great weapon of the Apostles and of all workers after them in the same field of labour, was to be prayer—as we have already seen that they themselves knew, by their words when they proposed to the faithful the choice of the seven deacons to relieve them from other distracting business, however charitable. Our Lord seems to promise here that their prayers will have that efficacy with the Father which might be expected in the case of those whom He Himself had so carefully selected and consecrated to the work of preaching the Gospel, for whom He had prepared the work and the souls to whom they were to address themselves, the graces on both sides needed, and the like. The Father to Whom is specially attributed the providential direction and protection of the conversion of the world by the Church, could not but hear them and grant them whatever they asked, in accordance with the rules of the Kingdom. When our Lord says that He has appointed them that they shall bring forth much fruit, and that their fruit shall remain, and that whatsoever they shall ask of the Father in His Name, He may give it them, He seems to imply that His Father will, as it were, do His part in the gracious process of which He is speaking, as well as the Apostles their part in the preaching and particularly the prayer. This they were to do by making duly and earnestly the prayers that it is their office to make for their work, and these prayers are to be made in His Name, through Him the chief Shepherd, according to His inspiration and in His Name, as for the work which He began Himself and then entrusted to them to carry on till the end of time. No work therefore can have a greater claim on the gracious assistance of the Father, Who will take a loving pleasure in acknowledging the prayers made in the Name of the Son of His love by those who have the fullest right to use that Name, to unlock as it were all the treasures of His clemency.

Our Lord then sums up this part of His discourse in the words which are now again repeated. 'These things I command you, that you love one another.' The repetition of the injunction to brotherly love may be understood in more than one way. It may be that the commandment is simply repeated again and again, for the sake of showing its importance and necessity, and the importance and necessity of the close union between them which was to be the condition of the preservation of their own souls in the perfect love of our Lord Himself, as well as of the success of their work. Or it may be that these things are enjoined on the Apostles as means to secure that tender burning love among them which our Lord so much desires, and without which all their efforts for the glory of God by the conversion of the world would turn out to be vain and fruitless, or at least wanting in that measure of fruitfulness which is requisite for the accomplishment of the work. As if He had said, 'All this I tell you about your great vocation, I tell you in order that you may love one another more.' And experience shows us, in the case of the saints of God, how much the having been called 'in one hope of their calling,' to use the words of St. Paul, to have the same work to do for God and to use the same means to attain success therein, and the like, knits the hearts of men together with the most ardent and intelligent love, so that although they may have to work, as after a time was the case of the Apostles, in distant parts of the world, with few occasions of companionship and of the happiness which the intercourse with congenial souls brings, they come to love one another with a tenderness which has few parallels here below, and, what is more wonderful, to be of one mind as well of one heart, to think in the same way and to use the same methods. The Apostles were no doubt specially guided by the Holy Ghost in all their labours and prayers, and were kept by a special grace, if that were needed, to teach and govern and found the Churches committed to them according to one and the same Spirit. What we are saying now is, that the faithfulness with which each one of them carried out His commission as Apostle, wherever his lot was cast, was a distinct principle in his heart generating the love of his brethren in the same work. Each labour which any one of them accomplished was an increase to him of the burning love which he bore to our Divine Lord, in Whose Heart they all met, and became more and more one than had been the case when they were with Him in Galilee or Judæa.

This in some kind of degree is reflected in the experience of the holy members of fervent religious orders, whether active or contemplative, who have not many opportunities of showing their affection one for another according to the ordinary methods of human love, but who are found to have an amount of brotherly love in their hearts which surprises those who watch them labouring in silence according to the same rule, though with few breaks in the hard work and constant occupation with which that rule furnishes them. Our Lord may have wished this to be the way in which the mutual love of the Apostles grew daily more and more in their hearts. In this sense it may be thought that He means to tell them that He had dwelt on their high vocation, and on the duties and the privileges which it involved, with a particular purpose in His Heart that the consideration of the work to which they were called, and of the rank in His Kingdom which it implied, and of the personal love for each one of them, on His part, which it embodied might be to each and all, not merely a joy and encouragement in their several labours, but also an external source of mutual love, binding them closely in one as their Lord and Master was one and the same, and their work and its reward one and the same.

The context of which we have already tried to explain the dominant idea and connection, begins and ends with almost the same words, 'This is My commandment, that you love one another.' 'These things I command you, that you love one another.' It is not our Lord's way to repeat His commandments without necessity or reason, and it seems natural to understand that the repetition here is connected with the great importance in His Heart of the injunction which is given three times over in this context, and it has been repeated not long before this. It seems fair to conclude that this repetition of the precept of charity has some special reference to the bearing of the whole of the portion of the discourse to which it belongs, especially as it is not elsewhere repeated in the same way, as if the joy and the fruitfulness and the power in prayer of which we have mention within a few verses, were to be dependent on their obedience and faithfulness to this command of mutual charity. The command itself is general, and undefined as to any particular exercise of mutual love, it is not specific, as it is for instance in the Epistle of St. John, where the exercise of charity which consists in the relief of others, who may not have the goods of this world when we are able to supply their wants, is mentioned as the test whereby true charity may be known. It seems natural enough to conjecture here that our Lord may have wished to turn their thoughts over and over again to the duty of that love of which the saying already quoted tells us that 'no one can have the charity of God who does not love the unity of the Church,' and that this renewed urgency of the precept of unity makes this passage of the discourse a sequel on what our Lord has been saying before. It is not that the special charity which consists in the love of Catholic unity is more important in the eyes of our Lord than the same virtue in its other operations, but that the time was to come in the Church when this precept of unity was to be practically forgotten by whole masses of Christians, who would deceive themselves into a false belief on the subject of schism, which would paralyze the work of the Church in the world, and be the ruin of countless souls who would have to be excluded, like the foolish virgins in the parable, from the wedding-feast of the Lamb, with the sad words, 'I know you not.''

When it is said that no man hath greater love than to die for his friends, our Lord speaks of what is in general ordinary among men, for certainly it is a proof of wonderful friendship for a man to die for his friends, although, as St. Paul reminds us, our Blessed Lord died for us while we were yet His enemies. But He is speaking of human love, not Divine, and

St. John reminds us of this very saying of His when he says, ' In this we have known the charity of God, because He hath laid down His life for us; and we ought to lay down our lives for the brethren.'[8] The mention of the Passion seems to fall from our Lord naturally, as if it were that kind of charity which He especially desired to see prevalent among His children, after His pattern, and He seems to rejoice in this opportunity of giving occasion to such a remark as that which we have just quoted from His Beloved Disciple. Our Lord goes on adding line after line to the list of His great acts of love for them, as if each one of these were a fresh motive to them for the mutual love and union which He has been so strongly and so repeatedly urging upon them. He first takes up the blessings which they have received in the character of His friends, to which they are raised by their position in the new Kingdom, which is that of sons instead of servants, as compared with that of the saints of the Old Law. But instead of calling them sons He chooses the name of friend, which was the title given to Abraham, who was admitted to share the counsels of God that he might intercede with Him for mercy to sinners. When our Lord adds that He will no longer call them servants, for the servants do not know what the Lord doth, but they have heard from Him all that He had heard from the Father, He seems to mean that it was among the privileges of the Apostles that they were made partakers of the counsels of God in the dispensation of the redemption of the world by the Incarnation, the benefits of which were to be brought home to mankind by means of their ministry and preaching, and they were to be the instruments,

<hr>

[8] 1 St. John iii. 16.

but the conscious, deliberate, and most willing and happy instruments, under God and with God, of the salvation of the world by means of the dispensation of the Incarnation, the treasures of which were to be placed in their hands, like the five loaves in the miracle, to distribute to the world. When He says that all things whatsoever He had heard of His Father He had made known to them, He may perhaps include among these mysteries some of those matters which we have supposed may have been touched upon in the course of the discourses of this evening, which have not been mentioned by the Evangelist. But in any case, even if there were many secrets of the counsel of God to be revealed to them for which the proper time had not come, this would not make the words of our Lord less true, because it must be understood that their knowledge as His friends was not all to be communicated at the same moment, and only in proper time and degree, as they were prepared for it.

This, then, is one of the great privileges which He declares to have been communicated to them as His friends, and, like the others, we can easily see that the possession of this knowledge of the ways and designs of God would be meant by Him to be a most powerful motive in them for mutual charity and union among themselves, just as the intimate confidants of any great king on earth would, if they loved him and were devoted to the cause of his kingdom, be necessarily very much united among themselves for his sake. There could not be imagined any higher honour than to be so trusted by the sovereign, and in the case of the Apostles the plans confided to them were the very choicest inventions of the loving wisdom of God, for the happiness and glorification of His creatures, the most tender and exquisite contrivances of the Divine condescension that has ever been displayed to the wondering inhabitants of Heaven since the first dawn of the ages. It cannot be wondered at that to be sharers and workers together in such magnificent operations of merciful compassion should have been hailed by the Heart of the Redeemer as likely to knit the Apostles and their followers in the Church in the bonds of the most perfect union.

If such was to be looked for as the result of their marvellous enlightenment, such also, as our Lord goes on to tell them, was to be the fruit also of their extraordinary richness in the fertility with which they were to labour for Him in the great harvest of the Gospel Kingdom. Here again He reminds them that the fruitfulness is not theirs, but His. ' You have not chosen Me, but I have chosen you, and have appointed you that you should go and should bring forth fruit, and that your fruit should remain, and that whatsoever you should ask the Father in My name He may give it you.' The Apostles then are to remember that the whole work and fruitfulness of the Apostolate is originally and wholly His gift to Him from His Father for the design of His own greater glory, which He has allotted to them in His free choice and personal love to them, when He might have chosen any others and left them aside. He adds that He has appointed them as well as chosen them, by which it seems to be meant that, first they were chosen for their work, and then, by another act of His choice, were invested with their office and equipped with all the graces that belonged to it in the design of God, then to be sent forth on its execution, and then blessed and prospered with the fertility which would flow naturally on those so sent forth by the great Lord of the harvest, and then again blessed with abundance of fruit, on which in addition He says that the special blessing of permanence should be vouchsafed. For indeed the Church in all the world is to the present day the witness to the abiding fruit of the labours of the Holy Apostles, teaching the same truths, administering the same sacraments, ruled by the same hierarchy, guided by and drawing its life from the same Divine Spirit. And yet He adds a further great boon, which seems to place in their hands and in the hands of those who come after them an almost indefectible power, 'And that whatsoever you shall ask the Father in *My* name, He may give it you.' For the whole work of the Church is to be carried on by prayer. It is not meant that the boons which He has just mentioned were to be given them without prayer, or rather if they neglected that duty, but that their life was to be one of perpetual prayer, as that of the whole body of the Twelve became after the Day of Pentecost, *e.g.* when they withdrew from many active occupations of charity in order to give themselves to prayer and the preaching of the Word, in the largest sense.

And then once more our Lord repeats the same commandment, 'These things I command you, that you love one another.' Cardinal Toletus tells us that all these last magnificent promises or gifts which are so to say heaped up, one upon another, in these sentences which follow on the Parable of the Vine and its Branches, are as a succession of arguments by which our Lord enforces His precept of charity. He seems to have left no motive to charity unmentioned, in order that the law of Unity which is set forth so strongly in the words about abiding in the Vine, abiding in Him, should be enforced in every possible way, and we shall see as a matter of fact that this insistence on the duty of Unity is kept up by our Lord to the very end, and is the last desire of His Heart, as is shown in the solemn words of His prayer to the Eternal Father, which flowed from His lips when He was on the point of leaving the Cenacle, which had witnessed so many wonderful mysteries that evening. What more can be wanted that we may know what was at once the tenderest desire of the Sacred Heart for the Church for which He was to shed His Blood, and at the same time the clearest conviction of His wisdom, as the thing which now more than any one thing else He judged to be the most essential provision required for its welfare and for the accomplishment of the great work for the glory of the Father, which He looked to her to accomplish in the world, and which was only to be completely achieved on the condition which He was Himself to lay down, that of perfect visible Unity maintained in the face of the world to the end of time? Reason and common experience of mankind tell us plainly that there is no evidence like this of the presence of God with any collection of the children of Adam. Reason and experience combine to witness that a house divided against itself cannot stand, while on the other hand there is no power that makes a body like the Church strong and energetic for great works—able to triumph over the world and subdue it by the manifold evidence of the Divine Majesty within it, the love of God shed abroad in the hearts of men, raising them as individuals to the highest perfection, healing all diseases and imperfections in their souls, uniting them and keeping them united, and by their union enabling them to labour efficaciously and perseveringly and patiently and fruitfully for the salvation and perfection of their own souls first, and then of their neighbours—except the power of mutual charity, kindling the whole body and every member of it with a heavenly and supernatural life, making them truly citizens of a country which is above the world, and giving them the secret of transforming this miserable valley of exile into what may truly be called an ante-chamber of Heaven.

CHAPTER III.

The Hatred of the World.

St. John xv. 11—27 ; *Story of the Gospels,* § 156.

THE topic to which our Lord now proceeds is very different from that of which we have been speaking, yet it may still be said to have been suggested by and to grow out of the other. In contrast to the close union and love which He wished to see prevailing among His Apostles and their followers, there must have come before His mind, as He looked forward to the future of the Church, the intense hatred and furious persecution which she was to meet with from the world, although her mission and her work were to bring home to the latter the priceless benefits which were to be purchased by the Precious Blood. He foresaw the treatment that the Apostles were to experience at the hands of the world, and He now said something to prepare them for this and to arm them against it. This had some connection with the former topic, because the enmity of the world would call forth a great amount of union and sympathy and mutual love among Christians, and in that way would tend to strengthen the principle of charity among the true children of the Church, even though there might be some instances in which the sufferings and trials were to have a contrary effect in those

children of hers who were weak in faith and inclined
to yield to the fiery trial which was upon them. For
calamities and persecutions sometimes produce a
want of cohesion and a consequent falling off from
unity among certain portions of the body on
which they fall with great violence, but generally
they have among the more faithful members a
bracing and purgative effect. It is not necessary
to suppose that our Lord now turned to this point
for the sake of the truth contained in the connection
between persecution and the strengthening effects
which it is able to produce in knitting together more
closely those who have had to suffer together. After
speaking of the principle of brotherly love which was
to distinguish His children internally, it was natural
that He should say something concerning the sufferings which they were to endure at the hands of the
world, and the reasons for which those sufferings
were inevitable.

'If the world hate you, know ye that it hath
·hated Me before you. If you had been of the world,
the world would love its own, but because you are
not of the world, but I have chosen you out of the
world, therefore the world hateth you. Remember
My word that I said to you, the servant is not
greater than his master. If they have persecuted
Me, they will also persecute you, if they have kept
My word, they will keep yours also. But all these
things they will do to you for My Name's sake,
because they have not known Him that sent Me.
If I had not come and spoken to them, they would
not have sin, but now they have no excuse for their
sin. He that hateth Me, hateth My Father also.
If I had not done among them the works that no
other man hath done, they would not have sin, but

now they have both seen and hated both Me and My Father. But that the word may be fulfilled which is written in their law, They hated Me without a cause.'

The chief purpose of this whole passage seems to be to prepare the Apostles for that practice of patience in the discharge of their office in the Church and with the world outside, which was to be one of the greatest fruits and exercises of that charity which He had been so much insisting upon. He seems to suggest one motive after another for this most essential virtue. At the same time our Lord gives a clear and calm statement of the reason why He had been so treated by the world, a reason which was to be a consolation to the Apostles in their own trials, which came originally from the same causes as His own rejection, and which would serve to strengthen them, when their turn came to be the rejected of the world while they were endeavouring to enrich it with ineffable blessings at the cost of the greatest labours and sufferings of their own. He first puts before them the unspeakable consolation of His own example—they were after all only to be treated as He had been treated, and to generous and loving hearts this was enough. Would they wish to fare better than their Lord in doing their Lord's work? So to fare would not only be the most happy thing for their own hearts, it would also secure them the strength and the guidance which were sure to be theirs when they were treading in His footsteps. 'Know ye,' or you know, 'that it hath hated Me before you.' Their work was to be a continuation of His, their objects, their methods, and their aims the same. It is not to be wondered at that their treatment at the

F 14

hands of the foolish world should be the same as
His.   The reason why our Lord was treated as He
was, lay in certain elements in His character and
teaching which touched the wounds of the world, as
some healing but irritating medicine, which is applied
to the sores of a sick man, whose state requires that
the sores should smart before they can be cured.

'This,' as He said to Nicodemus, 'is the judgment,
because the light is come into the world, and men
loved darkness rather than the light, for their works
were evil.   For every one that doth evil hateth the
light, and cometh not to the light, that his works may
not be reproved.   But he that doth truth, cometh
to the light that his works may be made manifest
because they are done in God.[1]   Our Lord could not
have fulfilled His Mission of being the healing of
the world unless He had touched its sores and
made them smart, and the smart was sure to ripen,
either into healthy conversion, or into hatred of
the physician, according to the state of the souls in
which it was occasioned.   The same treatment of
themselves by the wicked world was to be a proof
to the Apostles that they were the true followers and
servants of their Master.   It was to be a recognition
on the part of those who had been His enemies and
were to become theirs, of those same qualities in
them which had provoked hostility in Him.   To
those who loved our Lord so much as the Apostles
loved Him, it was a great honour and a great consolation to be hated by the world for being so like to
Him.

On the other hand, if the Apostles had met with
any other kind of treatment from the world than
that which their Lord had received, it would

---

[1] St. John iii. 19—21.

have been a sign that they were not loyal and faithful representatives of Him. ' If you had been of the world, the world would have loved its own. But because you are not of the world, but I have chosen you out of the world, therefore the world hateth you.' The hatred of the world is a recognition of the character of the Apostles as the disciples of our Lord, and any other treatment of them would have been just as much a sign that they were the world's own, that is, enemies of God and our Lord. Something seems also to be specially implied by the further reason given by our Lord, that He had chosen them out of the world. He says not only that they are not the children of the world and do not belong to it. They have been rescued from it. 'I have chosen you out of the world.' They had been, like others, and as much as others, the world's own by birth and right, as far as that can be truly said of any, as far as anything that is evil and corrupt can have any right over any of the creatures of God. Our Lord had rescued them from the bondage of the world, a bondage which was founded on a lie and which was therefore a usurpation. The world was the strong armed man, of whom our Lord had said that a stronger than he was to come upon him and take away his goods and despoil him of his prey. The world therefore saw in them those who were once its own, a prey which had been torn from its hands. And our Lord's words signify even more, for they signify that their lot in being saved out of the world was singular. They had been taken out of the multitude of those who had not been so taken. The despoiler of the world has chosen them and has left others unchosen. This word, chosen or elect, occurs over and over again in the New

Testament, signifying the blessed lot of those who have been the objects of that blessed choice which makes them heirs of salvation. The Church is the assembly of the chosen.

Our Lord speaks to them in the glow of His love, fresh from all the wonderful outpourings of His Heart in the mysteries which He had been celebrating, and we can feel that His tone reveals to us that their hearts were glowing with love as well as His. They were full of love in their measure. These reasons for patience in the discharge of the laborious task and under the hatred of those to whom they were sent, are all appeals to their personal love for Him. 'The world hated Me before you,—the world would love you if you were its own. I have chosen you out of the world, therefore the world hateth you.' All such words have greater or less force and power in proportion to the warmth or coldness of the hearts to which they are addressed. Our Lord then goes on to remind them of the great charge which He had addressed to them at the outset of their Apostolic career, and in them to the ministers of the Church in all time. We must remind ourselves as we read what He says now, that He may mean, in these as in other quotations, to recall to their minds not only the particular words which He quotes, but the whole context to which they belong. In that discourse[2] He had told them of the persecutions and trials which awaited them. 'You shall be hated by all men for My Name's sake, but he that shall persevere unto the end, he shall be saved. When they shall persecute you in this city, flee into another. Amen I say to you, you shall not finish the cities of Israel until the

[2] St. Matt. x.

Son of Man come.' And then He had used the words of which He now reminds them. 'The disciple is not above his master, nor the servant above his lord. If they have called the good man of the house Beelzebub, how much more them of his household?'

What our Lord now says is, 'The servant is not greater than his master.' Instead of the words about Beelzebub, He says, what is clearly more appropriate to the present occasion and leads more naturally to what is to follow, 'If they have persecuted Me, they will also persecute you, if they have kept My word, they will keep yours also.' Again, there is the same tacit appeal to their devotion to Himself as their Lord and Master. They can be patient under the treatment which they receive from the world, because He has received it before them, and because it identifies them with Him. He mentions two distinct shapes which that treatment takes, the persecution of His own Person and that of the Apostles, and the neglect and contempt of His doctrine and theirs. In the former, the persecution of outrage and injury to the person, His active enemies take part. They were to bring Him to the Cross, after numberless acts of violence and the infliction of all the pains and the shame which their malice, aided by the instigations of Satan, could devise, and outrages of the same kind have been the lot of those who bear His Name in all generations and all countries in innumerable cases. In the second kind of ill-treatment, not the open enemies alone of our Lord take part. For all Christians who are in any way on the side of the world, and have caught its spirit, and who therefore do not keep His word nor obey the precepts of the

Church, may be guilty of this kind of persecution to Him and His representatives.

He puts the case hypothetically, but it is plain that His words convey a most distinct and certain prophecy. The Apostles had not yet witnessed the extent to which the enemies of our Lord, the children of the world, were to go in their violence and the brutality of their treatment of His Sacred Person, and it is probable that, when the Passion actually came about, it was a revelation to them of which they had no expectation. So also it must be a revelation to the servants of God in all ages, how many are the Christian souls who take part in that persecution of our Lord and of His Church, which consists in the neglect and contempt of their words.

'But all these things will they do unto you for My Name's sake, because they have not known Me nor Him that sent Me.' He seems to refer to the discourse to the Apostles which has already been quoted, and which contains many other details, besides those which have been mentioned now, concerning the persecution of His followers. Or He may simply refer to what He has just said, that all the suffering and contempt was to be inflicted on them for His Name's sake. By this He may mean two things. First, the world may treat them ill for the sake of His Name, which they will preach and proclaim as that of the Saviour of the world. Again, they may be persecuted because they bear His Name and are known to belong to Him as members of His Body, the Church. Thus, when the Apostles, soon after the Day of Pentecost, were scourged by order of the Sanhedrin, for preaching our Lord, we are told that they went forth with joy from the presence of the Council because they had been counted worthy to suffer contumely for the Name of Jesus. In that place it may be either the preaching or the companionship of our Lord which may be meant, though it seems more natural to understand the words of the former. St. Peter, in his first Epistle, speaking of the persecution of the Christians, says, 'Let no one of you suffer as a murderer, or as a thief, or as an evildoer, as a busy body in other men's matters, but if any man suffer as a Christian, let him not be ashamed, but let him glorify God in this name,' that is, as it seems, for bearing the name of our Lord, and in that passage it is difficult to understand the words as referring to the preaching of His Name.[3] It was then either the preaching of His Name as the Saviour of man-kind, or bearing His Name as members of the Church, that was to bring upon the Apostles the enmity and persecution of the world.

Our Lord goes on to add that this result was to follow, on account of the ignorance of men concerning God, and concerning His having sent our Lord into the world to save men from their sins. The Jews had some knowledge of God as the object of worship, but they were ignorant of the truth that our Lord was the promised Messias, Whom God had promised and sent. He had been abundantly predicted for them in various ways, and yet they shut their eyes to the truth, for which so many prophecies and types and the whole figurative system of the Law, and the sacrifices of the Temple, ought to have prepared them. There was this blind-ness, not only on the part of the more ignorant and uneducated people, but on the part of the Scribes and Priests, to whom, our Lord says, was entrusted

[3] 1 St. Peter iv. 15, 16.

the key of knowledge for the benefit of their own souls and of the souls of those of whom they were the teachers and leaders. The moral reasons for this blindness our Lord had touched upon, but He passes them over in this place. But He goes on to explain shortly the two reasons for which their treatment of Himself was inexcusable in various degrees.

 ‘ If I had not come and spoken to them they would not have sin, but now they have no excuse for their sin. He that hateth Me hateth My Father also. If I had not done among them the work which no other man hath done, they would not have sin, but now they have both seen and hated both Me and My Father.’ When He says they would have no sin, or not be guilty, unless He had come and spoken with them, and unless He had done among them works which no other man had done, He means, not that they would have been free from guilt on any other account, for their lives might have been bad, and there is reason for thinking that the lives of many among the Scribes and Pharisees were so, but that they would not have been guilty of that particular sin of unbelief, in the face of evidence on which it was intended by God they should believe. Their sin consisted in the rejection of the proof with which God furnished them for the salvation of their own souls and of many others, whom they were meant to help by their example and authority, a proof which must have been beyond all doubt sufficient to convince them if their hearts had not been hardened by wilful malice. If the evidence had not been set before them by our Lord, as He says, they would not have been guilty in rejecting it ; as it was, they had no excuse for their sin. All excuse was taken away by the two-fold evidence which our Lord here mentions, the evidence of His words concerning God and Himself, and the evidence of the miracles by which it was made clear that what He said concerning both was true, because God could not by any possibility have confirmed by such miraculous signs and teaching a claim which did not come from Him.

Of the first head of this evidence our Lord had said, when He was closing His preaching among them, ' He that believeth in Me doth not believe in Me but in Him that sent Me. I am come a light into the world, that whosoever believeth in Me may not remain in darkness. And if any man hear My words and keep them not, I do not judge him, for I came not to judge the world but to save the world. He that despiseth Me and receiveth not My words, hath one that judgeth him. The word that I have spoken, the same shall judge him at the Last Day. For I have not spoken of Myself, but the Father Who sent Me, He gave me commandment what I should say and what I should speak. And I know that His commandment is life everlasting. The things therefore that I speak, even as the Father said to Me, so do I speak.'[4] In this passage it is distinctly said by our Lord that His own word was sufficient as a foundation of faith in Him, and thus in despising it a certain guilt was incurred, for which guilt an answer would have to be given at the Last Day. The word of St. John Baptist was to be received with faith, and it was a sign of reprobation in the Chief Priests that they had rejected it. Yet St. John Baptist had not worked a single miracle. In the first great disputation with the priests which the Evangelist records, and which took place, as it appears, at the Pasch of the second

[4] St. John xii. 44, 46—50.

year of our Lord's Ministry, He claimed their faith first on His own word, and then on the witness of St. John Baptist,[5] then on that of His miracles, one of which He had just wrought at the Pool of Bethsaida, and also on that of the voice of the Father which had been heard at the time of His Baptism. Lastly, He referred them to the witness of Holy Scripture, saying: 'Search the Scriptures, for you think in them to have life everlasting, and the same are they that give testimony unto Me. . . . Think not that I will accuse you to the Father, there is one that accuseth you, Moses, in whom you trust. For if you did believe Moses, you would perhaps believe Me also, for he wrote of Me. But if you do not believe his writings, how will you believe My words?' These words certainly seem to show that the Jewish priests were guilty for not believing our Lord's words, as He says here, independently of His miracles, because they had before them, in His Person, and in His teaching concerning God and Himself, the fulfilment of prophecy and of the whole system of the Old Testament, without more, much in the same way as persons who profess themselves to be Christians and yet reject the Catholic Church are guilty, even though she does not in these days ordinarily prove her claims by the same marvellous miracles as were vouchsafed in the early ages, and are still met within her occasionally at times when there is fitting room and occasion for them.[6]

We may consider our Lord as certainly implying that, although the full evidence presented to the Jews for the rejection of which they were inexcusable, included both His words and His miracles, still there was enough in His words, speaking as

[5] St. John v.   [6] See 1 Cor. xiv. 22.

He did with authority as from His Father and from Himself, to make the rejection of Him by them sinful. We know that the miracles were in an especial sense 'the works of the Christ,' as St. Matthew calls them, when He speaks of the appeal to them which was brought about by the mission of two of the disciples of St. John by their master to our Lord, when they were instructed to ask of the latter, 'Art Thou He that is to come, or do we look for another?'[7] St. John, as has been said, wrought no miracle himself, and perhaps for that among other reasons he arranged this sending of his disciples to our Lord, Who immediately worked a great many miracles of healing in their presence and bade them 'Go, and tell John what they had seen and heard,' using language which showed that He meant to draw their attention to the passage in Isaias in which these very signs had been prophesied of the Messias. It is clear that the people were meant to know our Lord by these miraculous signs. But when St. John at the beginning of our Lord's preaching had spoken to his own disciples about our Lord, he had not dwelt on His miracles, but on the inherent authority with which He spoke: 'He that cometh from above is above all. He that is of the earth, of the earth he is, and of the earth he speaketh. He that cometh from Heaven is above all. And what He hath seen and heard that He testifieth, and no man receiveth His testimony.'[8] The rejection of our Lord's words then had begun at that earliest stage of His preaching. St. John adds, 'He that hath received His testimony hath set to his seal that God is true. For He Whom God

---

[7] St Matt. xi. 3.   [8] St. John iii. 31, 32.

hath sent speaketh the words of God, for God doth not give the Spirit by measure. The Father loveth the Son, and He hath given all things into His hands. He that believeth in the Son hath ever-lasting life, but he that believeth not in the Son shall not see life, but the wrath of God abideth on him.'

It is clear from these words of the Precursor that the disbelief of our Lord's words was a sin of itself in the Jews, though it became much aggravated when it became also disbelief in the evidence of the miracles. Our Lord said of Himself at the feast of Tabernacles, 'In your Law it is written that the testimony of two men is true. I am one that give testimony of Myself, and the Father that sent Me giveth testimony of Me,'[9] and again on this last evening He said to St. Philip, 'He that seeth Me seeth the Father also. Do you not believe that I am in My Father and My Father in Me? The words that I speak to you, I speak not of Myself, and the Father Who abideth in Me He doth the works. Do you not believe that I am in the Father and the Father in Me? Otherwise, believe Me for the very works' sake.'

This must be enough to enable us to grasp the truth set forth by our Lord about the guilt incurred by the Jews, and especially the priests and those in authority, by their rejection of Him, a guilt which would not have been incurred if they had not had Him sent to them by the Father, and His Mission confirmed by the works which showed that that Mission was Divine. He adds other words which may strike us as reaching still further in the reve-lation which they contain of the evil state of these enemies of our Lord. For He adds, 'But now they

[9] St. John viii. 17, 18.

have both seen and hated both Me and My Father.'
That human malice can rise to such a pitch as to
involve the positive hatred of God the Father and
of our Lord, enhances our intelligence of the black
ingratitude of which He is speaking.

But the truth is contained in what our Lord said
to Nicodemus, at the very outset of the history—
that the judgment was that 'the light had come into
the world, and men loved darkness rather than
the light, for their works were evil, for every one
that doth evil hateth the light, and cometh not
to the light that his works may not . be reproved.'[10] Our Lord speaks of Himself as the
object of . their hatred before the Father, because
it was His presence, as the Light of the world,
which forced on them the alternative of either
accepting His teaching or turning upon Him in
anger and hatred, and the support, so to speak,
which He received from His Father forced them,
in the next place, to hate the Father also. What
our Lord said about the hatred of the light by men
who do evil, is drawn out more fully in a famous
passage in the Book of Wisdom. 'Let us lie in
wait for the just, because He is not for our turn, and
He is contrary to our doings, and upbraideth us with
transgressions of the Law, and divulgeth against us
the sins of our way of life. He boasteth that He
hath the knowledge of God, and calleth Himself the
Son of God. He is become a censurer of our
thoughts. He is grievous unto us even to behold,
for His life is not like other men's and His ways are
very different.'[11] The hatred began in their souls,
first with the preaching of St. John Baptist, from
which these priests turned away because it was a

<hr>

[10] St. John iii. 19, 20.   [11] Wisdom ii. 12—15.

call to repentance and the confession of sins. That
was the first step, and it involved all the rest.

The reproof contained in the preaching of St. John
was repeated and continued in our Lord, Who stung,
moreover, their jealousy by the great influence which
He gained by His character and miracles, and by the
open line He took in defiance of them when they
attempted to oppose Him. The more clear His
claims became, and the more irresistible the accu-
mulation of evidence by which they were supported,
the more obstinate became their determination not
to acknowledge the call upon their faith and submission, until at last it came to the resolution of
getting rid of Him at all hazards, even though their
only way of doing so was by His murder. It is not
difficult to understand how men in such a condition
came to hate the Person of our Lord and to hesitate
at nothing that was requisite for His destruction,
and this could not be, without the love of God
dying out in their hearts, Whom they had been
taught from their youth to worship, but Who as they
could not feel was on the side of our Lord, Whose
wonderful miracles were a continual appeal to the
witness of His Father, so that they might be truly
said to hate the Father also. It became continually
more and more plain that the witness of prophecy
was on the same side with the witness of miracles,
that the whole Divine system under which they had
been brought up was a foretelling of our Lord and a
preparation for our Lord, that the new system of
which He was the Prophet and the Messenger was
the fulfilment of the old, and therefore the God
Whom alone they knew before our Lord came, was
only to be made better and better known and more
intelligently honoured under the new revelation.

Those, then, who were determined to reject the claim of our Lord to be the Messias, were driven gradually, more and more as the light increased, to reject His Father as their God. We sometimes see the same process repeated in a certain manner by those who begin by a general belief in the Christian religion and are afterwards confronted with the claims of the One Catholic Church which they have been taught to hate. Such men not unfrequently find themselves driven to choose between accepting the entire revelation as the Church presents it to them, in one harmonious and consistent whole, and rejecting what they have already been accustomed to believe as true, because they are led irresistibly to the conclusion that the claims of the Church which are new to them are as true as that part of her teaching which they already admit.

Our Lord had before His mind the whole Counsel of God, as He had dealt with His people, and especially with the generation in which it had been determined that the Incarnation should take place and the redemption of the world be accomplished. He could see, as no one else ever saw, how full of love, and wisdom, and patience, had been the whole dispensation, both that part of it which had preceded His own Advent, and that which had come after. In one sense God the Father had taken to Himself the preparation of the chosen people for the great boon that was to be given, and our Lord, Himself the Incarnate Son, had then come among mankind and spoken and taught them Himself in His Human Nature. In both parts of the wonderful economy God had been rejected and rebelled against, and thus they had seen and hated both the Father and the Son, the Father in His providential government of the world, and the Son as a man among men striving to bring them back to God, and revealing to them what they could not have known so well before, the immense mercifulness and compassion of the Godhead. Looking forth upon it all, our Lord sums up the whole conduct of the Pharisees in the words of one of the Psalms,[12] and says that 'they have hated Him without a cause,' that is, gratuitously, and when there was no reason for their hatred. This is indeed a very gentle and inadequate statement of the intensity and malice of their hatred against Him, and of the outrageous violence in which it was about to vent itself in the Passion. Indeed, it says nothing of all this. It is only a complaint of ingratitude and wantonness of their rejection of Him.

We have more than once found it useful to refer to the passages of the Old Testament which are quoted by our Lord, on occasions like this, for He seems to wish to direct our attention, not only to the words which He cites, but to the whole context in which they occur. The Psalm from which these words come is one of those in which there is much anticipation of the Passion, and parts of it are frequently applied to our Lord in the New Testament. It is the Psalm which St. John quotes early in His Gospel, when he applies to our Lord the verse, 'The zeal of Thy house hath eaten me up.'[13] Our Lord Himself quotes it of Himself here. St. Paul quotes it of our Lord in Romans xv. 3: 'For Christ did not please Himself as it is written, "the reproaches of them that reproached thee fell upon Me,"' and he applies to the case of our Lord's enemies the imprecations or prophetical denunciations which this Psalm contains in Romans

[12] Psalm lxviii. 5.   [13] St. John ii. 17.

xi. 22, 23. It contains the prediction concerning the Passion which our Lord had in His mind when He spoke on the Cross the word, ' I thirst,' in order to bring about the fulfilment of the prophecy, ' In My thirst they gave Me vinegar to drink.' This is enough to show that the Psalm, now quoted, is full of reference to our Lord. There is about it a peculiar tone of injured friendship, of ill-treatment from persons from whom gratitude and kindness might have been expected. It is thought with much probability that it reflects the feelings of David at the defection of some of his oldest friends, men on whom he had heaped favours and benefits, as Joab and Abiathar, who, at the close of the aged and penitent King's life, took part in the conspiracy to place Adonias on the throne as his successor instead of Solomon, the son of Bathsheba, to whom the succession had been promised. This strain of complaint makes this Psalm suit very well as a prophecy of our Lord's feelings about the Jewish priests.

' But when the Paraclete cometh, Whom I will send you from the Father, the Spirit of Truth Who proceedeth from the Father, He shall give testimony of Me, and you shall give testimony, because you have been with Me from the beginning.' As the discourse of our Lord after these words returns to the subject of the ill-treatment of the Apostles by the Jews, it seems sometimes difficult to understand how this clause is connected with what precedes it and with what follows it. For our Lord, after some more words about the sufferings of the Apostles, seems to return to the Mission of the Paraclete. The connection seems to be something of this kind. We might have thought that after the complaints against

G 14

the Jews for their hatred against Him without a cause,
our Lord would have left them, as it were, to themselves, except perhaps to speak of the great judgments which they were to bring on themselves.
As has been said, there are many verses in the
Psalm from which He had quoted which might
have served the purpose of strong declaration on
this point. But we know that in the Heart of our
Blessed Lord there were thoughts not of vengeance
but of mercy, rising higher and higher in proportion
as the floods of their ingratitude and malice mounted
up more and more. He was lovingly reckoning up
all the sufferings of the day which was in a few hours
to dawn, sufferings which were to be intensified by
the ingratitude and hatred of which He had been
speaking. But of all this He says not a word to the
Apostles now. All the malignity displayed in the
Passion only drew from Him greater manifestations
of the tenderest love. Instead of leaving the Jews to
themselves, or sending at once the armies that were
to root out their name among the nations, He
offered up all that He suffered for their redemption,
and prayed for them on the Cross. Then He sent
the Holy Ghost, the promised Paraclete, to the
Apostles and the Church, for them, and by the
witness of the Paraclete to Him, with which was
to be joined, as He says, the witness of the Apostles
themselves, He gave them a new and most fruitful
opportunity of learning Who He really was, and of
having their share in the salvation which had been
wrought for the whole world on the Cross. This,
then, He' mentions first of all, as if to show how little
their ingratitude had made Him forget that they
were His own kindred. Our Lord then, as we see,
passes in silence over all that is to take place

between the persecution and rejection of Himself,
even the bitter outrages of the Passion, and the
Mission of the Paraclete, and goes on to speak
tranquilly of what He was to do for the deliverance
of the ungrateful people after that supreme wicked‑
ness of theirs had been accomplished.

'But when the Paraclete cometh Whom I will
send you from the Father, the Spirit of Truth Who
proceedeth from the Father, He shall bear testimony
of Me, and you also shall bear testimony because
you are with Me from the beginning.' He has
already spoken to them of the Paraclete, Whom He
had called another Paraclete, that is a comforter
and strengthener like Himself, and Who was to take
His place. Then He had said that He would ask
the Father, Who at His prayer would send them
another Paraclete, for He was Himself the Gift of
the Father to them. And He then added that this
other Paraclete was to abide with them for ever, and
thus to supply His own visible withdrawal. The
Paraclete was then said to be given at the prayer
of our Lord, for it was the merits of the sufferings
of the Sacred Humanity that gave efficacy to that
prayer, and won that great boon. But as our Lord
is One with the Father in the possession of the
Divine Nature and Substance, He says here that
He will send the Paraclete, Who proceeds from the
Father and from Him by one Spiration, and is said
to be sent by the Father and the Son from Whom
He proceeds, to bring about the effects which result
from His presence with creatures. He says that
He will send the Holy Ghost from the Father to
them, for He has before said that the Father would
give or send the Paraclete, and that there might be
no apparent diversity in the statements, as if He

had said that He would send Him without mention
of the Father. For the Son sends the Paraclete
from the Father, because He has from the Father
the Divine Essence, by reason of which He is able
to send Him. The Father is said to send the
Paraclete from Himself, because He Himself proceeds from no other Divine Person. The Son sends
Him with the Father, and by one and the same
Mission, because He proceeds from the Father, from
Whom He has the Divine Essence.

Our Lord next speaks of the promised Paraclete
as the Spirit of Truth. He is the Spirit of Truth
in more ways than one. He cannot possibly be
ignorant of any truth or teach anything but the perfect
truth, for He knows God and all that God knows,
having the whole Divine Essence communicated to
Him by the Father, from Whom, with, and through
the Son, He proceeds. The subject-matter of this
discourse is the witness which the Holy Ghost is to
bear, and therefore we may call this the chief meaning of the words about the Spirit of Truth. He is
also the Spirit of Truth, in that His office is to
make clear the obscure figures and promises of the
Old Law. Our Lord says that He proceeds from
the Father, not adding that He proceeds from the
Son, in order to avoid repeating His own words.
For He has already said that He will send the
Paraclete to them from the Father, and when it
is said that one Divine Person is sent by another,
it is meant thereby that He that is sent proceeds
from Him that sends. The truth of the Procession
of the Holy Spirit from the Son had thus been
sufficiently stated, but it was necessary to state that
of His Procession from the Father, lest it should
seem to be left out, and there were to be heretics

in later ages, who were to call Him the Spirit of the Son and not of the Father.

'He shall give testimony of Me.' Our Lord here speaks of the Mission of the Holy Ghost on the Day of Pentecost, which, as He presently tells them, was to be the fruit and recompence of His own going away. By His going away He seems to signify the Passion and Death itself which He was to undergo, and then the Ascension and Sitting on the Right Hand of the Father, which were the ineffable exaltation which was to be purchased by His Passion and Death. The Mission of the Holy Ghost was to be both external and visible, and also internal and invisible, showing itself by the marvellous effects which it produced in the hearts and lives of men. It was externally seen in the flames of fire which sat upon the Apostles and others at the coming of the Paraclete, and in other supernatural manifestations of the same kind, and it was internal also, proved by the spiritual graces which flowed so abundantly on the children of the Church. All these things were so many witnesses to our Lord, and especially to the great truth of all, the truth of His Mission as the Messias, the Son of God. He does not describe these manifold heads under which might be summed up this Divine witness to the truth of His Mission, for He is here speaking very concisely, and on a subject concerning which the Apostles and the Church after them were to possess abundant evidence.

He adds, however, that there was to be another testimony to Him besides that of the Holy Ghost, the witness of the Apostles themselves. 'And you also shall give testimony, because you are with Me from the beginning.' As our Lord's own testimony to Himself, as He speaks in the passage lately quoted, was one witness, and the testimony of the Father to Him by the miracles was another, so also the testimony of the Apostles and the Visible Church is to be distinguished in all ages from that of the Holy Ghost, although there can be no doubt that this testimony is inspired and guided by Him. Thus in His speech before the Sanhedrin, after the first Apostolic miracle, the healing of the impotent man at the Beautiful Gate, St. Peter after speaking of the Resurrection of our Lord, of His Ascension and Session at the right hand of the Father, says, ' We are witnesses of these things, and the Holy Ghost, Whom God hath given to all that obey Him,' meaning partly the invisible witness of the Holy Ghost and partly His visible manifestations. They bore witness, because having been with Him from the beginning, their testimony to His Resurrection was the best that it was possible to conceive. We find this condition of having ' companied with us all that time that the Lord Jesus went in and went out among us, beginning with the Baptism of John until the day wherein He was taken up from us,' assigned by St. Peter as the qualification of the one of the faithful who was to be elected in the place of Judas as a witness of the Resurrection.[14] In his speech on the Day of Pentecost, St. Peter first explains to the multitudes that the wonders which they saw were the visible witness of the Holy Ghost, according to the prophecy of Joel, which he quotes at length, and he adds the personal testimony of the Apostolic band to the fact of the Resurrection of our Lord.

The same insistence on the two-fold testimony

[14] Acts i. 22.

runs throughout the whole of the New Testament, the testimony of the Holy Ghost and of the human witnesses, whose evidence is continuous in more ways than one. The Sacred Scriptures of the New Testament are the evidence of their human authors, as well as of their Divine author, as St. John says, in the opening of his Epistle, which has been more than once referred to here. ' That which was from the beginning, which we have heard, which we have seen with our eyes, which we have looked upon, and our hands have handled, of the Word of Life—for the Life was manifested, and we have seen, and do bear witness, and declare unto you the Eternal Life, which was with the Father, and hath appeared unto us, that which we have seen and have heard we declare unto you, that you, also, may have fellowship with us, and our fellowship may be with the Father, and with His Son Jesus Christ.'[15] And besides the human testimony of Scripture, and of tradition, which is human and Divine like Scripture, and the unwritten Word of God, there is here foreshadowed by our Lord the perpetual official witness of the Church to the end of time, as a regular part of the dispensation which He was to introduce. Thus does our Blessed Lord in these few words sum up the whole history of the future, as it may be said, until His own second coming, the Church representing Him and bearing His Name, commissioned with His message and assured by His power, the world treating the Church as it had treated Him, and for the same reason, its ignorance of God and His Incarnate Son sent upon earth to redeem mankind, the Church distinguished by its notes of Unity and Charity, in which two characteristics her whole system is summed up, the

[15] I St. John i. 1—3.

Holy Ghost abiding in her and with her, and witnessing in her and through her to the truth of His Mission and the Divine authority of His Kingdom.

After this short description of the witness of the Paraclete and the Church to Himself, our Lord seems to return to the topic on which He has already said something, namely, the ill-treatment of the Apostles by the world. They must have been generally prepared for this from what He had already said, that if men had kept His word, they would keep theirs also, and if they have persecuted Him they would persecute them also. Now, as we shall see, He makes the matter more specific and plain, especially by adding that particular which must have been the hardest for them to bear in some respects, the separation of His follower from the body of the holy nation, which answers to the Christian excommunication. For the Apostles could hardly have expected this as a practical result of their adherence to Him, although we have seen that the confession that He was a prophet had brought this severe sentence on the man born blind whom He had cured.[16] They had been accustomed to recognize the Synagogue as the assembly of the faithful, the body in possession of the exclusive privileges of the people of God. To be told that they were to be cut off from God's people might even scandalize them, and our Lord therefore now clearly and calmly tells them that this thing was to happen to them. Perhaps they had not hitherto been able to bear the revelation of what was to be, externally at least, the future which their work in the world was to entail upon them, as they certainly had not witnessed

[16] St. John ix. 34.

and were in no degree prepared to witness, what was to happen in the next few hours to our Lord Himself. Hitherto His enemies had never been able to lay their hands upon His Sacred Person, but now He was to be given over to the fury of savage executioners, and to die upon the Cross in the deepest humiliation and contempt, as well as in the most terrible pain. The history of the Church was to be a repetition of the history of the Sacred Passion, and it was to last, not a few hours only, but through all time till the very end of the world. They were to be engaged in carrying on His work in the world under conditions identical with those under which He had Himself carried it on, misunderstanding, misrepresentation, persecution, sterility, and disappointment. Our Lord warns them of this briefly, in order that it may not be too much for their courage or their faith to bear unshaken. He no longer leaves this to be inferred from His words, but sets it forth with the greatest plainness.

'These things have I spoken unto you that you may not be scandalized. They will put you out of the synagogues, yea, the hour cometh that whosoever killeth you will think that he doth a service to God. And these things will they do to you, because they have not known the Father nor Me. But these things have I told you that when the hour is come you may remember that I told you of them. But I told you not these things at the beginning, because I was with you.' When our Lord says that He tells them these things in order that they may not be scandalized, the words have the full meaning which is contained in their etymological significance. A scandal is properly a thing that causes the feet to stumble or trip, and so fall, and here our Lord seems to mean the kind of stumbling of which He speaks soon after this, when on His way to the Garden of Gethsemani with His disciples, when He tells them that they are all to be scandalized in Him, 'for it is written, I will strike the shepherd and the sheep of the flock shall be dispersed.' The sudden overthrow of their confidence in Him by the manifestation of weakness and helplessness which broke upon them in His arrest in the Garden, led them to fall in various ways by cowardice, failure of open profession of the truth, and the like. The same might be the effect of the persecution which was to fall on themselves after His leaving them at the Ascension, although their faith had been so immensely strengthened and elevated, and then it would be a great support to them that He had told them beforehand what was then to happen.

Our Lord speaks of what the Apostles were to suffer under two heads. 'They will put you out of the synagogues, yea, whosoever killeth you will think that he doth a service to God.' The first kind of persecution was that which was to fall more immediately on the Apostles and disciples from the Jewish nation, in which, as has been said, to be put out of the Synagogue involved exclusion from civil rights as well as from religious privileges, and was in truth a kind of civil, social, and religious death. No doubt the Apostles themselves, as devout Jews, loved the Temple worship and the prerogatives of the people of God. Besides the forfeiture by excommunication of spiritual and ecclesiastical advantages, there were other consequences which seem to be summed up by our Lord in the Sermon on the Mount, though He does not use the technical language which would have required no explanation to Jewish hearers. He says, 'Blessed are ye when men shall hate you, and when they shall separate you and shall reproach you, and cast out your name as evil, for the Son of Man's sake.'[17] He sketches here a kind of persecution very difficult to bear, the hatred of those among whom they have to live and work, the separation involved in the denial of social rights and friendly intercourse, sometimes extending to the refusal to furnish them with the ordinary necessaries of life which are sold in the shops and markets, the reproaches which consist in the upbraiding them as renegades and apostates, both from their religion and their nationality, and the continual speaking evil of them when not present, producing a general feeling of dislike and contempt against which even those who are most charitably disposed towards them would find it hard to struggle. All these and other forms of social prescription are included in the simple phrase of casting out of the Synagogue. This kind of persecution had already been put into play before the time at which our Lord was speaking—at least St. John tells us that before this many of the chief men believed on Him, but because of the Pharisees they did not confess Him, that they might not be put out of the Synagogue, for they loved the glory of men more than the glory of God.[18]

The fear of which St. John speaks could operate for a time with men even like Nicodemus and Joseph of Arimathea, and afterwards with others, as it seems, as Gamaliel and the like, who ultimately became martyrs for the faith. This doubtless was the reason why the Apostles were careful not to give offence to the 'believers of the Circumcision.'

<hr>

[17] St. Matt. v. 11.   [18] St. John xii. 43.

It seems likely that in Jerusalem the Christians always kept up to some extent the practice of the Mosaic Law, and frequented the Temple as long as the Temple remained, and in every lawful way appeared to be like other Jews.[19] St. Paul, in the Epistle to the Hebrews, who were at the time under the very severest possible persecution of this kind, touches on more than one point in which they were in great need of encouragement and consolation.

If all the hints scattered over the Acts and Epistles which point to this kind of persecution were collected, we should have many materials for a complete picture of the sufferings of this sort to which Christians, and, first of all, the Apostles, were to be exposed, and which are predicted in this passage by our Lord Himself. It is hardly necessary to point out the great hindrance which was thus placed in the way of the progress and well-being of the Church by conversions to the faith.

It is a mistake to suppose that persecution is not a powerful weapon in the hands of the enemies of the Church, and perhaps this particularly applies to the social persecution of our own times. Persecution is often used for political purposes, and it often recoils on the heads of those who so use it, by engendering national hatreds, and by the decay which results to the social fabric from the arraying of class against class. But persecution often succeeds after its miserable fashion, for not all men have the courage for the great sacrifices which are required for the open profession of a severely proscribed and persecuted faith, and the oppression of consciences may often be successful in making men fear to follow the right path. Persecution, when thus successful,

[19] See Acts xxi. 20.

is generally avenged by the miserable moral degradation of whole masses who have been intimidated, and who are made thereby bad Christians and bad subjects, useless or mischievous members of the social community. To speak only of the Jewish commonwealth, in which the persecution of which our Lord here speaks was probably seldom inactive until the destruction of Jerusalem by Titus, we cannot tell how many of those who failed under that fiery trial after the Day of Pentecost, became afterwards the men of blood and rapine, the partisans of one or other of the maddened factions which tore the nation to pieces in its last agonies, when the clemency of the Romans would willingly have spared them if they had not themselves made all peace impossible. It is unnecessary to point out how our Lord's words have been verified in all the succeeding ages which have passed since He spoke them, and how strong and powerful the kind of persecution of which He speaks has been, in successive generations, for placing heresy and schism on the throne which belongs of right to the one true Church.

The other kind of persecution which is here mentioned is the persecution of violence and brute force, the persecution which comes from secular rather than ecclesiastical authorities, or even individuals, and which is often carried on under the forms of law against persons accused of transgressions of the civil law, rather than of simply religious opinions proscribed by the dominant sects or parties. Such was probably the persecution of Herod in which St. James the Great suffered, and the greater part of the Roman persecutions, or again those of Japan or China, in after times, or in England in the days of Elizabeth or the earlier Stuarts. The fanatics who bound themselves by an oath not to taste food till they had slain St. Paul, were instances of persons deceived by this spirit of persecution, and there may have been many men in all times who have really thought that their religion really required the removal by violence of those who preached the doctrine of our Lord. Our Lord foreknew all this, and now He mentions it as a thing for which it was well that the Apostles should be prepared. He assigns as the cause for both kinds of persecution, the ignorance of God and of Himself as sent by God. 'And all these things will they do unto you because they have not known the Father nor Me.'

A great Catholic commentator on the Gospel of St. John, to whom, perhaps, more than to any other single writer, these pages are indebted, has drawn out in one of his annotations what he considers to have been the chief causes to which the persecutions which have been suffered by the Church may be attributed. They are causes which we can easily see to lie in the nature of things and the condition of the world, and they consequently cannot be expected to be ever altogether inactive or inoperative. The first of these he finds in the never sleeping or relenting activity of the spiritual enemies of God and man, working through and on their instruments among mankind themselves, at one time rulers, whom they excite to persecution or to hatred of the truth, or of virtue, or to others whom they stir up in various ways to whatever may seem to them likely to bring dishonour to God and to hinder the salvation of men. St. Paul speaks most earnestly of this in the famous passage at the end of the Epistle to the Ephesians, where he addresses himself more especially to the priests, urging them to be strengthened in the Lord and in the might of His power. The language is of itself a proof how much he thought of the adversaries with whom the Christian ministers had to contend. 'For our wrestling is not against flesh and blood, but against principalities and powers, against the rulers of the world of this darkness, against the spirits of wickedness in the high places.'[20]   And in other passages he shows that he has continually in his mind the activity of the devil in opposing, by all means in his power, the merciful work of redemption committed to the Church. It cannot be said of the devils that, in one sense, they have not known the Father and the Son, though it appears likely that their fall from Heaven was brought about in consequence of their refusing to acknowledge the supreme majesty of the Eternal Son, dwelling among men in the Incarnation.

The Fathers echo the thought of St. Paul, and constantly attribute the persecution of the Church to the malice of the devil. It is the policy of Satan to hide himself in his warfare against the Church, not only using human instruments for her enslaving, or for the hindrance of her beneficent operations, but taking care that the workings of his malice appear to be the natural effects of human policy. On the other hand, it is the true instinct of the saints of God to discern, in what seems merely human opposition, the craft and deceit of the enemy of God. We are sometimes struck by the cleverness and cunning by which the opposition to a scheme of good is raised of a sudden, and in some unexpected quarter, especially among good men. But few of us are as watchful and cautious as we ought to be against the

[20] Ephes. vi. 12, seq.

powers of evil, and we let pass many opportunities
of guarding against their devices, and so often enable
them to succeed in their attempts *ad minorem Dei
gloriam.* For the prevention of a great evil does not
always involve the prevention of a less evil, and the
enemies of all good are well pleased to content themselves with small gains, when they cannot get greater
successes, while yet we might, by more prayer and
vigilance, have prevented them from having any
at all.

Cardinal Toletus mentions four other causes which
he assigns to the persecutions of the Apostles and
their followers. We have said something already of
the historical facts, especially in the earlier persecutions. But it is well to see if we can trace the
influence of the general cause which our Lord
Himself gives as the root and principle of all
reasons for the persecution, that is, the ignorance
of God and of Himself as sent by God. Next to
the activity of Satan and his evil angels, Toletus
places the ambitious jealousy of the persecutors, the
rulers of the Empire and their subordinates, who were
always ready to suspect the religion of our Lord as
being something inimical to their power as already
established. It cannot be doubted that the root of
this suspicion on the part of civil rulers was the fact
that the Church presented herself to the world as a
sovereign power, a kingdom, an organization, with
its own laws and principles, claiming allegiance from
man as its right, and thus apparently superseding
the systems which it found in possession. This was
enough to stir up the jealousy of the rulers of the
world, and their hostility to His Kingdom. This
was already visible before His Passion, when it is
plain that, among the Chief Priests, there were at

least some who were moved to bring about His ruin from the fear that His power with the people would lead the nation to revolt against the Empire, and then that the Romans would come and take away their place and nation. Our Lord Himself met this suspicion, when Pilate asked Him if He was a King, and He explained that His Kingdom was not of this world, giving the true answer to the question, and showing that there was no ground for the fear implied, seeing that His servants would not fight, that is, that His Kingdom was never to be defended by external force. We find St. Paul and the other Apostles taking great pains to inculcate obedience to the civil government, setting this matter also on the right basis, that the powers that be are ordained of God. No doubt a part of the motive for teaching this so plainly was the desire to shield the Church from the suspicion of which we are speaking. The same motives of hostility have been in action ever since, and even in the Christian systems of government men are constantly showing their fear lest their rights should be endangered by the free and unfettered action of the Church. There is no need to draw out this part of the picture further. It is enough to say that the fear is false, as our Lord showed to Pilate. It is clearly grounded on a mistaken thought as to God Himself in His providential government of the world, and is equally inconsistent with a right view of our Lord's teaching and character.

Another cause which is assigned by the writer whom we are following, as an explanation of the feelings which prompted, especially in the early centuries, the persecution of the Church, is found in the opinion which often prevailed, that public calamities, plagues, pestilences, famines, wars, and other such signs, as was commonly supposed, of the anger of Heaven, followed on the preaching of the Gospel. The expressions of some of the early Christian writers complaining of this false impression are well known. It may be remembered that such calamities may often have been brought about by the malice of the devils, for the very purpose of producing the impression of which we speak. Thus we are told in the Gospel history of the legion of evil spirits, who asked our Lord's permission to enter into the herd of swine, after He had cast them out of the furious demoniac, and who immediately proceeded to drown the herd in the lake. The owners of the herd came at once to beg of our Lord that He would depart out of their coasts, as if His presence there had produced the destruction of their property. In cases such as this a true intelligence of the ways of God would at once have set men right. The rules by which the Providence of God over the world in the arrangement of temporal chastisements, whether of persons or families, or nations, is guided, are very beautiful and wise and merciful, but they are not always understood. In spite of a thousand warnings, men will go on looking on temporal prosperity as the uniform reward of good, and temporal calamities as the direct punishment of evil in those on whom they respectively fall. They forget that such chastisements are often another form of blessing, as removing occasions of sin and as warnings to repentance. They forget that chastisements due to a family are often delayed, for some wise reason, such as the unfitness of the living members to profit by them, and that they are often sent on an innocent generation for the sins of their fathers, because they are to the good great opportunities of spiritual good. The wicked are often also rewarded for some slight good in them they may have had once, and which is repaid by temporal well-being or success, which is perhaps the only reward that such persons are capable of receiving from the hands of God, Who foresees that in the next world they are to be the objects of His just anger.

A further cause for this feature in history of which we are speaking, the readiness with which the world persecutes the Church, is to be found in the intense corruption of the great mass of mankind, the tendency to lawlessness, sensuality, and indulgence of every kind, to the worship of every foul passion, the love of the good things of this world, and to men giving themselves to their enjoyment with the most unbridled activity. Perhaps it is not well to call it altogether unbridled, because we are here met by a phenomenon which implies that there is some kind of restraint, even among the wicked, who do not do evil for evil's sake, but under the name of good, and are seldom so entirely lawless and shamelessly depraved as they might be. For the voice of conscience makes itself heard in many cases, even in the midst of the most ribald enjoyment and excess. But this very fact gives occasion to fresh fury in the persecution of all whose life and whose words seem to oppose some obstacle to the overflowing tide of evil, the votaries of which are spurred on by an uneasy instinct to the destruction of whatever witnesses to the truthfulness of the claims of conscience, of the supreme authority to which it is always an appeal, and the reality of retribution with which it is always threatening them. Our Lord said of Himself, ' Me the world hateth, because

I give testimony of it that the works thereof are evil.'[21]   Light had come into the world and men loved darkness rather than light because their works were evil.   Apart from all diabolical instigation, the hearts of the wicked are perpetually divided against themselves, and they have to carry on a continual struggle to suppress the threats of conscience. Thus any external witness that takes part in the struggle rouses against itself all the animosity of men, because it takes the part of the weaker principle, which men still instinctively feel to have the right on its side. The Church witnesses to the truth in matters of faith and to the high standards of pure and austere morality, and this is enough to array against her all the evil elements in the nature of man and of society.

The last cause of the hostility which has always waited on the faithful teachers of the Church from the Apostles downwards, is, as we are told by Toletus, the zeal of men for false religions and forms of worship. The religion of our Lord was indeed the legitimate growth and development of the original revelation of God to mankind, and in that sense it was the oldest religion in the world. But it came into the world in the ' fulness of time,' as the Scripture says, not at the beginning, and it found mankind enslaved by a number of spurious systems of belief and worship which had sprung up in the intermediate ages in various parts of the world, and were then in full possession. None of these false creeds or systems of life were without some shreds and fragments of ancient and traditional truth, but all of them, with the exception of the Jewish religion, had more or less hideously disfigured the portions

[21] St. John vii. 7.

of the original truth which they may have inherited, and they had overwhelmed those portions beneath a multitude of foul and degrading inventions, in which the Christian mind has no difficulty in tracing the handiwork of human passion and of diabolical hatred of God. This may be what St. Paul speaks of as 'detaining the truth of God in injustice.'[22] Men were given over by the just anger of God to these false beliefs and rules of life, which were steeped in the lowest moral degradation, for their ingratitude and inexcusably wilful ignorance of Him, and of the truths concerning Him which were taught by the visible creation, which, as well as the primitive traditions of the race, witnessed continually to Him, while man was always conscious of the guiding voice of conscience within himself, which was a perpetual appeal to the sovereign judgment of God. In various ways these false systems pandered to the lowest passions of men, which the devils had taken care to make the objects of worship. For man requires something to worship, and has instincts within him which reach forth to something to whom he may have recourse as his Maker and Lord. This place, as St. Paul tells us in another place, was occupied in heathendom by the devils themselves under the name of false deities. Systems like these naturally required a regularly organized worship, the priests of which became not only the teachers of the falsehoods, but also deeply and personally interested in their maintenance. Thus the Church found herself in the presence of a whole host of false religions, having a strong hold on the masses by the low morality which they sanctioned, the practice of which was deeply interwoven with the

[22] Romans i. 18.

worship itself of the false divinities, while it also supported a large class of adherents who lived on and profited by the foul delusions which the people believed to be true.

Here, then, were abundant sources for that hostility and persecution against the Church of which our Lord speaks, and with regard to which it is not necessary here to go into greater detail. The enemies of God and man, who had themselves invented these systems of falsehood and imposed them upon the world, had little difficulty in working on the superstitions, the passions, the vices, and the interests of their own priests and of the people who held them in veneration, against the preachers of the new religion, the servants of God, who taught them the alarming truth of the supremacy of conscience, the law of pure morality, the strictness of the account that all men must render to the all-seeing and all-powerful Judge, at the same time that they spoke of the glad tidings of salvation offered to all that believed, repented of their sins, and embraced the easy commandments of the God Who had died for them. It is not necessary to point out how the hostility to the Gospel under such circumstances was founded, as our Lord pointed out, on ignorance of God the Father and of Himself, nor how the conflict that ensued was inevitable, the ignorance and the passions of men being what they are.

It is also well to note that the conflict must last as long as the world is what it is, and that it rages with not less violence when the combatants against the Church are no longer the heathen of the first centuries, but the false philosophers of modern times, and the schismatics and heretics who have broken off from the Catholic unity for so many successive generations. One of the things which it is most sad to witness in the times in which we live is the spectacle of so many good men, engaged, without being conscious of it, or at least with a partial consciousness of the truth as to their position in the eyes of God, in carrying on the warfare against the Catholic Church which they have inherited from a former generation, the members of which were far more responsible for the evil than those are who come after them. It is not for us to apportion among individuals the blame of what is certainly, in itself, direct opposition to the Church, while the men who are thus her opponents may be quite as unconscious of the mischief they do as Paul was when, as he says of himself, ' I, indeed, did formerly think that I ought to do many things contrary to the Name of Jesus of Nazareth, which also I did at Jerusalem, and many of the saints did I shut up in prison, having received authority of the Chief Priests, and when they were put to death, I brought the sentence,' and the rest. St. Paul found mercy, as he tells us, because he did it in ignorance and unbelief, but the memory of his past was always in his heart, and was no doubt a spur to him for continual zeal for the advancement of the Gospel Kingdom.

But St. Paul had at least what seemed to him to be still the appointed Hierarchy of the holy nation, the body to which the Jews were taught almost to look as Catholics to the Church, who were Israelites, ' to whom belongeth the adoption as of children, and the glory, and the testament, and the giving of the Law, and the service of God, and the promises, whose are the fathers, and of whom is Christ according to the flesh, who is above all things God blessed for

ever.   Amen.'[23]   There was much in his case to
explain his repugnance to look, as we should say, at
the Christian evidences at first, and it is not to be
denied now that the immense mass of misrepresen-
tations which are accumulated around the common
idea of Catholicism, may be for a time the excuse
of men in good faith outside the Church.   But the
more that ignorance of which we speak is dispelled,
the more difficult their position becomes in the eyes
of Catholics, against whom they have to use the very
arguments of which they have more than half learnt
to know the fallacy.   May the God of mercy save
them from opposing her too long, for the safety of
their own souls !   And in the meantime may they
learn, which too many are reluctant to do, the real
history of the bodies outside the Church to which
they belong by birth—a history which they certainly
are bound not to be ignorant of, but which, on the
contrary, they seem to think is a treason against God
to inquire into.

   ' But these things I have told you, that when the
hour shall come, you may remember that I told you
of them, but I told you not these things from the
beginning, because I was with you.'[24]   It seems best
to take these two sentences together.   Our Lord says
that He has told them of the persecutions which they
have to endure, and of their cause, in order that they
may be able, and glad to be able, to remember when
the persecution comes, that He had told them.
The meaning seems to be a continuation of what He
had said a few moments before, that what He
had told them was to prevent their being scandalized.   It was inevitable that the hostility of which

[23] Romans ix. 4, 5.
[24] See Toletus in Joannem, cap. xvi. annot. 5.

He speaks should come upon them, and yet, when it did come, if they had not been forewarned, they might have been shocked, alarmed, surprised, and likely to lose heart or take offence. Thus we find, when the persecution was actually breaking out upon the Christians, St. Peter exhorting them almost as if he had these words of His Master in his mind, ' Dearly beloved, think not strange the burning heat which is to try you, as if some new thing happened to you, but if you partake of the sufferings of Christ, rejoice, that when the glory shall be revealed, you may also be glad with exceeding joy. If you be reproached for the name of Christ, you shall be blessed, for that which is of the honour, glory, and power of God, and that which is His Spirit, resteth upon you.'[25] Our Lord here says that He tells the Apostles these things now that they may remember that He has done so. This should certainly preclude them from taking scandal. They could say to themselves that their sufferings were just what He had told them beforehand. To remember this, would assure them of His prescience of the future, and turn their thoughts to His own sufferings, which had followed so closely on the prediction of their own resemblance to Him in having to suffer, and the thought that this was exactly the witness to Him that they were appointed to bear, that He was pledged to support them in their trial, which He could have prevented if it had so pleased Him, and that He would abundantly reward them and make their sufferings fruitful to themselves and to others for His glory. At the same time He adds that He has not told them before, because He was with them, and was always able to strengthen them and

[25] 1 St. Peter iv. 12—14.

console them by His presence, and moreover could always draw on Himself the greater part of the suffering. Now, as the time was drawing near for His leaving them, He told them of their future treatment by the world, which could not be otherwise than it was to be, without some violent change in the nature of things, and the conditions under which the Gospel Kingdom was to be launched on society, that the remembrance of His prediction might give them strength and courage.

It has sometimes been a difficulty to expositors that our Lord should here have said that He had not told the Apostles of these things before, because He was Himself with them. For there are some passages in the Gospels which seem to be at variance with this statement. Our Lord, in His great charge to them when they were sent out for the first time to preach, had told them of the persecutions which awaited them, and that they should be hated of all men for His Name's sake. He had encouraged them to great fortitude, telling them not to fear those who could only kill the body, and the like. Again, He had used much stronger language in His prophecy on the Mount of Olives, and He had said something to the same effect before on this same evening. The difficulty is more apparent than real. In the sentences on which we have now been dwelling, our Lord has been speaking of the persecution which they were to have to bear, more explicitly and at the same time more gravely than ever before. He goes to the root of the matter, as it were, and they must have felt that the treatment which they were to receive at the hands of the world was nothing extraordinary or not to be expected considering the circumstances of the case.

They would see that it was no longer merely a party among the Jews, the Sadducees who were in power, or the Chief Priests who denied the Resurrection, that were jealous of His influence with the people, and were to be stirred up to hostility against Him. The persecution was not to be partial, or transitory and fitful in its manifestations, an enmity which could be appeased as well as aroused, and which might be conceivably changed into friendship more or less cordial. The followers of our Lord were to be treated as renegades and apostates, aliens from the holy nation, and indeed, as the Roman historian says of the Jews, the enemies of the human 'race. And they would soon enough have a commentary on this prediction in what they were to witness before the setting of the morrow's sun, in the treatment, of which they had at that moment no anticipation whatever, of our Blessed Lord in His own sacred Person at the hands of Jew and Gentile, priests and people and governor and king, high and low, rich and poor, nobles and populace.

CHAPTER IV.

The Holy Ghost and the World.

St. John xvi. 5—15 ; *Story of the Gospels*, § 156.

In the last chapter we examined at some length the warnings which our Lord gave to the Apostles, in very few and pregnant words, concerning the treatment which awaited them at the hands of the world on which they were to be so soon launched as His representatives, charged with the carrying on of the great commission which He had received from the Father for the salvation of the human race. Our Lord enlarged but very little on the treatment of which we speak, as indeed He had said but very little in this whole discourse on the still more important subject of the treatment of Himself which was to follow immediately on His exit from the Cenacle, in which these words were spoken. A word here and there is left to show us how continually the Passion was before His mind and how uppermost in His thoughts, but He does not enter upon any details, though, while He was speaking of the manner in which His enemies had hitherto dealt with Him, it would have been very natural to add some words about the extreme enormity to which their ignorance of the Father and of Himself was about to carry these same men on within the next few hours. They had refused to hear Him, they had

rejected the truth which He taught them about Himself. They would not listen to the evidence of His
wonderful works—but what was all this when compared to the excesses of their hatred, as it was to
be let loose in full fury before the next day's sun
was to set ? It was enough for Him to have given
the Apostles the great source of strength contained
in the knowledge that their treatment at the hands
of the world was but to be an echo of His own,
and the lesson that the behaviour of the world to
both could not have been different, 'because they
have not known My Father nor Me.'

But He had something more to speak to them
about, especially with regard to the effects of that
mission of the promised Paraclete in His own place,
of which He had already said somewhat. He had
an immense mass of truth to tell them, as to the
results of the presence of the Holy Ghost in the
world, and we shall see how He sums up those
effects on the world itself in a few clear and most
weighty words. The world could not persecute
the Holy Ghost, Whom it could not see, but it
was to turn against Him and against the Apostles,
who were to act under His guidance. The world
refuses to believe, and is convicted of sin by the
Holy Ghost when He comes, and the mention of
that coming explains the connection of the sentences
that follow with those that immediately precede
them in the report of St. John. Our Lord introduces
the subject in His own gracious way, by a gentle
complaint, which is meant to attract their attention
to the truth that He was now very nearly at the
point of taking leave of them.

'And now I go to Him that sent Me, and none
of you asketh Me, Whither goest Thou ? But

because I have spoken these things to you, sorrow hath filled your heart. But I tell you the truth, it is expedient for you that I go, for if I go not, the Paraclete will not come to you, but if I go, I will send Him to you.' If they had known the truths of which He was about to speak, they would have been most glad to ask question after question concerning them. They had avoided them because they were afraid to hear something that might give them a momentary pain. So we often shrink from knowledge which we might receive concerning the will and the arrangements of the Providence of God for ourselves or others, because we have not the perfect confidence that whatever He ordains must be most truly for our good. His present departure from them was, He tells them, expedient for them, because it was a necessary prelude to the mission of the Paraclete, which was to be an inestimable blessing to them. This is all He says directly on the subject at present.

The 'going to Him that sent Him' is the phrase which He uses all through this discourse for His cruel Death and Passion, which were immediately to take place, by means of which and by the merits of which He was to achieve the stupendous victory, for Himself and for them, which was to be the reversal of the world's triumph and the establishment of the Kingdom of God. His words express nothing of the triumph, nothing of the fruits of the victory, any more than of the sufferings by which these are to be purchased. He simply says that if He does not go away the Paraclete would not come. He had already said some words about leaving them, in the former part of the discourse, but now He brings up the matter once more, to close with it finally. He desires to tell them what He was perhaps more desirous that they should ask Him, for an answer obtained by a question sinks more deeply into the mind than the mere mention of a fact, and friends expect to be asked about things which interest them greatly, and are of high importance, when they are about to do them. So He puts the instruction which He desires to give them in the form of an answer to a question which He puts into their own mouths, and which they were perhaps afraid to ask Him, notwithstanding their great love, fearing that it might receive an answer which they did not wish to hear.

In the first place He tells them the reason which it concerns them so much to know, why He was going away, and thus takes occasion to reveal to them the immense benefits to His Kingdom and to themselves, which were to be the result of His departure. The first thing He tells them is that He is going to Him that sent Him, that is, to the Father, and under these words lies hidden the whole doctrine of the redemption of the world by means of the Sacrifice which He had been sent by the Father to accomplish. He does not blame the sorrow which He saw filling their hearts, because it came from the great and natural love for Him, Who, to the hearts that could appreciate Him, was the object of the deepest and tenderest and most intense love that human nature is capable of conceiving. What He had already said on the subject had to some extent prepared them for the truth, but He now says plainly that on His departure to the Father, from Whom He is to ask the boon, for the sake of the merits of His Passion, depends the immense and inconceivable blessing of the Mission of the Holy Ghost. It was ordained in the Divine Counsels that so it should be, that the Holy Ghost was to be given on that condition. The giving of the Holy Ghost was to be a new Creation, in which the fruits of the Passion of the Incarnate Son were to be brought home and administered to men. And our Lord seems to take up again, and explain further than before, what He had already told them about the witness of the Holy Ghost, in which witness they were to join with a testimony of their own.

The passage which now follows, which is confessedly one of the most difficult to explain in the New Testament, as is seen by the great variety of interpretations which have been assigned to our Lord's words, must be approached with a word of preliminary caution, without which some confusion as to its meaning will not unnaturally occur. The difficulty has been caused, as it seems, by a prevalent supposition that He is speaking, more generally than is the case, of the whole effects of the presence of the Paraclete in His Mission, whereas the words are distinctly limited by Him to a particular effect of that Divine presence, which He specifies as the confutation or conviction of the world which He is speaking of as His own great enemy and persecutor, and, by implication, as the great enemy and persecutor of those who bear His Name and carry on His work. It is of the effect of the Holy Ghost in this matter of the confutation or conviction of the world that our Lord says what He does say, not of any other effects which may follow from His presence, although the confutation or conviction of the world, which is the main subject of the passage, may be produced by the various operations of the Holy Ghost, of which an account is given in later portions of the Sacred Volume, as in the passages of St. Paul, which we have had occasion to quote or to refer to in the first chapter of this volume. Our Lord has already spoken of the witness to Himself by the Paraclete, which is quite distinct from that conviction of the world of sin of which He is now speaking, though that is involved in it as its consequence.

He describes this witness of the Holy Ghost by three effects, which His presence and working in the world was to produce upon the world itself, and which He characterizes generally as its conviction. The word used by St. John signifies the result which is produced on a man against his will, when something which he dislikes and is not prepared for is brought home to him by irresistible evidence which he cannot gainsay or evade. He may have been accused of a crime, and have denied it, and he is convicted of it, when it is clearly proved against him. He may have denied the possibility of some work, and when it is shown to have been achieved he is convicted, or he may have refused to believe a statement, and when it is clearly demonstrated to be true, he is convicted of ignorance, or of a mistake, or of a lie, as the case may be. This is the result which our Lord says is to be produced on the world by the coming and presence of the Holy Ghost. He proceeds to mention the matters as to which the conviction is to take place, and He gives in each case a different reason for the conviction. It is clear that the right interpretation of the whole passage depends on our keeping in mind the distinct statements of our Lord. All three results are to be produced by the presence of the Holy Ghost, and they are to be produced on the world, and therefore they must be produced by the presence of the Holy Ghost, as far as that presence is to be perceptible and recognized by the world. The result in each case is distinct, and is to be produced by certain effects of His presence in the world which are specified by our Lord. It seems, then, that our Lord has taken pains to make His meaning as clear as possible for us, and we must correspond to that care of His, by attending very diligently to the distinctions which He makes, without which diligence we may easily miss the full meaning of this most important passage.

But the first part of this great declaration on the part of our Lord consists of the truths which are here conveyed concerning the Mission of the Holy Ghost. 'If I go not,' our Lord says, 'the Paraclete will not come to you,' and then He repeats the statement positively, 'but if I go I will send Him to you.' He speaks as the Incarnate Son of God, when He says that if He does not go, the Paraclete will not come, for, as we have already said, it was to be by His going to the Father by His Passion and Death that the Paraclete was to be sent. Not that the Father and the Son could not send the Holy Ghost without the sacrifice of the Passion having been previously accomplished, but because it was the Divine counsel and ordinance that so it should be brought about. He says, moreover, that if He goes He will send the Holy Ghost, thus making it clear that it is His, as One in the possession of the Godhead with the Father, to send the Holy Ghost, Who proceeds by One Spiration from all eternity from the Father and the Son.

One object which may be supposed to have had a

place in the Divine counsels as to the Mission of the Holy Ghost, may have been the manifestation of His Divine Person Himself as God. We have said more than once that the Third Divine Person was not as yet known clearly, even to the mass of the servants of God throughout the world. We can trace through the whole of the Old Testament indications of His Personality and Divinity, but it cannot be said that He was so fully revealed as the Father and the Son. He was to manifest Himself more fully by the wonderful gifts and graces, as well as the external signs of His Presence, with which the world which He had created was now to be filled. There was therefore a certain fitness in the removal of our Lord's visible Presence from among men, that the work of the Holy Ghost might be more signally and clearly recognized as His own, instead of being attributed to our Blessed Lord. Not that the One could eclipse or obscure the other, or that there could be, as it were, any rivalry between them, but that men might recognize the power and divinity of each One, by the marvellous love and wisdom with which each One showered upon them His gifts and blessings, to the greater glory and more complete manifestation of the Adorable Trinity.

Another thing which might contribute to this greater manifestation, and which may be found in the decree of which we speak, is that thereby it became more clearly known that our Lord Himself, as He says, sent the Holy Ghost from the Father. If our Lord had remained upon earth when the Holy Ghost was sent, it might have been thought that He had been sent by the Father for the sake of our Lord, but it would not have been so clear that our Lord had Himself sent Him. But He withdrew His own visible Presence among men, and after that withdrawal, the Holy Ghost came. A third reason for our Lord's departure in His visible Presence is found in the office and work which the Apostles were to discharge for the propagation of the faith and the foundation of the Christian Kingdom throughout the world. They were to scatter themselves over the whole earth, preaching the Name of their Master in a hundred different countries in succession, whereas when our Lord was on earth they must have been bound to cling to His sensible and visible Presence by an invincible attraction, which would have kept them indeed in unity and charity, as it had kept them hitherto, but not in so manifestly Divine a communion of heart and mind, and thought and method, as was to be seen when they were separated indeed in place, but one in the most perfect harmony through the One Spirit who animated them all. Here again we are reminded of that wonderful truth to which St. Paul alludes when he tells the Corinthians that ' henceforth we (the Apostles) know no man after the flesh, and if we have known Christ according to the flesh, but now we know Him so no longer. If then any be in Christ, a new creature, the old things are passed away. Behold all things are made new.'[1] It seems strange indeed, at first thought, that there can be anything better or sweeter to the Christian soul, than the visible presence of our Lord, or conversation with Him. But it is seen on reflection that the communion with Him which was possible to the Apostles during His Life on earth, even when they could talk with Him most familiarly, and listen to His words, and watch His every action, was something that they must have felt would pass

[1] 2 Cor. v. 16, 17.

away, and be superseded by something even better, and, at the same time, more consistent with the conditions of a life of laborious activity, varied by unceasing prayer and by much suffering of various kinds. The Gospels and the Epistles also are wonderfully silent on many points which have filled a very large portion of the thoughts and lives of the Apostles, but, with the lives of the saints before us, we learn to take for granted many things which St. Peter, St. Paul, and St. John thought it well not to mention to the communities for whom they wrote, or to commit to letters which were to pass from hand to hand, even though they may have been originally addressed to familiar friends, themselves saints, like St. Timothy or St. Titus.

With our modern ideas, living under conditions of society under which communication with the outside world is facilitated and multiplied to an enormous extent, we are led to suppose that it would be impossible to carry on any large amount of active work, even for God's service, without such communication. Thus it becomes difficult to understand the great isolation from human sympathies and intercourse under which the lives of the Apostles must have been led, after the time when they went forth to convert the world, one by one, or at the most, each with a single companion. But no doubt they were sufficiently and abundantly supplied with the best kind of companionship, of that kind which is so little thought of by men of more modern times. They learnt by experience the meaning of the promise which our Lord had made in the earlier part of this discourse, in answer to the question of St. Jude, ' If any one love Me he will keep My word, and My Father will love him, and We will come to him, and will make our abode with him.'[2] We must not forget that our Lord was to have new ways of communication with the souls dear to him, especially through His intercourse with them in the Blessed Sacrament, which may have made them less dependent on what had formerly been their greatest privileges, and so able, in the case in which they had to work in great solitude as far as human converse was concerned, to guide themselves continually and securely by the same spirit and the same principles and methods.

It is easy to see that, even in the discourse on which we are now commenting, there were many things on which our Lord would not say more than was necessary, and much less than He would have said, if it had not been that He was speaking at the very outset of the long intercourse, which was to be the life of the Church and of individual souls most dear to Him, between Himself and those souls in the Blessed Sacrament, and, again, the outset of the active and most multifarious dealings of the Holy Ghost in His various gifts and fruits with the souls in which He was to come and dwell. We see by the peace and calm which possessed the souls of the Apostles at the Ascension, how much they must have already grown in the use of the new life imparted to them by the sacramental presence of our Lord, and the other great gifts which are hinted at rather than explained here.

Considerations such as these may help us somewhat to see that when our Lord said that it was expedient for them that He should go away, for if He did not go away, the Holy Ghost would not come, He touched lightly on a truth which would become soon intelligible to the Apostles, and to all

[2] St. John xiv. 23.

who truly caught their spirit, with a light and power
of comprehension which would go on ever and ever
increasing more and more in faithful hearts like
theirs, until it merged itself in the clear intelligence
of beatitude itself. The prayer which St. Paul pours
forth for those whom he addresses in the Epistle to
the Ephesians, sums up the continual advance from
clearer to clearer light in which the progress of the
saints consists, and which is the truest interest of
the faithful soul, the most perfect glorification of
God therein, as well as the consummation of peace
and joy. 'I bow my knees to the Father of
our Lord Jesus Christ, of Whom all paternity in
heaven and earth is named, that He would grant
you, according to the riches of His glory, to be
strengthened by His Spirit with might unto the
inward man, that Christ may dwell by faith in
your hearts, that being rooted and founded in
charity, you may be able to comprehend, with all
the saints, what is the breadth and length and
height and depth, to know also the charity of
Christ, which surpasseth all knowledge, that you
may be filled unto all the fulness of God.'[3] St. Paul
in this passage does not attempt to describe in
particular what the treasures are which he prays the
Eternal Father to communicate to the Ephesians,
and he seems to give us to understand that they can
become intelligible only to those on whom that
Heavenly Father will bestow them. This is nothing
new with regard to the gifts of God of this kind, and
we may suppose that our Lord left them to be
revealed in due time by the teaching of the Father
to the Apostles. This, then, is all that He now says
to them on the subject.

[3] Ephes. iii. 14—19.

He proceeds to resume, as it were, the subject on which He had been engaged. He had been speaking to them of the reception which He Himself had experienced from the world, which, as He tells them, was to be repeated in the treatment of His messengers by the same world. They were to fare as their Master had fared. He does not, therefore, tell them that the Holy Ghost was to convert the world, though His beneficent presence was to produce in and through the Church the most marvellous and far-reaching effects to the glory of God. He describes in the three concise sentences which we have already quoted what these effects are to be. These we are now to endeavour to explain. The Holy Ghost was to convince or convict the world of three different things—of sin, of justice, and of judgment.

This conviction of the world of these three things must be taken as summing up what our Lord wished the Apostles to understand from Him, as He looked forward with the whole future before Him, from the moment of the Mission of the Paraclete to the end of the world, the effects of the presence of the Blessed Paraclete on the world into which He was to come. Our Lord, then, sums up the witness of the Holy Ghost to Him, as far as relates to the conviction of the world which had rejected Him, under these three heads. The world is to be convicted of sin by the Holy Ghost, Who will prove irrefragably that it has sinned and continues in sin, ' because they believe not in Me.' He uses the present tense in the original, as if the unbelief and the sin were o continue. This conviction, therefore, is to be produced on the world, by something that the Holy Ghost points out and makes manifest in the world itself. The second conviction, concerning justice, cannot be grounded on anything in the wicked world itself. Our Lord assigns as the ground of this conviction, the faith of the disciples, 'Because I go to the Father, and you shall see Me no longer.' The world is not to believe, and there is a clear contrast implied in the words now used, because His going to the Father removes Him from their sight, and the faith of the disciples becomes possible by the fact of the removal of His presence. The words, 'You see Me no more,' contain equivalently the other statement, 'You do believe Me.' The ground of the third conviction is neither in the world itself nor in the disciples, but in the evidently judicial chastisement and overthrow of the prince of this world—of judgment, because the prince of this world is judged—that is, in the evident overthrow of the kingdom of Satan, that is, a kingdom founded on usurpation and deep deception, and a misuse of the power permitted to him in consequence of the fall of our first parents. We hope to explain in what this kingdom consisted, and what is meant by the judgment inflicted on the prince of this world of which our Lord speaks.

The single word convince or convict which our Lord uses, seems to have the same general meaning in the three cases, modified according to the sense which the sentence in each case requires, as we shall see. To convince or convict the world of sin is to bring home to it the charge of sin, to convince or convict the world of justice is to make the world convinced that justice is working in it or in others by the operation of the Holy Ghost, and to convince or convict the world of judgment is to prove to it that judgment also is at work by the same means on its ruler, of whom our Lord speaks as the prince of this world. In all cases, as we have said, it is the work of the Holy Ghost that is to produce the conviction, and it is the world itself in which the conviction is produced. That blessed work is no doubt the delight and admiration of the saints and angels in Heaven, whom St. Peter, as we have seen, describes as gazing down in astonishment at the marvels of the grace and glory of God which are wrought by Him in the Church. But that is not the conviction of which our Lord is here speaking, which is a part of the witness to our Lord to be borne to the world by the Holy Ghost. It would not be against the meaning of the original Greek to translate the phrase by the word 'contradict,' but the proper sense includes the notion of a contradiction which contains also the proof of the truth of the contradiction, in which sense the word is used by logicians.

The first part of this witness which is to convict the world consists in its conviction of sin. 'Of sin because they believe not in Me.' The English version uses the past tense, 'Because they have not believed in Me,' and this is the reading of the Vulgate, but the original seems to be in the present tense. The meaning, however, is the same,—the world had not believed in our Lord, and in a historical statement the present tense might be used of all the time that the witness of the Holy Ghost was to continue. That witness, at the moment at which our Lord spoke, was imminent, and it was to last on throughout all ages. The present tense might, therefore, well be used. For the world always refuses to believe, in the nineteenth century as in the first, and is always convicted of sin for so refusing, and in this it is in contrast to those of whom our Lord speaks in the next sentence, as 'you,' the Apostles and their followers, who do believe. The world refuses to believe, and is convicted of sin by the Holy Ghost when He comes, because that coming is the evident demonstration that our Lord should have been welcomed with faith in His Mission and submission to His authority. The power of the Holy Ghost in the hearts of men, and the wonderful manifestations of that power even externally, by the marvellous signs which accompanied His Presence, and the conspicuous graces and virtues which were seen in the lives of the faithful, all was directed to the bearing witness to the truth of our Lord's Mission, and of the teaching which was committed to Him. The multitude which came together to witness the prodigies of the Day of Pentecost, and to whom the nature of the prodigies was explained by St. Peter, as we are told, ' when they had heard these things, they had compunction in their heart, and said to Peter and to the rest of the Apostles, What shall we do, men and brethren ? But Peter said to them, Do penance, and be baptized every one of you in the name of Jesus Christ, for the remission of your sins, and you shall receive the Gift of the Holy Ghost. And with very many other words did he testify and exhort them, saying, Save yourselves from this perverse generation.'[4] We here see the natural effect of any great display of certainly preternatural power on men whose consciences have been awakened and enlightened thereby. They become at once disposed and fit subjects for exhortations to enter into themselves and acknowledge their sins. We have a similar instance in the keeper of the prison at Philippi,[5]

[4] Acts ii. 37—40.   [5] Acts xvi. 27.

who was awakened by the earthquake at midnight, and found all his prisoners freed from their chains, when St. Paul and St. Silas had been singing their praises to God. 'And bringing them out, he said, Masters, what must I do that I may be saved?' The prodigies had either led to or been accompanied by a strong conviction of the sinfulness of their state in these persons, and this was the natural result, as it may be called, of the presence of the Holy Ghost.

The manifestation of the Holy Ghost did not change as to this purpose and effect after His first coming on the Day of Pentecost. The world was convicted by the witness of the Paraclete to our Lord, and this is the reason which our Lord here assigns, 'Of sin, because they believe not in Me.' The rejection of our Lord was the great sin of the generation to which He was sent, and the rejection of the Gospel as preached in His Name by the Church has been the great sin of the world in all successive generations since. It has been the sin which shuts the door of pardon to all other sins, which cannot be forgiven without faith in the Gospel message, witnessed to by the Church and the Apostles from the beginning, who are the dispensers and organs of the Word of God, His ambassadors, as St. Paul calls them, through the Holy Ghost, Who animates and guides the whole organization of the Body of Christ. The whole system by which grace is administered and applied is His work, and to turn away from and reject the means of grace, is to choose to remain in sin rather than accept the gracious offer of salvation. Thus it is that the world is convinced, by the workings of the Holy Ghost, of sin which consists in refusing to believe in our Lord. Our Lord must be considered as embracing in these few words all the manifold operations of the Holy Ghost, some of which are enumerated by St. Paul in more than one passage, and as declaring generally that the effect of these operations which are manifest to the world in themselves, or in their effects, is to witness to the truth of His Mission, and of His teaching with so large an amount of overwhelming evidence as to leave men without excuse for continued and obstinate rejection of Himself, and at the same time to touch the hearts that are ready for grace with affection and contrition.

It must also be remembered that the sin of which the world is convicted by the Holy Ghost is not to be limited to the single initial sin of unbelief, or refusal to believe. Our Lord's words may be taken as referring to the world of which He had been speaking as having rejected Himself, the generation to which He was sent in Palestine, and which was to be immediately confuted for its rejection of Him by the work of the Holy Ghost from the Day of Pentecost. But the words may also be taken more generally, as applying to the world in general, the mass of mankind generation after generation as long as human society lasts, for it is always true that the work of the Holy Ghost among men is to convict them of sin, and in a particular manner of the sin of unbelief, and the rejection of the evidences by which the Providence of God confirmed His claims to be considered as a Divine messenger. The world as such is always rejecting Jesus Christ, and is always being convicted of sin for that rejection, for there is always in every age the amount of evidence for the Church which God sees to be more than sufficiemt to make those who reject her, guilty of sin. Our Lord said to His enemies among the priests, ' If you believe

not that I am He, you shall die in your sin.'[6]   This
was said before some of His greatest miracles, and
before the Passion and Resurrection.   It implies
that they had evidence enough, even then, to convict
them of sin, and this was before their conviction by
the Holy Ghost of which we are speaking.

The same kind of guiltiness may be induced in
those who refuse any sufficient evidence in favour
of the truths set before men as the evidence on
which they are to believe, although it is not for us
to determine in particular cases as to the sufficiency
of the manner in which the evidence is set before
individual souls, so as to make the guilt inevitable.
As to the other matters on which our Lord is speaking
in connection with these three confutations of the
world, we may consider that He intends to refer in
the first place to the world which had rejected Him,
and secondarily of that confutation on some points
which was to come by the witness of the Holy Ghost
in after times, as we shall presently explain. On these
other points there was to take place, by the operation
of the Holy Ghost, the same confutation and contradiction of the world.   Our Lord speaks first of the
immediate proof furnished by the Holy Ghost on and
after the Day of Pentecost.   And there can be no
doubt that the effects of the presence of the Holy
Ghost were felt at that day by the people in
general, and even the enemies of our Lord in
particular, as a proof to the truth of His claims
and the wickedness of those who had brought
about His rejection by the nation and His murder.
The High Priest said to the Apostles, after the
great outburst of miracles which followed the
preaching in the name of our Lord, 'You have

[6] St. John viii. 24.

a mind to bring the blood of this Man upon us.'[7] That was the inevitable result of the Apostolic preaching in Jerusalem at the commencement, and the world, represented by the high priests, made no attempt to confute the truth by argument or evidence, they simply went on in their unbelief and the persecution of the Church. The miracles of the Apostles confirmed their teaching and their witness to the Resurrection of our Lord, and the evidence was no doubt immensely enforced by the holy lives of the first Christians, who were of one mind and heart, and had all things in common, and among whom there was conspicuous to the world the mutual charity and the unity on which our Lord laid so much stress. It is unnecessary to add how the weight of evidence in favour of this conviction of the world of which we are now speaking increased day after day and year after year in the Apostles' own time, spreading at first through Judæa and Galilee and Samaria until, in a very short time, the door of the Church was opened to the Gentiles by St. Peter, and the Gospel was carried over the Greek and Roman world by the work of St. Paul and the rest of the Apostles. The same process may be said to have been always going on in the struggle of the Church under the guidance of the Blessed Paraclete. He is that blessed Light of whom she sings, He is the Spirit of Truth, as our Lord calls Him, and He cannot be confronted with falsehood and darkness without scattering them and annihilating them, by the mere fact of His presence. Our Lord is here speaking of a condition of things in which no constraint is put upon the freedom of man, and therefore He does not say that the world

[7] Acts v. 28.

was conquered or convinced, it is not convinced in the sense of being converted, but that it is confuted though it chooses to adhere to its old lie.

We may also remember that it is a part of the office of the Paraclete, not only to bring to the knowledge of men the new truths concerning our Lord, and which had not been given to mankind before, but also, in a very true sense, to reawaken in their hearts, as is taught in the Epistle to the Romans, a good many truths which belonged even to the natural law, and which in many nations had become overlaid or buried by the progress of human corruption. This is a subject of large extent, to which we can only now refer. The description of heathenism which the Apostle gives in the first chapter to the Romans shows that in the times in which he wrote, and among the most cultivated nations of antiquity, many of the precepts of the natural law which was written in the hearts of men from the beginning, were absolutely or partially obliterated. The same phenomenon is found in various parts of the world in our own time. Men have not an idea that certain sins are such, in consequence of the darkness which has fallen upon them, and this is true even in some cases in Christian countries. The revival, so to speak, of the knowledge of the natural law, is the work of the Holy Ghost, and this seems to be another sense in which He convicts the world of sin, that is, of having been ignorant of the true character of many acts or habits which were in fact sinful, though men had lost the sense of their true moral turpitude. It is difficult to imagine the extent to which the enlightenment of the conscience on these points has been carried in the world of humanity since the Day of Pentecost by the Holy

Ghost, and the elevation and purification which has been the result. We find that savage tribes, who have inherited from their forefathers some of the most degrading and immoral customs of which men are capable, have been in one or two generations transformed by religion into communities in which it is rare for the law of God in respect to purity or justice or charity to be violated in any material degree. And we gather from history that it has always been the same where the work of the Blessed Paraclete has not been hindered.

The conviction of the world is not anything arbitrary or occasional, but a result which is involved in the nature of the two powers brought into conflict by the presence of the Holy Spirit of God in the false and miserable world. From the beginning, as soon as the world became what it is by the fall of Adam and the usurped power over it which is signified by the name by which our Lord, here and elsewhere, designates the Evil One, the strife of the Holy Ghost against the world has ever been waged. The history of man begins with his fall, and although the Holy Ghost was never in the world before the Day of Pentecost in the sense in which He has been in it since that day, He was always, as the Scripture says, 'striving with man.' The fall was immediately followed by the promise of redemption, and from that moment it became possible for man to please God and obtain the benefit of the promised salvation by the exercise of faith and repentance. In the sense which these words convey, it was possible to escape from sin, and where there was no faith, there could be no escape from sin. In this sense the presence of the Holy Ghost in the world was always the conviction of men of sin, if

J 14

they did not believe in the promise of salvation, which was handed on by tradition to all generations of the children of Adam, because the bringing home the conviction of sin to the hearts of men is always one of the works of the Holy Ghost, and when that conviction is produced, the souls thus awakened are already disposed to welcome the promise of salvation held out to them by revelation in whatever degree of clearness the revelation reaches them. Many thousands of men in all times do not believe, because they do not feel the need of the salvation which is held out to them, from their want of light about sin. This light it is the work of the Holy Spirit to produce.

Our Lord could have told the Apostles a great many more truths about the conviction of the world of sin, but it is clear that He speaks with studied brevity. This indeed is the case with the whole of His teaching concerning the Holy Ghost, which gives merely the main outlines of the great Gift, with which they were gradually to become familiar by the presence with them of the Paraclete Himself. Our Lord is equally brief in the description of the two other convictions of the world by the working of the Holy Ghost. The next on which He speaks is its conviction of justice. It seems at first sight a strange thing that the world is to be convicted of justice as the next step in the process, the first step of which was a conviction of sin, as if the justice and the sin, of which the proof was to be given, could be inherent in the same subject, and that subject, moreover, what our Lord calls the world. The world is in one sense the great enemy of our Lord, and in another sense it is the world that He came to save, and which He has, in fact, saved in thousands of millions of its children. Thus the world itself, which in its unconverted condition and in its unregenerated children is the enemy of God, pays its own tribute, as we see in the history of the Acts and in the Epistles, to the truth as it is in our Lord, as when our Lord speaks of those who are to believe in Him through the word of the Apostles, and thus we find that it can be quoted as joining in a sense of its own in the witness borne to Him after the coming of the Holy Ghost, as when St. Paul quotes of the work of the Apostles the verse of the Psalm: ' Their sound hath gone forth into all the earth, and their words unto the ends of the whole world.'[8]

For in truth the same blessed light of the Holy Ghost which brings home to the world the overwhelming proof of its sin in the rejection of Jesus Christ, has fallen in gracious and healing streams on the hearts of those out of the world who have believed, and in them this light has called into being all the manifold and marvellous fruits of the Christian virtues in fertile and luxuriant growth. No garden in the most favoured clime has ever teemed with beauty and fecundity that can be compared to this. The souls of the faithful under the touch of the life-giving Paraclete have bloomed into a new Paradise. Even in the natural order the soul of man is capable of immense and multitudinous fruitfulness, its gifts of intelligence and imagination give it almost a creative power, the results of which are works of the noblest kind. But the most glorious fruits which have had their birth in the human mind, when perfectly cultivated and most highly elevated, are as nothing at all to the magnificent fruits of grace in the souls of the saints. The highest achievements of genius and the noblest works of philosophy and

[8] Romans x. 18.

science are but as the dust of the earth in comparison to the grand creation of grace in the souls of God's servants, in which it may certainly be said that the Holy Ghost convinces and convicts the world of justice, as He convicts it of sin in its refusal to submit to our Lord.

This result, as we all know, may come about in the weakest and simplest of mankind. There is no natural power in the saints of God which is not possessed equally with them by the sinners who make themselves a disgrace to their nature. Human nature is the same in all, and thus the glories of the kingdom of grace in the chosen children of God are a conviction by which it is incontrovertibly brought home to the world by the Holy Ghost that justice and virtue, in their highest expressions, have been placed within the reach of mankind in the dispensation of the Redemption. In this sense the world is convicted of justice, because our Lord has gone to His Father, and His children see Him no more. He has gone to the Father, and His so going has been the meritorious cause for the effusion upon mankind of the wonderful gifts of the Holy Ghost, and these gifts are the reward of faith in Him, no longer seen by them, no longer present visibly to draw their hearts to Himself by the strongest attachment, but rather putting them to the trials and persecutions involved in the profession of their belief in Him in the face of a persecuting world.

It almost seems as if St. Peter had had these words of our Lord in his mind when he wrote his first Epistle, at least his language seems to be founded on the truth here set forth. He tells the faithful, just then, for the first time as it seems, under persecution, ' Blessed be the God and Father of our

Lord Jesus Christ, Who, according to His great mercy, hath regenerated us unto a lively hope by the Resurrection of Jesus Christ from the dead, unto an inheritance incorruptible and undefiled, and that cannot fade, reserved in Heaven for you, who by the power of God, are kept by faith unto salvation, ready to be revealed in the last time—wherein you shall greatly rejoice, if now you must be for a little time made sorrowful in divers temptations, that the trial of your faith (much more precious than gold which is tried by the fire) may be found unto praise and glory and honour at the appearing of Jesus Christ, Whom having not seen, you love, in Whom also now, though you see Him not, you believe, and believing shall rejoice with joy unspeakable and glorified, receiving the end of your faith, even the salvation of your souls.'[9] Thus, as the unbelief of the world in the former instance brought home to it the condemnation of sin, so does the faith of the children of the Church bring home to the unbelieving world the proof that justice has been placed within its reach, justice which is the fruit of the trials to which the faith subjects those who have it, and who display under those trials the most beautiful fruits of virtue.

It need hardly be pointed out how clearly and logically these two convictions of the world are connected with and correspond one to the other. The presence of the Holy Ghost brings out the difference between the wicked and the good, as the rays of intense light gild with their own brilliancy the hills and rocks and trees on which they fall, whilst they cast into the darkest shadow the surfaces that are turned away from them. The light of grace in the world was immensely intensified and magnified

<hr>

[9] 1 St. Peter i. 3—9.

when the Paraclete came, and as the evil became more conspicuous and more hideous thereby, so did the glory of justice and virtue become more splendid. The sin of the world was said to be in the rejection of our Lord and of the preaching concerning Him afterwards by the Church. It is natural and reasonable that as sin is the opposite of justice, and unbelief of faith, so the justice of which there is here question should consist in faith and the fruits of faith in the souls of men. This is what our Lord's words seem to convey.

He does not, indeed, in speaking of the operations of the Holy Ghost, omit the meritorious and formal cause of the justice which these operations are to produce. Thus we have a two-fold cause assigned for this justice. 'Because I go to the Father and you see Me no more.' Our Lord went to the Father in His Passion, and then He merited the great out-pouring of gifts and graces of the Holy Spirit for mankind. He went to the Father also in His Ascension, and then the fruits which had been merited in the Passion were given Him to be out-poured on mankind in the coming of the Holy Ghost. St. Paul, when he speaks of one great class of these gifts, says, 'To every one of us is given grace according to the measure of the giving of Christ. Wherefore He saith, Ascending on high He led captivity captive, He gave gifts unto men.' And then after some other words he goes on to com-memorate the gifts bestowed, particularly in order to the service of the Church—'some apostles, and some prophets, and other some evangelists, and other some pastors, and doctors, for the perfecting of the saints, for the work of the ministry, for the edifying of the Body of Christ '—not meaning of course to limit the multiform effusion of grace to the particular gifts which he has occasion to mention in the passage of which we speak. St. Paul's words are enough to explain why our Lord here mentions His own going to the Father in connection with the justice shown to and in the world by the Holy Ghost.

Our Lord's words, moreover, seem to contain a direct allusion to His own departure as making Him the object of the faith on which the justice and holiness of the saints is grounded, and in this He is echoed by the words of St. Peter in the Epistle we have lately quoted, about their not seeing our Lord, but loving Him and believing in Him, ' Whom not having seen you love.' Thus all the sin of the world comes from not believing our Lord, so the justice of the saints comes first indeed from the wonderful gifts and graces given by Him as the fruit of the Ascension, but also on their own part it comes from their faith in Him, as no longer seen, of which St. Peter speaks. And the conviction of the world of sin is not so glorious a result as the display to all the world which continues to the present day, and will continue to the end of time, of that transcendentally beautiful justice of which our Lord here speaks as the work of the Holy Ghost in the hearts and lives of those who believe, and in the Christian society into which they are formed in the Church.

As we have already hinted, the world had not long to wait for the verification of this prediction as to its own confutation on this point of justice. Indeed, it would not have suited the greatness of the gifts here foretold, if they had been left to a gradual manifestation. The members of the Church were comparatively few indeed in her early years, but within a short time from the Day of Pentecost, there began in her children the manifestation of that supernatural perfection and continual growth in the highest and purest virtue, which was the consolation of the Apostles and the cause of immense joy to the Sacred Heart. Palestine was soon peopled with small collections of faithful in the various cities, each one of which was more or less a reflection of the original Church of Jerusalem, a sketch of which is given in the first chapters of the Acts. The Church of Jerusalem was soon exposed to the storm of persecution, which it was the lot of that Church to bear up to the very time of the siege by the Romans, which ended in the destruction of the city. Jerusalem was also the chief seat of the party among the Jews that gave so much trouble to St. Paul. They were not content with persecuting the Church among themselves. They were not satisfied unless they forced the Christians not to admit the Gentiles into their own body. 'Who both killed the Lord Jesus and the Prophets, and have persecuted us,' St. Paul says of them to the Thessalonians,[10] 'and please not God, and are adversaries to all men, forbidding us to preach to the Gentiles that they may be saved, to fill up their sins always, for the wrath of God is come upon them to the end.' But notwithstanding the extreme hardships of their position, which made some among them inclined to yield to the persecution, which was aggravated by their being treated as socially excommunicated, and deprived of any share in the abundant alms sent to the Holy City by the Jews from all parts of the world, the picture drawn by St. Luke of the Christians of Jerusalem continued to be true to the end.

[10] 1 Thess. ii. 15, 16.

It was the same elsewhere. All through the Roman Empire, wherever the messengers of the Gospel found their way, there sprung up Christian communities, in which the practice of every virtue became the rule. Not many great names stand out to sight, for the history is very scanty, and in those days men were so constantly in expectation of death, and of the speedy ending of the world, that they did not take the pains to chronicle the virtues that were so common among them. It is more of a fulfilment of the prediction of our Lord that the Christian virtues should be practised in perfection by large masses of the faithful, than that there should be records remaining to us of a few conspicuous saints who were pre-eminent for extraordinary sanctity. But we can gather enough on this subject from the Epistles and the Acts of the Apostles to convince that this particular confutation of the world was one of the salient features of the first age of the Church, and so it has continued in all subsequent ages. It is particularly in the note of sanctity, which is one of the marks of the Catholic Church to which no other one of her rivals and counterfeits ever has laid claim, that we find the fulfilment of the glowing descriptions of Isaias of the beauties and glories of the Kingdom of the Messias, which seem far to surpass any earthly magnificence or prosperity.

Our Lord Himself seems to hold His breath, and to forbear enlarging on the subject, which might have been incongruous at the time when all these glories were as yet unpurchased by the only price that could have adequately earned them, that of His own Precious Blood, and when the Holy Ghost Who was to work all these wonders was not yet given.

For the present it may be well to pause before any attempt to describe them, however imperfectly. We may remind ourselves of the short passage in which St. Paul sums up the fruits of the Spirit, showing how familiar to his mind, and also to the minds of his readers, these matters had become. It really seems as if it was as easy to him to give a catalogue of these beauties of grace as of what he calls just before the works of the flesh. 'But the fruit of the Spirit is charity, joy, peace, patience, benignity, goodness, mildness, faith, longanimity, modesty, continence, chastity.'[11]   Although a full commentary on these few lines would furnish us with a general description of some part of the wonderful confutation of the world of which we are now speaking, everything of the kind must be more or less imperfect in human language, and it must always be qualified by the recollection that the Church and Christian society are always, as long as this world lasts, in the condition of that field of the householder in which an enemy sows cockle amid the wheat while men sleep, and that therefore the fruits of the Spirit in the children of the Church are always liable to the hindering of their growth and full fecundity, by the chilling and dwarfing influence of the neighbourhood of an atmosphere of evil. Then only will their growth be freed from all that may impede its full development and power and magnificence, when the just shall shine like the sun in the Kingdom of their Father.

We proceed now to the third effect of the presence of the Holy Ghost in and on the world which our Lord here mentions, which is said by Him to be that He shall convince or convict the world of judgment, 'because the prince of this world is

11 Galat. v. 22, 23.

judged.' These words naturally carry our minds back to the former passage in this same Gospel, where it is mentioned that on the Day of Palms, after the application of the Gentiles to see our Lord, and voice from Heaven which was afterwards heard, He had said, ' Now is the judgment of this world, now shall the prince of this world be cast forth, and I if I be lifted up from the earth will draw all things unto Myself.' This passage has been already explained, and little further need be added here by way of commentary. But it should be remarked that what is spoken of on that former occasion is the judgment of the world, not exactly of its prince, and that it is one thing for Satan to be judged and another thing for him to be cast out. The judgment of the world is the condemnation of the false goods, the false maxims, the false principles, the lies and impostures of the world whereby men have been deluded, and the like. The judgment of the prince of the world is the condemnation and chastisement of Satan, the overthrow of the usurped kingdom he has set up, the systems of false religions and false traditions which he. has imposed upon men, putting himself and his angels in the place of God. The work of the Holy Ghost was to be the dispersion of the kingdom of darkness, as the mists and vapours and glooms of the night are scattered by the advancing rays of the sun.

It must be quite clear that our Lord can only be speaking of the judgment of Satan, as far as the effects of that judgment are to be perceptible to human eyes, in the effects produced by the working of the Holy Ghost on mankind, in whom the empire of Satan over the hearts and wills and minds of men is to be seen to be comparatively broken and destroyed. In order to understand this completely, we must place ourselves, as far as may be, at the point of view from which the Christians of the first centuries regarded the wonderful history which had passed before the eyes of men like themselves since the Day of Pentecost. There was no doubt at all in their minds that the whole system of paganism had been the kingdom which Satan had set up in the world, that the heathen deities had been, as the Apostle tells the Corinthians, devils, who were literally worshipped, and they would probably say the same of the objects of worship and veneration which are still to be found in various parts of the world, where false religions still exist, in consequence of the non-fulfilment on the part of Christians of the precept of Unity, on the observance of which the perfect triumph of the Gospel Kingdom is made by our Lord to depend. This is a vast subject, but it must be enough to say here that if the Church, under the guidance of the Holy Ghost, had been able to do far less than she has actually done for the perfect conversion of the world, she would still have proved her Divine Mission, because she has produced results which no power but that of God could have enabled her to achieve.

It is true, therefore, that the supernatural chastisement of Satan is to be found in the destruction of his system of falsehoods before the truth and might of the Gospel, and among all the empires which have been in succession overthrown and brought to nought in the world there has been none so completely pulverized as the empire of the devil before the Kingdom of Christ. For spiritual forces are of an order entirely superior to those which are only material, and when a system of spiritual strength, such as that which Satan had been permitted to organize all over the world for the enslaving of men's souls, is broken to pieces by the agency of weak and simple men like the Apostles, assisted of course by Divine grace, but still in themselves but as children making war upon giants, the triumph then achieved is one to which none of the conquests which fill the annals of the world can be compared. It is the Holy Ghost Who brings this about to the glory of God and our Lord, and this is the third great effect which our Lord foretells as the result of His presence in the world, a display of power in the sight of all men which forces itself with irresistible might on the mind so as to convict the world. It is the judgment of the prince of this world, because it consists of his being deprived of power, which he had been allowed to usurp as a punishment for the sins and ingratitude of mankind. But he had ventured beyond the limits of the power conceded to him in endeavouring to stretch it by bringing about the persecution and death of our Lord, over Whom he had no claim as over the rest of mankind, and having thus endeavoured to use it where there was no foundation for it in the permission of God, it was broken in his hands and taken away from him altogether. Then in place of the kingdom of evil which Satan had set up, the weak children of men were made by the Holy Ghost the founders and fathers and rulers of the new Kingdom of the Church against which the gates of Hell are never to prevail, although the powers of evil still carry on the struggle, and are sometimes partially successful, on account of the unfaithfulness of Christians to the doctrine and example of our Lord and His own precept of Unity.

Perhaps the following somewhat long extract may be permitted as an illustration of the passage before us. It is quite clear that the judgment of the prince of this world, of which our Lord speaks, is not meant to be taken in the sense of the entire destruction of the power of Satan, which is not to be absolutely annihilated, as far as it affects men in their state of probation, as long as that state of probation lasts. But some readers may find it difficult to understand that a very real and effectual limitation of the powers of evil has been the effect of the introduction of the Gospel Kingdom, and that where the Church has had what we may call fair play, those powers have been very much curtailed. This is in effect what our Lord promises as the result of the coming of the Paraclete. The quotation is from a course of sermons, published more than twenty years ago :

In that old heathenism of the Roman world, into which it was the will of God that the Christian religion should be introduced by the Apostles, there were three diverse and often conflicting elements. There was a good element, which came from God, there was a thoroughly bad element, which came from Satan, and there was a corrupt element which was the fruit of the workings of unre-generate human nature upon society, and upon the objects of sense and intelligence with which man is placed in relation. The good element we see embodied in great part of the laws and institutions of the ancient world, as also in much of the literature, the poetry, the philosophy of Greece and Rome, which literature consequently—after having been purified, and, as it were, baptized—has always been used by the Christian Church in the educa-tion of her children. This element, I say, was originally the gift of God, the Author of Nature, to man, the offspring of reason and conscience, the tradition of a society of which God was Himself the founder. It enshrined whatever fragments of primeval truth as to God, the world, and man himself, still lingered, in whatever shape, among the far-wandering children of Adam. St. Paul alludes to this element in the first passage on which we dwelt to-day, and his words altogether seem to imply that God watched over it, supported it, and fostered it, as far as men were worthy of it, and that it might even have been expanded into a perfect system of natural religion and of reasonable virtue, had men been grateful enough to earn larger measures of grace from God, Who left not Himself without witness in His daily providence, and was ' not far from '.any one of His children.

But now we come to another element, which just now I placed the last of the three, the workings of which we may distinguish in the heathen world. All flesh had corrupted its way upon the earth, and man had shut out the knowledge of God from his soul, and had let his passions lead him instead of his conscience. The unre-generate instincts of nature gradually overpowered the moral law in the heart of man, and their victory reflected itself in the rules of society, in the customs and maxims by which human life was guided. In proportion as man became more and more the master of the world, as wealth and power, and knowledge and experience increased, as civilization (so to call it) and means of communication advanced, there grew up that great system of cruelty and immorality, of the godless pursuit of pleasure and worldly ends, which we call paganism. For paganism is not properly a religion so much as a system of human life and human society, according to the impulses and unbridled lusts of the natural man, checked only by what remained of strength in the law of right as written in men's hearts, in the voice of conscience, and in the old traditions of better days, and also by the law of necessity which made it imperative that society should in some way or other be kept alive and held together. St. Paul, in the passage to the Romans on which we have dwelt, has described to us, my brethren, what sort of men they were who were penetrated by this pagan spirit. And now, as I have already said, when the same Apostle comes to describe the men of the latter days, he paints them, as to all moral degradation, in the same colours as the pagans of his own time. The two passages correspond as to this word for word, the latter text is almost a repetition of the former. Thus far, then, we have St. Paul's authority for saying that the apostacy of the latter days will be a return to heathenism, understanding by that word the godless system of life and manners which is the fruit of the unrestrained development and reign of the lower instincts of human nature.

These thoughts bring us to the third element of paganism—that which I call the work of Satan, the enemy of God and man. As to this, also, we have St. Paul's authority, in that passage where in a few short words he tells us that the gods of the heathens were devils.[12] We, my brethren, are often inclined to look upon the personages of which the heathen mythology is made up as a number of poetic creations, as the powers of nature symbolized, or perhaps, at the worst, as great men and famous heroes of fabulous times raised by a sort of natural canonization to the thrones of a higher world. This is the human part of the heathen religions, skilfully used by the authors of evil to disguise their own work for the delusion of men. But there was more behind those forms of apparent grace and beauty than the imagination of earthly poets. This might have been seen, we may truly say, by the base impurities in which they were steeped. No, my brethren, unless St. Paul is mistaken, unless thousands of Christian Martyrs were mistaken who treated the heathen idols as the forms under which the apostate angels were adored, the gods of the heathen were Satan and his associates, permitted by the just judgment of God to draw to themselves the adoration which men had denied to Him, and taking care to deify in themselves every shape of human vice and passion, and to exact from their worshippers impure rites and filthy mysteries, that man, made in the image of God, might learn from them to degrade himself even beneath the level of the beasts of the field. Or, if we want a still more clear proof of the Satanic agencies which underlay the pagan religion, we may find it in that other

<hr>

[12] 1 Cor. x. 20.

kind of worship which it exacted in the ancient world, and
is still found to exact—I mean the frightful tribute of
human sacrifice, a custom widely spread and almost
.universal among pagan nations, some of whom have
astonished even their Christian discoverers by their mildness and gentleness, their courtesy and simplicity, and
yet have been found to be penetrated to the core by
corruption, and to be in the habit of honouring their gods
by a frightful homage of hecatombs of human victims, a
homage enough of itself to proclaim as its author the hater
alike of man, and of God Who created him!

Here, then, my brethren, we have come to that part of
the comparison as to which it need not be said that
St. Paul's two descriptions are identical. We need not
exaggerate the miseries of our own time, nor draw in
darker colours than St. Paul the evil features of the last
great apostacy. The Son of God, as another Apostle
tells us, was 'manifested that He might destroy the works
of the devil,'[13] and I do not find, in any of the prophetic
descriptions of the restored paganism of modern days,
that the system of the worship of false gods is to revive,
with its abominable rites of blood and its mysteries of
licentiousness. Wherever the Cross has been once firmly
planted, we may surely hope that the world has seen the
last of the public worship of Satan. In St. Paul's description of the latter days, I find the blasphemy of the true
God substituted for the worship of devils. But, my
brethren, the Son of God was not manifested altogether
to destroy the works of man. He came to raise man,
change him, regenerate him, sanctify him, by uniting him
to Himself. He did not come to take away man's free
will, or to tear out of his nature those seeds of possible
evil which produced all the human part of the paganism
on which we have been reflecting. The empire of Satan
has been overthrown, but alas! man is still his own great
enemy, and though our Lord has armed him against himself, He has still left him the power to mar the work of
God in his own soul, and this power, which each one of us
possesses in his own case, is always fearfully active in the

<hr>

[13] 1 St. John iii. 8.

K 14

corruption of the Christian society, the character of which is the result and the reflection of that of the parts of which it is made up.[14]

It is needless to remark that it is quite consistent with the manner in which God deals with men, that having allowed the establishment among mankind of a great system of falsehood and immorality by the agency of the devils, He should make the destruction of that system one of the great achievements of the Church under the guidance of the Holy Spirit, an achievement conspicuous to all the world, and that at the same time, He should forbear from entirely taking away from the evil spirits their full natural powers of mischief, as long as the probation of mankind lasts.

The sentences on which we have been commenting are very remarkable even among the sayings of our Lord in more ways than one. They contain, like other passages of this great discourse to the Apostles, a most comprehensive and far-reaching prophecy, for He speaks of at least one of the

[14] The sermon here quoted is printed in Vol. I. of *Sermons by Fathers of the Society of Jesus,* 1870, pp. 41, seq. The passages quoted and referred to above are (1) St. Paul's speech at Athens (Acts xvii. 22, 23), where the Apostle speaks of the tolerance of God during the past ages of idolatry and superstition, and also of the witness to Himself He has always maintained in His Providence; (2) the great passage in the first chapter to the Romans, in which the vices and degradation of the heathen are touched upon, their neglect of God, of the natural law, and its punishment by the abandonment of men to their lowest and even most unnatural passions; (3) the other passage, in which is contained the prophecy of the men of the 'latter days,' is found in 2 Timothy iii. 1, seq. The features of this picture are almost identical with those of the picture of the heathen in the Apostles' time, with the exception of idolatry and its kindred abominations. The argument suggested in the text of this chapter is that the judgment of the prince of this world of which our Lord speaks, is the destruction of idolatry as the work of Satan, which is not included in the prophecy by St. Paul of the evils of the latter days.

results of the Mission of the Holy Ghost into the world, a mission which will last as long as the world lasts, and the account which He gives of the result of which He speaks must be as true now as in the first century, and at any intermediate point of the history, as it was at the first or as it is now. To the whole space of time which thus falls within the scope of the prophecy our Lord gives these three short sentences. The Apostles, as we have said, had not asked Him concerning the matter to which these words refer. He Himself introduces the subject, almost as if their silence was to Him a matter of surprise or gentle complaint. But He forbears dwelling, as He might have dwelt, on the many most glorious and consoling effects which were to follow on and flow from that Mission of which we are now speaking, and of which He had said something already, and was to say more before the end of the discourse. He seems to confine Himself strictly to the connection of thought on which He had just before been engaged, and which was suggested by what He had been saying of the treatment which He Himself had received at the hands of the world, and was yet to receive, and which they after Him were to experience. He does not say that the world is to be conquered or converted in the fullest sense of the words, but He says it is to be convicted, to be proved to be in error on the points which He mentions.

These few and grave words of our Lord, therefore, sum up in truth the whole history of the long conflict between the world and the Catholic Church. They give the salient characteristics of that history as they struck the eyes of our Lord, like the other words which He used to the Apostles on the Mount of Olives on the afternoon of the day before that of which we are speaking. And as they were spoken by Him unasked, it cannot be but they were seen by Him to be most opportune and greatly required for the furnishing the Apostles and the Church with knowledge concerning the future, knowledge which would be of infinite value throughout the whole duration of the time to which the prediction applied. Moreover, the very brevity and at the same time the great precision of the language in which they are couched are intimations to us that they not only call for our most careful attention and most reverent and prayerful study, but also that the truths which they convey are exceedingly pregnant and of manifold application, such as it may require long-continued meditation before all their secret treasures can be laid bare. There is no point of the history of the human race which is of such paramount interest to Christians as the dealings of the world with the Holy Ghost in the Church, and the manner in which she has been guided through all by the Blessed Paraclete. Our Lord, as we see, describes the whole multifarious history in these three sentences, and we have His word, therefore, for the fact that whatever may be the features of that history to mortal eye, in the eyes of Him Who knows all things there has been going on from the beginning, and there will go on to the very end, the conviction of the hostile world of 'sin, of justice, and of judgment,' because of its unbelief in our Lord, because of His going to and permanent Session with the Father, which has issued in the gift of the Paraclete, and has called forth the faith of the Church, and because of the conspicuous judgment which has fallen on the prince of this world.

CHAPTER V.

The Holy Ghost and our Lord.

St. John xvi. 12—15 ; *Story of the Gospels,* § 156.

IT is not the least remarkable feature about this part
of the discourse of our Lord, as we have it reported
by St. John, that the great teaching about the action
of the Holy Ghost in the reproval, or confutation, or
conviction of the world, should be summed up in the
three short and somewhat enigmatic sentences which
have been considered in the last chapter. It is very
possible that our Lord used no more words on the
subject than those which the Evangelist has recorded.
If the case was so, we may reasonably infer that this
conviction of the world, which was the effect of the
presence of the Paraclete on the enemies of God,
was not considered by Him a subject which it was
His business to draw out with any great fulness of
detail to the Apostles, although indeed it included
incidentally the great display of the beautiful works
and fruits of the Holy Ghost in the Church and in
the Saints of which we have spoken. But such
subjects as the judgment of the prince of the world
were not commonly chosen by our Lord, although
there is much in the history of the Christian centuries
which may be said to illustrate the glory of God in
the destruction of the kingdom of Satan. Perhaps
also our Lord had other reasons for leaving the

subject aside after the few pregnant words which He had spoken—perhaps He might foresee that there were to be some flaws in the picture, not of course in the work of the Holy Ghost, which could not but be perfect in its kind, but in the want of human co-operation, and consequently He might know that the history of the use of the magnificent powers set in operation by the mission of the third Divine Person, if the result of that mission were to be completely related, might contain some elements of disappointment on which it would not be well to dwell. The Passion itself was now close at hand, and the near prospect and detailed consideration of the Passion was to include the bitter Agony, which was to afflict His Heart so much that He was to allow Himself to frame the prayer that the chalice might pass from Him untasted. It seems the most probable explanation of this that He was to foresee how comparatively fruitless His Sacrifice was to be for the large mass of mankind. For a reason of the same sort He may not have chosen to speak at full length of the wonders worked for His glory by the Holy Ghost, Who was to be so often grieved by the unfaithfulness of Christians. For whatever reason, this history, which as soon as it began to be worked out in fact on earth, was the delight and admiration of the blessed citizens of Heaven, was to be contained in our Lord's own words in the three sentences of which we have been speaking. But it must be remembered that one of the convictions mentioned could have given no pain or dissatisfaction to the Heart of our Lord—that, namely, in which He might have spoken of the fruits of the faith of the believers who were to reflect so much of glory on His work in the world, and it is perhaps more probable that the silence in this case was occasioned by some other motive. The time was running on, and the hour of the betrayal was not far distant. The discourse, as we gather from the Evangelist, had already occupied much time. Our Lord had yet some things more to tell them, and He may have shortened other topics for the sake of dealing with those which were the most necessary.

'I have yet many things to say to you, but you cannot bear them now. But when He, the Spirit of Truth, is come, He will teach you all truth. For He shall not speak of Himself, but whatsoever things He shall hear, He shall speak, and the things that are to come He shall show you. He shall glorify Me, because He shall receive of Mine, and shall show it to you. All things whatsoever the Father hath are Mine. Therefore I said that He shall receive of Mine and show it to you.' This passage seems to conclude and to sum up the instruction which our Lord now gives to the Apostles concerning the office of the Holy Ghost. It is, in the first place, an additional reason for them to long for and to welcome the coming of the Paraclete, that He will supply many things which they had not been able to receive from our Lord Himself. He says that He had many things to tell them, but that at that time and occasion they were not able to bear them. It seems, therefore, that they were able to bear certain things at one time and certain other things at another time, and that it was a part of that exquisite prudence and consideration which belonged to our Blessed Lord that He taught them what He had to teach, just at the time when their minds were fit to receive certain truths, and that He forbore to press certain other things until the time when they were fit. This beautiful prudence and, as the Wise Man calls it, 'reverence,' of our Lord for His poor and feeble creatures, may be traced all through His dealings with man from the first beginnings of the revelation of the promise in the Garden of Eden to the end, and it is also reflected in the careful reserve of the Church and in her gentle wisdom in bringing forth into the full light the doctrines which she has to define, from time to time, in consequence of the opposition of heretics, which renders such definitions necessary for the protection of the faith.

The Apostles could hardly realize what must have been very plain to their Divine Master, that the difference between the facility and rapidity and perfection of instruction received by them from our Lord Himself in the days of their familiar converse with Him as man like themselves, and the characteristic qualities of the teaching they were now to begin to receive from the Blessed Paraclete, was to be immense, and their new method of learning was to be in many respects a very great advance upon the privileges they had hitherto enjoyed, great as those privileges had been. It had been a great thing to live with our Lord, to see Him and to hear Him, to be able to ask Him a question, and to hear from His own lips the solution of what they had not understood. But the instruction of the Holy Spirit would be something more—a light in their intelligence continually elevating them to higher truths, which did not require the statement of their difficulties or perplexities, bringing out to their minds what He had said and what they had not comprehended at the time, deepening every line of the teaching and placing each separate portion of it in a fuller and clearer light, while at the same time the relation of one portion of the truth to every other portion became clear, and the harmonies and right proportions of all shone out in their own brilliancy.

It may very well be the case that the Apostles may have been wonderfully enlightened on many points at the time when they received the teaching of our Lord from His own blessed lips, but there are many places in the Gospels from which it seems more natural to conclude that they failed to follow Him fully up to the last. They seem often to have been unable to comprehend Him, and indeed the Sacred Text seems here to tell us this in our Lord's own words, for He says to them, ' I have many things to say to you, but you cannot bear them now.' He does not say that the time presses, though that was probably so, but that they cannot bear them. But when the Holy Ghost came all things were changed. His method of instruction is without words or voice, but entirely spiritual, by means of lights and motions communicated to the intelligence and the will, and it is impossible for Him not to help the souls with which He deals according to His own wonderful power and life. He breatheth where He wills, there is no slowness or imperfection about His breathings, He can illuminate a thousand hearts instantaneously as well as one. Nor can there be any difficulty about His teaching, because He is the Creator Spirit, and His motions bear with them the light that they require as well as the force which the will needs to close with what He suggests. The whole of the Divine plan for the redemption of the world, and, as a part of it, the instruction and training of the Apostles for their part of the work of the conversion of the world, was clearly and fully possessed by Him, both that part of that instruction which had been performed by our Lord, as well as that part of which He had just said that they were not yet able to receive it. Now, as it were, they were to become His scholars, and with ineffable love and wisdom He was to set about the work of their formation. He could remind them of anything they might have forgotten, He could most perfectly supply what was yet wanting, He could light up in their minds the sayings and doings of their dear Master in a manner which made them glow with new beauty and force, He could bring out meanings in them which before were hidden, and He could abundantly add the portions of sacred truth which up to that time had been kept back. We think that our Blessed Lady had all along had a wonderful and singular intelligence of the full meaning and import of the mysteries of our Lord's life as they passed in succession under her eyes, and that she was wonderfully helped in this by her own habit of 'pondering these things in her heart,' as St. Luke says. The illumination of the minds of the blessed Apostles for their great work in the Kingdom of God may have been something which issued in the same kind of intelligence, though it may have been more immediate, and have been independent of their own industry, and extending to all the subjects which it belonged to them to know with the perfect comprehension which their great office required.

But these words of our Lord seem to be in some way at variance with those others which He had spoken to the Apostles not long before in this discourse, when He had said, 'I have called you friends, because all things whatsoever I have heard of My Father, I have made known to you.'[1] It

---

[1] St. John xv. 15.

seems that then He had said that He had told them all things which He had heard from His Father, that is, especially, the truths, and doctrines, and precepts which He had received as Man and as Redeemer, to reveal and commit to them as the ministers of the Church. Whereas He now speaks of many things which they are not able to bear, that is, unable, not from any want of will, but from want of robust spiritual perception, saying that when they have been strengthened by the light and power of the Holy Ghost, they will be able to bear these things, and the Paraclete will then reveal them. The fact seems to be, that the truths and precepts which our Lord received from the Father, for the purpose of revelation in time to mankind through the Church, may be considered in various lights. Our Lord received and receives from His Father throughout all eternity the whole Divine substance and Nature, and there can never have been, or can be, a time at which He does not perfectly have them. As Man, also, He has the perfect knowledge of all that is bestowed on Him in His Human Nature, and when this complete knowledge was given to Him at the first, it was in a measure and degree which know no limitation or possibility of increase. And the office of Mediator and Redeemer in which He is our Light and Life, involves a commission and precept to Him to impart to us all that knowledge of the truths of God which He intends us to receive, and which we are capable of receiving. And when in time it was the will of God that this or that truth, in due order, should be made known to us, the precept of revealing it to us became, as it were, actual, for the purpose of the revelation, and what it was before ordered that we should receive, was then and there ordered to be revealed to us.

We may well understand from these considerations that our Blessed Lord, Whose will as God is the same as the will of the Father, and Whose will as Man is perfectly conformed and obedient to that of the Father, might say at one time that He had told the Apostles all that He had received from the Father to tell them, and yet at another time that He had still many things to tell them, for which they were not yet fit, and which, therefore, had not yet come under the precept of the Father to be told to them, being kept back by their weakness, until they were made clear by the teaching of the Holy Ghost, Who, as He receives all the substance of the Divinity from the Son and the Father, so, also, teaches nothing to men but what He has received from the Father and the Son. Nor does our Lord say that He Himself will not reveal these things to them, even while with them upon earth, at a future time. For after the Resurrection He must, as we cannot doubt, have been both able and willing to tell them many things which related to the Church in particular, and of which the Gospels speak, as when He explained to the two disciples who walked with Him to Emmaus, 'beginning at Moses and all the Prophets, the things that were concerning Him.' Again, we are told by St. Luke that before the Ascension He opened their understanding, that they might understand the Scriptures, and that after the Passion 'He showed Himself alive by many proofs, appearing unto them and speaking of the Kingdom of God.' In the few words which follow in this place, it appears as if our Lord were taking pains, out of a tender consideration for them, to make it plain that the teaching of the Paraclete was not to be different from that which they had received from Him, as indeed it could not be.

'But when the Spirit of Truth is come, He will teach you all truth.' Our Lord is speaking of the Paraclete, as the Greek words show, and the sentence might be more strictly translated, 'He Who is the Spirit of Truth, will be your guide into all truth.' The difference of genders in the Greek language shows that the words, the 'Spirit of Truth' are used as a description of the Paraclete, suggested by the repetition of the word truth—as if it had been said, being the 'Spirit of Truth,' He will be your guide into all truth' Our Lord says of Himself, that He is the Way, and the Truth, and the Life, and the Holy Ghost is the Spirit of Truth, because He proceeds from Him. Thus there is a continuity of subject between this and the former sentence. Our Lord has many things to tell them which they are not able to bear now, but they will be led to them by the guidance of the Holy Ghost. The Greek word, which both in the Latin and in the English version is rendered will 'teach,' is the word which describes the action of a guide, who shows the way by going along it with the person whom he guides, not giving a number of directions and then leaving him to himself to carry them out, but accompanying him, step by step, along the path. The idea, therefore, of a gradual growth in truth in the minds of those who are guided by the Holy Ghost, is plainly suggested by the language of this passage. And indeed the contemplations which are suggested by the use of the word which our Lord here employs of the Blessed Paraclete may be worked out in a very beautiful way in holy meditation. The word contains the idea of the Holy Ghost as the companion of our pilgrimage, leading us on step by step with His 'kindly light,' which is the way in which He deals with individual souls who are approaching the full possession of the truth.

We find various ways suggested in which the Holy Ghost was to teach the Apostles, as their guide in the visible absence of our Lord. One way is that which our Lord has Himself mentioned in the former part of this discourse, when He said that the Paraclete would teach them all things ' and bring all things to your remembrance whatsoever I shall have said unto you.' St. John mentions more than one instance of this, when the disciples afterwards remembered words of our Lord which they had not understood at the time. In the same way, words and actions of our Lord which did not impress themselves on their memory when they were said or done, may have been recalled to them by the Holy Ghost, with full enlightenment as to the deep meaning conveyed or contained in them. Again, it has frequently been said in the course of these volumes, that it was our Lord's method with the Apostles to deliver to them great truths in a few and pregnant words which conveyed the doctrines which they were to teach to the Church, as it were, in seed, at least in a form which was afterwards to bear expansion and development, something in the way in which He spoke of the Kingdom of God as a grain of mustard-seed, which eventually becomes a great tree, filling the air with its branches. It may be considered that it was the office of the Paraclete to make the Apostles understand the many great truths which were thus at first wrapped up in a small compass, until at length the whole magnificent growth of truth was enabled to unfold itself in all its manifestations, connections, and bearings. Our Lord, for instance, as far as we learn from the Evangelists, said very little, at least before His Resurrection, about the Church, though we can gather from what He did say most of its chief gifts and characteristic qualities, and much about its hierarchy, its government, its law of unity, its prerogatives, and the special gifts with which it was to be endowed.

The truths thus imparted, as it were seminally, to the Apostles by Himself, were afterwards unfolded in their minds by the working of the Holy Ghost, and the whole system of Christian theology, on this as on other subjects, is founded on the marvellous outpourings of the Apostles in their Epistles, which again came from the fulness of knowledge implanted and fostered in them by the Holy Ghost. The Epistles do not formally legislate on all subjects, for the legislation was completed in principle before they were written, and is taken for granted in them, but they are the products of the great system of truth on the law of God, the obligations of Christians, social, moral, and political, which was the creation, in the mind of their writers, of the operation of the Holy Ghost, bringing, as has been said, to their remembrance hints, and words, and examples, dropped, as it were, on a most fruitful soil by our Lord Himself. And again, there was the whole system of truth contained in the prophecies, the Psalms, and the other books of the Old Testament, and in the traditions of the holy people, for which our Lord had conferred a special gift of intelligence on the Apostles when He opened their understandings, as St. Luke tells us. And the general guidance and agency by which all this beautiful system was to be worked out into practical and familiar knowledge, was the guidance and the agency of the Paraclete.

What has been now said may help to explain the words of our Lord which follow here in the text of St. John. 'For He'—the Paraclete—'shall not speak of Himself, but whatsoever He shall hear, that shall He speak,' as well as other words which follow closely on this passage. The Holy Ghost is said to hear what He is to speak, and not to speak of Himself, because He has His essence and His knowledge from the Father and the Son, His being and knowledge and speech is one with theirs. In the same way the Son is said by our Lord[2] to do nothing but what He sees the Father do, because He has His Essence and Power from the Father, one and the same as His. Not to speak of Himself is the same thing as to speak what He hears from another, and this is the same thing as to have His knowledge and Essence from another, and to be the same with that other in Being and knowledge. What is here said shows that the Holy Ghost hears what He speaks from the Son, because our Lord is engaged in declaring that the Paraclete was to tell them the same truths which He had Himself to tell them, and which they were not able at that time to bear. The whole tenour of the passage is to assure the Apostles of the same thing, the intimate resemblance, or rather the identity of the teaching of the coming Paraclete with that of Himself, of which we have been lately speaking.

And indeed this truth is forced on our attention in every page of the New Testament. The second part of that precious volume is occupied with the

2 St. John v. 19.

history and the writings of the Apostles, who were guided in all that they did, and inspired in all that they wrote by the Paraclete of Whom our Lord here speaks. It is plain to any one who attentively studies the relation between the first and the second parts of the New Testament, how completely the latter is founded on the former, not more by historical connection than by identity of spirit. The words of our Lord are but seldom actually quoted, and the actions of His life are mentioned with comparative rarity. But it is easy to see how deep and intimate an acquaintance with His character, His methods, His peculiar and distinguishing virtues, if we may so speak, underlies the whole of this part of the sacred volume, so that His presence in the minds and thoughts of the writers seems to be perpetually suggesting itself, as an atmosphere in which their souls habitually lived and breathed. If it be said that this was in truth the case with all, at least, who had personally known our Lord, and with His disciples, this is only saying the same thing in different words—that the Holy Ghost was continually at work to impress our Lord's likeness upon them, both individually and collectively, though He may have used in some cases more and in others less, the power of personal recollections founded on the memories of some, and the traditions received from them by others.

'And the things that are to come He shall show you.' Another office of the Paraclete is here mentioned, namely, the keeping up in the Church the spirit of prophecy, not exactly as it was kept up in the elder dispensation, for in that there was a great and distinct work to be done, in order to prepare the holy people for the coming of our Lord by prophecies

L 14

and figures and types, but, according to the spirit and character of the New Testament, one of the features was that familiarity of the saints with the ways of God which our Lord had spoken of earlier in this discourse when He had said that He called them His friends, 'for the friend knows what his friend doth,' the children of God being made acquainted with His designs and interests and projects, so that it is possible to say that His plans for the future are not hidden from them. It is in something of this way that St. Paul writes about the intelligence of the saints, 'We speak of the wisdom of God in a mystery, a wisdom which is hidden, which God ordained before the world unto our glory, which none of the princes of this world knew, for if they had known it, they would never have crucified the Lord of Glory. But, as it is written, that eye hath not seen, nor ear heard, neither hath it entered into the heart of man, what things God hath prepared for them that love Him. But to us God hath revealed them by His Spirit, for the Spirit searcheth all things, yea, the deep things of God. For what man knoweth the things of a man, but the spirit of a man that is in him? Even so the things also that are of God no man knoweth, but the Spirit of God. Now we have received, not the spirit of this world, but the Spirit that is of God, that we may know the things that are given us from God.'[3] And as the carrying out of the great counsel of God for our redemption by the application of the merits and work of our Lord was committed to the Church after the Ascension under the guidance of the Holy Ghost, it would seem inconsistent with the high commission of the Church that she should not have among the fruits of the

[3] 1 Cor. ii. 7—12.

indwelling in her of the Holy Spirit, that of the instinct of discerning the future and preparing her children for the things which were to come upon her and on them in this world.

We find in the writings of the Apostles, and in the history of the first age of the Church, more than one trace of this spirit of prophecy as a familiar and well-known gift. St. Paul, as is well known, had informed the Church of the Thessalonians, even in the very few weeks which passed between their conversion and his own enforced absence from their city, concerning the future coming of Antichrist and of its signs. And in his second Epistle to them, written soon after the first, partly to remove a false impression which had been received from the first, after explaining the truth more fully, he says, ' Remember you not that while I was with you I told you of these things?' In the first Epistle to St. Timothy, he speaks of the evils of the latter days as having been foretold, not so much by the ancient prophets as by the continual witness of the Holy Ghost. ' Now the Spirit manifestly saith that in the last days men shall depart from the faith,' and the rest. St. Jude in his Epistle, much of which is taken from the Second Epistle of St. Peter, speaks of the same evil as rife in the time at which he wrote, and as having been foretold by the Apostles: ' Be mindful of the words which have been spoken by the Apostles of our Lord Jesus Christ, Who told you that in the last times there should come mockers, walking according to their own desires in ungodliness,' and he specifies especially the schismatics, thereby echoing the words of St. John, ' These are they that separate themselves, sensual men, not having the Spirit.' There is also indication of the presence in the Church of the spirit of prophecy as to particular matters, as in the case of Agabus, who foretold to the Christians of Antioch the great famine, in consequence of which prediction the brethren there sent alms to the Christians in Judæa by the hands of Barnabas and Saul. Agabus also at a later time foretold the persecution of St. Paul by the Jews. The words of St. Paul himself are remarkable in his address to the priests of Ephesus, ' And now behold I go bound in the Spirit to Jerusalem, not knowing the things that shall befall me there, save that the Holy Ghost in every city witnesseth to me, saying, that bonds and afflictions wait for me in Jerusalem.' It would seem then that the spirit of prophecy was commonly to be found in the Christian communities.

Our Lord continues, ' He shall glorify Me, because He shall receive of Mine and shall show it to you. All things whatsoever the Father hath are Mine, therefore I said, that He shall receive of Mine, and show it to you.' He adds then another feature in the work which belongs to the Holy Ghost, namely, to glorify the Incarnate Son. In truth, our Lord had not sought or brought about His own glorification, as He had said, though that was in His own power, and was indeed due to Him. He had come into the world as the poor Child of a despised artisan, all His surroundings from the first had been in keeping with His first appearance, and after a life of obscurity and humiliation, He was to die as a malefactor on a Cross between two thieves. Nevertheless, within a few years His Name was to be raised above the highest of men, He was proclaimed all over the world to be the Son of God and the Saviour of mankind, His glory has gone on increasing in splendour age after age, and He has received the homage of all that has been best and greatest and holiest among men, a great light has been shed upon His character, His Divine attributes, the power which He has shown of winning the hearts of men of all nations and generations and lineage, so that His glory on earth has mounted up to an incomparable height. And at the same time the work of redemption which has been accomplished through the Church has engaged the rapt astonishment and wonder of the blessed citizens of Heaven, who have learnt from what has been wrought through His name and power continually more and more of the greatness and wisdom and goodness and power of God, and His ineffable counsels, which furnish them with ever fresh themes of praise and adoration. All this glorification of our Lord has been brought about in Heaven and on earth by the operation of the Holy Ghost in the hearts and lives of men.

The only thing which may seem to require explanation in the words on which we are now commenting, is the reason which our Lord assigns for the glorification of Himself by the Holy Ghost which is contained in the words, ' He shall receive of Mine, and shall show it to you,' which is further explained by the words which immediately follow, ' all things whatsoever the Father hath are Mine, therefore I said that He shall receive of Mine and shall show it to you.' The Holy Ghost proceeds from the Father and the Son, from Whom He receives the whole Divine substance, which belongs to each, and to say that He receives from each the Divine Essence, is the same thing as to say that He receives from each or either the Divine power or the Divine knowledge. It is the third Person Who produces in the hearts of any among men any effect of the divinity, any knowledge of force, or light, or life that is communicated to them, and thus the light and grace that He imparts is a proof of what He has received from the other Divine Persons. 'He shall receive of Mine,' our Lord says, 'and shall show it or declare it to you,' because it is not possible that they should have told or declared to them the whole of what He has received, whether light, or power, or anything else. Especially in regard to all that concerns or belongs to the glorification of our Lord, the knowledge of anything that belongs to Him, His work, or grace, or character, His office as Redeemer of mankind, the First-Born of the new creation, the power that He has left behind Him, the means by which His merits are to be applied, and appropriated, and the like, it is clear that such a revelation as made concerning Him by the Holy Ghost, may be most fitly described as a taking of what is His and declaring it to them, and what is His is the Father's, and what is the Father's is His, for they are One in essence and substance, and in all that they do in creation, and providence, and the government of creatures, and thus it is that our Lord, in speaking of the works of the Godhead, speaks of them as His own, as well as the Father's, at the same time that the words He uses are spoken to illustrate the close identity of what the Holy Ghost has to declare to them with what He Himself has taught and done.

The meaning here given to the passage before us is that supported by a greater number of commentators, among whom are some of great name. It does not perfectly satisfy others, who do not see how the truth that the Holy Ghost proceeds from the Son as well as from the Father, by a Spiration altogether invisible, can explain the words, ' He shall receive of Mine, and shall show it to you,' the effect of the Spiration being that the Son is glorified by this action of the Holy Ghost, which seems to include at least some revelation or manifestation to the world or to the Church. But our Lord does not say that ' He shall receive of Mine,' and nothing more, but ' He shall receive of Mine, and shall show it to you.' The writer on whose objection we are remarking, understands the passage to mean that the Holy Ghost shall speak in our Lord's name, as His legate or deputy, and shall propose to them the doctrine which He shall impart for that purpose.

There seems to be some difficulty about the context, perhaps on account of the great brevity of the language, and of the comparative fewness of the occasions on which this great doctrine concerning the Holy Ghost is set forth by our Lord. We may remember what has already been said on the subject. The doctrine of the Holy Ghost is not inadequately proposed by our Lord, but He speaks of it on few occasions, and in few and pregnant words, and each word and each occasion has to be counted and noted in order to build up the whole doctrine. Now in the place before us, our Lord is adding line upon line to the doctrine, but He speaks, as we say, very briefly, and mentions just the points which belong to the purpose before Him. On these He speaks fully, but not unreservedly, because the subject was to some extent a new one, and, besides, in all this part of the discourse He studies brevity greatly. His direct purpose is to tell them that the Holy Ghost is to glorify Him, make His name known, and honoured all over the world, as indeed has been the case, and was the case within a short time of the Ascension. This was fulfilled by the Holy Ghost taking of what was His, and showing it to them, as it seems, by enlightening them spiritually concerning the character, the history, the sayings and doings of our Blessed Lord, His work, and institutions, and designs in the Church, and other similar points. The whole system of the Church, to the first Christians and others since them, is a reflection and manifestation of our Lord. We have from time to time endeavoured to draw out how the Apostles, and chiefly St. Paul, have caught up, and enlarged, and developed, and expanded the seeds of thought and doctrine which had been dropped by our Lord in the Gospels. But on this subject we have no need to repeat what has been already said. We must remember that we have ground for thinking that the common and familiar instructions given by the Apostles and first Christian teachers to their own disciples were chiefly based upon the actual teaching of our Lord Himself, with of course the supplementary matter required by the great mysteries which had taken place since the Passion itself. But it must be remembered that this matter, for what we may call catechetical instruction, must have been increased indefinitely after the Ascension, as the great mysteries of the redemption of mankind took place after the time during which our Lord was Himself able to teach the people. The whole of this rudimentary instruction must have been committed to the Apostles under the guidance of the Paraclete. Our Lord now became the subject-matter of the teaching which the Church proposed to her children, and which consisted of what He had done, and suffered, and wrought, and instituted for their benefit, and in this sense also He was Himself the great substance of that teaching.

We have a very precious, though disjointed and disconnected mass of teaching in those beautiful passages in the writings of St. Paul and other Apostles, which are contained in those parts of the Epistles, sometimes a considerable part of the whole, in which they leave the doctrinal or occasional topics which have been the main causes for their writing, and turn themselves to practical instructions in daily duties. All students of the New Testament will know the peculiar charm and sweetness of these parts of the Apostolic writings, which seem to have a fragrance of their own, like that of the Sermon on the Mount, and of other parts of our Lord's own teaching. It seems likely that we have here the reflection of that kind of teaching of which our Lord may be speaking, when He says of the Paraclete that 'He shall receive of Mine, and shall show it to you.' Not that it is not true or most important, that the Holy Ghost has the whole Divine substance and Nature from the Son with the Father, but that it may not have been our Lord's purpose to set forth that truth in the words on which we are commenting, which evidently relate to something which the Paraclete communicates to the Apostles, and they to the Church, for the purpose of the glorification of our Lord.

The words of the passage before us would apply equally to all that knowledge of our Lord, of which St. Paul so constantly speaks as the great matter in which he is constantly praying that the faithful may be ever advancing, by a growth that knows no limit, or at least that can never increase enough to satisfy his desire for them. The Apostle says that he prays that ' we may in all things grow up in Him Who is the head, even Christ,' and just before, that we ' may meet into the unity of the faith, and of the knowledge of the Son of God unto a perfect man, unto the measure of the age of the fulness of Christ.' He speaks of our Lord's perfect character as a sort of norm to which all are meant ultimately to attain, or to which all were by their constant efforts to strive to attain. Thus, in the desires of the Apostle, there was one normal standard of perfection of grace and intelligence in spiritual things which was to be the object of ambition to all, what he calls the ' measure of the age of the fulness of Christ,' and to the attainment of this standard they were all to be continually pressing on. He sometimes calls it the fulness of the knowledge of Christ, or of the Son of God, as if the growth which he desires to see was of the knowledge of our Lord. It was, as it appears, the office of the Paraclete, in a thousand different ways, to pour in and foster this knowledge of Him in the hearts and minds of the faithful, and it may fairly be considered that no office was dearer to Him, or more important in itself, and again that we have the fulfilment of the same office in the wonderful knowledge concerning Him of which the apostolical Christians were so full.

This perhaps may help also to the explanation of what our Lord says in the same context with the words immediately before us of the Holy Ghost, ' He shall receive of Mine and shall show it to you,' of which He gives the explanation that all that is the Father's is His. We have already said some-thing on these words, and may here add something more in connection with what we have been lately saying. It may be remembered, then, that there is extremely little mention of the Holy Ghost in the earlier Gospels, and that our Lord Himself does not speak of Him except rarely. The mentions made of Him are enough to prove that this was not from any imperfect appreciation of His dignity and majesty, for which the manner in which He is spoken of by the Angel at the Annunciation is sufficient. But if that is true which we have more than once had to say—namely, that the doctrine concerning the Third Blessed Person was not fully possessed by the mass of the sacred people of God in the days in which our Lord came, it is only a part of the same truth that the mention of the Holy Ghost should be comparatively reserved, even to those who were the people ordinarily instructed by our Lord. We find a kind of growth in this respect from the earlier parts of our Lord's teaching up to the later, and it is natural that that teaching should become more explicit and fuller in these later chapters of the Gospel of St. John on which we are now engaged. We can remember the much earlier passage in St. Matthew, in which, after mentioning the occasion on which our Lord is said by Him to have rejoiced in spirit and given thanks to His Father, He used the words, ' All things are delivered to Me by My Father, and no man knoweth the Son but the Father, neither doth any man know the Father but the Son, and he to whom it shall please the Son to reveal Him.'[4] Here some might be inclined to say that some mention of the Holy Ghost is required. But it might not have suited our Lord at that time to have introduced it. In the same way, when our Lord said, about a year before this date, ' No man can come to Me except

4 St. Matt. xi. 27.

the Father, Who hath sent Me, draw him. . . . Every one that hath heard of the Father, and hath learned, cometh to Me,'[5] in those words there is no mention made of the Third Divine Person, Who nevertheless cannot be excluded from any knowledge that is attributed to the Father or the Son. But the coming of the Holy Ghost was the great feature, if we may so speak, in the dealings of God with His creatures which was to follow on the Sacrifice of our Lord in His Passion, and it is natural that our Lord should now begin to multiply His instructions to the Apostles concerning Him, and especially to bring out more clearly to their minds how large a part He was to take in the manifestation of Himself, the Incarnate Son, by Whom He was to be sent.

We may, therefore, consider that passages such as that before us may be thought to be silent intimations to the Apostles that the doctrine concerning the Holy Ghost was no longer to be taught reservedly as before, and that it was on account of the reserve hitherto maintained that some things which were true concerning Him had not been explicitly mentioned. Our Lord was now engaged in preparing the Apostles for the coming of the Holy Ghost in place of Himself, and it was His object to enhance their notions of the immense blessing they were to receive in this new Presence with them of the Third Divine Person by every word that He said. The knowledge they had received concerning their Master had been the work, as He had told them, of the Father Himself, not without His own co-operation. Now He tells them the Holy Ghost will take of His, and show it to them, and that all things that are the Father's are His. The know-

[5] St. John vi. 44, 45.

ledge concerning our Lord brought into the world by the glorification of His name, belonged to the Father and to Himself, and now He insists on the truth which had not before been so much proclaimed, that it was brought home to them by the Holy Ghost.

CHAPTER VI.

Parting Words.

St. John xvi. 16—33; *Story of the Gospels*, § 156.

THE last words of our Lord, on which we have been commenting, seem to have been the conclusion of that part of His discourse in which He dealt with certain great subjects which it was important that He should Himself put before His Apostles before proceeding to His Passion. After the giving to them the priceless boon of the Blessed Sacrament, He had most naturally insisted on the all important matter of union with Himself, and had gone on to speak to them of that doctrine of Unity in His Body, the Church, which flowed from the union with Himself, that abiding in Him of which He had almost spoken as if, that one thing being secured, the perfect triumph of His scheme for the redemption of the world would be completed. He had spoken in the tenderest manner of the persecution which they were to suffer after His own example from the world, which might perhaps surprise them or even scandalize them, and against which they might require fortifying and comforting by the knowledge that it was in the nature of things, the world being what it is, as well as a mark to them of their resemblance to Himself, which would be in many ways dear to their hearts. He had gone on to tell them of the Mission of the Paraclete and the great work which He was to do for the glorification of His own Name and the advancement of His Kingdom. He had spoken, moreover, of the great office of the Paraclete in the confutation and exposure of the wicked and lying world, and of the witness which they were on their own part to bear to their Master. The full glories which were to be the fruit of the presence of the Paraclete were as yet kept back. But He said enough to give them an idea of His dignity and greatness, which were to be more fully made known after the Day of Pentecost.

There is, however, one remark which may fairly be made with regard to what may seem to us omissions of obvious topics, which we are naturally inclined to wonder at in discourses or conversations of our Lord like that on which we are now engaged. It cannot be doubted that our Lord had, at the time at which He spoke, present to His mind the fact that after a certain fixed time in the life of the Church the Gospels were to be written, and various documents were to be committed to writing, by means of which many of His own words and actions were to be preserved for future times for the benefit of the faithful. Records of this kind were to be the natural and almost spontaneous results of the system which He adopted of oral teaching, and would have their value and necessity in proportion to the importance of the teaching thus communicated and the estimation in which that teaching was held by those who heard it. But there are no traces of the anticipation beforehand of the formation of these treasuries of the Christian body, or of anything being directly said or omitted, because they were in time to come into being. If we consider the few immensely precious words which our Lord uttered, for instance, on this evening, concerning some of the most vitally important of the comparatively new gifts which He was to leave behind Him for the support and consolation of the faithful, we are struck with the manner in which He has confined Himself to the laying down clearly the matters of doctrine which seem most vitally important, so that the Church has not been left without words of His own on which her future edifice of authoritative teaching may be reared. His utterances in these chapters concerning the Person of the Holy Ghost are a case in point. They are very few, but they suffice for the foundation of Christian theology.

It may also be remembered that there was to be in some measure a difference between some of our Lord's institutions and gifts to the Church and others. The development of the Christian Hierarchy for the government of the Church all over the world was naturally a matter of time and gradual growth, except as to its essential elements, and the organization of the One body, as St. Paul says, by that which every joint supplieth, must have been likewise a process of time. But there were certain things in the system which our Lord came to establish which did not wait for a gradual unfolding, and among them we may certainly reckon the operations of the Holy Ghost, by which the Church was ·filled at once in all the communities where she existed. It would not have suited the manner in which this great gift had been announced if there had been any delay in making the effects of the presence of so mighty an agent known to the world, at least as far as it was in contact with the Church. Thus we conceive there was nothing gradual about the manifestations of the promised Paraclete when He came, except as far as such reserve was required by the circumstances of the Christian body. *Spiritus Domini replevit orbem terrarum*, is the language used concerning Him by Sacred Scripture. In the same way we suppose it likely that the great gift of the Blessed Sacrament was at once universally frequented among Christians, and we are supported in this opinion by the language of the Acts.

On the other hand, there must have been many points as to which doctrine and practice certainly unfolded themselves much more gradually. And there is less to surprise us in the fact that there is a comparative silence in the Gospels themselves which record only our Lord's promises and prophecies about these great and Divine gifts, than about certain other matters that were to become the heritage of the Christian people, but which were not communicated to them so instantaneously and unreservedly almost as soon as the Holy Ghost was given on the Day of Pentecost. Our Lord may have seen less need to give long explanations about the coming of the Paraclete and all His gifts and fruits, when within so short a space of time the whole country was to be filled with them. When He told the Apostles that they were to be baptized with the Holy Ghost not many days before the prediction was to be fulfilled, it would have been out of place to describe the tongues of fire or other particulars of Pentecost, or to have the prediction recorded in details and circumstances in any Gospel.

But it is time to return to this last conversation of

our Lord with His beloved Apostles. The next words recorded of Him are those in which He did what it yet remained for Him to do, that is, to break to them His own immediate departure, and this He does in the words which immediately follow. 'A little while and now you shall not see Me, and again, a little while and you shall see Me, because I go to the Father. Then some of the disciples said one to another, What is this that He saith to us, A little while and you shall not see Me, and again a little while, and you shall see Me, and because I go to the Father? They said therefore, What is this that He saith, A little while? We know not what He speaketh. And Jesus knew that they had a mind to ask Him. And He said to them, Of this do ye inquire among yourselves, because I said, A little while and you shall not see Me, and again a little while, and you shall see Me? Amen, amen, I say to you, that you shall lament and weep, but the world shall rejoice, and you shall be made sorrowful, but your sorrow shall be turned into joy. A woman when she is in labour hath sorrow, because her hour is come, but when she hath brought forth the child she remembereth no more the anguish, for joy that a man is born into the world. So also you now indeed have sorrow, but I will see you again, and your heart shall rejoice, and your joy no man shall take from you.'

Thus in the most tender way did our Lord proceed to hint at the imminent nearness of His leaving them. He had spoken in very plain words of His Passion and of His Resurrection also, from the time at which their faith in His Divinity had become firm and clear, that is, from the time of the Confession of St. Peter. He had, indeed, several times over, and with ever increasing distinctness, spoken even of the details and circumstances of the Passion, the betrayal, the scourging, His being mocked and spit upon, and the like. But now that the time was drawing so near, He said not a word of all these. He speaks as if He were merely about to depart, and come back again. 'A little while and you shall not see Me.' Under the little while He includes all that He had formerly predicted of the sufferings which were to end in His death, which He speaks of as His not being seen. 'And again a little while and you shall see Me.' Under this second little while He includes all the wonderful triumphs which were to ensue between His Death and Resurrection, after which they were to see Him again. He calls both the mysteries which He has in His mind by the same simple term of which He was so fond, especially on this last night of His Life—His going to His Father. For in truth He went to His Father through His Passion, on which followed the Resurrection and Ascension. By His Resurrection He took up again the glory of His Body, which He had laid aside that He might die, and thus His Passion and Death were the causes and necessary preludes of His going to His Father as He did. Perhaps our Lord used this language for the purpose of keeping back everything that might disturb or alarm the disciples, perhaps it was simply the language which it was most natural to use at the time, when the recent institution of the Blessed Sacrament, and the discourse which had followed on so many Divine mysteries of the faith, had created an atmosphere of peace and rapturous calm which would have been broken in upon rudely by the mention of the violences and outrages of the Passion.

Catholic critics will be aware that there exists another strain of interpretation of this passage which is maintained, after St. Augustine and St. Bede, by one of the most brilliant and ingenious of modern commentators, Maldonatus. According to this, the little time which our Lord speaks of in the first place is the interval which was to elapse between the time at which He spoke and the date of His leaving them at His Ascension, and the second little time was to be the period between the Ascension and the Second Advent at the end of the world. The time between the last days of our Lord's earthly course and His return to His Father was certainly not long, although we understand thereby not His Death, but His Ascension. Nor is there any great difficulty in understanding that He might speak of the interval between the Ascension and the Second Advent as a little time, for there are several texts of the New Testament which speak in that way, although they are qualified by others. The first generation of faithful certainly thought ordinarily that the Day of Judgment was to come in their own time, or in the days immediately after them, and we know that the Apostles had sometimes to warn them that they must not be misled by the common misconception, which might involve some errors. There is a good deal in our Lord's language which may seem to support the view of which we speak.

But He seems rarely to have spoken of His Ascension till after the Resurrection, when it became the next of the great mysteries to follow in order of fulfilment. It seems most natural to think that, in these words about the little time, He was breaking the truth as gently as He could to the disciples, who would think so much of the interval beyond which their immediate separation from their Lord was not to extend, and with that thought in His mind He is not likely to have omitted what would console and encourage them so much as His Resurrection after three days and His conversing with them for forty days from that date. In this part of His discourse He was specially occupied in giving them all the consolation and in sparing them all the pain in His power. There is the same strain of loving consideration and delicate forbearance as to touching any sore point, as it were, running through the whole context.

We cannot therefore think that it is quite in keeping with this consideration of our Lord that He should be supposed to have kept silence on a point which was so important to the consolation of the disciples as His revisiting them after the three days, and indeed it may be fairly said that the language in which He speaks in this passage of the affliction of the disciples is hardly consistent with the theory of which we are speaking. 'You shall weep and lament, but the world shall rejoice, and you shall be made sorrowful, but your sorrow shall be turned into joy.' This is intelligible of the condition of the Apostles before the Resurrection of our Lord, but not so easily intelligible of the whole period up to the Day of Judgment. In a certain sense it was true, as our Lord said, that in the world they should have tribulation, but at the same time He warned them that they were to have confidence because He had overcome the world. This sentence seems truly to describe their state during the period after the Ascension, when they certainly were not always weeping and lamenting, as a woman in travail, but had great tribulations to suffer, in the midst of which they were rejoicing and giving thanks.

The Apostles did not understand Him, as it is easy to imagine, when we remember how little they had realized the many warnings which He had given them on these subjects. Moreover, ever since the departure of Judas, all that they had heard and seen must have produced an unbroken peace and sense of security in their minds. They may have understood in a general way that our Lord's departure was at hand, but it was quite new to them that He was to go immediately, although some of His words to St. Peter, earlier in the evening, might have aroused their fears. Then in His tender way He broke the truth to them in the words on which we are now commenting, and it seems that He spoke enigmatically, for the very purpose of arousing their attention and provoking their questions. But at this time perhaps the great solemnity of the mysteries which He had been celebrating, and the unwonted fervour and Divine majesty of His language and actions, hushed them into silence to Him, although they spoke of their perplexity among themselves.

As our Lord wished to be invited to explain Himself more fully, He took their desire that He should speak more, as a direct request that He should do so. 'Jesus knew that they had a mind to ask Him, and He said unto them, Of this do you inquire among yourselves,' as it is said above, and without telling them exactly what was to happen to Himself, He spoke sufficiently plainly of its effect upon them. 'Amen, amen, I say [unto you, that you shall weep and lament, and the world shall rejoice, and you shall be made sorrowful, but your sorrow shall be turned into joy.' He goes on to explain how true His words were to prove, for He had said not that joy should succeed unto sorrow, or overwhelm it, or be substituted for it, or make them forget it, or have any similar effect to do away with or efface it, but that their sorrow shall be turned into joy. That is to say, that the very elements of their sorrow were to become the elements and causes of their joy. He illustrates this by an example within the common experience of all.

It is the characteristic of God in redressing sorrows and afflictions, that He turns sorrow into joy, instead of substituting the one for the other. The image which our Lord uses is very apposite, because in the troubles of childbirth it is the presence of the unborn child that causes the pains of the mother, and when the birth has taken place, that which has been the cause of pain becomes itself the cause of her joy, and the joy caused is greater than has been the pain. It is not so with ordinary sorrows, in which the sorrow is removed but nothing more—it is exchanged for joy, not turned into it. Where there is well-founded Christian hope, indeed, there exists some anticipation of this, as when we have to mourn for the loss of a parent or child or friend who has died happily and holily, and we have the remembrance of his happy end to dwell upon instead of the spectacle of his sufferings and last agony. A mother losing an only child is comforted after her loss by the consolations of religion, especially when the last illness has, by the mercy of God, been made a succession of evident proofs that the sufferer has been continually aided by grace, and has been able to show that he has died in peace with our Lord. It is needless to say that no sorrow of an ordinary kind could equal that of the Apostles at the loss of our Lord under all the circumstances under which they had to part with Him, for never was there affliction like that which then fell on our Blessed Lady and our Lord's friends, but it is equally true that never was there joy on earth like that into which the sorrow was turned. There was no single feature of His humiliation which had not its own corresponding reward of joy and triumph. And what then was repaid for the afflictions of the Passion to Him and them, has ever been repeated in principle since to those who have anything to suffer for Him, so that it has become the law of His Kingdom that sorrow shall be turned into joy.

'A woman when she is in labour hath sorrow because her hour is come, but when she hath brought forth the child, she remembereth no more the anguish, for joy that a man is born into the world.' The pains and anguish of the childbirth are, under the present rule of God's government, the natural and necessary conditions of the entrance of the child into the world, and for the sake of that they are loved by the mother. 'So also you now indeed have sorrow, but I will see you again, and your heart shall rejoice, and your joy no man shall take from you.' The source of the anguish of a mother is short, and the joy remains long, for a child is born into the world, and that will remain true, and a comfort to the mother, as long as the child lives. The sorrow of the Apostles for our Lord's Death was indeed greater than the sorrow of any mother in her travail could be. But it came to an end at the moment when He manifested Himself to them after the Resurrection. Moreover, the joy of their hearts was in proportion

to the bitter sorrow they had undergone at the death
of their Master, made perfect by their perfect faith
in His Divinity, and their intelligence of the greatness of the redemption which had been wrought
for them and for all mankind by the death which
had been the cause to them of so deep, though
momentary, a pain.   It was a joy that could be felt,
in its fulness, only by holy hearts which had been
made partakers of the graces which that redemption
conveys and is based on, shared by them in proportion to their love for Him, and their charity to all who
with them are made glad thereby.   And He adds
a last touch, too, when He says, 'Your joy no man
shall take from you.'   For all earthly joy can be
taken away, but this joy cannot cease, because that
on which it rests for its foundation can never cease,
that is, the victory over sin and Hell and death
which was accomplished in our Lord's Resurrection.
St. Paul may have had these words in his mind
when he wrote the glowing passage in the Epistle to
the Romans: 'What then shall separate us from
the love of Christ? shall tribulation, or distress, or
famine, or nakedness, or danger, or persecution, or
the sword?   But in all these things we overcome
because of Him that hath loved us. For I am sure that
neither death, nor life, nor angels, nor principalities,
nor powers, nor things present, nor things to come,
nor might, nor height, nor depth, nor any other
creature shall be able to separate us from the love
of God which is in Christ Jesus our Lord.'[1]

'In that day you shall not ask Me anything.'   The
words are ambiguous in our language, in which the
word to ask has the double signification of questioning and petitioning, and although the Greek word

[1] Romans viii.

which is here used by St. John may sometimes be used in both senses, it appears from the context of the passage that it is to be taken in the sense of asking a question. For the whole sentence is our Lord's reply to a question which the Apostles wished to put to Him, on account of what He had said about the little time during which they were not to see Him, and the little time after which they were to see Him. It is therefore more natural to suppose that these words mean that, in the time of which He is speaking, they shall not require to put questions to Him because they will be living in a new atmosphere, as it were, of truth clearly understood, that they will not need the perpetual answers from our Lord by which they had been accustomed to have their difficulties solved.

The time of which our Lord speaks may be understood as including the time of the forty days after the Resurrection, but it seems clear that our Lord is referring to the new life which will be theirs after they have received the great gift of the Holy Ghost which is uppermost in His mind at this time. This was a new and greatly higher stage of spiritual enlightenment for them, though He conferred some portions of what they were then in possession of before the Ascension, as when He opened their understanding that they might understand the Scriptures. Our Lord says that at the time of which He speaks they will not need, as we say, to have recourse to Him as of old. It seems clear that, as the conversation which He is now holding with them draws on to its close, He seems to speak more and more as if He had present in His mind that future condition of His Apostles which was to be their life after the Day of Pentecost, and which was to have about it so many new and more wonderful elements, making it in truth the enjoyment of a new creation, on account of the presence with them of the Divine Paraclete.

Our Lord's language here seems sometimes to leave it uncertain whether He is not speaking of a condition of things which cannot be perfectly realized till after this world has passed away, and they are already His companions in the possession of God. But there is nothing in these sentences which we can certainly apply to their state then. Still, the language seems intended to hint to us the very great elevation of state on which they were to enter after the Day of Pentecost. Then He continues, 'Amen, amen, I say to you, if you ask the Father anything in My Name, He will give it you. Hitherto you have not asked anything in My Name. Ask, and you shall receive, that your joy may be full.' In this sentence our Lord uses the other Greek word, which is commonly used for prayer, and He tells them that whatever they ask the Father in His Name, which they do not seem as yet in the habit of doing, will certainly be granted them by the Father. He does not mean of course that the Father is not to be addressed in prayer, but that they are now to use the Name of Him, the Incarnate Son, in their petitions to God, asking through His merits, and in right of all that He has done for them, by making Himself their Mediator, conferring upon them the whole might of His mediation and sacrifice and intercession, which took effect, as it were, formally, from the Passion which He was now to undergo out of obedience to the Father, as the Saviour of the world. It is clear that the difference must have been very great as regards the ordinary power of impetration, when the prayers were no longer made through a future sacrifice, and again when the sacrifice was to be pleaded as already accomplished, and the difference must have been still greater as to the confidence and hope with which the petitions were made in the several cases, and there was to be something new also, adding immense weight to the Christian prayer, when the prayer became so very much the pleading of the Adorable Sacrifice of the altar renewed day after day, and becoming, by the frequency with which that Sacrifice was offered in the Church, an almost unceasing stream of representation before the throne on high. This, too, was one of the great novelties given to the Church after the Day of Pentecost, of which our Lord says necessarily so few words, which must not be left by Christian contemplation unhonoured. He wished this immense power now to become the ordinary instrument of their prayers, and the prayers of all Christians, which are thus to have a weight with the Eternal Father, which will be seen by His faithfulness in listening to the prayers thus made. While our Lord was with them, and while the Passion was as yet unaccomplished, the merits of His Sacrifice were indeed applied in countless ways, and what He now enacts is that they should be always formally or virtually pleaded in Christian prayers of any sort, from the offering of the Adorable Sacrifice, which is the highest and most perfect pleading of the merits of the Cross, to the simplest aspiration of the devout heart which may be made in any place or at any time.

It seems more natural to understand the words before us of this kind of prayer, which could not be made in perfection without a full and intelligent

faith in the truth and effects of the Sacrifice of the
Cross for the salvation of the world, as accomplished
· by our Lord, and which therefore was in truth a
thing of which even the Apostles might not have
had a perfect intelligence until the Passion was
completed, rather than of the more ordinary conditions of prayer, as that it must be made for things
connected with salvation, and in a state of grace,
and the like. Our Lord tells them that hitherto
they have not asked anything in His Name, which
would under that other interpretation mean that
they had never hitherto made their prayers to God
with the perfect conditions of success. For He
says, ' Hitherto you have not asked anything in My
Name. Ask, and you shall receive, that your joy may
be full.' The prayer is henceforth to be made in
His Name, in the sense in which we now speak, and
then they will receive what they ask to an extent
and in a way which will fill them with joy. We are
told of the seventy-two disciples, who were sent out
to preach in the last year of our Lord's Ministry,
that they returned to Him with joy, saying that even
the devils were subject to them in His Name. Then
our Lord had told them that they were not to rejoice
because the devils were subject to them, but rather
because their own names were written in Heaven.[2]
In this place He had just said that after He had
returned to them after the Resurrection they should
have joy which no man could take away from them.
His present words seem to promise something more
than this, for their joy is to be made full, that is,
complete, by their habitual exercise of successful
prayer through His Name. He had said something
like this when He had spoken of them as branches

2 St. Luke x. 17—20.

who abode in Him. For in the sentence in which He contrasted such branches with those that did not abide in Him, and were to be cast forth and withered and gathered up and cast into the fire, He had said as a blessing opposed to this sad lot, that if they abode in Him and His words abode in them, ' You shall ask whatsoever you will, and it shall be done to you.'[3]

Now He says, ' Ask, and you shall receive, that your joy may be full.' For there can be no more perfect joy for Apostolic men than to be continually pleading before God the merits of the Sacrifice of our Lord on the Cross, and to find that their prayers are continually prospered and successful in the impetration of what they have asked. The petitions which they have made have been for things to the glory of our Lord, which have come into their hearts as matters of prayer by the loving inspiration of the Holy Ghost. The attainment of such requests must be a joy to them in itself, for the service of our Lord and the good of souls is advanced thereby. The exercise itself of prayer is an act of love and confidence shown to our Lord, Whose blessed merits are thus pleaded in obedience to His own command. It is an exercise of faith in Him and the power of His merits, and an exercise of love and confidence, to the Father in Heaven to Whom He so delights to send us as suppliants in His Name. It is a fresh joy to see the particular persons or objects for whom the prayers were made benefited and blessed by the granting of the petitions. There is a special joy in the continual exercise of thanksgiving in such cases, for thanksgiving is one of the most joyous exercises and affections of the heart. And the heart of an

[3] St. John xv. 7.

Apostle or Apostolic man goes onward to the next design for God's glory for the good of souls with fresh strength and joy after having received the answer to a petition made in the Name of our Lord, being moved by the Paraclete by Whom the prayer was prompted to conceive greater and greater designs for the honour and service of so good a God, Who gives ever fresh and fresh proofs of the power of our Lord's Name.

Although we cannot doubt that the Apostles were already what is understood to be meant when men are commonly spoken of as men of great prayer, before the time when these words of our Lord were spoken to them, still it is easy to see that after they had witnessed the Passion and Resurrection, and even more after the Ascension and the Day of Pentecost, the whole character of their lives must have been changed in this respect, and it may have been a part of our Lord's purpose in these last moments of His intercourse with them before closing this instruction, to lay the foundation of their new life in this respect, a life which must have been so full of subjects of the happiest anticipations to His own Sacred Heart. The light shed by the Passion on the truths which regarded His Sacrifice and its effects; the new powers breathed into them by the Holy Ghost; the new offices of which they became fitted and bound to discharge in His Kingdom; the views opened to them of the magnificence and immense work reserved for them in the world, their new knowledge as to the objects and ways and means which were to be sought and to come into play in that Kingdom,—all must have helped them to rise to the loftiest ideas as to their position in the world as His representatives and emissaries, and the effect of the whole must have been a perfectly new realization of the great things that were to be wrought by them by prayer, and a new intelligence of its power with God.

When our Lord had said to them, as we may remember, earlier in this evening, ' If you abide in Me and My words abide in you, you shall ask whatsoever you will, and it shall be done unto you,' they may have expected Him to say instead something abòut their great fruitfulness in the service of God which would have been naturally expected from the form of the sentence to which He was replying by an antithesis. But He framed the antithesis as we have seen, and in doing so He probably anticipated what they would very soon come to know as the most profitable boon to be conferred on faithful servants of their Master. Our Lord could now hail with immense gladness the thought of the many thousands of souls, of all nations and generations, who would live this new life of more or less perpetual prayer, and find therein a support and light and strength and elevation which would enable them to have, as the Apostle says, their conversation in Heaven, and which was to be one of not the least novelties and marvels of the new Kingdom, and one of the greatest works of the Holy Ghost in the souls of men, ' Likewise the Spirit also helpeth our infirmity, for we know not what we should pray for as we ought, but the Spirit Himself asketh for us with unspeakable groanings. But He that searcheth the hearts knoweth what the Spirit desireth, because He asketh for the saints according to God.'⁴ Our Lord may have spoken as He did in this place, without further explanation, as knowing how soon

⁴ Romans viii. 26, 27.

the time would come when the treasures of the immense kingdom of prayer would become comparatively familiar to the Apostles.

'These things I have spoken to you in proverbs. The hour cometh when I will no more speak to you in proverbs, but will show you plainly of the Father. In that day you shall ask in My Name, and I say not to you that I will ask the Father for you, for the Father Himself loveth you, because you have loved Me, and have believed that I came forth from God. I came forth from the Father and am come into the world, again I leave the world and I go to the Father.'

When our Lord says that He has spoken certain things to them in proverbs, He means that He has put them parabolically or figuratively, or in other ways obscurely and enigmatically. In the Gospel of St. John the word 'proverb' is used in the sense of parable, as in the case of the description of the Good Shepherd in chapter x. The things which He seems to mean as having been spoken in proverbs may have been many in the course of His teaching, but in this place it seems that He refers to what He has lately been telling them about prayer made in His Name in the sense which we have been explaining. It seems as if the full doctrine about the power of Christian prayer at which He is here hinting might require many heads of teaching in order to be fully explained —the necessity of the atonement by a Person Who could suffer because He was Man, and the merits of Whose sufferings could be infinite because He was God, all that we are taught in the Epistle to the Hebrews about the priesthood of our Lord, and his perpetual Session at the right hand of the Father

to make intercession for us, the doctrine too of
the priesthood which is communicated to men, the
priests of the New Covenant, and also that of the
spiritual priesthood of which St. Peter speaks,[5] and
the efficacy of prayer made in His Name by those
who have a right so to make it.

All these things were perhaps not completely
imparted to the Apostles at this stage of the instruction, and yet these and others would require to be
unfolded, before they could entirely comprehend the
immense power placed in their hands to which our
Lord seems to allude in this passage. The Christian
prayer and priesthood of which we speak was
perhaps, in all its fulness, one of those doctrines
which He said He had to tell them beyond what He
had already told them, but which were to be taught
them either after the Resurrection or by the Holy
Ghost when He came. If this be so, it is comparatively easy to understand how our Lord now
says that in that day they are to ask in His Name,
with more full intelligence, perhaps, of what they are
then doing.

It seems safe to suppose that He is here speaking of the doctrine which He has just laid down
on this particular point of prayer. The full doctrine
which is here put forward involves the whole truth
of the necessity of the Atonement as carried out
by our Lord, a Divine Person in human nature,
having taken flesh in order that He might suffer,
and in order that, being God, He might efficaciously
atone for sin by His Sacrifice, with all the fruits
of ineffable efficacy which it involved. It is said by
some of the Fathers that He prays for us now in
Heaven as He was wont to pray when on earth,

[5] 1 St. Peter ii.

N 14

though in a different way, for the effects of the redemption can and must still be applied more and more, and they understand in this way the text to the Hebrews, 'That He is always living to make intercession for us,'[6] and that of St. John, that we have Him an advocate with the Father, where he adds, ' And He is the propitiation for our sins, and not ours only, but also of the whole world.'[7] Moreover, the full knowledge of the privileges of Christian prayer is perhaps hardly to be possessed by any one except by experience. The persons who fully understand those privileges are those who have for some time been accustomed to their use, and then they come to know the strengthening and growth of the soul which follow from the faithful and persevering use of this great key of Heaven. Our Lord may leave a good many things unsaid on this subject, which He may have been sure that the Apostles would soon come to know for themselves in this most blessed way. It might have been well to explain, for instance, how His own prayer in His Sacred Human Nature would always accompany theirs, and the footing with God on which they were in future to stand, when confirmed and strengthened by the presence of the Paraclete and all the graces which He was to bring with Him, so that they would not need any special and independent intercession on His own part as before. He had said earlier in this discourse, ' I will ask the Father and He shall give you another Paraclete, that He may abide with you for ever,' and now He seems to speak as if that Gift having been won, it was not necessary that He Himself should make a number of particular requests for them, and He speaks also, as has been said, as if

[6] Heb. vii. 25.   [7] 1 St. John ii. 1, 2.

the Sacrifice of the Cross had been completed and its effects secured. What our Lord says here is, that He does not think it necessary to tell them that He will ask the Father for them when they ask in His Name. This may mean that the Father will be already so ready to hear them that a special pleading of our Lord Himself will not be needed, or that His own intercession will certainly accompany the prayer made by them in His Name. What He seems to insist on is the reason which He gives for what He says, namely, that the Father Himself loves them, and that for two reasons which He specifies, first, because they have loved Him, and second, because they have believed that He has come out from God, that is, that He is the promised Messias, the Son of God, Incarnate as Man for the salvation of the world. But the doctrine of which we speak as not fully explained as yet, implies a closer union still of the Apostles with our Lord, for they are branches of Him as the true Vine, they are members of His Body of which St. Paul speaks, their prayers are His prayers, and they have a right to claim that the power of impetration which belongs to His Sacrifice on the Cross may be imparted to them. In this sense the rights of the Sacred Humanity itself are made over already to the Christian prayer, especially, as we see, in the Adorable Sacrifice of the Altar in the Church. The dignity of the Christian priesthood may have been in our Lord's mind when He said here that He does not say that He will ask for them, because the Father Himself loves them, and the rest.

' I came forth from the Father, and am come into the world, again I leave the world, and go to the Father.' These words contain a plain declaration of our Blessed Lord's Divinity, and also of His Incarnation. The Fathers are fond of explaining the first statement, about coming forth from the Father, of the Eternal Generation, and the second statement of the Incarnation, the coming into the world by the assumption of the Human Nature. And when our Lord says that again He leaves the world and goes to the Father, they understand Him of His departure from the world by His Passion, Death, and Ascension, taking with Him the Sacred Humanity inseparably and for ever united to the Divinity. Thus the words sum up briefly the whole of our faith as to our Lord. The truth is the same as to His Divine Person as that which St. Peter expressed in his confession, ' Thou art the Christ, the Son of the living God,' and Martha, ' Yea, Lord, I have believed that Thou art Christ, the Son of the living God, Who art come into this world.' This is what the Apostles under-stood to be conveyed by our Lord's declaration concerning Himself, and when Caiphas asked Him, before the Council, ' Art Thou the Christ, the Son of the Blessed God ? ' he meant nothing short of the same question, as we see by the condemnation of our Lord for blasphemy which immediately followed. It was not His wont to express the truth so clearly, on account of the many snares that were always laid for Him.

The answer, therefore, was an abundant declara-tion for the Apostles, and cleared up the meaning of what had perplexed them in His words about a little time, and the rest. We must note, however, that He says nothing about that which was imme-diately to follow, namely, His Sacred Passion and Death. He had spoken of that before, and often,

but in this great discourse He says little or nothing
directly about it. The disciples could not control
their satisfaction at the plainness of His words.
They say unto Him, ' Behold, now, Thou speakest
openly, plainly, and speakest no proverb. Now
we know that Thou knowest all things, and Thou
needest not that any man should ask Thee. By this
we believe that Thou camest forth from God.' He
had answered their question while they were still
afraid to put it, and the plainness of the answer
made them break out into expressions of joy. They
knew by His answering them so clearly that He
had read the thoughts of their hearts, and the fact
that He had done so had been a cause of their
conviction of His Divinity.

There is something at once touching and sur-
prising about this outbreak of joy on the part of the
disciples at the plain declaration now made by our
Lord. The Jews were continually, as we know,
putting questions to Him, with the object, as it
seems, of inducing Him to tell them plainly Who
He was, but He always refrained from answering
them openly, because He saw that it would do them
harm by forcing on them the alternative of treating
Him as an open blasphemer, or accepting the truth
which He must have told them concerning Himself.
As we read the history, we are astonished at what
we deem the slowness of the disciples themselves in
arriving at the full truth concerning Him. In truth,
they had the true faith, but our Lord wished it to
ripen and grow in their hearts under the teaching of
the Father. It could have been flashed in a moment,
if He had chosen, over their hearts and minds, as it
was afterwards in the case of St. Paul—although we
do not know the full history, and are not told whether

it was not the case with him to submit on a sudden to a truth which had been for some time forcing itself on his intelligence, with some resistance on the part of his will, on account of the strength of the prejudices in which he had been brought up. In the case of the Apostles, at the time of which we are speaking, they had to have their perfect faith in our Lord ripened against the many difficulties with which they were surrounded. But we must remember the true saying of a great convert of our own time, that a great many difficulties do not make a doubt. As our Lord had just said, they had believed that He had come forth from God. But they had all the difficulties which His own humble and unassuming character created for them, all the difficulties caused by the strong opposition to Him of the whole hierarchy of the holy nation, all the difficulties which arose from imperfect knowledge of the system of prophetic anticipations which, in truth, bore witness to Him, and in some degree were supported by what seemed His own forbearance to declare Himself openly and plainly. These difficulties are constantly paralleled in the experience of converts, who, in days like our own, have to fight their way against much opposition to the threshold of the true Church, on whom those who have already the gift of faith sometimes look in alarm lest they should fail to endure their trial, and in wonder that they do not see what seems so plain. So, when the light comes in fulness, their hearts are filled with a sudden joy, because our Lord seems to them to have spoken plainly, and they seem to have no more need of further questioning. When the Apostles told Him that they were at rest, and that now they believed, they could not have meant that they had then for the first time passed from a state of incredulity to one of faith. But they found themselves so happy and secure in the conviction which His last words had produced in them, that it seemed to them that they no longer had any difficulties to overcome as to their faith in the Divine truths relating to His Person.

Although our Lord was so careful not to speak of the terrible blows that were so soon to fall on them, He does not seem to have omitted any occasion of reminding them of their great weakness and need of prayer to strengthen the spiritual forces. ' Jesus answered them, Do you now believe? Behold, the hour cometh and it is now come, that you shall be scattered every man to his own, and shall leave Me alone, and yet I am not alone, because the Father is with Me. These things I have spoken to you, that in Me you may have peace. In the world you shall have distress, but have confidence, I have overcome the world.' The words, ' Do you now believe?' may of course be read as an affirmation instead of a question, but the sense is nearly the same in either case. He means that they think they believe and have a certain firmness in their faith, but that they are not strong enough to stand firm in all that a perfectly fearless faith will require of them, and this weakness of faith will be shown very soon in the hour of trial, when they will see Him in the hands of His enemies, and will, out of cowardice, forsake Him, at the same time separating themselves from one another in their panic. Then He renews His declaration that He will always have the Father with Him, and thus He encourages them as well as shows His own source of strength.

. . ' Jesus answered them, Do you now believe?

Behold the hour cometh and it is now come, that you shall be scattered every man to his own, and shall leave Me alone, and yet I am not alone, because the Father is with Me. These things I have spoken to you, that in Me you may have peace. In the world you shall have distress, but have confidence, I have overcome the world.' The words which our Lord now addressed to the disciples about their being scattered and fleeing every man to his own, are repeated again by Him after a short interval, when He had already gone forth from the Cenacle, at the beginning of the first part of the actual Passion, before the Agony in the Garden. It may seem to us strange that He should not have uttered them earlier. But that He did not do so is another proof of His tender consideration for them, as they could not flee and leave Him without some apparent desertion of Him on their parts, and He was anxious to spare them as far as possible any subject of self-reproach, or anything that might disturb them. But it is clear, from what He now says, that He saw that the mention of His being left alone by them, considering all that He then added, was not calculated to disturb them too greatly. The remark with which He answered their protestation of faith in Him may be taken either as an affirmation or as a question, You now believe, or Do you now believe? In either case it has the same force as a gentle protest against their profession of faith, which was so soon to be liable to question. In truth, our Lord does not seem to mean that their profession of faith was not genuine, but He spoke to them a gentle warning not to trust too much to their feelings of personal affection and devotion, which might not stand all the strain which might be put on them to bear. ' Do you now believe ? Behold the hour cometh and it is now come, that you shall be scattered every man to his own, and shall leave Me alone, and yet I am not alone, because the Father is with Me.'

The words which He added will be considered afterwards. The scattering of the Apostles every man to his own, seems simply to be their dispersion one by one, which actually happened, although they may have come together in small separate parties before any long interval, for our Lord, by His words to the armed band which was sent to arrest Him, secured them from all pursuit or molestation. They were allowed to depart as seemed good to each, and they had no natural centre of union apart from our Lord. We know that ere long St. Peter and St. John found themselves together in the house of the High Priest. The prominent fact about them was their dispersion and abandonment of our Lord, which probably had been already accomplished before they had had time to think. A common panic seized them, and in a moment they were scattered according to our Lord's prediction, and found themselves free and without danger, unless it were such as they exposed themselves to of their own accord. Our Lord went on to add a few words on which we are now to comment. He says first of all that He was not to be truly left alone, even after their desertion, because the Father is with Me. The words seem to imply both what was obviously true, that He never could be separated from the Father, and also that when He was to be left alone by men on whom He might have reckoned not to forsake Him, and also that the Father would be present with Him in some special way of consolation, and companionship, and support of the Sacred Humanity, such as that which was withdrawn for a season when He said, 'My God, My God, why hast Thou forsaken Me?'

Indeed we find the thought of the Father uppermost in our Lord's mind at the moment before the desertion of the Apostles, when He turned to St. Peter and bade him put up his sword into the sheath, when He added the words which St. Matthew records, 'Thinkest thou that I cannot ask My Father, and He will give Me presently more than twelve legions of angels? How then, shall the Scriptures be fulfilled that so it must be done?' It may have been a point on which our Lord thought it well to instruct the Apostles specially at this time, that He was always not only one with His Father in the Divine unity, but by the special kind of assistance which may have been supplied to Him ordinarily in times of trial, as it would probably be habitually supplied, even in the case of the saints. For we should expect the words of our Lord to be verified to any one who was unusually abandoned by friends and destitute of human succour. The communication which our Lord thus made to the Apostles was meant to let them see that He had abundant comfort for Himself, and it was meant also to give them comfort and peace in another way, as He says, but as there is not perfect unanimity among those who have undertaken to explain the passage before us, it will be necessary to pause here awhile to explain the cause of difficulty.

Our Lord continues: 'These things I have spoken unto you, that in Me you may have peace. In the world you shall have distress, but have confidence, I have overcome the world.' The question here naturally arises, what the things are of which He says that He has spoken them in order that the

Apostles may have peace in Him, for that object may have been in His mind with regard to many of the things which He had said to them. The words may be true of the whole of this great discourse which He is now closing, or He may mean them to apply to the instructions which He has been lately giving in particular, especially those on the subject of prayer, or of the Holy Ghost, or of the love which .the Father bears to them, and the like. Expressions of the kind are not uncommon in our Lord's discourses, and the safest way may be to compare the places where they occur one with another, and see if we can get any guidance from the general use in such passages. We may confine ourselves to two or three instances which occur in the latter portion of this discourse.

After the celebration of the Blessed Eucharist, in chapter xv. we find Him saying, 'These things I have spoken to you that My joy may be in you, and your joy may be filled.' In that place it will be remembered that our Lord had just before been speaking of some things which were very close to His Heart, such as the precept of abiding in Him, of the love of His Father for Him and His love for them, and of their keeping His commandments, and it seems clear that when He says that He has told them these things that His joy may be in them, and the rest, He refers, not to His teaching in a general way, but rather to the last few words which He had spoken. Another place in which He uses the same language is at the beginning of the sixteenth chapter, where He has just before been telling them of the great persecution they are to undergo for His sake, to the extent of what was probably, at that time, a very alarming prospect to them, the excommunication from the Synagogue, the fear of which, as we know, kept back many who were inclined to believe in Him from avowing their faith. Then He had said to them, 'These things have I spoken to you that you may not be scandalized,' words which have certainly reference to what He has just said, or was going to say, and not to any general instruction. We conclude therefore, that in the passage before us, our Lord's words are meant to refer to what immediately precedes, and are not merely general in their application.

'These things I have spoken to you, that in Me you may have peace. In the world you shall have distress, but have confidence, I have overcome the world.' If we rightly understand the meaning of the words, 'These things I have spoken to you,' and the rest, as referring to what He had just before said—that is, to the words about their leaving Him alone, and 'yet I am not alone, because the Father is with Me,' these words, if deeply pondered, are certainly calculated to give great peace to the devout soul. They seem to set before us on the one hand the state of utter dereliction as far as created consolation and support are concerned, in which we may be placed, and on the other hand, the ineffable comfort and strength which are then to be found in the thought and the close presence of God, and the infinite strength and security which come to those who have no other to lean upon but God. It seems sometimes as if it were greatly better for them to have nothing to look to from any creature, in the way of companionship or help or comfort of any kind or degree, even as if such things were an embarrassment and an impediment to their perfect peace, which almost required their absence. They seem like the armour of Saul, which David felt he was stronger without, and more able to battle with the giant for having no one but God with him. The knowledge and experience of this immense source of spiritual strength was therefore something which our Lord might wish the Apostles to be able to acquire for their own sakes, and to learn from His example as one last lesson from their beloved Master at this stage of the history. He was now about to leave them indeed, but as He said of Himself, not alone. He was to leave them in the world, in which they were to have distress. He had not hidden from them that the world in which He was to leave them was to be as much their enemy as it had been His, their enemy because it had been His, and for the same reason. But the world could do them no real harm, it was an enemy already conquered and whose strength had been taken away by Him. All through these last words of His He always speaks as if the great conflict on which He was about to engage, the conflict of the Passion, was already over, as it was already over in the eyes of God. The struggles and trials to which they were to be exposed were great indeed, but the battle had been won and the foe conquered, and the sufferings already secured of their triumphant reward. ' In the world you shall have distress in order that you may earn thereby your share of the fruit of victory, but have confidence, I have overcome the world.'

CHAPTER VII.

The Prayer for the Church.

St. John xvii. ; *Story of the Gospels*, § 157.

WE gather from what we are sometimes told of our Blessed Lord's habitual manners with His disciples, that it was not uncommon for Him, after any great conversation or instruction—especially when it had had some particular importance in the unfolding of His plans for the work of the service of God—to withdraw from all human company, and spend the night hours alone in prayer with His Eternal Father. The last words which He had uttered on the occasion with which we are now dealing, would naturally prepare us for some kind of leave-taking for a time from the Apostles, and we might have expected to hear that He then turned from men and spent the night in prayer, especially as we are, to some extent, prepared for this by the few last words He had spoken, that although the Apostles were to flee and leave Him alone, He was not alone, because 'the Father was with Him.' But what we should not have ventured to expect just at this time, would have been that He should admit them to a participation of what we should, humanly speaking, call His confidences with His Eternal Father, from Whom He had just said that nothing could separate Him, and His companionship with Whom was His one great and never-failing resource and consolation, having which, He could never be alone. And yet so it is, the blessed Evangelist, whom Jesus loved, and who lay on His bosom during the Last Supper, and we know not how long after that, on this memorable evening, has been chosen to add this one still greater treasure to the many priceless boons for which we are his debtors in the Church of God, and to give us out of the faithful stores of his memory, assisted by the Holy Ghost, the comparatively long prayer which our Lord now poured forth to His most beloved and adorable Father.

Certainly, nothing of the kind can be a subject of astonishment to us from our Blessed Lord. At the outset of his account on which we have been dwelling, of the acts and words of this Holy Thursday, St. John has summed all up in the words that, 'having loved His own who were in the world, He loved them to the end.' It would take a very long commentary, as we know, to exhaust, even as far as it would be in our power to do so, the deep meanings contained in that short expression. But we can see that there was this one thing which He had never done before, as far as the Gospel records tell us— to let us hear Him communing with His Father regarding the affairs of our salvation, and His own thoughts and affections concerning them, and this not only for the time at which He was speaking, but with the whole future before Him, as it lay in the counsels and wishes of His Heart, providing for times and generations yet to come, and embracing thousands besides those who had already learnt in some measure to deserve the tender name of ' His own.' Surely nothing more is necessary to commend these words of His to the continual study of the

devout Christian. All the words of our Lord are
infinitely precious to the hearts of such, and few will
question that, even among His words, there are
none more weighty than those which were uttered
in the great discourse on which we have been commenting in these last chapters. But the words which
yet remain to us for examination have certainly an
importance of their own. They come at the very
end of the great discourse of the Thursday evening,
and are, as it were, a sequel and a corollary to it.
But they are more than that, for they deal with God
rather than man, and refer to the counsels and
designs of the Most Holy Trinity for the present
and the future, in relation to the salvation of mankind by means of the redemption wrought by our
Lord. No passage of Sacred Scripture breathes
more intense Divine love, or illustrates more perfectly the compassion of God for His wandering
creatures. The prayer of which we speak is in truth
the solemn oblation of the Sacrifice by which the
redemption of the world was wrought out, made by
the great High Priest Himself to the Father, as the
price of the reconciliation of God and man, by Him
Who could suffer because He was Man, and suffer
with infinite merit, and in a way adequate to the
offence, because He was God. It may also be
noticed that this prayer is in one respect unique as
a model of the manner in which God should be
addressed in this kind of supplication, the way in
which considerations and affections of various kinds
may be used in making our needs known to Him, and
presenting them humbly and reverently before the
throne of His merciful and most compassionate
Majesty. On this point we shall take occasion to
remark in the course of the following paragraphs.

It may be thought that the very momentous importance of the great sacrificial act of which we speak, between our Lord and His Father, may have made it less convenient for this prayer of our Lord to have been recorded in the earlier Evangelists. It is not possible to think that this prayer could have been forgotten by St. Matthew, or by St. Peter, who guided the pen of St. Mark, or have been unknown to those who were the authorities consulted by St. Luke, but it is clear that if the chapter of the Gospel which we are about to consider had taken a place in any of the three first authoritative Gospels, the Christian reader would have welcomed it with adoring reverence, but would not have felt so much at home with its sublime strains as when he reads it as the utterance of the Eagle of the New Testament, the Beloved Disciple himself. The laws according to which certain things are found allotted to one Evangelist and certain other things to another, are not to be traced out by us. But all such arrangements are by us to be reverently adored. Our attention may well be drawn once more to the incalculable importance of the additions which the knowledge of the Church received when, not long before the close of our first century, the Gospel of St. John was put into the hands of the faithful by the last survivor of the Apostles. The words of which we shall have to speak must have lingered in the hearts of St. John and of the other Apostles during the years, in the case of some of them, like St. James, short, in the case of others, as St. John himself, very long, during which they were to labour for their Master in the Church on earth. But we know that they never became the common property of the faithful till towards the close of the

Evangelist's life. We find in them many things which seem to have been echoed by words of the Gospel which he wrote, as it seems, about the same time, and there is no mistaking the identity of tone, and sometimes of expression, between the two documents. As we read over the first Epistle of St. John, we find ourselves often carried back into the Cenacle. 'That which was from the beginning, which we have heard, which we have seen with our eyes, which we have looked upon, and our hands have handled, of the Word of life, for the life was manifest, and we have seen, and do bear witness, and declare unto you the life eternal, which was with the Father and hath appeared unto us, that which we have seen and heard we declare unto you, that you also may have fellowship with us, and our fellowship may be with the Father, and with His Son, Jesus Christ. And these things we write unto you, that you may rejoice, and that your joy may be full. . . . Behold what manner of charity the Father hath bestowed upon us, that we should be called and should be the sons of God. Therefore the world knoweth not us, because it knoweth not Him. Dearly beloved, we are now the sons of God, and it hath not yet appeared what we shall be. We know that when He shall appear, we shall be like Him, because we shall see Him as He is. And every one that hath this hope in Him, sanctifieth himself, as He also is holy. . . . We know that the Son of God is come, and He hath given us understanding, that we may know the true God and may be in His true Son. This is the true God and life eternal.'[1] Many more passages might perhaps be cited, in which the words of this prayer are not exactly quoted, for the prayer is an address

[1] 1 St. John i. iii. v.

to the Father, and in the Epistle the Apostle is exhorting and instructing and warning the faithful people to whom he writes, and the language could not necessarily repeat the exact words which He had used. But it shows the thoughts of our Lord as expressed in the prayer to have been present to the mind of the Apostle, and this is the kind of resemblance between the two documents which the nature of the case admits of.

It was something unusual in our Blessed Lord to address His Eternal Father in this way. The whole life of the Sacred Heart was a continual converse with Him, but it was a life which was wrapt up in perpetual silence, and the acts of which were kept shrouded from mortal ears, as far as we can gather from the Evangelists, who but very seldom have been guided to reveal to us the words which passed between our Lord and His Father. We may conjecture that if they had more of this kind to tell us, we should not have been left by them without the consolation and instruction which such Divine words must have given us, and which it is but natural to suppose must have been listened to by the Apostles with an amount of reverence and awe quite surpassing even what was their habitual attitude of mind when listening to our Lord's words to themselves. We have noticed that in the earlier parts of this great discourse on which we have been for some time commenting, the Apostles were not afraid to interrupt Him by the questions which occurred to their mind from time to time, but that this was not so towards the end of the same discourse. As it drew towards the end of the evening there seems to have been no interruptions, and we are told that when they were perplexed about His words as to the 'little times' which were to intervene between His presences with them and His absences, they had not ventured to ask for an explanation.

We may gather from this that there was a certain air of unusual solemnity and majesty about the demeanour of our Lord on this occasion, which produced a corresponding impression on the Apostles. The earlier Evangelists must have felt themselves restrained from relating these Divine words, and indeed they felt that it was not their office to report any of the sublime sayings and doings which occupied so large a portion of time on this last night before the Passion, and which were kept back by the Holy Ghost till the time came for the Beloved Disciple himself to be their chronicler. With regard to the words on which we are now about to comment, there are certain things to be remarked as to their peculiar character among the utterances of our Lord Himself, which are suggested by the unique nature of the occasion on which they were spoken, which we have occasion to remark upon in the course of the prayer itself. It is enough to have said these few words by way of preface before entering on the consideration of a chapter which is without any parallel as to the outpouring which it relates of the tenderest and most intimate affections of the Sacred Heart as manifested to His Eternal Father, and also as opening to us the matters concerning which He chose to treat in prayer with the same beloved Father, at the very moment when He was about to offer to Him the appointed Sacrifice of Himself for the satisfaction of the sins of the whole world.

But without following out these thoughts more into detail at present, it will suffice for us to keep in mind, as we read over and ponder with the deepest reverence the words of this great prayer, the many various lines of thought which are here collected for us. Sometimes it may seem as if our Lord was meaning to instruct us as to things which He had not yet spoken of to the Apostles, as when He mentions the glory which is to be His, and which He calls the glory that He had with the Father before the creation of the world. Sometimes He seems to be adding other and more tenderly earnest expressions to commandments or counsels which He had already urged on them, as when He makes the unity, which He has already enjoined so strongly, the subject-matter of a new and special petition for the Church to His Father, and more than once implies that His motive for desiring that unity is that the world may believe in the truth of His own Mission by the Father. Sometimes He kindles their love and raises their hope to a higher pitch than ever before, as when He draws the contrast between the Apostles with those who are to believe in Him through their word, praying for them, and not for the world, and asking for them that consummation of blessedness which is to consist in being where He is, and seeing His glory, and as when He utters those mysterious words about the glory which the Father has given to Him, and which He in turn has given to them, that they may be one, as His Father and He are one, that the world may believe. There is also much implied prophecy in the course of these sentences, and of revelations which are not made elsewhere.

It is only natural that the more this Divine document is examined and pondered by the Christian contemplative, the more should there be found in it to reward the devout study which it deserves. The prayer of which we are to speak, although we have no other longer prayer strictly so called from our Blessed Lord's lips, is not of any great length in itself, and it admits of being arranged in some few and obvious divisions. It may be well, in the first instance, to point out what these divisions are, for the sake of noting the continuity and at the same time the onward flow and progress which can be traced. It is one continuous and most loving out-pouring of the Sacred Heart, beginning from the immediate subject of the accomplishment of the work on earth which had been committed to Him by the Father (for He speaks of it as accomplished), and a part of which has consisted in the manifes-tation of the Name of the Father to the men whom that Father had given to Him, and then passing to the petition which He begs for them, who are now to be left by their Master in the world, and are in consequence the objects of His special care and more than one special request, which we shall have to dwell on in particular.

The prayer begins by an action of our Lord which must have arrested the attention of the Apostles, His lifting up His eyes to heaven, which implied of itself that the words which followed were addressed not to men, but to God. Our Lord told His Father that the hour was come, and begged Him to glorify His Son, that His Son might glorify Him in return. The mode or manner of the glorification which He has in His mind is signified by the mention of the fact that He had already given to the Son power over all flesh, that He may give eternal life to all who have been given Him, and, as to this eternal life, it is added that it consists in their knowing Him, the true God, and Jesus Christ Whom He has sent. He adds that He has Himself glorified the Father upon earth, and has finished the work that His Father has given Him to do. As a consequence of this, He asks that now, the hour having come, the Father will glorify Him with Himself, 'with the glory which I had before the world was with Thee.' This may be considered as forming the first portion of the prayer before us.

The second portion embraces the prayer which our Lord makes, not any more directly for His own glorification, but for the disciples who had been the objects of His care and labours while He was in the world which He was now about to leave. He tells His Father that He has manifested His name to the men whom He had given Him out of the world. They had been the Father's, and He had given them to Him, and they had kept His Father's word—they had received that word, and had come to know the Mission of the Son by the Father, and had believed 'that Thou didst send Me.' He says that He prays for them, not for the world, as all things that are His are the Father's, and all that is the Father's are His, and He is glorified in the men of whom He is speaking, and is going to the Father, leaving the world. What He prays for them is that the Father will keep them in His own name, 'that they may be one, as We also are.' He says that while He has been with them He has kept them in His Father's name, and no one of them has been lost, save the son of perdition, that the Scripture may be fulfilled. Now He is going to the Father, and He says what He now says in the world, that they may have His joy fulfilled in themselves. He has given them His Father's word, and the world has hated them, because they are not of it, as He was not. Then

He names His petition, not that the Father should take them out of the world, but that He should keep them from evil. They, as He, are not of the world. He asks His father to sanctify them in truth, adding that His word is truth. They have been sent into the world, as He was sent by the Father, and for their sake He sanctifies Himself, that they may be sanctified in truth. Here we may consider that the second portion of the prayer ends.

A third section then follows, in which our Lord says that He prays not only for His Apostles, whom He has sent into the world, as He has been Himself sent by the Father, but for those who are to believe on Himself through their word. For them He asks the same boon as for the Apostles, 'That all may be one, as Thou, Father, art in Me and I in Thee, that they also may be one in Us,' and here He adds to what He has before said in His prayer for their unity, by subjoining the motive for which He asks this precious gift, 'That the world may believe that Thou hast sent Me.' He adds another thing, namely, that He has given to them, the Apostles and those who are to believe in Him through their word, what He calls the glory which Thou hast given Me, and this for the object that they may be one, 'as We also are One. I in them and Thou in Me, that they may be consummated into one, and that the world may know that Thou hast sent Me.' This petition had been made before, but now there is added to it the further clause, 'And hast loved them as Thou hast also loved Me.'

The last section of the prayer expresses a desire or resolution of the Sacred Heart which is not exactly a petition. Our Lord says, 'Father, I will that where I am those also whom Thou hast given to

Me may be, that they may see My glory which Thou hast given Me, because Thou hast loved Me before the making of the world.' And He adds a declaration that the world has not known the Father, but that He Himself has known Him, and that those of whom He speaks have known the truth of His Mission by the Father. He says that He has made known to them the name of the Father, and will continue to make it known, 'that the love wherewith Thou hast loved Me may be in them, and I in them.' It is easy to see how carefully each single word here deserves to be considered, and how necessary it will be to ascertain, as far as possible, the precise meaning of each, and the bearing and connection of each several clause. For the present we may be content with a slight analysis of the whole, and with the general remark that if the Apostles could have wanted an explanation of our Lord's words just before, that He could not in truth be alone, because the Father was with Him, as a sufficient commentary on those words would have been furnished by their being permitted to listen to this disclosure of the communing which was habitual between the Sacred Heart and the most loving Father, Who was ever, as He says, in the bosom of the Father.

We must allow ourselves one more preliminary remark before we proceed to deal in full detail with this most important prayer. The prayer before us appears to be reported with singular fulness of detail by the Evangelist. We have therefore an opportunity of studying it as a specimen of the class of prayer to which it belongs, that is, of using it as a model of the manner, so to speak, in which our Divine Lord was accustomed to lay His wishes before His Father, if we may say so, to choose the

matters which He urged as petitions for Himself or
for others, and the way in which He was wont to
urge His requests by various considerations, and by
the use of the various affections which belong to this
holy exercise. This reason for studying the prayer
before us with peculiar interest and attention has
been already hinted at above. We shall find that
it is not our Lord's way to make a great number
of distinct petitions in prayer of this kind, but
rather to present the subject-matter of His petition
in a few words, and then to urge it on various
grounds, with great fervour. There is so much to
be learnt in various ways from the words before us,
that we shall not forbear from pointing out what
occurs to us, even though it may involve a repeated
dwelling on the same words or thoughts in dealing
with the present chapter, which is unique in this
respect also among the records of the New Testament. It can hardly be thought a loss of time to
examine the prayer before us in this light also.

Such, in brief outline, is the prayer on the explanation of which we are now to enter. What we
have called the divisions into which it seems
naturally to fall, are easily discerned. There is also
a close unity of thought throughout, and a certain
order and growth in the whole, which starts from
the state in which He is about to leave the little
flock confided to Him by the Father, and comes to
its natural end when He has provided for their being
with Him where He is in the glory of eternity. It
will not fail to strike the devout reader that all
through this prayer the earnest desire for the unity
which has been so often spoken of by us of late
seems to present itself, almost as if the whole migh
be entitled, the Prayer for Unity. We may now

proceed to examine the clauses of the prayer one by one.

The Evangelist introduces it, as we know, in his usual simple way. ' These things spake Jesus, and lifting up His eyes to heaven, He said, Father, the hour is come, glorify Thy Son, that Thy Son may glorify Thee.'

We know our Lord's habit of lifting up His eyes to heaven on solemn occasions, that men who saw Him might understand the reverence and devotion with which He spoke to His Eternal Father. It was His custom generally to keep His eyes on the ground for an example of modesty and recollection, and thus it is that, when He departed from His usual attitude in this respect, the Evangelists notice it more particularly. We must keep in mind that this was an occasion which was pre-eminent in solemnity in His Life. Not long before this He had for the first time celebrated the Adorable Sacrifice of the Altar, in anticipation of His Passion, and besides instituting the Blessed Sacrament of His Body and Blood and the other sacraments that it was appointed should be now established in the Church, He had instructed His Apostles concerning those and the other chief mysteries of His Kingdom. He had opened to them His whole Heart, we may surely say, and spoken of Its most intimate secrets, and the things on which He set the most store for the satisfaction of His love and for the salvation and perfection of souls, charity, mutual union, the precious gift of the Holy Ghost, of which He had before said so little. It is impossible to fathom the depths of the love and affection which had now been poured out. We see by the last words of the Apostles that they were themselves kindled to a glowing joy and enthusiasm of love and confidence when He came to cease speaking. But His Heart was glowing with a love that infinitely surpassed any conception even of the holiest hearts among them, for it was the love which He bore to His Eternal Father, and this, as we know, was always the paramount love in His Heart, a love seldom expressed in words of which any communication was ever made to man, though it was the spring of all His actions and dominated every thought and every word of His. But now by the mercy of God we are allowed to listen to this outpouring of the affections of that Sacred Heart, which is absolutely unique in Its tenderness and copiousness. The first word of the prayer is the name which was ever uppermost in His Heart and on His lips, 'Father.'

As it is as Man, and not as God, One in substance and power with the Father, that He can pray, we understand the word to be used by Him as Man. But in this prayer especially, wherein He sometimes uses language which expresses an Almighty will, we must not forget that He speaks as the appointed Mediator between God and Man, as the great High Priest after the order of Melchisedec, uniting both natures in His one Divine Person, Who is presenting His own sacrifice of infinite merit before the throne of God. This gives His words a power of impetration which they could not have as only the words of a mere man. And this prayer must all through be considered in this light, as an exercise of the priestly power of our Divine Lord, praying, indeed, as the Mediator in the two-fold nature which He was to possess in order that He might suffer, but at the same time suffer with infinite merit, as One Whose merits were enough to atone fully and perfectly for the sins of a thousand worlds. It is, then, the Eternal Son speaking in the Human Nature which He had assumed out of obedience to the Father for the redemption of the world, that He now asks what He does ask, for the full accomplishment of the design of the Eternal Trinity, in the decree that had made Him Man for our sakes and for our salvation.

'Father, the hour is come.' In the original it is that hour, the hour long foreseen and prophesied, and long delayed, but now at last arrived, in the fulness of time, as He had said of it more than once, that it had not yet come, and now changes His language and declares it is come. We may remember that St. John more than once uses the expression with which this prayer of our Lord begins, about His hour, at times when certain measures against Him were contemplated but not efficiently carried out by His enemies, and then the Evangelist gives the reason that they could not do as they designed, because His hour was not come. And at the feast at Cana, when He wrought His beginning of miracles, He told His Blessed Mother as an explanation of the delay, that His hour was not yet come. Some of the Fathers on that place understand the words as implying that it was not yet the time for Him to show that He treated her as His Mother, by a public acknowledgment of her influence over Him, and that this acknowledgment was to take place at the time of the Passion. Whatever may be thought of this commentary on the words, as if they contained a reference to our Blessed Lady, it may be safely assumed that the hour of which our Lord spoke on so many different occasions, and of which St. John more than once makes mention, was the hour of His great humiliation by His sacrifice of Himself on the Cross, and that He now refers to that hour as bringing with it an occasion on which in the Providence of the Father, He had, as it were, an especial· right to look to Him for a corresponding exaltation and vindication of His honour, in proportion to the humiliation which He was about to receive. What He asks with the deepest reverence, and also the fullest confidence, is that the decree of which we have spoken may be carried out in perfection.

That decree had ordained the sufferings and humiliation of the Incarnate Son, and, as the fruit of those sufferings and that humiliation, the salvation of vast multitudes of the human race, not only as regards the intrinsic merit of the sacrifice, but also as regards the application of those merits actually to the souls of the saved. In this was included what our Lord here speaks of as the glorification of the Redeemer of the human race, by the action of the Father in His Providence. Hitherto He had glorified the Father by His obedience, and He was still more to glorify Him in His sufferings, endured so lovingly and with such a display of the highest virtues. But now the coming of the hour, to which He had so long looked forward, was to prevent Him from appearing before men as One distinguished by any qualities which they could honour or which would draw to Him that faith in Him which was necessary, in order that they might accept Him as sent from God to save them. In the approaching Passion all that was conspicuous about Him was to be overwhelmed in infamy and disgrace. He was to be silent when accused, helpless when assailed, dumb as a sheep before her shearers, falsely charged, yet answering nothing, betrayed by one disciple and then forsaken by all, deserted by the people who had been accustomed to hang on His words as on those of a prophet, shamefully sacrificed by the judge, who knew His innocence, with no one to lift a voice in His favour save a thief crucified by His side, to have a robber and murderer preferred before Him, to be subjected to the most ignominious punishment as well as the most painful, jeered at and mocked even in His agony, and to have gall given Him to drink in the last torments of His terrible thirst. There was much about Him before which gathered round Him honour and reverence, even though men could not penetrate the secret of His Divinity, but now there was to be nothing. He was to become despised and rejected of men, and so He asks His Father, Who had continually borne witness to Him in His humiliations, to take upon Himself the vindication of His honour and to glorify Him before men, in a manner fitting to the work for which He had been sent into the world by His Father, and the full accomplishment of the salvation He was about to win for men.

Our Lord's words include in their meaning the prodigies by which His Death was to be attended, the darkness over all the earth, the earthquake, the rending of the rocks and the veil of the Temple, which were all so many witnesses ordered by His Father to testify to His dignity, and which, when taken together with His most adorable patience, forced from the Roman officer himself who had charge of the details of the Crucifixion, the declaration that He was the Son of God. But perhaps our Lord was thinking more directly of the witness to Him which was to be borne, in so many different ways, all through the Christian ages, to the truth of His Mission and work in the Church and also in the world, for He speaks these words when He is no longer to appear among men, no longer to preach and to teach in His own Person, no longer to work miracles, whether of healing or of chastising power. For even His Resurrection was to have no eye-witness, and He was to work no wonders as before among the people, indeed, He was to hide Himself from the gaze of the world as much after His Resurrection as during His Passion, and the witness to the truth of His claims and the dignity of His Person, was to be borne to the world only by the few chosen for that purpose. He was to withdraw altogether from appearing before the world, which was to learn whatever it was ordained that it should learn concerning Him from the working of the Father's Providence, which our Lord now invokes. This, then, is the prayer which He now makes, that, as has been said, His Father will take up His cause and glorify Him in His Passion, Death, Resurrection, Ascension, and in all the many ways in which His Name has been honoured and exalted from that time to the end of the world.

Our Lord adds another clause to His prayer, which is not only for the glorification of His Name by the Father, but that by means of that glorification the Father may Himself be glorified. For the more the Name of our Blessed Lord is known, honoured, and glorified among men, the more is the Name of the Father glorified. The nature and character and attributes of the One Godhead become more and more clearly revealed and recognized, the mystery of the Ever Blessed Trinity in Unity is more and more known, with the work of each one of the three Divine Persons in the great dispensation of the salvation of the world by the sufferings of the Incarnate Son, and the like. God becomes known as Creator and Provider and Governor more and more clearly, and He is also revealed as redeeming His fallen creatures, as elevating them and sanctifying them and glorifying them, with a splendour of illumination fresh even to the heavenly citizens themselves, much more therefore to the poor and feeble children of man. This is the work of the whole Christian dispensation, a work which began at once with the Incarnation itself and which will continue with an ever widening blaze of light for ever. The whole of the great revelation is contained in the Person of our Lord and what He has done, for it is He that has purchased for us the gift of the Holy Ghost, Whose office it is, as the Church sings, to make known the Father and the Son and Himself. Our Lord therefore prays that His Father will bring about in the first place the glorification of His Name and the knowledge of the redemption which He has wrought, that through that and all its consequences the glory of the Father Himself may be continually increased and manifested, ever more and more, and, as the words which follow imply, the salvation of men and their consummation in the knowledge of God may be wrought out.

It may occur to us to remember what had happened a few days before this, when, as it seems, on the afternoon of the Day of Palms, the Greeks mentioned by St. John[2] as wishing to see our Lord, gave Him occasion to utter His remarkable words about the grain of wheat that must fall into the ground and die in order to become fruitful, and He

[2] St. John xii.

P 14

spoke certain words which disclose a kind of trouble in His soul, calling on the Father first to save Him from that hour, but afterwards asking simply that the Father would glorify His own Name. Then the answer came from Heaven, ' I have both glorified it and will glorify it again.' What our Lord prays for now does not seem to be quite the same thing, at least we may learn something from the difference in the words on the two several occasions. Then He asked simply that the Father would glorify His own Divine Name, now He asks Him to glorify His Son, that His Son may glorify Him. The glorification in the first case was to be a continuation of that succession of Divine acts, such as the miracles, by which the Name of the Father had come to be known and honoured among men, and especially in the course of our Lord's Ministry. It was in a manner the glorification and manifestation of our Lord Himself also, for the miracles were wrought in order that men might believe in Him also, and the Father by His voice from Heaven had promised that this should be continued. But now as we have seen, it is the glorification of our Lord as the Incarnate Son in His humiliation which is asked for, and we are reminded of the passage in which St. Paul speaks of His humiliation and consequent exaltation to the Philippians:[3] ' He humbled Himself, becoming obedient unto death, even to the death of the Cross. For which cause God also hath exalted Him, and given Him a Name which is above all names,' and the rest.

This indeed seems to be conveyed clearly in the words which follow, ' Now this is eternal life, that they may know Thee, the only true God, and Jesus

[3] Philipp. ii. 8, seq.

Christ Whom Thou hast sent '—that is, the eternal life which Thou hast given Him power to give to all whom Thou hast given to Him, consists in the knowledge of Thee, the only true God, and of Jesus Christ Whom Thou hast sent. But for this knowledge the glorification of the Name of Him Whom Thou hast sent is the means, because if His Name and His Mission and dignity are not made known to all, they will not be able to believe in Him, and receive eternal life from Him. The comparison which is implied between the power over all flesh and the glorification which our Lord asks for, implies that the desire of His Heart is that His Name may be most fully known and most widely glorified among men, in order that they may be as largely and as universally as possible the recipients of the eternal life which He has power to give. He desires that no man may fail to reap the boon which He has power to bestow, and for that purpose He asks the Father in His providence to bring about the immense glorification of His Name, that by means of that the Name of the Father also may be known to all. When our Lord calls the Eternal Father the only true God, He speaks to contrast Him with the false gods to whom divine honours were paid by the heathen all over the world, who were in truth no other than the devils whose malice was not satisfied in drawing men away from God, but went on further to impose themselves on mankind as the objects of their worship—a worship which they took care, moreover, to stain with the most infamous licentiousness as well as the greatest cruelty. He does not mention that He Himself is God, as well as the Father and the Holy Ghost, in the unity of Nature, for it is sufficient for Him to name the One Godhead which He has with

the Father and the Holy Ghost. But He names as
also necessary to eternal salvation that men must
know the truth of the Incarnation, in which God
sent His only-begotten Son into the world, that men
might be saved through faith in Him. He sets no
limits to the extent and universality of the knowledge
of these great truths which are necessary to eternal
life, because, according to the intention and desire of
our Lord, there is no one to be excluded from this
salvation, and therefore He prays the Father to exalt
and make known His Name everywhere, although
there can be no violence done to human liberty, and
therefore the actual result, as to the glorification of
His Name and the spread of the knowledge of God,
may be and is fearfully hindered by the faults of men
who may be, in the first place, unfaithful to the duty
of promulgating the Gospel, and, in the second place,
obstinate in rejecting it when it is proposed to them
by the Catholic Church.

The prayer of our Lord, then, is that the glorification of His Name and of the Name of His Father
which is to follow on His humiliation in the Passion,
may correspond to the power of giving eternal life
to all who have been given to Him by the Father.
This power, it need hardly be said, is not that which
He has as God and always had from the beginning,
but the power conferred upon Him as Man and in
His Humanity the Redeemer of mankind, by God
Who gives what He did not possess of right in
His Human Nature, but what it was fitting that He
should receive as having sacrificed Himself as Man
for man.

Our Lord continues, after having specified His
petition for the great extension of the knowledge
of Him among men, to speak of what He has hitherto

accomplished up to the time of the Passion. His work up to the present time is complete. ' I have glorified Thee upon earth, I have finished the work which Thou gavest Me to do. And now glorify Thou Me, O Father, with Thyself, with the glory which I had, before the world was, with Thee.' This is a different petition from that which He has just made. It is not for the glory of His Name, and the immense diffusion of His honour and Kingdom. What He asks is still for His Sacred Humanity, but it is that in that Humanity He may receive the glory which belongs to Him as a Divine Person, the glory of the ineffable Godhead. This was always His own by right, but it had been suspended in order to the sufferings and humiliations which He was to undergo, and now He asks that it may be given Him as Man, for all that He receives as Man is a matter of prayer, though He could take in and give it to Himself as God. In the whole course of His Ministry He had glorified His Father by teaching the truth, by revealing His character and especially His love for man, for whose salvation He had sent His only-begotten Son to save them. He had accomplished the work that the Father had given Him to do by showing how He was indeed His Son sent for the redemption of the world, by His preaching and His witness to the truth and faithfulness of God, and also by His Death and the execution of the decree of redemption, for although that was not actually accomplished as yet, He was on the eve of its accomplishment, and our Lord speaks of it as performed, for it was actually in course of being so. Judas was already, now for some hours, perhaps, arranging the steps which were to be taken for His apprehension, the false witnesses were being gathered, the wicked judges were being warned to hold themselves in readiness, the bands of armed men were being assembled, and the whole plot was ready for its execution. So our Lord Who is now praying aloud and in the presence of the Apostles, in order that they may hear His prayer and remember it afterwards, speaks of the work given Him to be done in the Passion, as already completed.

The language used by our Lord should be carefully considered, as it contains more truths than may at once appear. The glory which He asks as Man to be communicated to His Sacred Humanity is that which He had with His Father before the world was, and therefore it must be that which belongs to Him as God, and is therefore contained in the Divine Essence and Nature. When our Lord took flesh, it was with the intention and purpose of suffering for the sins of men, and the glory of which He speaks, if shared by His Humanity, would not have been convenient for that design. It was therefore suspended in the Sacred Humanity, the Divinity that united to itself that Sacred Human Nature would otherwise have shone through and permeated the whole of the Human Nature, and made it glorious. When the work of redemption was accomplished, and the Soul of our Lord once more united to His Body,—which, as well as the Soul, had never for an instant been separated from the Divinity,—at the Resurrection, the glory of which we speak became the property of the Body, and was only withheld from the eyes of those who saw Him in order to spare them the effects which it might have produced in them, carrying them out of themselves, and being something more than they could bear. It could not be that the Humanity of our Lord was transformed into the Divinity, but the inherent Divinity gave it a splendour and glory of its own, as the sun gives its splendour to the earth on which it shines, and as the blessed are made glorious with the light of the Divinity on which they gaze. There is, however, a difference between the glory of which our Lord speaks here, and that of any of the blessed inhabitants of Heaven. For to all these the glory which makes them glorious comes from without in the first instance, though it may be that their soul receives it and imparts it to the body. But in the case of our Lord's Sacred Humanity, the glory with which it is glorious comes from within, because our Lord is both God and Man, one Divine Person in two Natures. It is therefore His own glory which He had before the world was, and has not received, and Toletus tells us that from this language of our Lord it is fairly and truly argued that He is God. This is language which cannot be used of any of the saints who, before the world was, may have been chosen or predestined to receive it, but who have not had it till they have received it in the appointed time.

The words here used seem very exactly to correspond to the words in St. Luke in the account of our Lord's discourse on Easter Day to the two disciples on the road to Emmaus, 'Ought not Christ to have suffered these things, and so to enter into His glory?' Our Lord here speaks of His accomplishing the work given Him to do. This is the same thing as to say that it was ordained that He should suffer certain things. The suffering being over, the dispensation by which His glory was held in abeyance was accomplished. So He says, 'And now glorify Me, Father, with Thyself, with the glory which I had, before the world was, with Thee.' He asks to be glorified with the glory which is His own, as St. Luke says, He was to enter into His glory that is His own. He had never parted with His glory, for it was always His own, not only by right, as it were, but in act, but He had taken to Himself a body which had no glory, in order that He might therein be able to suffer for us. The word 'now' has a sense of illation and causation, as if it had been said, Now, therefore, the work of My humiliation being performed, I ask Thee to let My Body be glorified, as the reason for the suspension of its glory can no longer impede it from entering on its full possession.

We may perhaps pause here for a few moments, for the sake of making a few remarks on the prayer on which we are commenting, which admits of being considered both as to the meaning of the words of which it consists, and also as a prayer presenting certain subjects in humble and confident and loving entreaty to the Divine Person to Whom it is directed. There is of course a great deal to be learnt from it in every way, both from its considerations simply as an outpouring of supplication, and as an instance of prayer in the larger sense, in which it is spoken of as an elevation of the mind and heart to God, which is the old definition of prayer. The prayer before us contains comparatively few direct petitions, and in this we see the difference which distinguishes it from the Lord's Prayer, as we commonly call it, which consists of a string of very short and pregnant petitions. The Lord's Prayer was meant for daily and continual use, and it would not serve that object if it had been made longer and more diffuse. The prayer now before us is probably an instance of the loving and familiar though deeply reverent manner in which the Sacred Heart was

accustomed to open Itself on such occasions. There
are not more than very few matters of distinct petition
contained in the verses on which we have hitherto
dwelt, and as the prayer proceeds to its close we
shall not find the number greatly increased. The
language reminds us somewhat of that of the Psalms,
in which the various affections of the devout heart to
God succeed one the other, passing from petition to
what is called obsecration, and then to acknowledgment of need, or weakness, or fear of spiritual
enemies, and supplication against them, and the like.
The first petition here made is that the Father will
glorify His Son, and the clauses that inclose as it
were the petition, call on Him by that loving name
in which our Lord delighted, and which was in itself
a prayer of most winning efficacy, pleading to Him to
Whom it was addressed all the most powerful titles,
if we may so speak, of Him Who made the prayer,
on His justice, and His mercy, and the intense love
with which He was regarded by His Father, Who
had sent Him into the world. The next clause, in
which mention is made of the hour being now come,
is also a most forcible pleading for the granting of
what our Lord now asks. And then is added another
motive to the same effect, namely, that the Son may
in turn glorify the Father, Whom He asks to glorify
Him, for He seems to ask His own glorification for
the purpose that it may enable Him to increase the
glorification of the Father. What is meant by the
glorification which is here asked of the Son by
the Father has been already explained. We are
now engaged in pointing out how rich in spiritual
affections the words which are here recorded appear
to be. We cannot doubt that everything which is
mentioned or implied is meant to be subordinated to

the main object of what is said, which seems to be
the petition, made to the Eternal Father by our Lord
in His Sacred Humanity, for the granting of the
glorification which is asked almost as if it had been
said, ' Father, I ask this because the hour is come,
and because Thou hast given Me power to give
eternal life to all those whom Thou hast given Me,
and because this eternal life is nothing less than the
knowledge of Thyself, the only true God, and even
beyond that, the knowledge of Jesus Christ, Whom
Thou hast sent, and because I have given Thee the
glory which Thou hast received from Me on earth,
and because that great and most glorious work which
Thou hast entrusted to Me here below is finished—
for all these reasons, and by all these titles, I ask
now that Thou wilt glorify Me with Thyself with the
glory which I had, before the world was, with Thee.'

There is a strain of intense loving gratitude running through the whole context, which may also be
dwelt upon in meditation. Our Lord could not tell
His Father that the long looked for hour was now
come without a glow of thankfulness filling His
Heart, nor could the thought of the power over all
flesh of giving eternal life to those who had been
given Him, rise to His mind without the same
affection suggesting itself. These things are mentioned here for the sake of pointing out the multitude
and variety of affections which were probably included in any converse held by our Lord with His
Father in prayer, not of course with any idea of
exhausting this most fascinating topic. To attempt
this would be a task beyond our limits, but it may
have been well to open the field of such extraordinary richness, especially as it might not have
been self-evident that what we may call the con-

siderations by which the main object of petition in the few verses before us are supported by our Lord do not form, any more than in the Lord's Prayer itself, in which they are entirely omitted, a part of the prayer itself in the strictest sense, that is, they belong to the prayer in the larger sense of the name, as it is 'converse with God,' they do not belong to it as it is a simple petition and nothing more. We consider the thing asked in the few verses of which we have spoken, to be the glorification of our Lord by the action of His Father, in the sense which has been explained, and that the rest of the words in the paragraph before us are, as has been said, subordinate to that petition, breathing as they do the tenderest and most earnest love of the Sacred Heart. In the words which immediately succeed, our Lord seems to pass on to another subject of prayer.

The next words of our Lord speak of those for whom He is praying to His Father in this Divine prayer, and whom He has already mentioned virtually, when He has said that He has had power given unto Him to give eternal life to all that have been given Him, and that He has finished the work that He had been given by the Father to do. The disciples have been the subjects of the work of ministration which He had received. Of these, then, He says, 'I have manifested Thy Name to the men whom Thou hast given Me out of the world. Thine they were, and to Me Thou gavest them, and they have kept Thy word. Now they have known that all things which Thou hast given Me are from Thee. Because the words which Thou gavest Me I have given them, and they have received them, and have known in very deed that I came out from Thee, and they have believed that Thou didst send Me.' This is the foundation and beginning of the great prayer that follows, and it is well that we should consider it in the first place by itself. The first thing that He says of the Apostles is that they were the Father's own, and that He had given them to Him, the Incarnate Son, out of the world; then, that He had manifested to them, so given to Him, the Name of the Father Who gave them, and then they had kept the word of the Father which had been manifested to them. 'They have kept Thy word.' In the first place, then, they belonged to God, not simply as all created things and all men are His, good as well as bad, by virtue of His rights as their Creator and Sustainer, but because He had chosen them for certain great gifts and vocations, which it is always in the power of God to dispose of to whom He pleases. He tells us in another place that no one could come to Himself as a disciple unless the Father draws him, and the drawing is an effect of the power of His omnipotence and free choice.

Having thus received them from the hand of His Father, He had manifested the name of His Father to them. That is to say, He had taught them many truths concerning His Father which they knew before only indistinctly, for the Father was revealed to them with comparative incompleteness.

Such, for instance, was the truth that God was the Father of a consubstantial and coequal Son, Whom out of love He was to send into the world, in the nature of man, to be the Redeemer of mankind, that all who believed in Him might not be lost. Such were many other things concerning His will and law, such the truth that He was about also to send the Holy Ghost into the world in a new manner, to be the Sanctifier of men, and the like.

All these things, and many more, were a message of the Father to men concerning Himself, which message was to be delivered to them by the Son sent into the world, which would explain to them the purpose of the Mission and the Office of Him Who was thus sent to be the Redeemer and Saviour and Teacher of mankind. This great message was to shed a light, either not possessed by men before, or at least not fully possessed, concerning the fatherly character and love of God, Who seemed to be by many nations almost unknown altogether, and to the most enlightened, excepting the Jews, was hardly recognized fully as the Creator and Provider and Ruler of the world which He had made.

Our Lord adds, in the second place, that those whom the Father had given Him, and to whom He had manifested the name of the Father, have kept His Father's words. By this He seems to mean that they had received and accepted the doctrine which had been taught them by Him as from the Father, and had believed the claims which He had made on their faith by the evidence on which they had been supported. He had found them docile disciples, although they had been slow to understand Him and to take in the lofty spiritual truths which He had set before them. This is further expanded in the sentence which follows. 'Now they have known,' or come to know, 'that all things which Thou hast given Me are from Thee.' Their faith had grown so far that they had recognized that what He taught them was from God, the doctrines from God, the statements of fact from God, and the miracles and other proofs which they had received of His Divine Mission from God. Indeed, as we know, the Apostles had come, by the gradual guidance of

the Father in His Providence, to recognize in our Lord
no less a messenger than the Incarnate Son Himself,
Who had been promised as the Saviour of the world.
All that they had heard and seen, during their long
familiarity with our Lord, had tended to create this
blessed faith in their hearts—the beauty and gra-
ciousness of His character, the purity and heavenli-
ness of His doctrine, the splendour of the virtues
that He practised, His wonderful charity and condescension and humility, the agreement of His whole
history with the prophetic writings and the Law, and
the whole system which had prepared the chosen
people for so many ages for His coming.   After this
came the witness of the Baptist, of whom they had,
in many cases, been disciples before he sent them
to our Lord, and the miracles of mercy and power
by which the Father Himself had attested the truth
of His claims.   'Because the words which Thou
hast given Me I have given to them, and they have
received them, and have known in very truth that I
came out from Thee, and they have believed that
Thou didst send Me.'

For our Lord's words were not confined to simple
moral teaching, but they included also many statements about Himself, both direct and indirect, from
which it was natural to infer, if men's hearts were
not hardened, that He meant them to understand
more than He said of Himself.   For He always
called Himself the Son of Man, and spoke in other
ways humbly and lowlily of Himself.   Yet that He
was also more than Man might also have been understood by the authority with which He spoke in His
teaching, and which He showed also in His manner
of working miracles and casting out devils.   All
this led up to the faith of which mention was made

just now, that He was the Son of God. This is what is meant by the words that ‘they have believed that I came out from Thee, that they have known in very truth that I came out from Thee,’ not as a simple messenger as others sent by God, which is signified rather in the first clause of the sentence, but as directly proceeding, by generation and of the same substance with Him from Whom He thus came forth. Our Lord thus declares the fulness of the faith in His Divinity, which He calls in the Apostles knowledge, and also their faith in His Humanity.

What our Lord here states concerning the Apostles, that they have grown in their faith to the point of believing, not merely that He has been sent by the Eternal Father as a messenger or preacher of truth into the world, but that He comes forth from Him as His only-begotten Son, one in substance and Divinity with Himself, and also that He was sent from God, not only as a Prophet or Teacher, but as the Messias Who had been foretold of old as the Redeemer of the world, is a magnificent witness to their faith. These truths were contained in the words ‘that the Father had given Him,’ and the Apostles had received them, and had known in very truth that His Mission was nothing short of this, and that this was the fact concerning His character and His Person. His enemies, such as Caiphas, had divined that He would not deny that He claimed as much as this, though He would never answer them in so many words, until the time came when the High Priest adjured Him to tell them the truth, not for the purpose of believing it, but in order to found on His statement the charge of blasphemy. As we see from the words of St. Martha at the time of the miracle on Lazarus, this truth, which had been formally confessed by St. Peter long before, was the short form of ordinary confession of faith concerning Him among the near friends and disciples of our Lord. When this is kept in mind, we understand a little better the distinction which our Lord presently makes between His near disciples and the rest of the world, who had not any faith in Him of this kind.

'I pray for them, I pray not for the world, but for those whom Thou hast given Me, because they are Thine. And all My things are Thine, and Thine are Mine, and I am glorified in them. And now I am not in the world, and these are in the world, and I come to Thee.' Our Lord may have had other reasons for making the particular petitions which are here made for the disciples whom He was to leave behind Him in the world, but there is a peculiar tenderness in His making the prayer known to them while He was pouring it forth to the Father, that they might hear the words which express so much love and care for them, as well as the one principal thing which He asks for them, as we shall see. In a prayer thus made in the presence and hearing of those whom He so much loves, is conveyed to them the knowledge of what it is that He feels most anxious that they should receive, and if their hearts are like His, what it is that they should most of all pray for themselves and attempt to secure from God by every possible means in their power. His prayer cannot be made with any defect of reasonableness or propriety, such as would be a prayer for the pardon of sinners who do not repent of their sins, or for the salvation of unbelievers who will not believe. He Who knows the state of each one will ask for each one that particular grace for which there is a disposition in the soul, and which if granted may lead him on to others by fitting him for them. The things which our Lord here asks for those who are His own, He could not well ask for those who were not His in any sense, as we shall see.

This seems to be the reason why He here says that He prays for them and not for the world. Not that there were not many things to be prayed for for the world, or that any human souls, as long as this time of probation remains, are outside the care and therefore the prayer of the Redeemer of all, but that the prayer He is now making is for graces that His own are fit to receive, and others not fit. It is of no use to ask for men of the world given up to passions and pleasures, who have no faith in God, and no sense of religion, the special graces which are here mentioned as asked for those who were the Father's, and whom He had given to the Son as His Apostles and saints, while, at the same time, it is equally true that those who belong to God by a true faith and obedience may yet be raised continually higher and higher in the knowledge of what they believed and in the practice of the virtues which are enjoined on them by the law of God. But it is for such that our Lord now makes this prayer, seeing what they specially need and what they are fit to receive by virtue of this prayer of His, which cannot but have a special efficacy from the Person Who makes it, and the occasion on which it is made. He was about to offer Himself a sacrifice on the Cross for the whole world, and no one was to be shut out from the pardon which that Sacrifice was to win except by the fault of his own will, which was to be the case with but too many who might have had a share in the salvation so freely offered to them.

Our Lord, as we shall see presently, was about to ask certain special and great boons for His own, and He did not ask them for those who were not yet His own. These boons were what He calls the keeping of them in His Name by the Father, as He had hitherto kept them, while with them, and that through this they might be one, as He and the Father are one, as St. Paul puts it, by the preservation of the unity of the Spirit in the bond of peace, and other like graces. These things He asks then for the Apostles and those whom they represent. They had been and still were the Father's own, and the Father had given them to Him as the Incarnate Son in His Human Nature, but He adds words which signify His oneness with the Father in His Divine Nature, when He says, ‘And all My things are Thine, and Thine are Mine, and I am glorified in them,’ that is, by their faith in Me, that I came from Thee and am one with Thee. I receive in My Sacred Humanity the glory of which I have already spoken. This glory has accrued to Me from them already, and therefore it is meet to ask for them the further boons of which I am about to speak, and which will add so much to My glory, seeing I am now about to leave them. ‘And now I am not in the world, and these are in the world, and I come to Thee.’ The condition of the Apostles, left in the world among so many enemies and dangers, and without the visible presence of our Lord to protect, guide, and encourage them, was in itself enough to make them objects of pity, notwithstanding the continual care which God would have over them, and the many spiritual aids with which they were to be provided. They would feel themselves alone for the first time since they had known our Lord, and the hearing these words from Him would be an immense support and strength to them.

What He prays for them, then, is expressed in the words which follow. ' Holy Father, keep them in Thy name whom Thou hast given to Me, that they may be one, as We also are one.' It is worth while to notice that our Lord in this place in the prayer does as He does elsewhere in this same great teaching, that is, He calls on the Father by an especial attribute, which in this case is the attribute of Holiness. ' Holy Father, keep in Thy name those whom Thou hast given Me, that they may be one, as We are.' It is generally to be understood as to the attributes by which God is addressed in any prayer, that it is meant thereby that the petition is especially made for an exercise or display, in the granting it, of the attribute that is particularly mentioned. Thus the Omnipotence and the Mercifulness of God are the attributes which are the most frequently appealed to, because we most often ask that those attributes may be exercised when we address Him in prayer. In the case before us the prayer is that the Apostles may be kept in the name of the Father, so that they may be one, as the Father and our Lord are one. It would seem therefore that the boon asked for them is connected with the attribute of Sanctity, and indeed we cannot imagine any attribute which is more plainly exemplified than this in the perfect unity of the Church, which is the work of the Holy Ghost, the Sanctifier of souls, and which, as our Lord implies in the words which He uses a little further on, is to be the great evidence to the world of the perpetual presence of His Holy Spirit in the Church, a kind of evidence which the world itself cannot gainsay or evade.

'That the world may know that Thou hast sent Me.'

The prayer is two-fold, that the Father will keep them in His name, that they may be one, as He and the Father are. The latter portion of the sentence is the consequence of the former. The first question which occurs to us is what is the exact meaning of their being kept in the name of the Father? It seems to be much the same with what our Lord in the next sentence speaks. 'While I was with them I kept them in Thy name,' and it is much the same in the former words: 'I have manifested Thy name to the men whom Thou gavest Me out of the world, . . . and they have kept Thy word.' He says again that 'those whom Thou gavest Me, I have kept, and none of them is lost, save the son of perdition, that the Scripture may be fulfilled.' Our Lord asks the Father to keep the Apostles in the name in which He had Himself kept them while He was with them, and from which one alone had been lost, the son of perdition, in accordance with the Scriptures, which had foretold what God had determined to permit in the case of Judas, on account of his own bad correspondence to the great graces of the Apostolate which he had received.

When our Lord says that He has kept those whom the Father had given Him, and that none of them is lost save the son of perdition, that the Scripture might be fulfilled, the language requires to be carefully attended to. Judas, of whom He speaks, is numbered among those whom the Father had given to Him. But he was given to our Lord in a different sense from the others, for it was not the will of the Father that Judas should be kept permanently in His name, like the rest, as is shown by the manner in which St. John speaks of them in the following chapter, when our Lord provided for their safety by securing them an unmolested flight, on which act of our Lord's St. John remarks that it brought about the fulfilment of the word He had said, ' Of them whom Thou hast given Me, I have not lost any one.'[4] Judas therefore was an exception as the son of perdition, that is, the man preordained to incur perdition. Not that our Lord had not kept him, up to a certain point, as the rest, not that he might not have been kept as the rest if he had used the graces furnished to him faithfully, but that on account of his unfaithfulness he had been allowed to fall, and our Lord knowing that he was to be allowed to fall, had not exerted for him any extraordinary providence, which might conceivably have rescued him, even after his obstinate rejection of the graces which he had received, by some interposition of pre-ternatural power beyond the usual limits of mercy, but not beyond the absolute possibilities of God's great clemency. Our Lord seems here to give as His reason for not exerting this extraordinary power, His knowledge of the Divine resolve by which the fall of Judas was to be permitted and not prevented, a resolve embodied in the prophecy of which He speaks. The Scripture had registered the decree of God which was to have its fulfilment in Judas, and his obduracy in evil, against all the touching over-tures from our Lord by which his heart was con-tinually assailed, made it impossible that he should be saved from the consequences. But it was his own will and choice that determined the issue, not any hardness or want of mercifulness on the part of his Master. We may also remember that the per-

[4] St. John xviii. 9.

dition of the lost Apostle was not consummated at this time. It was not finally and irreparably accomplished either by the betrayal, or the kiss, or the condemnation of our Lord by the Jewish tribunals or the Roman Governor. It became irretrievable by nothing but by the despair and suicide of that miserable man, for our Lord's Heart was open to him till the very last.

To be kept in the name of God seems to mean, then, what our Lord had just before spoken of in the case of the Apostles, who had received the words which the Father had given our Lord to give to them, that is, the revelation and instruction which had been proposed to their faith, concerning God Himself and the Mission of our Lord, 'They have received the words, and have known in very deed that I came out from Thee, and they have believed that Thou didst send Me.' It was on this true faith concerning the Father and Him Whom He had sent into the world for the salvation of mankind that had been founded the whole of the spiritual progress, and growth in virtue and knowledge of the Apostles, and their formation into that moral and spiritual community from which Judas had separated himself already—though he was not hopelessly lost—when he went forth from the Cenacle, as the Apostle sent by our Lord on a temporary mission, as they supposed, but with his apostacy from the band of the disciples perfectly accomplished in will and in heart. So our Lord speaks of him as already lost.

With the true faith as revealed to them by the testimony of our Lord, there came to the Apostles a growth in virtue, in knowledge of the law of God, in obedience, in concord, and mutual charity, in what St. John in his Epistles calls 'fellowship' in all the qualities which constitute the character of the members of the One Body of which St. Paul speaks, or the branches of the One Vine of which our Lord has taught them in His last discourse. This is that Oneness which He here desires from the Father from them, 'that they may be one as We are One.' St. Peter sketches this process in his second Epistle,[5] where he says, ' And you, giving all diligence, join with your faith virtue, and with virtue knowledge, and with knowledge abstinence, and with abstinence patience, and with patience godliness, and with godliness brotherly love, and with brotherly love charity.' As our Lord came not only to teach and train the Apostles, but also to found the organized body which He left behind Him to carry on His work under the guidance of the Holy Ghost, the 'name' of the Father into which He had gathered His followers whom God had given to Him, was in truth that Body which afterwards was known to the world externally as the Catholic Church. And there is a reference to this Body wherever He speaks of their being gathered in His Name, or in the name of the Father, though He does not mention in detail the several parts of the organization, as the life of the whole was to be from within, and those who had the growth of virtues described by St. Peter, would not be at all likely to rebel against the external order and discipline of the living Body to which they belonged. Decay in virtue is certain to precede the outward breach of unity among Christians, and where the growth of virtue is perfect, there can never arise questions about authority, except through misunderstandings which are corrected with comparative

[5] 2 St. Peter i. 5—7.

ease. In a prayer like this to the Father, it would not have been natural for our Lord to speak of the preservation of the Apostles from sins which would have placed them at once on a level with the children of the world for whom He does not pray, such as disobedience to appointed rulers in the Church, heresies and schisms. Nevertheless, this prayer witnesses most strongly to the value which His Sacred Heart set upon external unity, as well as on purity of faith, both of which are absolutely essential to that unity of which He speaks, which is the great subject of the prayer, and which therefore we are . right in considering as the one thing beyond all others, as will be shown presently, on which His most ardent desires for the Church are fastened, and which He more than once in the course of these few verses, expressly mentions as the one visible characteristic—by the sight of which the world was to be converted to faith in Him, and to the acknowledgment of the truth of His Mission by the Father.

'And now I come to Thee, and these things I speak in the world that they may have My joy fulfilled in themselves.' This is not the first occasion on which we meet with this expression of joy being fulfilled in a person or in persons, and it does not seem always easy to explain what is meant. It may mean simply that the joy of the person who speaks may be fulfilled, because he sees in others the cause of joy which is made full. Or it may mean that the persons spoken of may have in themselves the fulness of that joy which the speaker feels on a certain account, into which they enter, to use an expression of our Lord's in one of the parables, that is, which they share and have in its fulness, because they share in that which causes it. Or it may mean that the persons spoken of may be the causes of joy in some very full and great measure to the speaker. In the first case the joy of which our Lord speaks here would be truly in the disciples, in the second case they would be the causes of it to Him. Early in this Gospel we find a similar expression used by the Blessed Baptist of his own joy in the success of our Lord in winning the hearts of men, where he compares himself to the friend of the bridegroom who stands and hears the voice of the latter conversing with his bride. 'This my joy therefore is fulfilled.' St. Luke tells us[6] of one of the few occasions of which our Lord spoke of His joy in the revelation of the tidings of the Gospel to the little ones to the exclusion of the wise and prudent, because so it had seemed good in the eyes of the Father. We cannot doubt that our Lord's Heart was habitually inundated with the purest and deepest joy, and that the first great source of it came from the thought of His Father, and from the fact that He was in every detail of His Life doing the things that were pleasing to the Father then and there. He said to His disciples, who had left Him wearied and exhausted by the side of Jacob's well, and who wished Him to take some refreshment after His long walk in the heat of the day, that His meat was to do the will of Him that sent Him, and to perfect His work. Next to the joy which was always present to the Sacred Heart in this fulfilment of the will of the Father in every detail of His human life, may be placed that of which He speaks in the passage just now quoted, in seeing the revelation which He was sent to proclaim communicated to and bearing fruit in the

<hr>

[6] St. Luke x. 21.

hearts of the little ones to whom it was preached by Him. This is especially the joy of apostolic hearts, and we find St. Paul more than once speaking of his disciples as his crown and joy.[7]

Toletus illustrates the passage on which we are engaged, by quoting some words of the Apostle to the Philippians[8] in which he seems almost to echo the very words which our Lord here utters. St. Paul is entreating his spiritual children to make his joy in them perfect by great union and peace with one another. ' Fulfil ye my joy, that you be of one mind, having the same charity, being of one accord, of one agreeing in sentiment, let nothing be done through strife nor by vainglory, but in humility,' and then he goes on to the celebrated words about the imitation of the humility of Christ. The great commentator whom we have named thinks that the words before us refer to the joy which our Lord derives from the perfect following of Himself by the Apostles. But the Greek words of the original hardly seem to permit of this interpretation, for it is not said that our Lord's joy may be fulfilled in them, but that they may have His joy fulfilled in them, and that He speaks these things in the world that so it may be. The words spoken in this world seem to be spoken that they may hear them, and our Lord does not simply ask this boon for them, as in other clauses of the prayer, but lets them know that He asks this in order that it may have a special effect upon them. It seems therefore more natural to think that the joy which He asks that they may have in its fulness in themselves, is the joy with which His own Heart was so familiar that He calls it *His* in some peculiar way, the joy of perfect

<hr>

[7] Philipp. iv. 1 ; 1 Thessal. xi. 19.   [8] Philipp. ii. 2.

obedience to His Father's will, and of seeing the fruit of His work among others. And we must not forget that He has just mentioned the consummate perfection of their obedience, and of their work in others, which He desires for them in order that their joy may be perfectly full, that is, that they may be One as He and His Father are One. This, again, is the perfection which St. Paul mentions in the passage just quoted from the Epistle to the Philippians. Our Lord then seems here to pray that the Apostles may have in their own hearts the perfect fulness of joy, which was in His caused by the continual consciousness of His own perfect fulfilment of the will of the Father, and of the fruitfulness with which that obedience was blessed.

We are tempted to think that the joy of our Lord may have some further special meaning in different passages in which the phrase may occur, though it may be safer to interpret it as has been done here, as that which was ordinarily and habitually the joy of the Sacred Heart. In the place before us, our Lord has particularly before His mind the great object of His special prayer to the Father, that the disciples may be kept in His Name, that they may be one, 'as We also are.' He is now urging this special petition for them by various considerations upon the Father, and He says that He speaks these things in the world which He is about to leave in order that the Apostles may have ' My joy filled in themselves.' Does it not seem natural that the words may refer to that peculiar joy which may have been in His Heart from the contemplation of this special subject of the unity and peace and mutual charity which He looked forward to as the characteristic features of the Body which He was to leave behind Him to bear His own and His Father's name in the world ?   There could be nothing in the result of His work or that of the Apostles which could fill His Heart with so much joy as this.   Nor could the Apostles for whom He asks this great boon find anything in their condition among the dangers of the world more likely to fill them with consolation than the possession of this gift of unity, whatever might be the storms which might assail their little flock from external enemies.   It is this which strikes us in reading the Epistles, that the general tone of the minds of those whose character they reflect must have been one of joy, founded on the possession of the ' peace which surpasseth all understanding.' And the children of the Church know in some measure the ineffable blessing and the joy that comes from the firm and unchangeable unity of which we are speaking.   ' Behold, how good and pleasant a thing it is for brethren to dwell together in unity ! like the precious ointment on the head that ran down upon the beard, the beard of Aaron, which ran down to the skirts of his garment, as the dew of Hermon which descended upon Mount Sion ! for there the Lord hath commanded blessing, and life for evermore.'

' I have given them Thy word, and the world hath hated them because they are not of the world, as I also am not of the world.'   Up to this point He has said nothing in this prayer about the treatment that the Apostles would be exposed to from the world, in which He was leaving them.   He now turns to this subject, of which He has already spoken in the discourse to the disciples themselves, preparing them for the great sufferings and persecutions which were in store for them from the world.   ' I have given them Thy word, and the world hath hated them because they are not of the world, as I also am not of the world.' The conjunction 'and' has here the force of causation, as if He had said, 'Therefore the world hath hated them.' This is the sufficient reason why there can never be men who truly belong to our Lord, and have His word and His commission to preach it to the world, whom the world can welcome gratefully and kindly. The reason is that the men who are sent with the Word of God in their mouths may be ever so amiable and sweet in character, they may have their hands full of gifts of mercy and charity, they may even be armed beside with power to authenticate their teaching with wonderful signs of power, as our Lord Himself was. But the world can never, as long as it remains what it is, forgive them for the message which they bring, which is indeed full of comfort and promise to the souls of men, but which is a sentence of condemnation upon the world, and of denunciation of punishment on its wicked ways. The world can never put up with men who do not belong to it. It may hesitate for a moment before it assaults them savagely, but when they have shown themselves in their true colours, the world must turn against them in all its fury, or deny its own character by submission and repentance, and then it becomes no longer the world in the sense in which our Lord speaks. As long as the messengers of God are faithful to the Word with which God sends them, however winning and beneficent they may be in themselves, the Word which they have to deliver makes the world feel that they are its deadliest enemies. It was this that set the world against our Lord, and it is this that sets it against His Apostles.

The Apostles might perhaps have thought that their own future was not to be any lot which would separate them from our Lord. Either they would be working with Him in the victorious establishment of His Kingdom, or, if they had penetrated the secret that He was not to be long on earth Himself, their wishes would have led them to ask that where He was there also they might be with Him. In the same way they probably longed for the continuation of their loving brotherly intercourse one with another. If during the months which had passed since their call into the community which had formed itself around Him, each one had become intensely attached to His personal presence, it may also be thought they had become much attached to the members who had shared his own privileges as a follower of our Lord. The one thing they would naturally shrink from the most would be the prospect of separation from one another and of the absence of their Master. The apostolical life was a lonely one, of which they were to learn by experience the trials, the labours, the anxieties, and the ineffable consolations, while it was to be at the same time the training of their souls in spiritual manliness and mature strength and perfection. It must have been a trial to them to hear Him say that He did not wish them to be taken out of the world, but that they were to be left in the world without Him, and to be kept and shielded from evil, or the evil one. In time they might come to see that the lot which He had chosen for them was the noblest, though the most laborious that they could have. They might come to understand that what was for their own spiritual advantage in so wonderful a degree was also the lot in which they could labour and suffer most for Him, and have the largest share in that which He was fond of speaking of as His own most full and perfect joy. But that time was not at first. The immediate prospect before them was that they were to be left exposed to all that the enmity of the world can bring upon them in the way of persecution and suffering, for their own greater sanctification and for the salvation of thousands of souls. They are to be left in the world without their Master as to His visible presence, though we have gathered in the discourse on which we have had to comment how many beautiful and tender and most powerful provisions He was to make, and had already made, for their comfort and support, so that their new condition was to be more abundantly supplied with helps and resources than their former condition before the Passion was accomplished.

He does not pray that they may be saved from danger and persecution, but that they may suffer nothing that can impair the beauty and purity of their souls in the course of all the trials and persecutions to which they are to be exposed. 'I pray not that Thou shouldst take them out of the world, but that Thou shouldst keep them from evil.' The life which they were to lead was to be full of the grandest opportunities of merit and increase in grace, if only no evil came near their souls. St. Peter and St. John must have longed to be delivered from the miseries of their exile, and this longing to be with Christ, which St. Paul says would be much better than staying on here, must have been felt, most of all, by our Blessed Lady herself, who had yet to wait fifteen years after the Ascension of her Son, before she passed to her throne in Heaven. St. Paul, in the passage we have referred to, speaks of remaining yet awhile for the sake of the faithful. This exile of the saints of God has always been greatly for the salvation of the world. The world always contains a number of saintly souls who are fit for Heaven, and whose hearts are already entirely there, who by their sufferings and prayers and example and influence are the salt of the earth. Some of them have said that if they had the choice given them of working yet longer for God on the one hand, and of being transplanted at once to Heaven on the other, they would prefer the former, even though there might be some uncertainty about their own salvation,— they would prefer the opportunity of suffering and working yet longer for God. Our Lord prays for the Apostles that the Father in His Providence will keep them from evil. He repeats here what He has said before, that 'they are not of the world, as I also am not of the world,' they have nothing in common with the world, which therefore hates them.

Not only so, but their not being of the world is to be the foundation in them of still greater and greater sanctification. This is one reason why they are left in the world, in this stage of their course, which gives them the opportunity of growing in grace. 'Sanctify them in truth. Thy word is truth. As Thou hast sent Me into the world, I have also sent them into the world. And for them also do I sanctify Myself, that they also may be sanctified in the truth.' Here are three statements made by our Blessed Lord concerning the presence of the Apostles, and of the Church, after them, in the world. The first is that as our Lord was not of the world, so also are they not of the world. The second is that, as is implied, they are to be in the world to be sanctified in the truth, or, as some copies have it in the Greek text, in the truth which is Thine, in Thy truth, and it is added, that the word of the Father is truth, or the truth of which He speaks. The third statement is that our Lord has sent them into the world, not merely left them in the world, but given them a mission in the world like His own—' As Thou hast sent Me into the world, I have also sent them into the world,' and this statement contains the further truth that their mission by our Lord is a continuation and sequel of His own mission by the Father. There is therefore every reason why they should be left in the world, notwithstanding the departure of their Master. For they have a work to do in the world, a continuation of His work and mission, and in which the process of their sanctification is to be brought about, for the profit of their own souls and for the glory of God, and this process is to consist or be connected with what our Lord speaks of as the truth of the Father, in which He prays that they may be sanctified.

One of our great commentators[9] remarks on this passage that it furnishes an instance of the manner in which our Lord was wont to use indefinite language which had some ambiguity to the hearers. It is perhaps true that the words are not quite clear in their meaning, as it seems, while a certain hidden doctrine is conveyed by them. But the very brevity of the sentence necessarily requires explanation. The words are meant to be pondered deeply, and then they will certainly repay any labour and thought that may have been devoted to them. Our Lord is speaking of the Divine reason which He had for leaving the Apostles behind Him in the world,

[9] See Maldonatus, in loc.

R 14

which was to be to them a scene of continual trial and persecution, and He prays for certain graces for them, which may make the remaining behind Him profitable to themselves and to the cause of God.   He has spoken of the joy which He wishes them to have fulfilled in themselves, and this joy of His we have endeavoured to explain as the delight with which His Heart was flooded in doing constantly, as He Himself said, the things which pleased His Father, and in seeing in others the fruit of His work for souls.   Of this joy He wishes the Apostles to be made partakers to the full.   It is for the carrying on of this work that the Apostles are to be left in the world.   Our Lord has also added that He has given to them the word of His Father, and that this is the subject-matter of the work which they are to do for Him and after Him in the world.   He says now, 'Thy word is truth,' or the truth, and that it is in this that they are to be sanctified, according to the prayer which He now makes, 'Sanctify them in the truth,' or in Thy truth.   'Thy word is truth.' We conclude, therefore, that their labour is to be devoted to the spreading of this word of the Father, which is the truth, and that it is for this that they are sent by Him into the world as labourers who are to follow in His own footsteps.

The prayer that He now makes, 'Sanctify them in the truth, Thy word is truth,' may mean that He asks that they may find their consummation and perfection in sanctity in the preaching of the truth and in working for the truth.   Or it may mean, according to the use of the word sanctify in various passages of Sacred Scripture which are quoted by those writers who have commented on this passage, that they may be consecrated, dedicated, set apart, as ministers and priests of the New Testament, to the work of the Word of God, the preaching and teaching of the Gospel truth. In this sense the word is used in the prophecy of Jeremias, where it is said of him, 'Before thou camest forth out of the womb I sanctified thee, and made thee a prophet unto the nations.'[10] We shall return presently to this interpretation. But it is very true that labours and sufferings which are incurred in the service of the truth, whether in direct propagation, or as a consequence of devotion thereto, must have a great effect on the character, and must bring with them very great increase in sanctity, except in the case of those who neglect their own souls while they are spending their time in the occupation of the Gospel ministry. Occupation of this kind, unless in such exceptional cases, fills men with the interests, the hopes, and the fears which belong naturally to the next world. It raises them above earth, and insensibly leavens the whole character, by the thoughts which belong to the Kingdom of God, and the efforts and exertions and aspirations familiar to a life of this kind, the ordinary tenour of which is conversant with the greatest truths and realities. This might be naturally expected—that a life devoted to the spreading of the truth should be elevated and strengthened thereby, and emancipated alike from the trivial cares and contemptible ambitions which are the daily food of the minds and hearts of worldlings.

But what might not be expected, except by souls who have had some experience of the ways of God with those who give themselves heartily to His service, would be the immense amount of careful

[10] Jerem. i. 5.

protection which He spends on such souls, in shielding them from sudden and unforeseen dangers, in bringing good even out of their mistakes, and victories out of their failures, in multiplying their fruitfulness, and giving an abundant reward in their own souls, while they have seemed to be toiling day and night for the souls of others. The labours of which we speak may seem sometimes to be thrown away, as far as great visible results are to be reaped, and nevertheless the fruit is felt in the souls themselves who seem to have been unsuccessful. For the growth of an apostolic soul in sanctity is an immense gain to the Church and to our Lord, and a process over which He watches with immense care and interest, for the sake of the soul itself and of the great issues which are at stake therein, which are so very dear to the Sacred Heart Itself. Nor is it uncommon for Him, Who was wont at times to give to His martyrs an abundance of exuberant pleasure, in the very torments which would naturally have been most excruciating to their bodies, which have been racked and torn to pieces for His sake, to fill the souls of such servants of His in the midst of what would naturally be most wearisome labours in the battle for souls, with joys and consolations which appear out of place in such conflicts, but are not out of place to Him, Who gave thanks to His Father and rejoiced in spirit, when He knew that the great truths of the Kingdom were being hidden from the wise and prudent, but revealed unto babes and little ones as it seemed to the world.

This may be said in explanation of the words before us, taken in their simplest sense. But the words may also be understood according to the use which is made of such expressions in various places of Sacred Scripture which are quoted by the writers who have commented on the text, in the sense of a prayer that the Apostles may be consecrated, dedicated, set apart, separated, as ministers and priests of the New Testament, for the work of the Word of God, the preaching and teaching of the Gospel truth, and generally, for all that is the legitimate sphere of the Christian priesthood. There is much in various parts of the Old Testament about the solemn consecration of priests of the Old Law, which it is natural to suppose may have been meant to prepare the minds of priests and of people for the far higher sanctity which was to be required in the Christian priesthood, in which the poor children of Adam are raised to so lofty a height, and have the 'powers of the world to come' placed in their hands. It is not unlikely that our Lord may have brought this subject into His prayer to His Father on this occasion. We may be here reminded of the words of the Prophet Jeremias, when it is said of him, ' Before thou camest forth out of the womb, I sanctified thee a prophet unto the nations.'[11] The Greek word in that passage is the same as that which is here used by St. John, and St. Paul seems to allude to the passage in the prophet, when he speaks of his own consecration, ' When it pleased Him Who separated me from my mother's womb, and called me by His grace to reveal His Son in me, that I might preach Him among the Gentiles.'[12] Although he does not use the word sanctify, the word which he does use, that is, separate, is used in the same sense as when we are told in the twelfth of the Acts that the Holy Ghost said, ' Separate me Saul and Barnabas for the work to which I have taken them.' The words

[11] Jerem. i. 5.   [12] Galat. i. 15, 16.

of our Lord about the Apostles may be understood in the same sense of dedication, setting apart, or consecration of those of whom He speaks, to the special work of the sacred ministry.

The consecration of the Jewish priest was performed with a number of ceremonies and sacrifices to which there may be some allusion in the place before us. And generally what was consecrated to the service of God in any special manner, was so dedicated by sacrifices and holy rites, so that the word sanctify in Scripture seems to involve the idea of sacrifice, and anything set apart to His service was by the mere fact considered as sacred and sacrificed to Him. Thus we come to understand how it is that the Fathers commonly interpret the words which follow next in this prayer of our Lord, 'For them do I sanctify Myself, that they also may be sanctified in truth'—of the oblation and sacrifice of Himself by our Lord which was to be consummated in the Passion. In whatever sense we take the former words, whether generally of sanctification, or of the special sanctification by the preaching the truth, we must carry on the same in the interpretation of this petition of our Lord, that they also 'may be sanctified in truth.' Our Lord thus makes the sanctification of the Apostles and of the ministers of the Church after them, the object of His own great oblation, and offers that as the price by which their perfect consummation in sanctification is to be purchased. He begs this of His Father to Whom the oblation is made, as one of the fruits which are to belong to His own sacrifice of Himself, and thereby lets us see how great store he sets upon the perfect discharge of the work of the Apostles and of those who come after them in the world.

For it is the work of the Christian ministry to bring home to the souls of men the whole fruits of the Sacrifice of the Cross, and it is by this means that it is appointed by God that men should reap the benefits of the redemption there wrought by the Saviour of the world.

The words before us are an instance of the manner in which our Lord's prayer, on which we are now occupied, sheds, as has been said, fresh light upon many truths which otherwise might not have come down to us with the same amount of distinct de-claration from Him.   The truth of the immense importance in His eyes of the Christian priesthood, and the whole sacerdotal and sacramental system of the Church, is naturally unquestioned among Christians, but it is not often spoken of by our Lord Himself before His Passion, and, in consequence, is not conspicuously prominent in the Gospels. For the Jewish system contained the idea of the priest-hood, and this was not a novelty introduced by the New Testament, so that the minds of believers had not to learn, for the first time, what a priesthood was, though they had to be raised, as to this and other subjects, to an elevation which had not been before conceived.   In the words before us, our Blessed Lord does not, of course, describe the Apostolate nor enlarge on its dignity. But He lets us see how great must be its importance and value, by showing that He makes it one of the main objects of His own Sacrifice and Oblation of Him-self. ' For them do I sanctify Myself, that they also may be sanctified in truth.' We suppose that the consecration, so to speak, of the Apostles took effect on the great Day of Pentecost, and that the Divine agency which produced their sanctification was the

Holy Ghost, Whose mission began on that day, and has continued ever since that time, in and through the Catholic Church, but the grace which was then poured out on mankind was the fruit of the Passion and Sacrifice of our Lord.

The Holy Ghost is the Spirit of Truth, and the words 'that they may be sanctified in truth,' may be thus interpreted in this passage, without excluding any other direct meaning—for in this prayer of our Lord to His Father there is no direct mention of the Third Divine Person, perhaps on account of the comparative lateness of the introduction of the full doctrine concerning Him. Christian minds would easily have conjectured from the analogy of the New Dispensation, that the Holy Ghost would find His most natural and congenial sphere of action in the guidance and inspiration of the sacred ministry to which the active work of the Gospel preaching and administration of the sacraments of the New Law were to be entrusted. But our Lord is not now engaged in drawing out the whole wonderful scheme, He is simply pouring out His wishes and designs to His Adorable Father, and only instructing us by the way, dropping words of living truth and ineffable power. We are to gather the treasures and beauties which fall from Him in this way, and to combine what He thus puts before us with other sayings of His and the Apostles, and especially St. Paul, who has said so much about the operation of the Holy Ghost, and the manifold and various forms which His grace chooses for its multifarious activity in the ministrations, all of which are the work of the One Spirit, to Whom the Apostle carefully attributes them. The whole system of which St. Paul speaks was before the

Sacred Heart at this moment, as well as the glories which were to follow to the Divine Trinity, and the wonderful fruits which were to be produced in the souls of the Saints.

It is now time once more to pause, and to endeavour to sum up what our Lord has been asking of the Father in these last paragraphs, which constitute, unless we are mistaken, the second great division of the prayer before us, that, namely, which contains what He begs for those whom He calls 'the men whom Thou hast given Me out of the world.' He says a great many things concerning these men, who, as we must remember, were then present with Him in the Cenacle, which had already witnessed so many Divine mysteries, and which was in the few years which were to follow, to witness many more. But, though our Lord here says so much about the Apostles, the petitions which He actually makes for them are not many, and indeed all may be summed up in a few words, as we shall see. He begins by saying that they are those whom the Father had given Him out of the world. He pleads this as a consideration why the Father should grant the prayer which He now makes for them, though the prayer itself is not mentioned for several verses. If the Apostles were, as it seems, listeners on this occasion to the words uttered by our Lord, His speaking of them as He did must have filled their hearts with the greatest love, gratitude, and confidence. They could hardly have ventured to hope that He Who knew all things, all the secrets of hearts, and the state of all souls of men before God, could have spoken to His Father so highly and so lovingly of them, and could, as it were, have reminded the Father of His own love for them in this way. They must have felt their own weakness and unworthiness, and have had many misgivings, which indeed were to be realized, as to their own stability and faithfulness. And yet our Lord omits all reference to their possible failures, and speaks only of those points in them which He could perfectly commend, as when in speaking of His executioners on the Cross He said nothing of their rudeness or savageness, but only pleaded, 'They do not know what they are doing.' He says of them that they had been the Father's in a peculiar way, more than others, for in a most true sense all souls and all His creatures are His, but these of whom He speaks were His own far more than others.

He tells the Father that He had given these men by a special act of love to His Incarnate Son, and He adds that they have kept His word. They have come to know, by the teaching of the Father, that all things which He had given to His Son came from Him, all the doctrine, all the power, all the miracles, and the rest. He had said to St. Peter, a few months before this time, that he was Blessed, because flesh and blood had not revealed to him the truth which he had professed concerning his Lord, but the Father Who is in Heaven. Now He bears to the whole body of the Apostles the magnificent testimony, ' The words which Thou hast given to Me, I have given to them, and they have received them and have known in very deed that I came out from Thee,' by an Eternal Generation, ' and they have believed that Thou didst send Me ' by My Incarnation. He does not praise them to the Father for their humility, or their obedience, or their charity, though He might have said much perhaps on these points, but for their faith. So great in the sight of God is the value of the true faith heartily received in a simple and humble soul, that as we see, our Lord makes it the condition on which the greater gifts which He desires to see conferred upon the Apostles may be imparted to them. No doubt the faith must have been strong in their hearts to enable them to believe against all the difficulties which beset them, but the prerogative of faith is not so much founded on its difficulty, which is more or less according to circumstances, as on the free choice of God Who has willed that the Kingdom should be for those who believe, and that that should be the key to His treasures. When the soul is about to take its flight into the presence of its Maker, and the Church has to speed the dying man on his last journey, a holy instinct tells her to frame her last prayers in the form of suppli-cation, indeed, for pardon for sins and offences, but she pleads only the merit of faith, *Licet enim pecca-verit, tamen Patrem et Filium et Spiritum Sanctum non negavit, sed credidit, et zelum Dei in se habuit, et Deum, Qui fecit omnia, fideliter adoravit.*

After our Lord has pleaded, as it were, the faith and docility of the Apostles, He appears to allege in their favour with the Father some other con-siderations founded on their relation to the Father Himself, and also to the Son. But He first speaks of what is the main subject before His Heart, though He has been so deliberate in introducing it, that is, that He is about to make His prayer for them. All that He has said hitherto for them is introductory to this. Now He says, 'I pray for them,' and He takes the pains to let it be quite clear that He does not, in what He is now about to make the subject of His prayer, include others, for whom He knew that it would be of no use to pray, as He is about to pray for the Apostles. Something has already been said in explanation of this, which need not be repeated here. ' I pray for them, I pray not for the world,' and if what has been said above be true, the reason alleged in the clause excluding the world, is of itself a commendation of those for whom He does pray, as it implies that the Apostles are fit to have the prayer made for them which cannot reasonably be made for those who are unfit. Then He adduces quite a chain of considerations in favour of the petition which He is about to make. These considerations are set forth one after another in the words which follow. He says that He prays for them whom the Father has given Him, ' for Thou hast given them Me, for they are Thine. And all My things are Thine, and Thine are Mine, and I am glorified in them.' The truth that He finds Himself glorified in them is, therefore, another consideration why His prayer for them should be granted, as is also the consideration with which He concludes the series of which we speak. ' And now I am not in the world, and these are in the world, and I come to Thee.'

The last words of the sentence conclude the considerations of which we are speaking, in the way of an appeal to the tenderness and compassion of the Father, which may serve to move Him to the granting of the prayer which our Lord is about to make for the disciples. ' I am not in the world,' the words seem to plead all that it is to cost Him in order to leave the world in the manner which obedience to the Father requires of Him. There is, therefore, all the Cross and Passion clearly before His mind, and not less, certainly, present to the knowledge of the Father Who had decreed them than of the Son Who was to suffer by His command. 'These are in the world,' words which set forth the desolation and weakness in which the disciples will be left without their Master. 'I come to Thee,' words which include the thought of the manner in which that coming to the Father is spoken is to be carried out, and the great and infinite merits of the passage to the Father, merits to which nothing that He asks of Him can be denied. And then at last our Lord makes the petition which has been so long burning in His Heart, and for the favourable reception of which all these considerations are adduced by Him. The prayer, as we know, is that the Father will keep them in His Name, 'that they may be One as We are.' He speaks for them as having from Him the same commission with which He had been sent by the Father, and implies that all those who are in any way concerned in the execution of this great design of love and mercy, become of course special objects of the love of God, they belong to a class of chosen instruments on which each of the Divine Persons necessarily looks down with very great affection and most watchful and beneficent care. All this is now pleaded by our Lord, and what He asks for them, is virtually asked for the sake of the mutual love of the Father and the Son, and also for consideration that our Lord is glorified in them.

The petition made for the Apostles is one which embraces, we cannot doubt, the very dearest and most tender wish of the Sacred Heart. What, then, is this prayer? Our Lord says very plainly, calling on His Father by His attribute of holiness, 'Holy Father, keep them in Thy name, whom Thou hast

given Me, that they may be one, as We also are.'
There are many things that follow on this prayer
in the words of our Lord here reported, as there
are many also that have preceded them, but this
is the substance of the petition which is here made.
We have already said enough on the meaning of
the prayer, and are now occupied in drawing out
somewhat the affections by which the petition is
enforced and urged on the loving tenderness of the
Father, and it is not difficult to see in the words
which follow quite a chain of considerations one
after another. The Father is urged by the thought
that this preservation in His name, which is asked
in order that the disciples may be one as the
Father and the Son are One, has been the great
work and occupation of the Incarnate Son during
the time of His sojourn among men. 'While I
was with them, I kept them in Thy name.'

He speaks of the poor single soul who has been lost,
but through his own fault, that the Scripture might
be fulfilled. That was a loss preordained for by
God for His own inscrutable purposes, but as far
as it went it was a defeat of the designs of God's
mercy and of the burning desires of the Sacred
Heart, Who felt it more keenly than the separation
of a limb from the body. No one of them whom
the Father had given Him as yet had been lost
except the 'son of perdition, that the Scripture
might be fulfilled.' Here was a consideration of
great weight to be urged on the Father, for the
preservation of the disciples in His name must have
been a matter of great importance in the counsels of
Heaven, and it had been committed to the Incarnate
Son while upon earth, and by Him secured hitherto
with one only exception in accordance with the pre-

ordained plan. And now He was to go. to His Father, the mention of which fact was equivalent to the setting forth to the Father Himself the whole decree by which the redemption of the world was to be carried out, by the Sacrifice on the Cross, to the immense glory of the Father. The disciples were to be left to themselves by the removal of our Lord, and thus the whole interests of this most glorious work of God were at stake, as it were, and the Father was called on to secure them against possible peril by making the provision which was asked of Him.

Our Lord seems to add another most touching consideration when He goes on to say, ' And now I come unto Thee, and these things I speak in the world, that they may have My joy filled in themselves.' This language has already been explained, but we may add a few words to what has been already said. Our Lord seems to speak of His joy, the joy that was familiar and so peculiar to Himself and His own Heart, whether in always doing the will of His Father perfectly, or in the knowledge that the work committed to Him in the souls of the disciples was prospering fruitfully according to the design of the Father, and this His own special · joy He desires to pass on to the disciples in its fulness, and in order that this result might be obtained, He says that He speaks the words now spoken in the world, before, that is, He leaves them. Perhaps we are to understand that the knowledge that this prayer for their being kept so that they may be one was to be of a peculiar fruit in the minds and hearts of the Apostles, and of those who were to come after them in the Church, in increasing and making more solid and strongly founded their joy in labouring for all that belongs to the work, especially of preserving, as St. Paul says, 'the unity of the Spirit in the bond of peace,' a task of which He may easily have foreseen the immense and continual difficulties, of which the history of the successive ages of the history of the Church was to be so full. He speaks, therefore, as it seems, as if His prayer to the Father, of which we are now speaking, might be of especial comfort and consolation to the Apostles and their followers, as well as the fact that they had been told of it beforehand by Himself. In the same way He told St. Peter that He had specially prayed for him that his faith might not fail in the night when all the Apostles were to be 'sifted like wheat,' and this no doubt was a consolation to the Apostle in his penitence, as well what He said at the same time about his strengthening his brethren, which charge was given to him in the hearing of the others.

We have already said something of the verses which next follow. They may be made wonderfully instructive if we could dwell on them as illustrating the affections of the Sacred Heart towards His Father in this His earnest supplication for the great boon which He had so much at heart to win for the Church, the boon of perfect unity, that the work for the sake of which all these preparations have been arranged may have its full fruitfulness in the conversion of the world. For this is the end at which all His plans and designs and gifts to the Apostles are meant to produce—that the world may believe that the Father has sent Him. We shall find the same end still uppermost as the desire of His Heart for the Church in the section of this same prayer which follows upon that with which we have been now

concerned. This last section begins with His declaration that He does not ask what He here asks for
the Apostles only, and His other followers, but for
all those who all over the world, and in all subsequent ages, are to believe in Him through the word
of the Apostles. It is for the sake of this that He
speaks of giving to them the glory which His Father
has given to Him, and which we shall presently try
to explain, ' I in them and Thou in Me, that they
may be made perfect in one.' This must suffice for
what can be said of the affections of the remaining
verses of this prayer.

' And not for them only do I pray, but for them
also who through their word shall believe in Me,
that they may all be one, as Thou Father in Me
and I in Thee, that they also may be one in Us,
that the world may believe that Thou hast sent Me.
And the glory which Thou hast given Me, I have
given to them, that they may be one as We also
are one. I in them and Thou in Me, that they
may be made perfect in one, and the world may
know that Thou hast sent Me, and hast loved
them as Thou hast loved Me.' These two paragraphs should perhaps be taken together, although
there is some difference between the subject of each,
for the second seems to be a continuation and enlargement of the first, and the whole doctrine which
they contain is best grasped when they are con-
joined. Our Lord says in the first place, that having
prayed in the former sentence for the Apostles and
the Church, He wishes to include in His prayer
those who shall believe in Him by means of the
preaching of both unto the end of time. It is easy
to see that He thus shuts out a possible cavil which
the heretics of coming generations might make,

S 14

according to whom the great boons secured to the Apostolic Church in this great and efficacious prayer might be supposed to have ceased with the generation which was immediately addressed by the first Apostolic teachers. For there is always an inclination in such men to limit the extent of the special gifts of the Church, in the same manner as they themselves limit the duration of her authority and power, and the duty of all Christians to obey her. It is the will of our Lord that the authority and the powers and the gifts of the Church should live on, always the same through the successive generations during which her existence on earth is to last till the end of the world. If this were not so, His words would come false, and the gates of Hell would prevail against her, in direct contradiction to His promise.

The Church, unless we are mistaken, has always considered that the gifts asked for in this prayer, made by our Lord at this time, are gifts on which she may count as having been certainly conferred on her by virtue of this great pleading of our Lord, and as resting on the most certain foundation of this expression of His will. The Father is not likely to refuse what is asked by our Lord with so much earnestness, at such a time, nor can we conceive our Lord to have asked anything that would not be granted. The fact also of the prayer having been made in the hearing of the Apostles, and having been specially recorded in the Gospel history by the Beloved Disciple so many years after the time at which it was made, gives us an additional security that it has not been recorded without having been granted. And our Lord may have made this statement for the sake of consoling and encouraging

the Apostles in whose hearing He was speaking,
as if to promise them indirectly that great fruitfulness of which He had spoken before, when He said,
' Herein is My Father glorified, that you bring forth
very much fruit.' And it is an immense consolation
and strength to Christians who live in these later
ages, to know that they were in our Blessed Lord's
Heart and had a share in this most powerful prayer
of His to His Father, on this night of His betrayal
when He was about, as He says, to sanctify Himself for us all. What He says, of those for whom
He now prays, and whom He classes with the
Apostles and their immediate followers in His
supplication, is that they have believed and are to
believe in Him through the preaching and word
of the Apostles themselves. The pure Apostolical
teaching lasts on in the Church of all successive
ages, and those who believe in our Lord by the
teaching of the Church of the nineteenth or
twentieth centuries are as dear to our Lord as
those who followed her in the first.

The prayer that He makes for these children of the
Church is, not that they may have the greatest
spiritual gifts and virtues, and be conspicuous in all
graces, ' all wisdom and all knowledge,' and have
' faith so that they can remove mountains,' and have
the gift of prophecy, and suffer greatly for the faith,
so as ' to give their bodies to be burned.' No doubt
our Lord would rejoice in the prospect of the
wonderful gifts of any generation of Christians, and
we do not doubt these great gifts will not be wanting
in the last generations of the Church, any more
than in the first. But our Lord has in His mind,
as the one thing above all others to ask in this
prayer to His Eternal Father, for those who are to

believe through the teaching of the Apostles in Him to the end of time, that one great characteristic note of the Catholic Church on which, if we are to gather the truth from these words of the prayer before us, the conversion of the world always depends. That is, the gift of unity. He speaks of this in these two consecutive paragraphs on which we are now engaged in two several ways. First He asks the boon itself, that all may be one, 'as Thou Father in Me, and I in Thee, that they also may be one in Us, that the world may believe that Thou hast sent Me.' Here, as we say, He simply asks for the boon, and in the following sentence He adds that He has done something to secure what He asks in giving what He calls the 'glory which Thou hast given to Me' to them, 'that they may be one as We are One.' He says a few words in explanation of this gift of His to them, which He says He has already bestowed, and then He repeats with some enlargement what He has already said about the purpose of the gift, 'That the world may know that Thou hast sent Me, and hast loved them, as Thou hast loved Me.'

It is easy to see that the boon for which our Lord prays, both for the Apostles and for those who are to believe after them through their word, is the gift of unity, and that the prayer is made with the special explanation, that, on their possession of that gift, our Lord says, the conversion of the world to faith in Him chiefly depends. 'That the world may believe that Thou hast sent Me,' 'that the world may know that Thou hast sent Me, and hast loved them as Thou hast loved Me.' What requires explanation is how the belief of the world in the truth of our Lord's Mission is to depend on this unity, and again, how it is that the glory which He says He has given to them is to be evidence of the same truth, for the words are plain, ' That the world may know that Thou hast sent Me, and hast loved them as Thou hast loved Me.' There is also a question as to what this glory is which our Lord says He has given the Apostles and those who come after them, that it may produce the conviction in the world of the truth of His Mission by the Father.

As to the gift of unity, it is twice described in this passage by our Lord, and the words are nearly identical in both places. First He says, asking for those who are to believe in Him through the preaching of the Apostles, for whom He has before made the same prayer, ' That they may all be one, as Thou, Father, in Me, and I in Thee, that they also may be one in Us.' And He adds also, ' That the world may believe that Thou hast sent Me.' The second time He has added the truth that He has given to the disciples and to those who are to believe, through their word, the glory which the Father has given to Him, and that the gift has been made that 'they may be one, as We also are One, I in them and Thou in Me, that they may be made perfect in one, and the world may know that Thou hast sent Me, and hast loved them as Thou hast also loved Me.' The additions which are thus made by our Lord to His own words must be carefully distinguished, and cannot have been made without a special intention.

Some have made a distinction between two stages and degrees of the unity which our Lord here asks for His faithful, and it is to be remembered that, before the last words which we have quoted, He has spoken of the gift of the glory which the Father had given Him, as has been said. The distinction made is between the union among themselves, in faith and charity and religious practice on the one hand, and their union with God and with one another in God on the other hand, that abiding in Him of which so much has been said in the discourse which preceded this prayer. There seems to be something added to the union of the disciples among themselves when it is said that they are to be one in God, as the Father and the Son are one in Nature and Substance. Not of course that the comparison is meant to be exact and complete, but only as far as that is possible. The grace of God, an identity in faith and religion, and in belonging to one external body with other Christians, makes us one with them, and we are united to God and our Lord by grace and faith and charity. St. John says that 'whosoever shall confess that Jesus is the Son of God, God abideth in him and he in God,' and in the same passage he says, 'God is charity, and he that abideth in charity abideth in God, and God in him.'

These words are enough to explain what is here said, though perhaps they are not enough to exhaust our Lord's meaning. He here tells us that the disciples are 'to be one as the Father is in the Son and the Son in the Father, that they also may be one in Us.' The faithful might be united one to another in the way just now spoken of, by faith and charity and grace, without the additional feature of being one in God, as our Lord says, 'One in Us,' as if by the more perfect abiding in Him they were taken up and knit together by a kind of unity which was in itself larger, nobler, mightier, greater, and more perfect than any which may exist between man and man—a Divine Oneness penetrating them and strengthening their union with the force of an indissoluble and eternal life. It is clear that the language here used by our Lord implies some very great and close bond of union between the faithful among themselves, and the whole tenour of the request that He makes for them, and the manner in which it is urged by Him on the Father, leads us to expect that the gift to the faithful of which He speaks must be understood of something very sublime—'I in them, and Thou in Me, that they may be made perfect in one, that the world may know that Thou hast sent Me, and hast loved them, as Thou hast also loved Me.' Every word of our Lord must have its own sublime meaning, although it may not be easy for us to grasp it.

It is greatly worthy of remark that our Lord has taken pains, in this part of His prayer, which He has, moreover, taken care that we should possess, to put it on record that His desire for the unity of which His Heart is so full, is not to be limited in point of time, any more than as to place. The unity which is to be the great satisfaction of the Sacred Heart was not to die out with the first teachers of the Gospel, nor was it to prevail as the characteristic mark of the Church, as long as her range of influence extends itself no further than the people of one tongue, or the descendants of one nation, or the subjects of a single empire. It is to embrace all peoples and languages and nations and races, and above all, it is to bind them in one throughout all time. This is the truth specifically conveyed to us by this part of the prayer, 'Not for them only do I pray, but for them who through their word shall believe in Me.' And, as if to emphasize what He has said, He goes on in language such as He has not before used on the subject of unity, 'That they all may be one, as Thou, Father, in Me, and I in Thee, that they also may be one in Us, that the world may believe that Thou hast sent Me.'

It is obvious to a moment's consideration that the effect produced on the world, in the way of conviction of the truth of our Lord's Mission by the Father, must come with much greater force when it is seen that the faithful are knit together in the perfect unity of the Church, when there is no other bond of union between the members of the body into which they are gathered, but the faith only and the membership of the Church, when all other bonds of union are more or less superseded and subordinated, or even sacrificed to this—when our Lord becomes known to the world as the King not of one people alone, but the Author of a religion which is made equally for the whole world and all the various classes and characters of mind and national diversities, the results of almost innumerable differences and divergencies which have their origin in history, or ancestry, or geographical distance, or physical or climatical variations. The religion of our Lord sprang from a single people, which has preserved its exclusiveness as if it was incapable of blending with any other. And yet from the very beginning its most salient characteristic, as a religion, was its power of amalgamating the most various and discordant and far separated of the children of Adam into one great family. We need not pursue farther a line of thought which is so fertile, and which it is enough to have pointed out to the thoughtful reader. But it is conceivable that our Lord might have contented Himself with the prospect of the universality of the future Kingdom which was to be His, without going on to the truth that it was not only to be an universal religion, but that over and above that, it was to be a religion the subjects of which were to be united one to the other, millions upon millions, as in one externally cognizable Body, the unity of which, notwithstanding all natural tendencies to the contrary, was to be the great argument by means of which the world outside it was to be convinced, as by a peremptory proof, that its Founder came from God. And it is when He speaks of this unity that our Lord uses the strong expressions which we have already quoted, as if He intended to make it plain beyond all cavil that the unity here spoken of was not only to be visible to the world as a motive for its conversion, but also rooted in the hearts and minds of the faithful, binding them together by a bond of spiritual identity which has no parallel save in the union of the Divine Persons themselves, ' As Thou, Father, in Me, and I in Thee, that they also may be one in Us, that the world may believe that Thou hast sent Me.'

With the entire history of all the future years before Him, ages, it may be, to us unknown, as the centuries of the modern life of the human race were hidden from the ken of the early generations of the Church, He makes this prayer for those who were to inherit the teaching of the Apostles long after they had passed away, that—under whatever change of circumstances and history—there was to be for ever this one feature of identity perpetual in the body which is to bear His name in each successive generation and phase in human society, that it is to be conspicuously one, and one even as He and the Father are One. As we look back on the history of the Christian commonwealth, we see indeed the fulfilment of this desire of the Sacred Heart in the

Catholic Church, in which Unity has ever lived on in the maintenance of the faith of the Apostles, under the guidance of the One Pastor to whom our Lord committed the charge of strengthening his brethren. But while we rejoice with intense gratitude over the abiding peace which has reigned in the flock of St. Peter, we cannot but be aware of the many falls from the true faith, and the large rents that have been made from time to time in the seamless robe, by unfaithful and rebellious children, and we can understand in some measure the intense and most loving earnestness with which this prayer was poured forth from the Sacred Heart. We can see how the Christian Kingdom might have fared, in the perpetual storms and trials through which it has to pass, if it had not been for this most efficacious prayer, and the continual assistance of the powerful graces which it has brought to the aid of the Church in her direst need. We can in some measure enter into the desires of that Sacred Heart, which we cannot doubt must be as strong now, after so many centuries, as they were when these words were spoken in the hearing of the Apostles, and which the last survivor of the holy band has been commissioned to hand on to succeeding generations. The lapse of time since the words were uttered has only added continually fresh and fresh proof to the cogency of the argument which our Lord speaks of as to be deduced from the Unity of the Church.

It was a great thing in the first ages to point to the Church as already gathering, into her one fold, the children of all the nations included in what seemed the world-wide Empire of the Cæsars. It took some centuries to accomplish its ruin, and when it finally fell, the men of the time thought that the end of the world could not long be delayed. But the end was not yet. Like the successive waves of a long flowing tide, hordes of barbarous nations came into possession of what had seemed the world of civilization, nations which it seemed equally impossible to resist, or to tame and soften, or to keep at peace. Yet before long they were gradually tamed and made children of the Church, learning from her the truths of salvation and the laws of conduct, how to be good citizens and neighbours, as well as the useful arts of life, and also how to live as faithful children of the one true God, Who is dishonoured by breaches of the rule of unity of faith and by rebellion against the gentle sovereignty of the chair of Peter, as well as by the idolatry and superstition under which their ancestors groaned for so many generations. But it would be going beyond our province here to point out how powerfully the Church performed her blessed task of blending the descendants of all these various stocks into her own unity, and how she has continued ever since the same Divine process. The power of the Christian teaching when allowed its full scope has been always the same from the first generation of believers down to the present day, and it may fairly be said that, however long the world may last into future ages, there has already been time enough to make it clear, that there can be but few elements or phases, in the life of those who share the human nature which has remained the same from the beginning under all the changes which have come over its exterior, to which the religion of Jesus Christ has not provided a sufficient key and solace and remedy amid all the troubles and woes which have been the lot of the race since its first start in the world.

Here again we are in the presence of a great subject of thought and reflection which we have no time or power to exhaust. What may be said is that the Church has been able to cope with and find a key for every kind of change in society, every state and condition which has come to be the lot of the children of our race, the possibilities and capacities of which are well enough known to those who study its history. The time, then, of the trial of the Church has not been short, and the space over which it stretches has embraced every modification of varying fortune. She is always the same, always teaching the same truths for the healing of the nations, always setting forth the same laws and rules of conduct for man's well-being and happiness here, always guiding and helping him on to the world beyond the grave by the same hopes and fears, the same heavenly consolations and means of grace, the same worship and creed and the same sacraments, by means of which thousands all over the world, of every class, of every condition, of every degree of intellectual culture and gift, as well as of every nation and race and generation, have passed out of this world into the next to meet their great Judge and their eternal doom in peace and hope and confidence, trusting in the redemption to which she has taught them to look.

Among the physical wonders of the universe there are some which delight us more and more the more closely they are examined, and the more we scrutinize them the more wonderful do we deem the wisdom and care which have been expended on them, requiring all the resources of art to enable us to discover their ingenious and minute beauties. But what is to be said of the Kingdom of Sanctity, the laboratory of the Holy Ghost? It is most true that each saint is a special manifestation of that Divine Worker, and that each has his own peculiar loveliness in the eyes of Heaven, and yet here the law of unity prevails, in spite of the infinite diversity of human characters and of the circumstances under which they are formed and moulded to perfection by the Father of souls. And in the eyes of Heaven each one bears the likeness and the features of Him on Whom each one and all are formed as on their model. Every one is in a way and a degree a copy of the character and virtues of Him in Whom the Father is well pleased, and the words of St. Paul may be applied to each, though not exactly in the same sense in which they were originally used by the Apostle, when he wrote that 'it pleased Him Who separated me from my mother's womb, and called me by His grace, to *reveal His Son* in me.'[13] The true character of the work of Christian grace in the soul of man must be studied in those souls in which there has been no impediment allowed to hinder or mar the Divine work, and our Lord was able to see the glories and magnificence of the Kingdom as it was meant to be in the counsels of the Eternal Wisdom, as St. Paul says of Him, that 'He loved the Church, and delivered Himself up for it, that He might sanctify it, cleansing it by the laver of water in the word of life, that He might present it to Himself a glorious Church, not having spot or wrinkle or any such thing, but that it should be holy and without blemish.'[14] It is in the length of time during which she has been battling with the world, the supernatural force which she has displayed in surmount-

[13] Galat. i. 15.　　　　[14] Ephes. v. 27.

ing all difficulties and beating down all opponents, in her marvellous power of healing all ills, the ever fresh vigour which enables her to cope with every new invention of the evil one, in her recovering all losses and rising again after all blows, that the vitality of the Church has been shown age after age. All the time the ceaseless brood of her enemies find her still one and the same, the earthly reflection of the unchanging God.

We may further add some considerations which Toletus gives us as follows, deriving them from St. Cyril of Alexandria *in Joann.* xi. St. Cyril says that there are two unities here spoken of, one of which is a unity of souls, the other a unity of bodies. The souls of the faithful are united in the unity of the Holy Ghost, for all believers in our Lord partake of one and the same Spirit, and are united in Him, and through Him are said to be in God. They do not receive the Deity in itself, but they partake thereof by faith, hope, and charity, and He Who is thus partaken by them, is one and the same in them. Thus the souls of the faithful are one in one individual thing, that is, in the Holy Ghost, and their unity resembles that of the Father and the Son and the Holy Ghost, Who are one in substance. But there is a difference, for the Divine Nature is the same in the Father and the Son, and cannot but be so, and the Holy Ghost is the same in the faithful but by their participation of grace. The Scripture says of this union, ' In this we know that we abide in Him and He in us, because He hath given us of His Spirit.'[15] Through the Holy Ghost, then, God abides in us and we abide in Him. St. Paul says, ' He who is joined to the Lord is one spirit '[16] with

---

[15] 1 St. John iv. 13.   [16] 1 Cor. vi. 17.

Him, that is, he has the same Spirit Who is God, and Whom the Father and the Son have, but not equally with Them. In the twelfth chapter to the Corinthians the Apostle describes the unity of the Spirit working distinct gifts in all and in each, as He wills, and giving to each His diverse gifts, and collecting one Body out of many. This is the unity of the souls of the faithful, according to which they are all one, both with one another and with God, though it is a different thing to be one, and to be one with God. But what makes all the faithful one among themselves and one in God, is one and the same thing, that is the Holy Ghost, of Whom we all participate, and Who exists in us by grace and by faith and by charity. Through Him all are one with one another, and one in God Himself.

But there is another unity of bodies. For the bodies also of the faithful are made one in God, and this unity by which they are made one and united, is the very Flesh of Christ which is given to the faithful really and truly in the Blessed Sacrament, so that they are not one by any participation as was the case in the unity before-mentioned, in which the Holy Ghost was given to them in His gifts. In this case Christ Himself is really and substantially given to them as their food. On account of this unity there is here a greater resemblance to the unity of the Father and the Son, for by His Body and Blood Christ really abides in us and we in Him, as is said in St. John c. vi. and we are in a certain way so made one with Him corporally. It is of this that St. Paul writes to the Corinthians, ‘ The chalice of benediction which we bless, is it not the communion of the Blood of Christ? and the bread which we break, is it not the partaking of the Body of the Lord? For we being many are one Bread, one Body, all that partake of one bread.' His words are to be taken in their plain and full sense, and he goes on further to use another argument, from the truth that those who partake of these sacrifices in the temple are partakers with those to whom the sacrifice is offered, whether in the temple of the Israel after the flesh, as he says, or the heathen deities to whom sacrifice was offered, who were in reality devils. ' You cannot drink the Chalice of the Lord and the chalice of devils, you cannot partake of the table of the Lord and of the table of devils.' [17]

Toletus wishes to distinguish these two unities of which St. Cyril speaks, so that the words of our Lord's yrayer, when He says that they 'may be one as We are,' may be understood of the unity of souls, which is caused by the participation of the Holy Ghost by the faithful by faith, hope, charity, grace, and the gifts by means of which they are one with one another. And he wishes the words that follow, ' That they may be one in Us, Thou in Me and I in Thee,' to be explained of the unity which is produced by the same Holy Ghost, but with God, that the faithful may be one in God, and they in God, and God in them. Up to this point Toletus does not understand that anything has been said by our Lord about the unity of bodies which St. Cyril mentions, but he thinks that when He adds, ' The glory which Thou hast given Me I have given to them, that they may be one as We also are One,' our Lord proceeds to speak of this real union which is produced by His adorable Flesh. There are therefore three stages in this consummation of unity, and this remains to be further explained.

[17] 1 Cor. x. 21.

It is not difficult to see how the unity which has been already mentioned, that is, before there has been anything said by our Lord about the clarity or glory that He has given to the Apostles and all that believe through their word, is sufficient of itself to produce the effect which is here attributed to it, namely, that of showing to the world that He has been truly sent by the Father for the redemption of the world. For the unity among the faithful of which He speaks, which is the work and fruit of the Holy Ghost, is to a certain extent visible to the world, and it is clearly an effect which can only be brought about by a Divine power and agency. It is, in fact, the work of the Holy Ghost, and except for the power of God, it would be an inconceivable miracle to men as they are. It proves the presence in the Church and in the hearts of the faithful of the Divine Spirit of truth and peace and love. In this sense it is a permanent miracle of the highest order, and it is continually shown to be such, by the utter absence of love and peace and certain truth every-where outside the Church.

This unity is the work of the Holy Ghost, and like His other works, which make themselves known otherwise than interiorly, so as to be known to out-ward ken, it can only be partially understood and appreciated except interiorly. The fiery tongues which sat on the heads of the Apostles and others on the Day of Pentecost, the marvellous languages in which they spoke on that and other occasions, were but imperfect expressions, though real manifestations, of the wondrous gifts then imparted, figures of the spiritual effects then and there vouchsafed. So the external unity of the Catholic Church is a very wonderful phenomenon in itself, and it impresses

T 14

itself more and more on the mind the more it is studied and examined thoughtfully. The organi-zation of the Church is necessarily multifarious and elaborate, for it has to spread itself over the whole world, and embrace men of all kinds and classes and characters, and to be subject to the thousand acci-dents and variations which the multitudinous range of its subject-matter, and of the persons with whom it deals, imposes on it.

Even the decisions on moot points which are drawn from it on particular occasions, when some contro-versy has been moved, are liable to the delays required for consultation and discussion, and these delays are often prolonged by human imperfection, as well as by the malice of enemies, human or diabo-lical, nor is there any machinery in the world, so to speak, which is exposed to more jars and hindrances to its easy working than that of the government of the Church. And yet peace and order triumph and reign, and the result to those who study it fairly can lead to no other conclusion than that the hand of God is there, Whose characteristic gift it is to make 'men of one manner to dwell in a house,'[18] as one of the great prophetical Psalms says, that is, Who can give the grace to a number of men to live together in a house at peace among themselves, in the possession of one faith, in perfect charity, and in the observance of one rule of discipline, as the text is explained in the notes to the Catholic Bibles. For it is the acknowledgment of this truth that is required to make the unity of the Church possible and intelligible.

The Body which bears our Lord's name in the world is notoriously and conspicuously one in its

[18] Psalm lxvii. 7.

internal peace, and is distinguished from all other bodies by its complete separation from and exclusion of them, however much they may claim resemblance to it, and even origin from it. As St. John says of them, 'They went out from us but they were not of us, for if they had been of us, they would, no doubt, have remained with us, but that they may be manifest that they are not all of us.' Thus the Church at once blends all nations into one, but at the same time throws off, as by a natural revulsion, those who rebel against her laws of unity and obedience. The world has never seen a body at once so comprehensive in the fullest sense and so jealously exclusive. We take the words of a modern writer, whose words we are glad to quote. Speaking of the Kingdom of the Incarnation, Father Faber says, 'It has thrown down the partition walls of tribes, kindreds, and nations, and made Jew and Greek, barbarian and Scythian, bond and free, into one heavenly nation, one complete family in Jesus Christ the Head. As an Empire it has a government of its own, earthly and visible, yet like nothing else on earth besides.' He speaks of its ruler, the Vicar of our Lord, with an unexampled extent of power, and yet no source of worldly power of his own, of the manner in which his jurisdiction is acknowledged with delight by his subjects, and of the happy liberty which they enjoy. This kingdom has its own system of legislation, which 'embraces more of the secrets of government and more legislative wisdom than any other jurisprudence in the world, and it is peculiar and essentially so unnational, that it could not be applied to any other government than that of the Church.' This kingdom has its own councils, its own method of deciding controversies, and institutions, like the sacraments and religious orders, to which the world has no parallel, a literature, a poetry, a philosophy all its own.[19]

The unity of the faith, produced by the spirit of peace and love, is the most marvellous oneness in the history of the human race, and its beauty is enhanced by the absolute incapacity of the same result being shown anywhere outside the pale of Catholicism. Outside that pale, as we know very well, there are bodies without number who have broken off, some in ancient times, some in modern, nor does any considerable number of years elapse without the number being increased, for the instinct of independence is always alive in man, and Christians have to be as careful as others against its inveterate wilfulness. The manner in which each period or each generation of humanity shows the vitality of the instinct of separation is a proof, both of the power of this evil tendency, its depth of root in human nature, and the strength of the forces of grace which are required to keep it in check. Those who are familiar with the history, and who are conversant with the persons who form many of these separate bodies, will not in general be disposed to speak or judge severely of them. They number among them some of the most excellent of mankind for moral virtues, kindliness, activity in good works, and the like, they often make great sacrifices for the services of benevolence to which they are devoted, and the propagation of the imperfect creed, which in many cases are theirs by the accident of descent and nationality, rather than conscious and deliberate choice. In many cases the activity for good and truth, as they deem it, might be a reproach to the children of the Church, from

[19] See Faber, *The Blessed Sacrament*, bk. iv. sect. iii.

which they are not wilfully separated. We are very far indeed from saying that all these persons are living against their conscience.

But there is one thing they cannot show, with all their fair boasting upon the score of religious activity and zeal in works of good. They cannot show that they are in any sense which will satisfy the word of our Lord in this prayer, *one*, either one with what they consider the rest of the Catholic Church, or one with the members of the religious community to which in the eyes alike of God and of man they belong, from whose living teaching they receive their faith, and the sacraments to which they look as the channels of grace. And in the sense in which they do not venture to claim or assert their possession of this Divine gift of unity, men in general agree in acknowledging that it is possessed by the One Catholic Church. This, strictly speaking, is enough to prove the Catholic theory, because it tends to show that the world, in the common sense of the word, does see and believe that the Body which bears His name among men has, in common estimation, a kind of oneness about it as to which it is different from all other bodies. Many of these have distinctions of other kinds, learning, zeal, ecclesiastical power, a missionary enterprize by which they have spread themselves far and wide within the dominion of the state or nation to which they belong, but the words of our Lord to His Father do not speak but of one thing, ' That they be all one as We are.' This is nearly what St. Paul says, that he might speak with the tongues of men and of angels, might have all pro-phecy, and know all mysteries and have all knowledge and faith, so that he might remove mountains, dis-tribute all his goods to the poor, or give his body to be burned, all would avail him nothing if he had not charity. Our Lord's doctrine and that of His Apostle are really identical, and would that the good persons of whom we speak would learn the comparative futility of prosecuting with the utmost energy every most various scheme for His honour and glory, while they are afraid of taking up the simple question which is alone of vital importance, the unity of the Body of Christ !

The unity of the faith which gives the children of the Church certain knowledge as to the most sublime mysteries which surpass the limits of human intelligence, as well as the great splendours of Christian charity, of which society and the history of the world are full, are enough of themselves to explain how truly this implied promise of our Lord has been fulfilled to the Church. Still, it must be sorrowfully acknowledged that the Unity of the Faith and of the Body of our Lord have been most miserably assailed by His own children, and that the result has been a frightful impairing of this evidence of the truth of His Mission, which is quite enough to account for, though not to excuse, the refusal of those outside the pale of Christianity to acknowledge its cogency. It may be noted here again that our Lord uses the word world here, not in its worst sense, but for mankind in general, as when it is said that ' God so loved the world that He sent His only-begotten Son that all who believe in Him might not perish but have eternal life.' In that sentence the word is used of all those to whom the Incarnate Son was sent for their salvation, some of whom have believed, and some of whom have not believed. Our Lord here says that those who believe in His Mission from God will do so on the evidence of the charity and unity which His children will display, though there may be many who will refuse to believe in any evidence. In the following sentence He goes on to speak of the glory which He has given to those who belong to Him, which has now to be further explained.

' And the glory which Thou hast given to Me, I have given to them, that they may be one as We also are One. I in them and Thou in Me, that they may be made perfect in one, and the world may know that Thou hast sent Me, and hast loved them as Thou hast loved Me.' This sentence, as has been said, is a supplement, as it were, to what has preceded, and must be distinguished from it, as well as considered in connection with it. Our Lord has already asked the Father for that unity among His faithful with one another and with God and in God, which is produced by the presence in the Church and in her children of the Holy Ghost, and now He speaks of another gift which He says He has received from His Father and which He has given to them, for the same purpose and with the same effect of producing what seems to be a still more perfect and consummate unity among them, and which is said to have the same result on the world which witnesses it, of convincing it of the truth of His Mission by the Father. Our Lord seems to mention two distinct causes of unity, one of which He prays the Father to give and the other of which He says that He Himself has already given. That which He prays for has not yet been given, namely, the unity which is the fruit of the presence of the Holy Ghost in the faithful. But what He says He has already given is not duly prayed for, that is, the glory or clarity of which He now speaks, when He says, ' The glory which Thou hast given to Me, I have given to them, that they may be one as We are One.'

It has been already explained that when our Lord at the beginning of this Divine prayer asks the Father to glorify the Son, we are to understand it of the glory which rightfully belonged to the Sacred Humanity of the Incarnate Son, that He might be glorified both in Soul and in Body—but which glory has been suspended by Divine dispensation, as far as regards the Body, on account of the decree which required that that Body, which was to suffer for the redemption of the world, must be capable of suffering, which is inconsistent with the glorified state. When He goes on to say there, ' And now glorify Me, O Father, with Thyself, with the glory that I had with Thee before the world was,' this is, that glorification and exaltation of the Sacred Humanity of which our Lord spoke to the two disciples on the way to Emmaus, when He said, ' Ought not Christ to have suffered these things and so to enter into His glory?' This glory He there speaks of as His, because it belonged by right to that Sacred Humanity from the moment at which it was united to the Divine Person of the Son, and like the union itself with the Divine Person, it was the gift of God to that Sacred Humanity. It was the natural result of the union of the Body. This glory our Lord now says that He has given to the Apostles and the Church, because He had already given them His precious Body in the Blessed Sacrament, that is, the Body to which this glory belonged, and which was to be visibly possessed by it in the state of glory after the Resurrection and Ascension. Some of the Fathers understand that this glory, being the work of the Holy Ghost Who brought about the

Hypostatic Union, produces in the faithful to whom it is communicated that unity of which we have already spoken as His work. But Toletus, whom we are here following, thinks, as has been said, that there are two parts, so to say, of the union among the faithful of which our Lord speaks, as the evidence to the world of the truth of His Mission, the unity of souls which is the special work of the one Spirit Who dwells in them, and a 'certain real and bodily unity' which is the special fruit of their participation of the Blessed Eucharist. The following words of our Lord seem to insist upon this, 'I in them, and Thou in Me, that they may be made perfect in one, and the world may know that Thou hast sent Me, and hast loved them as Thou hast loved Me.' 'I in them,' for My Flesh has been given them as really and truly their food. 'Thou in Me' as Thy Divinity is united to My Flesh, the Deity in the flesh, and the flesh in the faithful, and so the Deity in the faithful by the means of the Flesh of Christ. The faithful, therefore, have in themselves the Flesh of Christ, and therefore the Deity, and they are made one, and have a certain unity through Christ by reason of His Flesh, and so are made perfect in one, that is, they are perfectly one with one another and with God, not only as to their souls, by the work of the Holy Ghost, but also as to their bodies.

The concluding sentences of this address to the Father are something more than a simple petition, and they refer rather to the reward which our Lord desires to give to His faithful servants, after their time of toil and suffering and laborious service to Him has come to its blessed end, than to the blessings He desires for them before that reward can be given. We are again struck with the tenderness and consideration of the Sacred Heart in taking care that those whom He loved so much should hear these things from His own lips, and should hear them as made the subject of a most loving prayer to His Father, rather than as a simple promise of His own. No doubt the Apostles would have believed, if He had simply said that they were to be with Him in His state of triumph in Heaven, but He has provided that they should have the additional blessing to look forward to of their joy and crown having been made a boon to be conferred by the love of the Father, after a special appeal to it on the part of our Lord, and an appeal, moreover, as we shall see, not asking it as a special favour, but with the claim of justice included in the request,— justice, inasmuch as what is sought for them is due to the merits of the Sacrifice which He was about to make. 'Father, I will that where I am, they also whom Thou hast given Me may be with Me, that they may see My glory, which Thou hast given Me, because Thou hast loved Me before the creation of the world.'

Our Lord uses the word, 'I will,' and not the word, 'I pray, or ask,' and some Fathers understand it as a more vehement and earnest prayer, but still a prayer. In the next sentence He uses the word 'just' of the Father to Whom He is speaking, and, as we have already said, in addresses to God it is natural to appeal to Him for an exercise of some particular attribute which befits the subject-matter, His omni· potence, or His mercy, or any other as the case may be. It may be thought that here He speaks of a Redeemer and the High Priest of the great Sacrifice, and perhaps the use of the epithet 'just' conveys a further allusion to the fitness and congruity, if we may use the word, of the request itself. For there was a certain suitableness in the fact that the Apostles, and indeed all the elect, had been given to our Lord by the Father, and had served faithfully in the work which He had received from the Father to do, and this might make it an act of Divine justice that they should be given to Him also to partake of His triumph and to be with Him where He is. This boon completes, in a natural way, their union with Him, which began when the Father gave them to Him, of which gift we have heard so much from His lips in the foregoing verses. And we may say that His words now spoken must have sunk down into their hearts, and we find an echo of them in the words of His Beloved Disciple, written many years after this, who says in his Epistle, 'Dearly beloved, we are now the sons of God, and it hath not yet appeared what we shall be. We know that when He shall appear, we shall be like to Him, because we shall see Him as He is.'[20] For it is the sight of God that constitutes the beatitude of the saints, and our Lord seems to speak with strict theological accuracy in describing their reward. The words of St. John implicitly reveal the further fact that the vision of the Godhead is not only their beatitude, but also the cause of their resemblance to Him, and his words remind us curiously of what St. Paul says to the Corinthians,[21] 'That we all beholding with open face the glory of the Lord are transformed into the same image from glory to glory, as by the Spirit of the Lord.'

What our Lord here says is that He wills or desires strongly, implying that He gives to His demand the utmost power of impetration, that those

[20] 1 St. John iii. 2.   [21] 2 Cor. iii. 18.

for whom He has been praying should be with Him in Heaven, and see His Divinity, in the sight of which the beatitude of that blessed home consists. This glory of which He speaks, He says His Father has given Him. For He has received it from the Father, though still as a necessary process essential to His Nature, the whole Divine Essence and Substance. He speaks with authority, and as Lord and Judge of all things, and as such His use of the words, ' I will,' does not of necessity imply that He does not speak as Man. For He has received power as Man, as He says in St. John v.: ' The Father hath given Him power to do judgment, because He is the Son of Man.' But His use of the words, ' I will,' implies more than an ordinary prayer, as has been already said. The same may be said of the words which follow in this place, those who are His own are to see ' My glory which Thou hast given Me, because Thou hast loved Me before the creation of the world.' These words, as we say, seem to be spoken as Man. For it is as Man that our Lord was chosen before the Creation, and it was then decreed that He should have the glory of the Divine Union conferred upon Him, although it was not actually conferred till the moment of the Incarnation, when the Sacred Humanity came into existence. His eternal generation was not an act of free love in itself, but a process of the Divine Nature, necessary and essential thereto. But the Sacred Humanity, as our Lord says, was beloved by God before the creation of the world, and it was an issue of that love which rested on it more than all creation, that it was chosen to have the Godhead united to it, and it was raised to the dignity and pre-eminent excellence that the Man Jesus Christ was God. This choice was no new thing, it was made before the world was made; the election was from eternity, although the Union was in time, and so it is true to say that the Sacred Humanity and the Man Jesus Christ was beloved from eternity. But our Lord had His Divine Nature by generation from the Father, not in time, but from eternity.

'Just Father, the world hath not known Thee, but I have known Thee, and these have known that Thou hast sent Me.' It belongs to the Divine justice that they should have the blessing of which He speaks as a reward for their docility to the teaching of the Father in His providence, and to the training of their souls in the knowledge and love of God during the months and years of His converse with them, which training and teaching had led them up to the height to which their souls had now attained. He seems to say that the difference between the Apostles and the rest of their generation as to the knowledge which the one had reached, and the other had not reached, was a kind of foundation for the claim which He now urges. For the disciples might have rejected, as well as the rest of the world, the evidence on which the truth of the revelation which the world had rejected was based, and the faith of the disciples was the condemnation of the world. He asks therefore that the disciples may be rewarded for their faith, as the world has been rejected for its unbelief. He speaks of Himself first as knowing the Father, His knowledge of the Father was inherent in His Divine Person, He knows the Father perfectly, and necessarily, but what the disciples have known is that the Father has sent Him. This knowledge, under the drawing of the Father and by means of the manifold and continuous instruction of various kinds,—by word of mouth, by example, by the revelation of His character, by illumination as to the Scriptures and prophecies, by the display of His miracles, by the whole Divine economy of His Life and history, and the many influences which pressed upon their souls from every side,—has ripened insensibly under the guidance of the Holy Ghost into the firm faith which they now possessed that the Father, about Whom they had been taught from their infancy, was the Divine Father of a Consubstantial Son, Whom He had sent into the world, not on any common errand as a prophet, but for the enlightenment and redemption of all mankind. This is the state of those for whom He asks the great boon that they may be where He is, and see His glory which had been given Him by the Father, Who loved Him, as has been explained, before the creation of the world.

He adds that His work in the revelation to the disciples is begun and not finished. For it is the office of the Son to reveal and declare the Father; and He had said that no one knoweth the Father but the Son and he to whom it shall please the Son to reveal Him. The words He adds imply that the knowledge of the Father which He has hitherto revealed to His Apostles is not yet complete, for He is about to add much more. In the discourse which precedes this prayer, He had said that the time would come when He would speak to them openly of the Father. We may suppose that He did this far more fully after the Resurrection than before, and still more openly, though in a different way, after the coming of the Paraclete, Whose office it is to make us know the Father and the Son and Himself also, and in truth we find the Epistles of

St. Paul and the other Apostles full of a knowledge of the Three Divine Persons, which we do not find in the earlier Scriptures.

The few words which follow, and which conclude this great intercession, show us that our Lord means to continue the work which He has begun in the Apostles and in the Church after them. The passage is a succession of affirmations which may perhaps escape our notice. He says, ‘I have known Thee, although the world has not, and I have made known Thy Name to them,’ that is, to the Apostles, ‘and I will hereafter make it known, that the love where-with Thou hast loved Me may be in them, and I in them.’ The words about the love of the Father convey the motive for which He declares His purpose of continuing the revelation of the Father to the Apostles, and of this we shall speak presently. It might be translated, ‘I have both made known, and will still further make known, Thy Name, that is, the knowledge concerning Thee, to them.’ The fact that He had communicated so much knowledge concerning the Father to them, and that they had believed in His teaching, was made, just before, the ground of His desire that they should have the enjoyment in the future of the vision of His glory, but it is not that of which He goes on to speak. He has mentioned just before the love which the Father had borne to Him before the creation of the world, and now He speaks of this love as the motive why He should continue the revelation of the Father to those to whom He had begun to impart it, that His Father may love His disciples, with that same love, or rather, in like manner, as He loves His only-begotten Son, ‘that the love wherewith Thou hast loved Me may be in them, and I in them,’ that the love wherewith the Father loves His Son may light upon and rest upon those to whom His Son has made Him known. We must remember that the love wherewith the Father loves the Son, and the Son the Father, is nothing short of the Holy Ghost, the Third Person in the Adorable Trinity, and what our Lord seems to say now is that the love with which the one regards the other is the Person of the Holy Ghost. So St. Paul says that the ' charity of God is poured forth in our hearts by the Holy Ghost, Who is given to us.'[22]

Toletus says that God loves all things that He has made with a general love, but does not communicate to all things His love. He showers benefits on them, but He does not give His own love to them. But the faithful He loves so much, that He not only confers benefits on them, and makes them the children of His adoption, but He gives to them His own love, so that it is in them really. This love of the Father is the Holy Spirit, Whom He gives to the faithful, and by Him they are made the children of God, and receive the blessings which proceed from that love of His for them. Our Lord here asks for the faithful, not only that common love by which God makes His sun to shine on the good and bad alike, but that love by which they are to be made the sons of His adoption, and heirs of eternal life, and also one as the Father and the Son are One, but also those blessings which would not be theirs unless by their receiving this love of the Father, by which He means the Holy Ghost. We have already quoted the words of St. John, ' Behold, what manner of charity the Father has bestowed upon us, that we should be called and be the sons

[22] Romans v. 3.

of God,' and St. Paul says also, ' You have received
the Spirit of adoption of sons, whereby we cry Abba,
Father.' [23]

But it must not be forgotten that our Lord ends
His prayer to the Father by some words which He
was fond of using in utterances of great affection
towards His own disciples. He not only speaks
of the love of the Father as being in them, but He
adds the words, ' And I in them.' The occasions
on which this phrase is used by Him are not so very
many, and it is probable that it is used by Him
with a definite meaning each time. In the great
discourse contained in the sixth chapter of this
Gospel, He uses it of the union between Himself
and the faithful in the Blessed Sacrament. ' He
that eateth My Flesh and drinketh My Blood abideth
in Me and I in him.' And in that place He adds
other strong words, as if He was careful to lay down
the truth of which He was speaking very plainly.
' As the living Father hath sent Me, and I live by
the Father, so He that eateth Me, the same also
shall live by Me.' [24]

In the fourteenth chapter, in the earlier portion of this
discourse, when He has made His great promises to
the Church through the Apostles, and speaks, as we
have supposed, of the blessings they are to have by
His presence with them in Holy Communion, He
says, after the promise of the Holy Ghost, and as
passing to a distinct gift, ' I will not leave you
orphans, I will come to you, . . you see Me because
I live and you shall live, or you also shall live,' words
which remind us of those just now quoted, that as
He lives by the Father, and he that eateth Him
shall live by Him. He then continues, ' In that day

[23] Romans viii. 15.   [24] St. John vi. 57, 58.

U 14

you shall know that I am in My Father, and you in Me and I in you.' Here again, unless we are mistaken, there seems to be implied a presence o our Lord in the faithful, which is a special blessing and to be distinguished by His language from His abiding in them, as does the Father and the Holy Ghost in the Godhead. In the same way, in the chapter before us now, which contains the great prayer for the Church, where He speaks of the glory which His Father has given Him, He says that He has given it to them 'that they may be one as We also are One. I in them and Thou in Me, that they may be made perfect in one, and that the world may know that Thou hast sent Me, and hast loved them as Thou hast also loved Me.' In all these passages there seems to be a distinct reference to our Lord's communication of Himself to the faithful in the Blessed Sacrament, and it is a gain to devout souls that it should be pointed out to them when it is the case.

APPENDIX.

Harmony of the Gospels.

§ 156 (*b*).—*Our Lord's discourse to His Apostles.*

St. John xv. 1—27; xvi. 1—33.

I am the true Vine, and My Father is the Husbandman. Every branch in Me that beareth not fruit, He will take away, and every one that beareth fruit, He will purge it, that it may bring forth more fruit. Now you are clean by reason of the word which I have spoken to you. Abide in Me, and I in you. As the branch cannot bear fruit of itself, unless it abide in the vine, so neither can you, unless you abide in Me. I am the Vine, you the branches. He that abideth in Me, and I in him, the same beareth much fruit, for without Me you can do nothing. If any one abide not in Me, he shall be cast forth as a branch, and shall wither, and they shall gather him up, and cast him into the fire, and he burneth. If

St. John xv. 8—15.

you abide in Me, and My words abide in you, you shall ask whatever you will, and it shall be done unto you. In this is My Father glorified, that you bring forth very much fruit, and become My disciples.

As the Father hath loved Me, I also have loved you. Abide in My love. If you keep My commandments, you shall abide in My love, as I also have kept my Father's commandments, and do abide in His love. These things I have spoken to you, that My joy may be in you, and your joy may be filled. This is My commandment, that you love one another, as I have loved you. Greater love than this no man hath, that a man lay down his life for his friends. You are My friends, if you do the things that I command you. I will not now call you servants, for the servant knoweth not what his lord doth. But I have called you friends, because all things whatsoever I have heard of My Father, I have made known to you. You have not chosen Me, but I have chosen you, and have appointed you, that you should go, and should bring forth fruit, and your fruit should remain, that whatsoever you shall ask of the Father in My name, He may give it you.

These things I command you, that you love one another. If the world hate you, know ye that it hath hated Me before you. If you had been of the world, the world would love its own, but because you are not of the world, but I have chosen you out of the world, therefore the world hateth you. Remember My word that I said to you, The servant is not greater than his Master. If they have persecuted Me, they will also persecute you, if they have kept My word, they will keep yours also. But all these things they will do to you for My name's sake, because they know not Him that sent Me. If I had not come, and spoken to them, they would not have sin, but now they have no excuse for their sin. He that hateth Me, hateth My Father also. If I had not done among them the works that no other man hath done, they would not have sin, but now they have both seen and hated both Me and My

Father. But that the word may be fulfilled which is written in their law, They hated Me without cause.

But when the Paraclete cometh, Whom I will send you from the Father, the Spirit of truth, Who proceedeth from the Father, He shall give testimony of Me, and you shall give testimony, because you are with Me from the beginning.

These things have I spoken to you that you may not be scandalized. They will put you out of the synagogues, yea, the hour cometh, that whosoever killeth you, will think that he doth a service to God. And these things will they do to you, because they have not known the Father, nor Me. But these things I have told you, that when the hour shall come, you may remember that I told you of them. But I told you not these things from the beginning, because I was with you. And now I go to Him that sent Me, and none of you asketh Me, Whither goest Thou? But because I have spoken these things to you, sorrow hath filled your heart. But I tell you the truth, it is expedient to you that I go, for if I go not, the Paraclete will not come to you, but if I go, I will send Him to you. And when He is come, He will convince the world of sin, and of justice, and of judgment. Of sin, because they believed not in Me. And of justice

St. John xvi. 11—20.

because I go to the Father, and you shall see Me no longer. And of judgment, because the prince of this world is already judged.

I have yet many things to say to you, but you cannot bear them now. But when He, the Spirit of truth is come He will teach you all truth, for He shall not speak of Himself, but what things soever He shall hear, He shall speak, and the things that are to come He shall show you. He shall glorify Me, because He shall receive of Mine, and shall show it to you. All things whatsoever the Father hath, are Mine. Therefore I said, that He shall receive of Mine, and show it to you.

A little while, and now you shall not see Me, and again a little while, and you shall see Me, because I go to the Father.

Then some of His disciples said one to another, What is this that He saith to us, A little while, and you shall not see Me, and again a little while, and you shall see Me, and because I go to the Father? They said therefore, What is this that He saith, A little while? We know not what He speaketh.

And Jesus knew that they had a mind to ask Him, and He said to them, Of this do you inquire among yourselves, because I said, A little while, and you shall not see Me, and again a little while, and you shall see Me? Amen,

St. John xvi. 21—29.

amen, I say to you, that you shall lament and weep, but the world shall rejoice, and you shall be made sorrowful, but your sorrow shall be turned into joy. A woman, when she is in labour, hath sorrow, because her hour is come, but when she hath brought forth the child, she remembereth no more the anguish, for joy that a man is born into the world. So also you now indeed have sorrow, but I will see you again, and your heart shall rejoice, and your joy no man shall take from you. And in that day you shall not ask Me anything. Amen, amen, I say to you, if you ask the Father anything in My name, He will give it you. Hitherto you have not asked anything in My name. Ask, and you shall receive, that your joy may be full.

These things I have spoken to you in proverbs. The hour cometh, when I will no more speak to you in proverbs, but will show you plainly of the Father. In that day you shall ask in My name, and I say not to you, that I will ask the Father for you. For the Father Himself loveth you, because you have loved Me, and have believed that I came out from God. I came forth from the Father, and am come into the world, again I leave the world, and I go to the Father.

His disciples say to Him, Behold, now Thou speakest plainly, and speakest no pro-

St. John xvi. 30—33.

verb. Now we know that Thou knowest all things, and Thou needest not that any man should ask Thee. By this we believe that Thou camest forth from God. Jesus answered them, Do you now believe? Behold, the hour cometh, and it is now come, that you shall be scattered every man to his own, and shall leave Me alone, and yet I am not alone, because the Father is with Me. These things I have spoken to you, that in Me you may have peace. In the world you shall have distress, but have confidence, I have overcome the world.

§ 157.—*Prayer of our Lord to His Father for the Church.*

St. John xvii. 1—26.

These things Jesus spoke, and lifting up His eyes to Heaven, He said,

Father, the hour is come, glorify Thy Son, that Thy Son may glorify Thee. As Thou hast given Him power over all flesh, that He may give eternal life to all whom Thou hast given Him. Now this is eternal life, that they may know Thee, the only true God, and Jesus Christ Whom Thou hast sent. I have glorified Thee on earth, I have finished the work which Thou gavest Me to do. And now glorify Thou Me, O Father, with Thyself, with the glory which I had, before he world was, with Thee.

I have manifested Thy

St. John xvii. 7—15.

name to the men whom Thou hast given Me out of the world. Thine they were, and to Me Thou gavest them, and they have kept Thy word. Now they have known that all things which Thou hast given Me are from Thee. Because the words which Thou gavest Me, I have given to them, and they have received them, and have known in very deed that I came out from Thee, and they have believed that Thou didst send Me. I pray for them ; I pray not for the world, but for them whom Thou hast given Me, because they are Thine. And all My things are Thine, and Thine are Mine, and I am glorified in them. And now I am not in the world, and these are in the world, and I come to Thee.

Holy Father, keep them in Thy name whom Thou hast given Me, that they may be one, as We also are ! While I was with them I kept them in Thy name. Those whom Thou gavest Me have I kept, and none of them is lost, but the son of perdition, that the Scripture may be fulfilled. And now I come to Thee, and these things I speak in the world, that they may have My joy filled in themselves. I have given them Thy word, and the world hath hated them, because they are not of the world, as I also am not of the world. I pray not that Thou shouldst take them out of the world, but that Thou shouldst keep them from evil.

St. John xvii. 16—23.

They are not of the world, as I also am not of the world. Sanctify them in truth. Thy word is truth. As Thou hast sent Me into the world, I have also sent them into the world. And for them do I sanctify Myself, that they also may be sanctified in truth.

And not for them only do I pray, but for them also who through their word shall believe in Me, that they all may be one as Thou, Father, in Me, and I in Thee, that they also may be one in Us, that the world may believe that Thou hast sent Me.

And the glory which Thou hast given Me, I have given to them, that they may be one, as We also are one, I in them, and Thou in Me, that

St. John xvii. 24—26.

they may be made perfect in one, and the world may know that Thou hast sent Me, and hast loved them, as Thou hast loved Me.

Father, I will that where I am, they also whom Thou hast given Me may be with Me, that they may see My glory which Thou hast given Me, because Thou hast loved Me before the creation of the world.

Just Father, the world hath not known Thee, but I have known Thee, and these have known that Thou hast sent Me. And I have made known Thy name to them, and will make it known, that the love wherewith Thou hast loved Me may be in them, and I in them.

QUARTERLY SERIES.

EDITED BY THE REV. H. J. COLERIDGE, S.J.

(The Volumes in Italics are at present out of print.)

1, 4. **The Life and Letters of St. Francis Xavier.** By the Rev. H. J. Coleridge, S.J. Two vols. 10s. 6d.

2. **The Life of St. Jane Frances Fremyot de Chantal.** By Emily Bowles. 5s.

3. **The History of the Sacred Passion.** By Father Luis de la Palma, S.J. Translated from the Spanish. 5s.

5. *Ierne of Armorica:* A Tale of the Time of Chlovis. By J. C. Bateman.

6. **The Life of Dona Luisa de Carvajal.** By Lady Georgiana Fullerton. Small Edition, 3s. 6d.

7. **The Life of St. John Berchmans.** By the Rev. F. Goldie, S.J. 6s.

8. *The Life of the Blessed Peter Favre,* of the Society of Jesus; First Companion of St. Ignatius Loyola. From the Italian of Father Giuseppe Boero, of the same Society. (A new Life by Father Goldie is in preparation).

9. **The Dialogues of St. Gregory the Great.** An Old English Version. 6s.

10. **The Life of Anne Catharine Emmerich.** By Helen Ram. 5s.

11. *The Prisoners of the Temple;* or, Discrowned and Crowned. By M. O'Connor Morris (Mrs. Bishop).

13. *The Story of St. Stanislaus Kostka.* Edited by the Rev. H. J. Coleridge, S.J. 3s. 6d.

15. **The Chronicle of St. Antony of Padua.** "The Eldest Son of St. Francis." Edited by the Rev. H. J. Coleridge, S.J. In Four Books. 5s. 6d.

16. *Life of Pope Pius the Seventh.* By Mary H. Allies.

18. **An English Carmelite.** The Life of Catherine Burton, Mother Mary Xaveria of the Angels, of the English Teresian Convent at Antwerp. Collected from her own writings, and other sources, by Father Thomas Hunter, S.J. 6s.

21. **The Life of Christopher Columbus.** By the Rev. A. G. Knight, S.J. 6s.

22. **The Suppression of the Society of Jesus** in the Portuguese Dominions. From documents hitherto unpublished. By the Rev. Alfred Weld, S.J. 7s. 6d.

23. **The Christian Reformed in Mind and Manners.** By Benedict Rogacci, S.J. The Translation edited by the Rev. H. J. Coleridge, S.J. 7s. 6d.

24. **The Sufferings of the Church in Brittany** during the Great Revolution. By Edward Healy Thompson. 6s. 6d.

25. **The Life of Margaret Mostyn** (Mother Margaret of Jesus), Religious of the Reformed Order of our Blessed Lady of Mount Carmel (1625-1679). By the Very Rev. Edmund Bedingfield. 6s.

26. **The Life of Henrietta D'Osseville** (in Religion, Mother Ste. Marie), Foundress of the Institute of the Faithful Virgin. Arranged and Edited by the Rev. J. G. MacLeod, S.J. 5s. 6d.

28. **Three Catholic Reformers of the Fifteenth** Century (St. Vincent Ferrer, St. Bernardine of Siena, St. John Capistran). By Mary H. Allies. 6s.

29. **A Gracious Life** (1566-1618); being the Life of Madame Acarie (Blessed Mary of the Incarnation), of the Reformed Order of our Blessed Lady of Mount Carmel. By Emily Bowles. 6s.

30. **The Life of St. Thomas of Hereford.** By Father L'Estrange, S.J. 6s.

32. **The Life of King Alfred the Great.** By the Rev. A. G. Knight, S.J. 6s.

33. **The Life of Mother Frances Mary Teresa Ball,** Foundress in Ireland of the Institute of the Blessed Virgin Mary. By the Rev. H. J. Coleridge, S.J. With Portrait. 6s. 6d.

34, 58, 67. **The Life and Letters of St. Teresa.** Three vols. By the Rev. H. J. Coleridge, S.J. 7s. 6d each.

35, 52. **The Life of Mary Ward.** By Mary Catherine Elizabeth Chambers, of the Institute of the Blessed Virgin. Edited by the Rev. H. J. Coleridge, S.J. Two Vols. 15s.

38. **The Return of the King.** Discourses on the Latter Days. By the Rev. H. J. Coleridge, S.J. 7s. 6d.

39. **Pious Affections towards God and the Saints.** Meditations for Every Day in the Year, and for the principal Festivals. From the Latin of the Ven. Nicolas Lancicius, S.J. 7s. 6d.

40. **The Life of the Ven. Claude de la Colombiere.** Abridged from the French Life by Eugene Sequin, S.J. 5s.

41, 42. **The Life and Teaching of Jesus Christ** in Meditations for Every Day in the Year. By Father Nicolas Avancino, S.J. Two vols. 10s. 6d.

43. **The Life of Lady Falkland.** By Lady G. Fullerton. 5s.

44. **The Baptism of the King.** Considerations on the Sacred Passion. By the Rev. H. J. Coleridge, S.J. 7s.6d.

47. **Gaston de Segur.** A Biography. Condensed from the French Memoir by the Marquis de Segur, by F. J. M. A. Partridge. 3s. 6d.

48. **The Tribunal of Conscience.** By Father Gaspar Druzbicki, S.J. 3s. 6d.

50. **Of Adoration in Spirit and Truth.** By Father J. Eusebius Nieremberg. With a Preface by the Rev. P. Gallwey, S.J. 6s. 6d.

55. **The Mother of the King.** Mary during the Life of our Lord. By the Rev. H. J. Coleridge, S.J. 7s. 6d.

56. **During the Persecution.** Autobiography of Father John Gerard, S.J. Translated from the original Latin by the Rev. G. R. Kingdon, S.J. 5s.

59. **The Hours of the Passion.** Taken from the " Life of Christ " by Ludolph the Saxon. 7s. 6d.

60. **The Mother of the Church.** Mary during the first Apostolic Age. By the Rev. H. J. Coleridge, S.J. 6s.

61. **St. Mary's Convent, Micklegate Bar, York.** A History of the Convent. 7s. 6d.

62. **The Life of Jane Dormer, Duchess of Feria.** By Henry Clifford. Transcribed from the Ancient Manuscript by the late Canon E. E. Estcourt, and edited by the Rev. Joseph Stevenson, S.J. 5s.

65. **The Life of St. Bridget of Sweden.** By F. J. M. A. Partridge. 6s.

66. **The Teachings and Counsels of St. Francis Xavier.** From his Letters. 5s.

69. **Garcia Moreno, President of Ecuador.** 1821—1875. From the French of the Rev. P. A. Berthe, C.SS.R. By The Lady Herbert. 7s. 6d.

70. **The Life of St. Alonso Rodriguez.** By the Rev. Father Goldie, S.J. 7s. 6d.

71. **Chapters on the Parables.** By the Rev. H. J. Coleridge, S.J. Price 7s. 6d.

73. **Letters of St. Augustine.** Selected and Translated. By Mary H. Allies. Price 6s. 6d.

---

74. **A Martyr from the Quarter-Deck.** Alexis Clerc, S.J. By The Lady Herbert. Price 5s.

75. **Acts of English Martyrs,** hitherto unpublished. By the Rev. John H. Pollen, S.J. With a Preface by the Rev. John Morris, S.J. Price 7s. 6d.

Works on the Life of our Lord.

BY THE REV. H. J. COLERIDGE, S.J.

THE HOLY INFANCY.

9. **The Preparation of the Incarnation.** 7s. 6d.

53. **The Nine Months.** The Life of our Lord in the Womb. 7s. 6d.

54. **The Thirty Years.** Our Lord's Infancy and Early Life. 7s. 6d.

THE PUBLIC LIFE OF OUR LORD.

12. **The Ministry of St. John Baptist.** 6s. 6d.

14. **The Preaching of the Beatitudes.** 6s. 6d.

17. **The Sermon on the Mount** (Continued). 6s. 6d.

27. **The Sermon on the Mount** (Concluded). 6s. 6d.

31, 37, 45, 51. **The Training of the Apostles.** Parts I. II. III. IV. 6s. 6d. each.

57. **The Preaching of the Cross.** Part I. 6s. 6d.

63, 64. **The Preaching of the Cross.** Parts II. III. 6s. each.

68, 72, 76. **Passiontide.** Parts I. II. III. 6s. 6d. each.

INTRODUCTORY VOLUMES.

19, 20. **The Life of our Life.** Harmony of the Life of our Lord, with Introductory Chapters and Indices. Second Edition, with Preface rewritten and enlarged. Two vols. 15s.

36. **The Works and Words of our Saviour,** gathered from the Four Gospels. 7s. 6d.

46. **The Story of the Gospels.** Harmonized for Meditation. 7s. 6d.

The Prisoners of the King. Thoughts on the Doctrine of Purgatory. By the Rev. H. J. Coleridge, S.J. New Edition. 4s.

The Seven Words of Mary. By the Rev. H. J. Coleridge, S.J. 2s.

The Seven Words on the Cross. By Cardinal Bellarmine. Translated from the Latin. Second Edition. 5s.

The Manna of the Soul. By the Rev. Paul Segneri. Meditations for every Day in the Year (Vol. I. out of print). Vols. II. III. IV. each, 7s. 6d.

The Charity of Jesus Christ. By Father Francis Arias, S.J. 3s.

The Virtues of Mary, the Mother of God. By Father Francis Arias, S.J. With Preface by George Porter, S.J., late Archbishop of Bombay. Price 2s.

Pietas Mariana Britannica: A History of English Devotion to the Most Blessed Mother of God. By the late Edmund Waterton, F.S.A. Net, 10s. 6d.

The Truth about John Wycliffe. His Life, Writings, and Opinions. Chiefly from the evidence of his Contemporaries. By the Rev. Joseph Stevenson, S.J. 7s. 6d.

The History of Mary Stuart, from the Murder of Riccio until her flight into England. By Claude Nau, her Secretary. Edited by the Rev. Joseph Stevenson, S.J. 18s.

Manual for the Use of the Sodalities of our Lady affiliated to the Prima Primaria. Cloth, 2s. 6d. net.

Bona Mors. Devotions for a Happy Death. New Edition, from the authorized Version, with Music. 1d.

BY THE REV. JOHN MORRIS, S.J.

The Condition of Catholics under James the First.
Second Edition (a few copies). 14s.

The Troubles of our Catholic Forefathers related
by themselves. Series I. (out of print). Series II. demy 8vo,
cloth, 14s. Series III. demy 8vo, cloth, 14s.

The Life of Father John Gerard, S.J. Third
Edition, re-written and enlarged, 14s.

The Letter-Books of Sir Amias Poulet, Keeper
of Mary Queen of Scots. 10s. 6d.

The Life and Martyrdom of St. Thomas Becket.
Second and Enlarged Edition. In one vol. large post 8vo,
12s. 6d. Or in two volumes, 13s.

The Venerable Sir Adrian Fortescue, Knight of
the Bath, Knight of St. John, Martyr. With Portrait
and Autograph. 1s. 6d.

Canterbury: Our old Metropolis. Price 9d.

**The Tombs of the Archbishops in Canterbury
Cathedral.** Price 1s. 6d.

Daily Duties: An Instruction for Novices. 6d. net,
by post 7d.

Meditation: An Instruction for Novices. 6d. net,
by post 7d.

Vocation: or Preparation for the Vows, with a
further Instruction on Mental Prayer. 6d. net, by post
7d.

These three Instructions together, in cloth, post free, 2s. net.

A Remembrance for the Living to Pray for the Dead. By Father James Mumford, S.J. Reprinted from the Author's improved Edition, published in Paris, 1661; with an Appendix on the Heroic Act by the Rev. John Morris, S.J. Third Edition. 2s. 6d.

The Heroic Act, printed separately, 1d.

The Devotions of the Lady Lucy Herbert of Powis, formerly Prioress of the Augustinian Nuns at Bruges. Edited by the Rev. John Morris, S.J. 3s. 6d.

The Order for the Dedication or Consecration of a Church. Translated from the Roman Pontifical. New Edition. 1s.

The Rite of Conferring Orders. Translated, with Annotations, from the Roman Pontifical. 1s.

The Text of the Spiritual Exercises of St. Ignatius, translated from the original Spanish. 2s. 6d.

The End of Man. By the Rev. A. J. Christie, S.J. Crown 4to, Library Edition, 10s. 6d.; fcap. 8vo. edition, 2s. 6d.

The Spiritual Exercises of St. Ignatius. Meditations for an Eight Days' Retreat. By the Rev. A. J. Christie, S.J. Cloth, 2s. 6d. The Meditations in loose papers, 2s.

Theodore Wibaux, Pontifical Zouave and Jesuit. By Father du Coëtlosquet, S.J., with an Introduction by the Rev. R. F. Clarke, S.J. Crown 8vo, handsomely bound in blue and gold. 5s.

The Existence of God: A Dialogue. By the Rev. R. F. Clarke, S.J. Fcap. 4to, cloth, 2s.

The Pope and the Bible. By the Rev. R. F. Clarke, S.J. Wrapper, 6d.

Records of the English Province of the Society of Jesus. By Henry Foley, S.J. Vols. I. to VI., Six Guineas. Vol. VII. in two Parts, price 21s. each. This Volume presents the entire English Province, from its commencement in 1620-1 to 1773, with Notices of Deceased Members to the year 1883. The entire set, £8 8s.

James Stanley, Manresa Press, Roehampton.